THE CARTERS: NEXT GENERATION SERIES

KERRY KAYA

B
Boldwood

First published in Great Britain in 2024 by Boldwood Books Ltd.

Copyright © Kerry Kaya, 2024

Cover Design by Colin Thomas

Cover Photography: Colin Thomas

The moral right of Kerry Kaya to be identified as the author of this work has been asserted in accordance with the Copyright, Designs and Patents Act 1988.

All rights reserved. No part of this book may be reproduced in any form or by any electronic or mechanical means, including information storage and retrieval systems, without written permission from the author, except for the use of brief quotations in a book review. This book is a work of fiction and, except in the case of historical fact, any resemblance to actual persons, living or dead, is purely coincidental.

Every effort has been made to obtain the necessary permissions with reference to copyright material, both illustrative and quoted. We apologise for any omissions in this respect and will be pleased to make the appropriate acknowledgements in any future edition.

A CIP catalogue record for this book is available from the British Library.

Paperback ISBN 978-1-83751-288-1

Large Print ISBN 978-1-83751-289-8

Hardback ISBN 978-1-83751-287-4

Ebook ISBN 978-1-83751-290-4

Kindle ISBN 978-1-83751-291-1

Audio CD ISBN 978-1-83751-282-9

MP3 CD ISBN 978-1-83751-283-6

Digital audio download ISBN 978-1-83751-284-3

This book is printed on certified sustainable paper. Boldwood Books is dedicated to putting sustainability at the heart of our business. For more information please visit https://www.boldwoodbooks.com/about-us/sustainability/

Boldwood Books Ltd, 23 Bowerdean Street, London, SW6 3TN

www.boldwoodbooks.com

For Elizabeth Tyler.

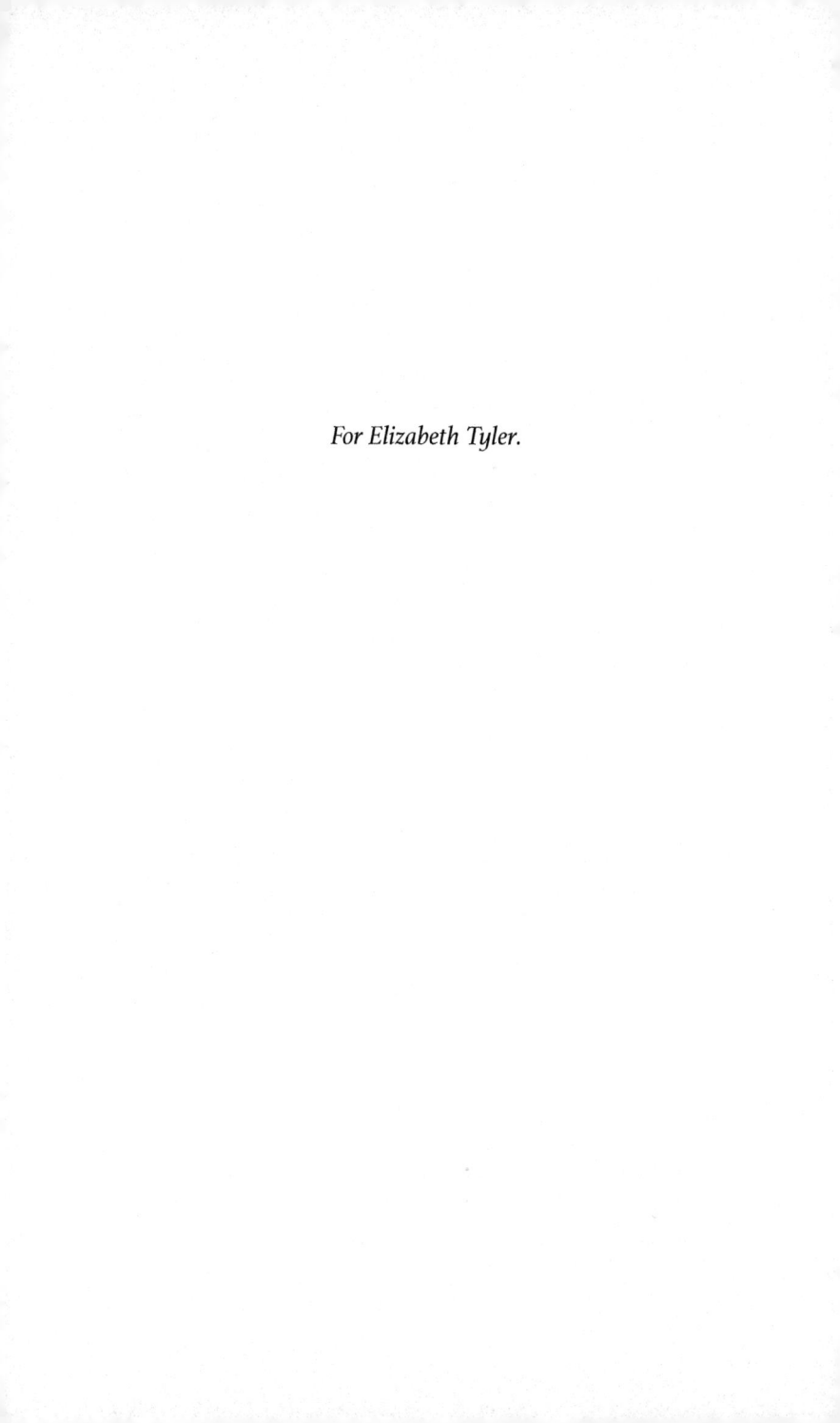

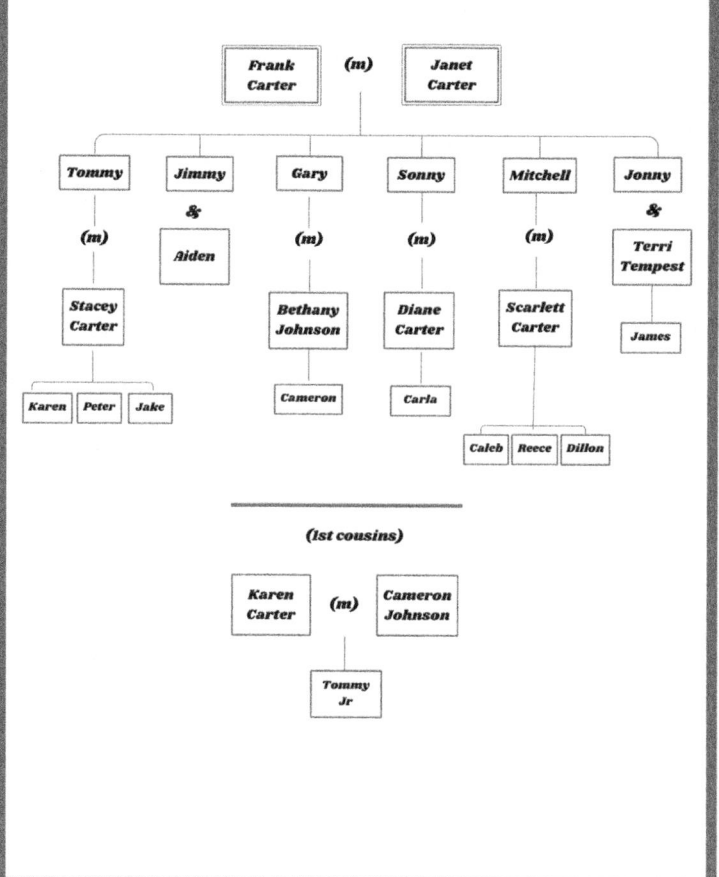

PROLOGUE
SEPTEMBER 2024

Thomas Johnson – or Tommy Jr as he was commonly known amongst his family – felt as though he were being strangled. Sliding his fingers underneath his tie he moved his neck from side to side, sensing relief for a moment. Not only were the clothes he was wearing uncomfortable, but he was also sweating buckets, although to be fair he had a feeling it was more so because of the circumstances rather than the temperature of the courtroom.

He swallowed deeply, nerves getting the better of him, and as he glanced up at the public gallery he locked eyes with his girlfriend, Aimee. She looked scared to death, her face pale and drawn, and her eyes red-rimmed. Tearing his gaze away from Aimee he looked at each of his family members in turn. First his mum and dad, then his nan, and great uncle Jonny, before finally casting his gaze upon his best mate and cousin, Reece. He looked worried, Tommy Jr noted, and considering the situation he had every right to be so.

His hands clammy, Tommy resisted the urge to fidget, he couldn't sit still and as he nervously bounced his knee up and down, he sucked in his bottom lip. He was starting to feel nauseous, and as an overwhelming urge to vomit swept over him, he swallowed the acrid bile down in one large gulp.

'All rise.'

Tommy's heart almost beat out of his chest and as he got to his feet, he stole a final look towards the public gallery before turning his attention to the magistrate, a pompous old bastard if he'd ever seen one. There and then Tommy's heart sank. His brief had already warned him that due to the seriousness of the charges against him the case would be referred to a crown court. And then there was the question of bail. In the beginning, his brief had been hopeful that he wouldn't be remanded into custody, until that was, he'd learned the name of the magistrate assigned to the case; he'd soon changed his tune then. 'He's a hard bastard, Tommy,' he'd said with a theatrical sigh. 'A hard nut to crack. You'd best prepare yourself for the worst.'

The magistrate's expression was stony and as he peered at Tommy over the top of his gold-rimmed glasses, his lips were pursed. It was at that moment Tommy knew that his fate had been sealed; that no matter how good his brief was, and he really was one of the best in the business – or rather the best that money could buy seeing as his family had gone all out in their attempt to see him freed – that he wouldn't be going home.

A deafening silence fell over the courtroom and as those in the public gallery leaned slightly forward to get a better view of the magistrate, Tommy stared straight ahead of him, his gaze fixed on a mark on the wall and his throat becoming so dry that he could barely swallow. He couldn't look at his mum, his nan, or even Aimee. Couldn't bear to see them so distraught.

This was it, Tommy decided, this was the moment his life was about to change forever. Taking a deep breath, he gripped onto the handrail before him so hard that his knuckles turned white.

And as the words 'bail denied' reverberated around the courtroom, his shoulders drooped. This couldn't be happening, he wanted to scream, you've made a mistake. Only he knew that nothing he said would make a difference, not now, it was too late, his future had already been decided.

As he was led out of the courtroom, Tommy looked up at the public gallery and gave his family a small smile, not that he actually felt like smiling; what was there even to be happy about? The only thing he had awaiting him was a concrete cell, his human rights all but taken away from him.

'It's gonna be alright,' Reece shouted as he jumped to his feet, his skin ashen. 'We'll get you out.'

Tommy nodded, what else could he do? Not that he actually believed his family would be able to get him out. They may have had money in abundance, may have had reputations as hard men, but it wouldn't be enough to help him, not now, not this time. His luck had finally run out; he was going down, and there was nothing Reece, or any other member of his family could do or say to change that fact. The only question at the forefront of his mind was whether or not his incarceration would end up bringing the rest of the family down with him.

1

TWO MONTHS EARLIER

Aimee Fox stuck her chin in the air, her eyes flashing with defiance. 'You don't understand,' she screeched at the top of her lungs.

'Oh, I understand a lot more than you think,' her mother Melanie screamed back at her. 'Boys like him are only after one thing and you mark my words, girl, once he's had his fill of you he'll soon have it away on his toes and move on to the next girl stupid enough to believe his lies.'

Tears sprang to Aimee's eyes, and as she swiped a lock of blonde hair out of her eyes she glared at her mother. 'He's not like my dad,' she shouted. 'He's decent, kind, and he loves me.'

'Loves you.' Melanie gave a high-pitched cackle. 'Is that what he told you?' she demanded, giving her only daughter a look of disapproval. 'It's the oldest line in the book; of course he told you he loves you, he wanted to get you into bed. And you, you silly little mare, fell for it hook, line and sinker.'

Aimee shook her head. It wasn't true; her Tommy did love her, she knew he did, he'd told her so enough times, and more importantly she believed him.

'Didn't I teach you better than this?' Melanie continued to shout. 'To not follow in my footsteps and drop your knickers for the first boy who looks at you?'

As her mother went on to rant about Aimee's father, she grew all the more frustrated. Tommy was nothing like her dad and no matter what her mum said about him, Aimee knew that Tommy had a good heart. 'You won't stop me from seeing him,' she sobbed as hot tears slipped down her cheeks. 'I mean it, Mum. I love him.'

Exasperated Melanie threw her arms up into the air. 'You're seventeen for crying out loud, what do you know about love?'

Wiping the tears from her eyes Aimee's hand wandered down to her stomach. 'I know a lot more than you think.'

As her mum followed the movement, for the tiniest of moments Aimee was filled with a sense of satisfaction. It wasn't often that she was able to get one over her mum, but this was one of those times, and no matter how right or wrong the situation might be Aimee couldn't help but feel a tiny bit smug. She was having a baby, Tommy Johnson's baby, and already she loved the tiny life growing inside her womb.

'No!' Melanie cried, her face turning white as she gripped the back of a dining chair for support. 'Please tell me you're not. That you're not up the duff. That you wouldn't be that stupid?'

A single nod from Aimee was enough to confirm Melanie's worst fears and for a few moments the soft tick-tocking that came from the clock on the mantlepiece was the only sound that filled the silence between them.

'Well, you can't keep it,' Melanie warned as she reached out for her cigarette packet with trembling fingers. 'I'm warning you now Aimz',' she said, plucking out a cigarette and popping it between her lips. 'Don't even think about going there. Having a baby at your age will ruin your life.' She lit up and inhaling deeply into her lungs, she hastily exhaled a cloud of smoke above her head. 'You'll have to get rid of it. There ain't no way you can have a baby, not here. This house isn't big enough to swing a cat, let alone bring up a baby. And what about college? Are you really that daft that you'd be willing to throw away a promising career, to be tied to man who'll end up betraying you time and time again? A man who'll shag anything with a pulse while you're stuck at home bringing up his kid.' She shook her head. 'He's going to end up breaking your heart, girl, and then what, eh? You'll end up just like me, working a dead-end job and up to your eyeballs in debt.'

Aimee swallowed down her tears. Her first year of college would soon be coming to an end and even though she'd initially wanted to stay on and complete a second year, there were plenty of salons that would be willing to take her on with a level one hairdressing qualification. Fair enough, the hours would be long, and the pay wouldn't be great, but she wouldn't need much. Her Tommy would provide for her and the baby; he had a good job and was never short of cash. And if she was really stuck then her dad might be willing to help her out, not that she actually wanted to ask him for money. As it was, he was always complaining that he didn't have a proverbial pot to piss in, although if Aimee was being truthful, she had a feeling it was more to do with the fact he wanted to get out of paying her mum child maintenance. He could be spiteful like that when the mood took him and despite pleading poverty, he always seemed to have the money to prop up the bar on a daily basis.

As for Tommy, her mum had always had it in for him. No matter what he did her mum would find fault; he could give her the moon and it wouldn't be good enough in her mum's eyes. But her mum didn't know him like she did. Tommy would never betray her; it would never enter his head to do so. He'd been brought up right and knew how to respect women. Neither would he go out shagging other women. Oh, he might look, but what man didn't? It was only human nature after all. Above all else she trusted him with her life; they loved one another. 'I'm keeping it, Mum,' she declared with a steely glint in her eyes. 'And nothing you or anyone else has to say on the matter will make me change my mind.'

Melanie shook her head and stubbing out her cigarette, she placed her hands on her hips. 'You think you've got it all sussed out, don't you?' She gestured around the lounge which, although clean, had definitely seen better days. The second-hand sofa was worn, and the carpet beneath their feet was so old and thin that it had begun to fray in places. 'Do you honestly think it will be that simple? Because believe me, girl, when you haven't got the money to feed and clothe yourself let alone a baby you'll soon realise what a big mistake you've made just like I did all those years ago.'

As fresh tears sprang to her eyes, Aimee angrily swiped them away. It wasn't the first time her mum had referred to her as being a mistake. If anything, her mother's words made her all the more determined that her baby wouldn't go without, that right from the start he or she would know they were wanted and loved. And when it came to Tommy, she knew in her heart that he would see her alright; they may be young, but he would take care of both her and their baby.

'And what about him?' her mother spat. 'What does he have to say about all of this?'

'He's got a name,' Aimee spat back as she pulled herself up to her full height and looked her mum in the eyes. 'And Tommy's happy about it if you must know. Over the moon about it in fact.' Although it would be fair to say that describing Tommy as being happy was a slight exaggeration. If anything, he was just as scared as she was, she would even go as far as to say he was terrified at the prospect of becoming a father.

'Well.' Crossing over the lounge Melanie paused in front of the door that led out to the kitchen. 'Let's just hope it stays that way because I won't be able to help you. I can barely afford to pay the rent for this place let alone find the cash to feed another mouth.' She gave a sigh and shook her head. 'I had such high hopes for you,' she added, her voice quivering. 'You're a beautiful girl, Aimz' and I really thought that you'd make something of yourself, that you were better than this.' She motioned around the lounge, her shoulders slumping as though she had finally come to the realisation that this was her lot in life. 'All I've ever wanted was for you to get away from here, away from this shithole of an estate, to have the life I could only ever dream of.'

With those parting words Melanie retreated into the kitchen, leaving Aimee to stare helplessly after her. She'd let her mum down, she knew that as well as she knew her own name, and as her hand wandered back down to her tummy, she fought the urge to cry again. Her mum was right; they had nothing, at least nothing they could be proud of. Her mum had more than just scrimped and scraped over the years; she had gone without just to make sure that her daughter had gone to bed with a full tummy. She'd even pawned her gold necklaces just so that she could pay for the hairdressing kit Aimee had needed for college and this was how she'd repaid her, by falling pregnant at the earliest opportunity. Following her mum into the kitchen she found her standing at the kitchen sink, her head bowed and her shoulders ever so slightly heaving. 'I'm so sorry, Mum,' she said wrapping her arms around her. 'I'm so, so sorry.'

Melanie sniffed back her tears and clasping onto her daughter's hand she nodded. 'I know darling,' she sighed, her initial shock of finding out she was to become a grandmother slowly ebbing away. 'We'll work it out.' She glanced around the dated kitchen, her gaze falling upon the broken cupboard door that still hung precariously despite the council coming out to fix it numerous times. 'I don't know how, but if you're determined to keep this baby then somehow, we'll manage.'

Aimee nodded. 'Tommy will help me, Mum, I know he will.'

Melanie raised her eyebrows, then opening a drawer she took out a potato peeler and motioned for Aimee to put on the chip pan. 'He's going to have to,' she said as she began to peel a potato. 'Because let's face it, girl, he's got no other choice in the matter. That baby you're carrying is his responsibility too and if he knows what's good for him then he'd best remember that fact.'

* * *

Tommy Jr switched off the ignition and surveyed the pub before him. He'd only ever been in The Cross Keys public house a couple of times and that had been when Aimee had taken him to meet her dad. With a sense of trepidation, he glanced around him. Other than a churchyard and a low-rise block of flats in the near vicinity, the area was desolate, and in Tommy's mind the perfect venue to give someone a kicking that they wouldn't forget in a hurry and God only knew after what he'd done he deserved a hammering.

A part of him still couldn't believe that he was going to be a dad. He was only nineteen, still a kid himself, he knew nothing about life let alone how to bring up a child. The mere thought of what was to come was enough to bring him out in a cold sweat. Not that he had anyone to blame for the predicament he found himself in, other than himself; he should have been more careful, should have made sure that he'd used protection.

'So, are you going to marry her then?' his cousin, Reece

Carter, asked, breaking his thoughts as he sat beside him in the passenger seat.

Tommy screwed up his face. 'Nah, fuck that. Neither of us wants to get married.'

Reece shrugged. 'So, what are we waiting for then?' Unclipping his seat belt, he nodded towards the pub. 'Are we going in or not?'

Tommy sighed and glancing towards his cousin he rubbed his hand over his short, dark, cropped hair and gave a weary smile. 'I suppose I'd best get it over and done with, eh?'

Reece returned the grin and stepping out of the car, he leaned his forearms on the open door and nodded across to the pub. 'I don't know what you're getting yourself worked up for, I mean what's the worst that can happen?'

'He could batter me,' Tommy replied.

'Leave it out,' Reece chuckled. 'As if that's ever gonna happen. The man's an idiot.'

Tommy screwed up his face. 'How would you know? You've never even met him.'

Reece gave a nonchalant shrug. 'Lucky guess I suppose. Listen,' he said, his voice becoming gentle. 'I've got your back and if he does kick off, he won't be able to take on the pair of us, he'd be a fool to even try.'

'Yeah, I suppose so,' Tommy sighed wishing that he had his cousin's confidence. 'Come on.' He slammed the car door shut and locked up. 'But if he swings for me,' he warned flashing a nervous grin, 'don't tell anyone or I'd never live it down.'

'I've already told you,' Reece winked. 'It's never gonna happen.'

Pushing open the pub door Tommy stepped inside and scanned the bar area. Exactly where he'd known he would find him, Aimee's dad was in his usual spot propping up the bar. He took a deep breath and moved forward, all the while resisting the urge to wipe his clammy hands down the length of his jeans. The fact Aimee's dad had called him asking for a meeting in the first place was enough to tell him that he knew about the baby. Perhaps he wanted to know what Tommy intended to do about the situation, or maybe just as he'd originally suspected, Aimee's dad wanted to batter the life out of him.

'Oi, Tommy,' Kevin Fox shouted out. 'Over here.'

As he neared the bar, Tommy offered a stilted smile while bracing himself for Kevin to start throwing punches. Not that he could say he would actually blame him if he did; he'd taken the piss, had got his daughter pregnant, and for that alone he deserved a slap.

He settled himself onto a bar stool, his shoulders remaining rigid. 'You alright mate?' he asked testing the waters. He jabbed his thumb in Reece's direction. 'This is my cousin, Reece.'

Kevin offered a wide grin, his teeth uneven and tobacco stained, and just underneath his left nostril was a smattering of white powder. 'Brought him along as back up did you, eh?' he winked before going on to shake Reece's hand. 'And as for me, Tommy lad, I couldn't be better.' He wiped the powder away then narrowed his eyes as he studied the bruises that littered Tommy's face. 'Which is a lot more than can be said about you.'

'It's nothing,' Tommy said as he reached up to touch the slit above his eyebrow.

'Don't tell me,' Kevin winked. 'The other bloke looks a lot worse.'

Tommy lifted his eyebrows. 'Yeah, something like that.' Which in all fairness was no lie considering Lenny Tucker, the man who'd inflicted the damage, was dead and had in fact been murdered by his and Reece's uncle, Jonny Carter. In Tommy's opinion Tucker's demise was a reason for him and his family to celebrate. And despite the so-called truce that had been drawn up between the two families the amount of bad blood between the Carters and Tuckers had remained the same. He would even go as far as to say that in recent months the animosity between them had begun to grow. It was only a matter of time until the situation came to a head. Lenny Tucker had been responsible for injuring Jonny's partner, Terri. And so it was only natural that Jonny, alongside Terri's two brothers and nephew, would want to retaliate, resulting in Lenny's death. Clearing his throat in a bid to change the subject Tommy dug his hand into his pocket. 'Can I get you a drink?'

Kevin continued to grin and downing the remainder of his lager he placed the empty glass on the bar. 'I wouldn't say no.' His gaze drifted towards the optics. 'And I'll have a whiskey chaser to go with it. Oh, and make it a double while you're at it.'

Resisting the urge to roll his eyes Tommy gave over his order. One of his earliest observations about Aimee's dad was that he was a ponce and nothing since then had been able to sway his mind. 'So, what was it you wanted to see me about?' he asked as he pocketed his change.

'I think you already know the answer to that.' Kevin ran his hand over the dark stubble that covered his jaw, his sly, beady eyes studying his daughter's boyfriend. 'A little birdie told me that my Aimee is in the family way, and in my book that makes us as good as family now.'

'Yeah, well.' Tommy's cheeks turned red. 'It wasn't exactly something we planned but I'm gonna—'

Kevin held up his hand. 'No need to explain yourself to me lad, I've been there, done it, got the bloody T-shirt. No,' he lowered his voice slightly and jerked his head towards a table across the far side of the pub, 'that's not what I wanted to have a word about.'

Once their drinks had been placed in front of them, Kevin downed the whiskey in one large gulp, wiped the back of his hand across his fleshy lips then led the way across the pub. Pulling out a chair, he took a seat then rested his forearms on the sticky tabletop. 'I can see that my Aimz' has fallen on her feet with you,' he winked. 'And from what I've heard, you're going places. Would be hard not to I suppose,' he said craftily as he looked between Tommy and Reece. 'Considering the family you come from.'

As Tommy gave his cousin a sidelong glance, he lifted his eyebrows.

'Has Aimee told you what I do for a living?' Kevin asked, breaking his thoughts.

'Yeah, I think so,' Tommy answered. Tearing his gaze away from his cousin he sank back in the seat and held up his hands. 'I can't get you a job if that's what you're after. My family won't allow outsiders to work for the business,' he said, looking towards Reece again for confirmation.

'Nah, you've got no chance,' Reece replied between mouthfuls of his drink. 'They barely trust us when it comes to the business, let alone anyone else – and we're family.'

Kevin chuckled. 'I'm not after work.'

Tommy heaved a sigh of relief. 'I think Aimee mentioned something about you being a postman.'

'I'm no postman lad,' Kevin grinned. 'Although admittedly, I do work for the Royal Mail.'

Tommy shrugged. 'Same thing, isn't it?'

'And I bet you didn't know this,' Kevin continued. 'In fact, not many people do,' he added tapping the side of his nose. 'I don't just deal with any old letters.'

'Nah, I suppose you sift through packages and parcels too,'

Tommy replied, wishing that Kevin would hurry up and get to the point.

'Not quite,' Kevin grinned. 'I look after parcels.' He looked between Tommy and Reece then puffed out his chest with a measure of self-importance. 'I'm talking about special parcels. Parcels that are worth a fair few bob.'

'Yeah, like what?' Tommy asked as he picked up his pint glass and took a sip of the lager.

Glancing around him, Kevin leaned across the table and lowered his voice. 'Gold bullion, diamonds, Rolexes. You name it and I look after it. Like I said – special parcels.'

Tommy choked on his drink. 'What did you just say?' he asked once he was able to catch his breath.

Kevin smirked. 'I thought that might get your attention.'

'But...'

'No buts, lad,' Kevin said, his demeanour becoming deadly serious. 'It's one of the Royal Mail's best kept secrets and you, sunshine,' he said, lounging back in the chair with a sly grin spread across his face, 'are going to help me to steal it.'

2

In the scrapyard office that the Carter family owned, Jonny Carter was feeling restless. As he twirled the chair he was sitting on from side to side, he drummed his fingers absentmindedly on the desk.

Sitting opposite him, Sonny Carter glanced up, his gaze going from the persistent drumming to his brother's face. 'Do you mind,' he snapped. 'You're starting to really wind me up now.'

Jonny sighed, and sitting forward, he leaned his elbows on the desk. 'I'm bored,' he complained.

'Bored?' Sonny's mouth fell open and as he gestured to the paperwork before them he shook his head. 'What the fuck is there for you to be bored about?'

'I don't know,' Jonny shrugged and as he begun tapping the desk again, he caught the look of warning his brother shot towards him. 'What?' he asked, flopping back in the seat. 'I can't help it can I.'

Sonny shook his head again, and as he went back to leafing through a pile of paperwork, his daughter, Carla cleared her throat.

'Maybe once Terri and the baby are home,' she said, referring to Jonny's partner and newborn son. 'Then you won't be so bored.'

'Yeah,' Sonny butted in. 'Just wait until you're knee high in nappies because believe me, you'll soon wish you were sitting here doing fuck all then.'

Jonny sighed. Perhaps Carla had just hit the nail on the head. With Terri still in hospital recovering after giving birth to their son, everything seemed so up in the air. The house was empty without her, too quiet, hence why when he wasn't at the hospital, he was spending his free time at the scrapyard bored out of his nut. 'Maybe,' he said glancing out of the window. 'Or maybe I just need something to focus on... like a job maybe. Something I can really get my teeth into.'

Sonny looked up again, his expression hardening. 'Please tell me that was a joke.' He glanced around the office that just days earlier had been peppered in their adversary, Lenny Tucker's blood. Three coats of paint it had taken to erase the fact a grisly murder had taken place, and even then, Sonny wasn't so sure that they hadn't missed a spot. After all it was no secret that blood was a bugger to get rid of, and he knew from experience that claret had a nasty habit of lingering no matter how meticulously you scrubbed away at it. In fact, if it had been left down to him, he would have burned the office down to the ground, at least then they would have covered their tracks and no incriminating evidence would have been left behind. 'Haven't you caused enough damage?' he asked. 'Seeing as the last heist you orchestrated turned out so well.'

Jonny clenched his jaw. Fair enough, he'd be one of the first to hold his hands up and admit that he'd made mistakes in the past, and a lot of them, but at the end of the day he'd still managed to pull off the one thing his elder brothers had never managed to achieve. All thanks to his expert planning, he was in possession of a bag of diamonds. Diamonds that were so hot he'd more than likely never be able to shift them, not to mention the fact he'd almost lost Terri and his newborn son in the process. He held up his hands. 'I was thinking more along the lines of a bank job, or...' He looked around him. 'I don't know, a security van maybe, something that won't take a lot of planning, something we could do with our eyes shut, something the boys could help with,' he said referring to their nephews. 'They could use it as a bit of practice, just until they've got some experience behind them.' Although if truth be told, he was bored to the back teeth of robbing banks. They'd targeted so many over the years that it had become all too easy, tedious.

Shaking his head Sonny went back to the paperwork before him. 'Or how about,' he said, eyeing his brother, 'we let the dust settle for a while and do nothing? We've got more than enough going on, what with the debt collecting and running this place.'

'Yeah, there is that I suppose,' Jonny reluctantly answered, not that the scrapyard was how they actually earned a living; if anything, it was merely a cover for their real line of work: armed robberies. As he went back to looking out of the window, he resisted the urge to drum his fingers again. He was more than just bored; he needed something to occupy his mind and seeing as he was now the head of the Carter family and in charge of the business, he needed to establish himself, to prove not only to himself but also to his brothers and nephews that he had what it took to lead them into the future.

'I'm going to head off home,' Carla said as she got to her feet and gathered her coat and handbag. 'Are you coming, Dad?'

Sonny glanced at his watch. 'Yeah,' he said as he followed suit and got to his feet. 'I'll probably nip over to the Fiddlers first before though,' he said referring to the pub his partner Rina owned. 'Do you fancy a drink?'

Thinking it over Jonny shook his head. 'Nah, you're alright. I'll finish what I'm doing here and then get off home.'

Sonny nodded, and as he shrugged on his coat, he gave his brother a pointed look. 'I meant what I said. Let the dust settle before you start planning another job.' He motioned to the freshly painted walls. 'Or at least wait for the paint to dry before you start looking for another target.'

Jonny groaned. Out of all his brothers, he'd known that Sonny would be the one to give him the most grief over the murder he'd committed. Admittedly, it hadn't been a wise move on his part in bringing Lenny Tucker to the scrapyard, but in the circumstances what other choice had he had, where else was he supposed to have taken him?

He waited for his brother and niece to leave the office then leaned back in the chair and closed his eyes.

'I was hoping you'd still be here.'

Jonny snapped his eyes open. 'What are you doing here?' he asked his great-nephew.

Tommy's face was flushed and as he bounded into the office, he flopped onto the sofa, the excitement in his voice when he spoke more than audible. 'You won't believe what I've just been told.'

Jonny narrowed his eyes.

'I was just with Aimee's dad,' Tommy hastily explained.

'And?' Steepling his fingers across his chest Jonny cocked his head to the side.

'Did you know' – pausing for breath Tommy then flashed his uncle a wide grin – 'that the Royal Mail transports gold bullion?'

'Yeah,' Jonny answered, sitting forward and resting his chin in his hand.

Tommy's face fell. 'But how?' he asked, screwing up his face.

Jonny let out a laugh. 'How do you think? We're armed robbers, it's our job to know what's out there ready for the taking.'

Still confused, Tommy's forehead was furrowed. 'Then why haven't you done it?'

'We thought about it,' Jonny shrugged. 'But in the end decided it wasn't worth the aggro. There're hundreds, maybe even thousands of Royal Mail vans out there, we can't keep tabs on all of them. It'd be like trying to find a needle in a haystack.'

'Yeah, but.' Tommy leaned back in the chair, his expression smug. 'What if I told you that rather than pay out extortionate amounts of money for insurance, that some jewellers use the Royal Mail to store their goods over the weekend?'

Narrowing his eyes again, Jonny studied his nephew. 'How the fuck would you know something like that?'

Tommy grinned, and tapping the side of his nose, he nodded towards his uncle. 'An inside man told me.'

'And let me guess,' Jonny groaned. 'This inside man of yours would be Aimee's dad?'

Tommy nodded. 'He reckons it'd be a doddle.'

'Carried out a lot of armed robberies then, has he?' As soon as the words left Jonny's mouth, he regretted them. He hadn't intended to come across so harsh, and at times it was easy to forget that his great-nephew had little to no experience when it came to carrying out heists. 'Look.' He got to his feet and perched his backside on the edge of the desk. 'Aimee's old man hasn't got the first clue. Having an inside man might make our job that tiny bit easier, but it would still need a lot of planning and believe me I'm speaking from experience when I say this; it's not as simple as you might think. It could be months before we're even ready to see a job through.'

'Yeah, but...' As he chewed on his bottom lip Tommy rubbed his hand over his forehead. 'I need the money; I mean, *really* need it.'

'What for?' Immediately suspicious, Jonny crossed his arms over his chest. 'Why would you need more cash, you get paid a decent wage working here, although I use the term "work" loosely considering you do fuck all,' he said in an attempt to lighten the mood.

'I just need it, alright?' Tommy snapped.

'No, it's not alright,' Jonny answered. 'So I'm going to ask you again – why do you need the money? Are you in trouble?'

Tommy glanced away.

'Tommy Jr,' Jonny warned, the tone of his voice more than enough to tell his nephew that he wasn't playing games. 'I asked you a question. Are you in trouble?'

Sucking in his bottom lip Tommy nodded. 'Yeah, you could say that.'

The nerve at the side of Jonny's eye twitched. The fact he and his great-nephew were so alike scared him half to death at times. When he'd been Tommy Jr's age, he'd been pretty much uncontrollable; he'd even been the sole reason that his brothers had been roped in to committing the murders of four men. 'What have you done? Because I'm telling you now if I so much as receive one phone call about you causing aggravation I'll swing for you myself.'

'I haven't done anything.' Tommy was quick to answer. 'At least not in the way you think I have.' He sighed then looked down at his hands. 'It's Aimee.'

'What about her?'

'She's pregnant.'

Jonny pinched the bridge of his nose. 'For fuck's sake, Tommy Jr,' he growled. 'Are you really that fucking stupid?' He pushed himself away from the desk then tapped two fingers none too gently against his nephew's temple. 'Is there actually a brain up here because believe me I'm beginning to suspect otherwise?'

Tommy shrugged his uncle away from him. 'It was an accident,' he protested.

Shaking his head Jonny gave a look of disbelief. 'Falling down the stairs after you've had one too many sherbets is an accident, but this,' he shouted, 'is nothing less than stupidity. What the fuck is wrong with you?'

'I didn't mean it to happen,' Tommy shouted back as he jumped off the sofa and made to bolt for the door.

'Oh no you don't,' Jonny said as he blocked his nephew's path. 'You don't get to run away from this.' He shook his head again. 'Your mum and your old man are going to go spare, and as for your nan.' He blew out his cheeks. 'Well, you can imagine what she's going to have to say about this.'

Tommy averted his eyes. 'I'm guessing that they're not gonna be happy.'

'You think?' Jonny rubbed his hand over his jaw as he thought the situation through. 'Look, if it's money you need then I'll give it to you. I can't say I know much about this kind of thing. I mean how much is a termination, a couple of grand? Maybe five, ten thousand if she goes private...'

'She's keeping it,' Tommy interrupted.

Jonny sat back on the edge of the desk, his shoulders slumping. 'Of course she is,' he said rolling his eyes. 'I should have seen that one coming.'

'And that's why I need the money,' Tommy added. 'The baby is going to need stuff.' He looked helplessly around him. 'Clothes, nappies.'

'It's going to need a lot more than just clothes and nappies,' Jonny sighed. 'I've forked out an absolute fortune on James,' he said of his newborn son. On seeing the look upon his nephew's face, he relented slightly. 'Tell me more about this Royal Mail job.'

Tommy took a deep breath. 'Kevin... that's Aimee's dad.'

'Yeah, I gathered that much,' Jonny groaned. 'Get to the main part,' he said impatiently.

'Well, it's mainly just him and some other bloke who are on shift of an evening. He would be able to tell us exactly how to get into the depot.'

Jonny narrowed his eyes. 'Nah,' he said. 'It can't be that simple.' He lifted his chin. 'Where's the catch? Because I can guarantee there is one.'

'Well, we'd need to get our hands on a post office van. Kevin reckons they just buzz them through the gates, they don't even ask for ID.'

Nodding his head, Jonny was deep in thought. 'Considering we both have nimble fingers and that stealing cars is our forte, I can't see that being a problem. What else?'

'That's about it. I mean of course there'd be CCTV, but you'd expect that.'

'And what about Aimee's old man? Do you trust him?'

Tommy thought the question over. The truth was, he didn't trust Aimee's dad, not one little bit. From a young age Tommy had been taught not to fully trust anyone from outside the family; it was a rule that they lived by and one that had stood them in good stead over the years. There were some exceptions of course, his nan's husband Danny McKay being one of them, and then Mad Dog Harris and his partner, Lillian who had worked for his Grandad Tommy being the other two. But both Danny, Mad Dog, and Lillian had known the family for decades, they trusted them tenfold. Whereas he'd only met Kevin a couple of times, and then there was the drink and drug problem to contend with. If it wasn't for the fact that Kevin was Aimee's dad, then he'd want nothing to do with him. They weren't mates, nor were they ever likely to be and other than Aimee, they had nothing in common. 'Nah.' He shook his head. 'I wouldn't trust him as far as I could throw him.'

'And that right there,' Jonny nodded, 'is your problem. Like the old saying goes, if it's too good to be true then it more than likely is.'

'True,' Tommy answered, deflated. 'What else am I supposed to do though?' He chewed on his thumbnail. 'I can't let Aimee down. I need the cash.'

Jonny sighed. 'Look,' he finally answered. 'Give me a few days to think it over.' He reached for his jacket, slipped it on, then grabbed his car keys from the desk. 'Go on, get off home. I've got a feeling you need to have an awkward conversation with your mum and dad.'

Tommy groaned. 'They're gonna hit the roof.'

'Yeah,' Jonny agreed. 'And that's putting it mildly.'

* * *

Kevin Fox banged his fist on his ex-wife's front door. In one hand he held a bunch of flowers that he'd picked up in the local supermarket, and in the other, a cheap bottle of sparkling wine. He knew Melanie like the back of his hand, and she'd always been like putty in his hands especially once she had a drop of alcohol inside of her.

'What do you want?' Leaning against the door frame Melanie crossed her arms over her chest, the scowl across her face enough to warn Kevin that he wasn't welcome.

'Come to celebrate the good news ain't I,' he grinned. 'To wet the baby's head.'

'She hasn't even had the baby yet.' She narrowed her eyes. 'And how do you even know anything about it?'

'How do you think?' Kevin answered with a wide grin as he slipped past Melanie and entered the house. 'Our Aimz' messaged me.'

Melanie raised her eyebrows and closing the front door she placed her hands on her hips. 'I can't think why,' she muttered. 'You're hardly dad of the year material.'

Kevin spun around. 'What are you talking about?' he scolded. 'I've always been there for Aimee.'

'Pity you weren't around when she needed new shoes, or clothes.'

'That's all in the past,' Kevin answered waving his hand dismissively. 'She's a big girl now and besides, she's got her bloke to buy her stuff now, hasn't she, and from my understanding he's loaded.'

Melanie flopped down on to the sofa. 'Oh, I can see where this is going,' she said rolling her eyes. 'You know that he's got a few bob behind him so you're going to try and sponge off him now. Bleed him dry like you bleed everyone else bleeding dry.'

'Of course I'm not.' Cocking his head to the side, Kevin eyed his daughter's mother. 'What's the matter with you, ain't I allowed to be happy? It's not every day I find out I'm going to be a grandad.'

Shaking her head Melanie snatched up her cigarette packet, took out a cigarette, and lit up. 'It's hardly something to be happy about, is it? She's only just turned seventeen.'

Kevin shrugged. 'She'll work it out. She's got her head screwed on, and with me and you guiding her she'll do alright for herself.'

An incredulous laugh escaped from Melanie's lips. 'You mean with me guiding her. You're about as much use as a glass hammer. You barely ever changed her nappy when she was a baby let alone took care of her. You were too busy down the pub, shagging anything that moved.'

'What is this?' Kevin growled, his expression hardening. 'Have a go at Kevin day?' He stabbed his forefinger in Melanie's direction. 'How many more times do I have to tell you that? I've sorted myself out, got a job, a decent fucking job for your information,' he seethed. 'So keep that buttoned,' he said pointing to his lips. 'And let me enjoy this moment in peace without you digging at me every two minutes.'

Melanie huffed out a breath, and taking a final drag on her cigarette she stubbed it out in an overflowing ashtray. 'Aimee,' she shouted. 'Your dad's here.'

Moments later Aimee padded down the stairs and entered the front room.

'Here she is.' Spreading open his arms, Kevin grinned. 'These are for you,' he said passing across the flowers. 'And this,' he said, turning to Melanie and handing over the bottle of sparkling wine, 'is for you, well for us.'

'Thanks Dad,' Aimee beamed. 'Ain't they lovely, Mum?'

Melanie reluctantly nodded. 'Go and put them in a vase of water.'

'Yeah, I will do,' Aimee said as she hugged her father to her again before walking through to the kitchen.

Kevin rubbed his hands together. 'And bring in some glasses,' he called out. 'We've got some celebrating to do.'

'Don't get too cosy,' Melanie remarked. 'You're not stopping here.'

Ignoring the comment, Kevin took a seat in the armchair and made himself comfortable. 'And that boyfriend of yours had better be looking after you,' he called out.

'Of course he is,' Aimee answered as she came back into the

room with the vase. 'He always does.' She placed the flowers on the sideboard then retreated back into the kitchen to fetch the glasses.

'Yeah, well,' Kevin answered craftily. 'He'll have me to deal with if he doesn't.'

Melanie burst out laughing. 'Give over, Kev. I thought we'd already established that the only person you've ever thought about is yourself.'

'Now that's not true,' Kevin replied as he began opening the bottle. 'My little girl has always been my top priority. Admittedly, I could have done more when she was a nipper but I'm here now,' he grinned as he handed his daughter a small glass of the alcohol. 'And what's more, I'm here to stay.'

'You're like a bad penny, you are. No matter how many times I get rid of you, you keep coming back,' Melanie said.

'Yeah,' Kevin chuckled. 'You know me too well.'

Taking a sip of the wine, Melanie pursed her lips and shook her head. 'Don't I just.'

* * *

As he climbed out of his car Tommy Jr looked up at his parents' house. Boasting six bedrooms, the house was situated in a tree-lined avenue in what was considered to be an affluent part of Chigwell in Epping Forest. With many of the neighbouring houses selling in the region of a million pounds and upwards, it was a far cry from the Dagenham council estate where Aimee lived, or even where his family had originally come from seeing as they had been born and bred in Barking, which was only a stone's throw away from Dagenham.

Entering the house, his stomach was tied in knots. The problem was, his parents had never even met Aimee. Oh, he'd talked about her, mentioned her here and there, but they had never actually come face to face. And the funny thing was he didn't even know why. Why hadn't he introduced them before now? He'd had ample opportunity to do so.

Only, deep down, he did know the reason why he'd never brought Aimee over to meet his parents. They were expecting him to find a local girl, someone who had had the same upbringing as himself. And although his parents didn't put on any airs and graces, they had money, and a lot of it. What did his Aimee have? Nothing, that's what; their worlds were a million miles apart. But that was what he liked about her. She wasn't flash, she didn't care about buying the latest designer handbag, or how much his car was worth. She liked him for him, not because of who he was or what he could give her. She was a grafter too. Not only did she attend college through the week, but she also worked in a hairdressing salon on a Saturday. It was at the salon where they'd first met; he'd walked past one day and spotted her inside. It had been a case of love at first sight, or lust, whichever way you wanted to look at it, although his Aimee preferred to say love, and in a way, he supposed she was right. He'd hung around for hours waiting for her shift to end just so that he could chat her up, not that she'd made it easy for him; she'd turned him down at first, told him to get lost, but in the end, he'd managed to charm her into giving him a chance, and the rest, as they say, was history. Now all these months later he was about to tell his parents that they were going to become grandparents, the mere thought was enough to make him feel sick.

'Tommy Jr, is that you?'

Tommy momentarily froze, then taking a deep breath he answered. 'Yeah, Mum.'

Karen Johnson walked out into the hallway, a wide smile

plastered across her face. They looked alike Tommy noted, same colour hair, same blue eyes, only he'd never really noticed the similarities before now. Not that he should have been entirely surprised by their likeness; his entire family were like clones of one another, so much so that people often presumed he and Reece were brothers rather than cousins once removed. In that instant he wondered who his baby would take after, himself or Aimee?

'I was just saying to your dad that I hadn't seen you today,' Karen grinned. 'Are you hungry? We were thinking of getting a takeaway. What do you fancy, Chinese or a curry?'

'I don't want anything.' Tommy shook his head. 'I'm not hungry.'

'What's the matter with you?' Karen gave a small laugh. 'You're always bleeding hungry.'

Tommy averted his gaze. 'Nothing.' He tapped his foot, his stomach doing somersaults. 'It's...' He looked up, swallowed, then offered a weak smile. 'It's...'

'It's what?' Alarmed, Karen stepped forward. 'What's wrong? Are you feeling unwell?' She pressed the back of her hand to her son's forehead. 'You don't feel hot.'

'For Christ's sake, Mum, leave it out, will you?' Gently swatting his mum away from him, Tommy gave an irritated sigh. He hated it when she treated him like a baby, something his cousins, Reece in particular, liked to take the piss out of him for. 'I'm fine. Will you just stop fussing over me?'

Stunned by her son's reaction, Karen dropped her hands to her sides, her face instantly falling.

Shame washed over Tommy. As an only child, his parents had given him everything his heart had desired. That wasn't to say he'd been spoiled though because he hadn't. As soon as he'd hit his teenage years they'd made him work at the scrapyard in the school holidays to earn a bit of extra cash. 'I'm sorry.' He rubbed at the nape of his neck. 'I didn't mean to snap.'

'Then, what's wrong?' Karen probed. 'Has something happened? Cam',' she shouted out to her husband, Cameron. 'Come out here, will you?'

Still studying a takeaway menu, Cameron walked into the hallway and looked up, his gaze going between his wife and only son. 'What's up?'

'I don't know,' Karen said as she nodded towards Tommy. 'But something's not right. You know as well as I do that he can eat us out of house and home. His head is always stuck in the fridge or kitchen cupboard looking for something to eat.' Her hand fluttered up to her throat. 'Is it your nan? Has something happened to her?'

'Of course it hasn't,' Tommy retorted, screwing up his face. 'I haven't even seen her.'

'Thank Christ for that. Blimey Tommy Jr, between you and your father you're going to end up putting me in an early grave.'

'Stop being so dramatic,' Cam laughed. 'The boy's not hungry, that's all.' He turned to look at his son and flicked his chin towards him. 'So, what's going on?'

Tommy swallowed. He wasn't only scared about becoming a father, but he was also scared for his baby's health. His parents were first cousins and after they'd had him they'd never tried to have another baby; they'd been too afraid that any future children they might bear could be at risk of having a genetic disorder. So what did that mean for him, were his kids at risk too?

'If I was to have a kid, what would the chances be of it having something wrong with it, like a genetic problem?'

Karen and Cameron glanced towards one another.

'Where's this coming from?' Karen asked with a shake of her head.

'Would it be alright?' Tommy asked again, his voice becoming desperate. 'You and dad are cousins, and I'm the result, so what does that mean for my kids? Would they be born with birth defects?'

'For fuck's sake,' Cameron muttered underneath his breath. 'Is this something to do with that mouthy bastard, Lenny fucking Tucker?' He stabbed his finger forward. 'How many times did I tell you not to take any notice of the prick? You're not inbred.'

'Inbred!' Karen gasped. 'He's not bloody inbred.'

'I know he's not,' Cameron answered in an attempt to calm his wife down. He turned back to his son, the muscles across his shoulders flexing. 'Is that what this is all about?'

Tommy shook his head. 'No, not really. Well maybe a little bit.' He took a step back in an attempt to create a reasonable distance between himself and his parents. If he knew his mum as well as he thought he did then she was about to go ballistic. She had a wicked temper on her and despite the fact she liked to baby him, she wouldn't be averse to thumping him if needs be. Time and time again she'd warned him to be careful, to not go getting any girls pregnant. And he had been careful, he'd always made sure to use a condom, or at least he had until he'd met Aimee. 'It's...' He paused, swallowed, then began again. 'It's my girlfriend, Aimee.'

'What about her?' Karen's voice ever so slightly trembled and despite the small smile she gave, unease radiated off her.

'She's...'

'She's what?' Karen asked, her voice coming out as a squeak.

Tommy swallowed again, and momentarily closing his eyes, he took a deep breath. 'She's pregnant.'

'What do you mean, she's pregnant?' The colour drained from Karen's face. 'But.' She glanced towards her husband barely able to comprehend what her son was telling her. 'She can't be, you're too young.'

'Karen.' Lifting his eyebrows Cameron gave his wife a knowing look. 'He's not a little boy, he's nineteen.'

'I know how bloody old he is,' Karen shrieked back at her husband. 'I gave birth to him. And as for you,' she said, glaring at her son, 'what the hell were you thinking?' She took a step closer filling the gap between them, her hands clenching into fists. 'This isn't some game you're playing,' she shouted. 'Something that you can walk away from once you've grown bored or when you realise just how difficult life has become. A child is for life, Tommy Jr.'

'I know that.' Averting his gaze again, Tommy shrugged. 'It wasn't planned. It was an accident.'

'I should hope it wasn't planned.' Throwing her arms up into the air, Karen's face was set like thunder. 'I can't believe this,' she cried. 'I can't believe that you'd be so careless, so stupid.' She turned to look at her husband, tears pricking her eyes, her expression one of despair.

Placing his arm around his wife's shoulders, Cameron sighed. 'And it's definitely yours?'

'Of course it is,' Tommy snapped. 'Aimee's not like that, she's not some tart.'

'I didn't say she was.' Cameron held up his free hand. 'It's just a lot to take in that's all.'

'Will it be alright though?' Tommy urged as he looked between his parents. 'I mean what if my genes... well, you know, what if it's born with problems?'

Still dumbstruck, Karen shook her head. 'Of course it will be alright, you daft sod.' The tears slipped down her cheeks, and she wiped them away as Cameron pulled her even closer.

'This is all a bit of a shock, eh?' he said. 'A lot for us to get our heads around.'

Karen nodded. 'I could bloody kill you, Tommy Jr,' she said through her tears. 'And as for this Aimee.' She gave an exasperated sigh, half contemplating swinging for her son, to knock some sense into his head. 'You'd best bring her around to meet us.'

'You'll like her, Mum,' Tommy said. 'Honest you will.'

'Yeah, well,' Karen answered. 'I don't suppose I'm going to have much choice in the matter seeing as she's the mother of my grandchild.'

* * *

Aimee clutched her mobile phone to her chest. 'Tommy's mum and dad have invited us over to their house,' she said, her eyes as wide as saucers. 'They want to meet us.'

'And so they should.' Lounging back in the armchair, Kevin guzzled down his wine. 'It's the least they can do considering their son knocked you up.' He pointed the empty glass towards his daughter. 'They owe you, girl, and that baby you're carrying is gonna be your meal ticket out of this dump.'

'Dad!' Aimee gasped, her mouth dropping open. 'I'm not going to use my baby as a bartering tool.'

'Oi,' Melanie butted in, her body bristling at the insult. 'That's my house you're talking about,' she said, gesturing around the front room. 'I know it might not be the Ritz but at least it's clean and tidy.'

Kevin waved his hand dismissively. 'It's a shithole and you know it. The place is falling apart. Besides,' he said craftily, 'you said yourself there isn't room for a baby.' He nodded towards his daughter. 'With a bit of luck, they'll see you alright, and if you're really lucky they might even buy you a house, something a darn sight better than this dump,' he said, motioning around him. 'They're not going to want their only grandchild brought up in squalor. That baby's a Johnson and you'd best remember that; they look after their own that lot.'

'She's seventeen,' Melanie seethed. 'She can't live all by herself.'

'She won't,' Kevin grinned. 'She'll have us living with her.'

'I knew it.' Melanie shook her head. 'This is so typical of you. This isn't even about our Aimee,' she scolded. 'This is about you and what you can get out of the situation. As per fucking usual,' she added with a roll of her eyes.

'That's where you're wrong,' Kevin smirked. 'I only want the best for our girl, always have done. And as for me.' He tapped the side of his nose. 'I'm about to come into some dough myself, a lot of dough,' he said rubbing his thumb and forefinger together. 'You just wait and see, I'm gonna be rolling in it.'

Lifting her eyebrows, Melanie returned the smirk. 'Well in that case you can take care of Aimee, buy her a house, see that she's alright. You are her dad after all.'

About to refill his glass Kevin paused, his back stiffening. 'She's Tommy's responsibility now,' he said, sulking. 'He's the one who got her pregnant. It's fuck all to do with me.'

'Yeah, I thought as much,' Melanie barked back. 'You'll never change, Kevin Fox, not as long as you've got a hole in your arse.'

Kevin couldn't help but chuckle. 'As I keep on telling you,' he grinned. 'You know me too well.'

* * *

A few days later as Karen Johnson busied herself around the kitchen she was on tenterhooks. 'I still can't get my head around this,' she stated to her mother, Stacey McKay. 'He's too young to be a father, he hasn't got the first idea how to look after himself, let alone a baby. As it is, I still do his washing for him. I don't think he even knows how to boil an egg.'

Stacey sighed, and as she pulled kitchen foil away from a plate of sandwiches, she gave her daughter a gentle smile. 'It's like history repeating itself all over again. I wasn't much older than Tommy Jr when I had you. And believe me when I say this, me and your dad soon had to learn how to grow up.' She looked into the distance as she thought back to her first husband, not that she could say he was ever far from her mind. She'd loved Tommy Snr with all of her heart and had never envisioned a day when he wouldn't be by her side, nor a day when he would be cruelly torn away from her, murdered in cold blood. That wasn't to say that she didn't love her second husband, Danny, because she did, but her Tommy would always hold a special place in her heart. She gave a small smile. 'Not that your dad ever had much of an input when it came to looking after you or your brothers, it wasn't the done thing back in those days. Looking after children was seen as the woman's responsibility while your dad's job was to put food on the table and keep a roof over our heads.'

'Yeah, but,' Karen argued. 'It was a different world back then. You and my dad had no other choice but to get on with it.'

Stacey lifted her eyebrows. 'I'm not so sure about that. Kids today have a wealth of knowledge at their fingertips, much more than we ever had.' She patted her daughter's arm. 'It's going to be alright, darling, and he's got a lot of family around him to help out.'

'I suppose so,' Karen huffed. She glanced up at the clock on the wall. 'They should be here soon,' she said referring to Aimee and her parents. 'I actually feel sick to my stomach. What if they don't like us, or what if we don't like them?' She clutched her hand to her chest. 'What if it doesn't work out between Tommy Jr and this Aimee? What if she refuses to let him see the baby, you know how spiteful women can be? It would break his heart, Mum. And no matter how old he is, he's still my baby.'

'Stop,' Stacey warned. 'You're worrying yourself sick over nothing. Here take this.' Passing across a glass of wine she couldn't help but laugh. 'You look like you could do with a drink, you're a nervous bleeding wreck.'

Taking the glass Karen gulped at the liquid. 'I can't help it,' she protested. 'I've been like this ever since Tommy Jr told me about the baby. It's the "what ifs" that worry me the most. I mean what do we do if she decides she doesn't want him or us around the baby?'

'As if that's going to happen,' Stacey answered.

'But what if—'

Placing her hand on her daughter's arm, Stacey shook her head. 'I said stop,' she scolded. She took a deep breath and sighed. 'If the worst was to happen then we get a solicitor involved, take her to court if need be. Fathers have equal rights nowadays, and there are even steps grandparents can take so that they play a part in a child's life – mediation and that sort of thing.'

'Yeah, you're right.' Somewhat placated, Karen nodded. 'Is uncle Jonny here yet?' she asked, glancing in the direction of the lounge.

Stacey shook her head again. 'I'm sure we would have heard him if he was.' She gave her daughter a wink, and as both women giggled the doorbell rang.

'Speak of the devil and he appears,' Stacey laughed. 'You finish doing this.' She motioned to the buffet that was in the process of being laid out. 'And I'll let him in.'

Moments later, Jonny Carter and his partner, Terri Tempest

entered the kitchen. 'You alright, darling?' Jonny asked as he kissed his niece on her cheek.

'I've been better,' Karen admitted. 'I could happily throttle him for this,' she said of her son. 'Not that it would change anything.'

'Yeah well, I've brought this little one along,' Jonny gestured to the car seat containing his newborn son. 'Might as well let them see what they're letting themselves in for.'

Karen rolled her eyes. 'It's a bit late for that don't you think?' she answered as she crouched down to make a fuss of her youngest cousin. 'They can hardly do anything about the situation now, can they?'

'True,' Jonny sighed. 'So, what's she like, this Aimee?' he asked, turning to look at his nephew Reece as he entered the kitchen.

'She's alright,' Reece shrugged as he helped himself to a drink. 'She's nice. And she could do a lot better than him, I know that much,' he winked, jerking his thumb in Tommy's direction.

'Oi, I heard that,' Tommy huffed.

'I'm only playing,' Reece laughed, slinging his arm around Tommy's shoulders. 'Let me put it this way,' he said, his voice becoming serious. 'She's a lot better than that old man of hers.' He tipped a bottle of beer towards his uncle before taking a sip. 'I might have only met him the once, but it was enough to tell me that amongst other things the bloke's a ponce.'

'Yeah,' Jonny answered thoughtfully. 'I had a feeling you might say that.'

* * *

Kevin Fox stepped out of his car and surveyed the house before him. Whistling through his teeth he resisted the urge to rub his hands together. 'So... This is how the other half live, eh?' he stated as he glanced over his shoulder to look at his ex-wife.

Melanie looked up at the house, then smoothing down her short blonde hair she turned to look at her reflection in the car window. 'Do I look okay?' she asked in a moment of uncertainty. She'd bought the linen trousers and fitted white shirt from the market especially for the occasion, and she'd thought she looked smart but on seeing Tommy's parents' house she wasn't so sure any more. 'I don't look a state, do I?' She nodded towards the iron gates that led to the house. 'I knew they had money, but I wasn't expecting it to be as fancy as this, and I don't want them to think we're riff-raff.'

A nasty gleam twinkled in Kevin's eyes. 'They're hardly gonna be looking at you, are they? Not when our Aimz' is the star of the show.'

'Give over, Dad,' Aimee groaned as she joined her parents on the pavement. 'I feel nervous as it is.' She clasped hold of her mother's hand. 'And you look lovely, Mum.'

'There ain't nothing for you to be nervous about,' Kevin retorted. 'This lot ain't no better than us. And I'll tell you something else for nothing – I remember them Carters from back in the day when they were living over in Barking and trust me when I say this: once upon a time they had fuck all to their names.'

'They've done alright for themselves since then,' Melanie observed.

'Of course they have,' Kevin hissed as they walked down the driveway, the brickwork under their feet immaculate and free from weeds. 'They're villains, the whole bloody lot of them.'

At the front door Kevin straightened out his shirt. He'd taken extra care of his appearance that morning. Not only had he had a bath and a shave, but he'd also laid off the gear. He wanted to make a good impression, and seeing as he wanted young Tommy Jr to put in a good word for him it was in his best interests to stay off the coke.

* * *

As the doorbell rang, Tommy Jr jumped out of his seat.

'Fucking hell,' Jonny chuckled. 'That's the quickest I've ever seen you move.'

Tommy rolled his eyes, and as he went to open the door he missed the knowing look that his father and uncle shared.

A short time later he walked back into the lounge. 'Mum and Dad,' he said, his voice holding a hint of trepidation. 'This is Aimee and her parents, Melanie and Kevin.'

Karen stepped forward. 'Well, he said you were pretty,' she commented, pulling Aimee into her for a hug. 'But I wasn't expecting you to be this stunning.'

Aimee's cheeks flamed red, and gripping onto Tommy's hand, she glanced around her. 'I thought you said your parents' house wasn't anything that special,' she hissed in her boyfriend's ear.

'It's not,' Tommy laughed. 'And if you think this is special, just wait until you see my nan's house,' he winked.

Aimee gulped, and as she looked nervously towards Tommy's grandmother, she forced her shoulders to relax. She'd heard the stories about Stacey McKay, or Carter as she'd once been known. And if she'd thought those were bad, they were nothing compared to the rumours she'd heard about Stacey's second husband, Danny McKay.

Once the introductions were complete, Karen nodded towards the kitchen. 'Can I get anyone a drink?'

'I wouldn't say no,' Kevin was one of the first to answer. 'Whiskey if you've got any?'

Karen nodded. 'I'm sure that we've got some somewhere. And what about you, Melanie?' Karen smiled.

'Just Mel is fine,' Melanie answered waving her hand in the air. 'And wine would be nice.'

Karen nodded, and as she made her way into the kitchen, Melanie followed.

'It's a beautiful house you've got,' she said, looking around the state-of-the-art kitchen that had to be at least four times the size of her own kitchen, the solid oak kitchen cabinets and granite worktops gleaming; there was even a display of fresh flowers in a crystal vase on the windowsill that by her estimation must have cost an arm and a leg. 'Puts my little council place to shame. I dread to think what your Tommy must think of it whenever he comes over, especially when he comes from this,' she added.

About to pour out their drinks, Karen paused, and placing the bottle back on the granite counter, she turned around and sighed. 'I didn't bring him up to judge others.' She offered a warm smile. 'My mum and dad had absolutely nothing when they started out, they couldn't even afford a place to live when they first got married. Nothing was handed to them on a plate, my dad worked his arse off to buy them a house of their own. And as for Tommy Jr, he'll have to do the same. Admittedly we'll help him out where we can, but he won't get much else out of us, he'll have to learn to stand on his own two feet, same as the rest of us.'

'Maybe we're not so different after all,' Melanie laughed, her nerves slowly dissipating. 'I've been saying the same thing to my Aimee. I can't afford to feed and clothe a baby; it'll be down to her to provide for him or her.'

'Well don't you worry about that.' Karen handed over a glass of wine. 'That baby is as much Tommy Jr's responsibility as it is

Aimee's.' She glanced towards the lounge and bit down on her bottom lip. 'I just wish that they weren't so bloody young.'

'Yeah,' Melanie sighed. 'Talk about babies having babies.' Her forehead furrowed and she looked thoughtfully to where her ex-husband was standing. 'The only one who seems over the moon about all of this is him,' she said, nodding towards Kevin.

* * *

Standing centre stage in Cameron Johnson's lounge, Kevin was in his element, and as he greedily gulped down the whiskey, he eyed up the drinks cabinet, although to call it a cabinet would be the understatement of the century. The shelving unit that spanned the entire length of the back wall was encased behind glass doors that had been polished so vigorously they sparkled, and to top it off, spotlights had been placed strategically to illuminate the bottles of alcohol housed there. From Kevin's position he could see that the alcohol was not your average run-of-the-mill booze that could be bought from the local off-licence or supermarket. No, unless he was very much mistaken the bottles on display were worth hundreds of pounds, perhaps even thousands. Nothing would surprise him when it came to this lot; they had more money than sense.

Still, he reasoned, once he had his share from the robbery then he too would have a drinks cabinet, not that the alcohol would last very long. He liked a drink, liked a bit of charlie even more. He was a man's man, much the same as the Carters and Johnsons in that sense. And back in the day, he himself had had a bit of a reputation, not in the same league as the Carters of course, but people had been wary of him. He was shrewd, knew how to play the game, and what's more he knew how to look after himself when he needed to.

Using the back of his hand, he wiped it underneath his nose all the while wondering if Tommy's family were partial to a bit of coke. He could do with something to loosen him up a bit and wanted to kick himself for not having the hindsight to bring a wrap along with him. He stole a glance towards the hallway, and in particular the door that led to the bathroom: the marble worktop would be the perfect surface to cut a line. Yeah, he decided, he and Tommy's family weren't so different, they were cut from the same cloth, and he wouldn't be surprised if they had a stash of cocaine hidden away. They could certainly afford it, he knew that much, and what's more he had a feeling they knew how to let their hair down and have a good time. He looked around him wondering how best to broach the subject. Maybe he should pull Tommy aside and ask him outright if there was any sniff in the house, or perhaps he should bite the bullet and ask Tommy's father, Cameron Johnson? He was in the mood for a party and seeing as his daughter's pregnancy was a reason for them to celebrate it was only right that they supply the goods.

* * *

Jonny Carter eyed Kevin Fox over the rim of his glass. Reece had been right, the man was a ponce, not to mention a braggart, and if that wasn't bad enough along with the constant sniffing and wiping of his nose, the more the drinks were flowing the more Kevin was becoming loose-lipped. In other words, Kevin was a liability, if ever Jonny had seen one.

'And if you're ever after chisel,' Kevin said tapping his nose, his sly eyes twinkling. 'Then come and see me and I'll see you alright. I've got a contact,' he continued to brag. 'It'll be the best fifty notes you've ever spent.'

Glancing towards Cameron, Jonny lifted his eyebrows.

Drugs had never been his scene, or rather hard drugs anyway, and the fact that Kevin was boasting about the narcotics that he could supposedly get his hands on was all the more reason for Jonny not to like him. 'So, Tommy Jr was saying that you work for the Royal Mail,' Jonny said, keen to change the subject.

Kevin's eyes lit up and taking a step closer he made a show of looking over his shoulder, as if to check that no one else was within ear shot of their conversation. 'That's right. And did he tell you about the items I look after?'

Jonny gave a nonchalant shrug. 'Yeah, he mentioned it in passing.'

Kevin beamed. 'So, what do you reckon?'

Jonny shrugged again, his forehead furrowing. 'About what?'

'The goods,' Kevin urged. 'The special parcels.'

'Why the fuck would I have an opinion about it?'

Straightening up, Kevin's mouth fell open. 'But it's gold,' he said, confusion sweeping over his face as he looked between Jonny and Cameron. 'Gold bullion to be precise, not to mention Rolexes, diamonds, and every other gemstone you can possibly imagine.'

'And,' Jonny answered nonchalantly, 'what makes you think I'd be interested in something like that?'

As the atmosphere between the men became considerably frosty, Kevin's face paled. 'But you're Carters,' he exclaimed.

Cameron gave a hollow laugh, and holding up his hands he shook his head. 'I'm a Johnson, mate. Although to be fair, my old man was a Carter.'

'But...' Kevin looked aimlessly around him. 'That's what you do, you're armed robbers.'

'Says who?' Jonny answered with a menacing growl, his stance enough to alert anyone with half a brain cell that he wasn't impressed that Kevin had been made privy to their personal business.

'But...' Stumbling on his words again, Kevin swallowed deeply. 'I thought... Well, what I mean is, it's common knowledge that...'

'What?' Taking a step closer, Jonny's eyes hardened.

'I thought...' Kevin swallowed again, and as he glanced in the direction of his daughter and Tommy, his already ruddy cheeks turned a deeper shade of red. 'I thought that was your game, bank jobs and the like.'

'Well, you thought fucking wrong,' Jonny barked out. 'And the same goes for any other tosser out there spreading rumours about me and my family. We run a respectable business; and what's more we've even got the business accounts to prove it.'

Kevin swallowed deeply, his expression instantly falling. 'I'm sorry,' he said, holding up his hands, thoroughly humiliated. 'My mistake.'

'Too fucking right you made a mistake.' Jonny continued to glare. He didn't like Kevin Fox, not one little bit, and like both Tommy Jr and Reece, he didn't trust the man as far as he could throw him. Neither did he trust Kevin to have any insight into how the Carter family actually made a living. As for the gold, Rolexes, and gemstones, oh he was interested alright, not that he was prepared for Kevin to get a look in. Knowing just how loose-lipped the man was, he didn't trust Kevin not to throw them under the bus should the police come knocking on his door. He took another sip of his drink, thinking the situation over. The problem was though, how were they going to get their hands on the goods? As much as he didn't like to admit it, they needed Kevin to a certain degree and without him they wouldn't be able to get into the Royal Mail depot. Of course there was a simple solution to the problem, they could put the hard word on him, maybe even rough him up a bit. He gave Kevin a surreptitious glance as a second idea sprang to his mind; they could use him for their own gains, lure him into a false sense of security. After all Kevin had been right about one thing, they were Carters, and as such they were ruthless and allowed nothing to stand in their way. And when it came to armed robberies, they had decades of experience behind them and, as it just so happened, that experience also included murder. With the idea firmly planted in his mind Jonny turned his attention back to his great-nephew and his girlfriend. 'I reckon this calls for a toast,' he said raising his glass in the air. 'To another little Carter.'

'You mean Johnson,' Karen called out, her voice jovial.

'Yeah.' Holding up his hands Jonny joined in with the laughter. 'My mistake.' He raised his glass a second time. 'To another little Johnson,' he corrected.

As those around him lifted their glasses, Jonny couldn't help but sneak a glance in Kevin's direction. The drooping of Kevin's shoulders was enough to tell him that he wasn't a happy bunny, that perhaps his bubble had been well and truly burst. Not that Jonny cared one iota about the man's feelings. As far as he was aware Kevin was nothing more than a means to an end. In fact, he'd go as far as to say the worst thing Kevin could have ever done was to tell them about the goods kept overnight in the Royal Mail depot, because one way or another, they would be taking them, with or without Kevin's input.

3

Kevin was raging, and after climbing into the car, he slammed the door shut with such force that the car windows rattled.

'Are you sure that you're alright to drive?' Melanie asked from the passenger seat as she snapped the seat belt into place. 'You've been knocking the drinks back tonight.'

'Been keeping tabs on me, have you?' Kevin spat. 'Watching my every move?'

'Would be hard not to,' Melanie answered, her forehead furrowed. 'Every time I looked over at you, you had a drink in your hand.'

'Of course I'm alright to drive,' Kevin barked back. 'I'm not an idiot.' He gave the Johnsons' house a final glare. 'I wouldn't be surprised if they watered the booze down anyway. The fucking arseholes.'

Melanie's mouth dropped open, and glancing over her shoulder, she took note of her daughter's stunned expression.

'Dad,' Aimee gasped.

'Well.' Kevin screwed up his face, and starting the ignition, he pushed his foot down on the accelerator and screeched away from the kerb. 'They really think that they're something special. They're nothing but flash fucking cunts. That drinks cabinet alone must be worth thousands. Even the khazi was decked out better than the shithole of a room that I'm forced to live in.' He looked up at the rearview mirror and locked eyes with his daughter. 'Worst thing you ever did was to get knocked up by one of that lot.'

'Mum,' Aimee cried, tears welling up in her eyes. 'Will you tell him to stop?'

Melanie snapped her head towards her ex-husband, all the while keeping one eye firmly fixed on the road ahead of them. 'You've changed your bloody tune,' she exclaimed. 'You've been singing their praises all week. And will you slow down?' she all but screamed. 'Are you trying to get us all killed?'

Easing his foot off the accelerator, Kevin clenched his jaw. He'd been made to feel like a fool, and for all intents and purposes he was pretty sure that he'd looked like one too. Jonny Carter had made him feel so small that it had taken everything in Kevin's power not to smash his fist in the man's face, to teach him a lesson he wouldn't forget in a hurry. Just who the fuck did he think he was? And as for pretending the Carters and Johnsons were holier than thou, well that was utter tripe. Kevin had heard the rumours and knew for a fact that they could be held accountable for at least a dozen armed robberies, if not more. And as for Carter claiming that they ran a respectable business, well that was bollocks an' all. Kevin wasn't as green around the edges as some might think and he knew for a fact that running a poxy little scrapyard wouldn't be enough to generate the vast wealth the Carters and Johnsons had gained over the years; to even suggest otherwise was ludicrous.

'Well, I thought they were very hospitable,' Melanie said breaking his thoughts. 'And that spread Karen put on was out of this world.' She turned to give her daughter a warm smile. 'Tommy has got a lovely family.' She reached out to clasp Aimee's hand and give it a reassuring squeeze. 'I know that I had my reservations, but I've got a feeling you and Tommy can make this work, he's besotted with you,' she said with a laugh.

Aimee smiled through her tears. 'Thanks, Mum, the feeling's mutual.'

'Besotted with her,' Kevin muttered as he flicked the indicator to turn onto the motorway. 'Fat lot of good that'll do her when he's banged up.'

'Mum,' Aimee cried again.

Pulling her hand free, Melanie turned in her seat. 'What on earth is wrong with you?' she demanded of her ex-husband. 'I thought you liked Tommy?'

'Well, that's exactly where he's headed!' he bellowed. 'Him and that family of his.' Kevin's lips curled into a snarl, his earlier humiliation all too fresh in his mind. And that was another thing – he'd specifically told Tommy to put a good word in for him. Instead, the no-good bastard had done the complete opposite and contributed to his shame. 'I should have put my foot down,' he growled. 'Should have warned the fucker to stay away from her the very moment he started sniffing around.' He gave Melanie a sidelong glance. 'I blame you for this,' he spat. 'You've allowed her to run wild. Taught her to spread her legs for all and sundry.'

Melanie's mouth dropped open. 'Well, that's charming,' she huffed. 'And what a way to talk about your only daughter.'

Kevin pulled his shoulders up into a shrug, and as Aimee began to weep, he ignored her sobs. Anger flowed through his veins. He'd been counting on that money from the Royal Mail robbery. He'd had plans, big plans. That money was to set him up in life, to give him a standing in the local community. Why should Tommy and his family live a life of luxury while he had nothing? He didn't even have a home to call his own. After Melanie had kicked him out of the council house they'd once shared, he'd had no other choice but to rent a box room in a crowded house that was both cramped and stank of mould and stale sweat. Bitterness and jealousy engulfed Kevin. Jonny Carter had messed with the wrong man, and if it was the last thing Kevin ever did, then it would be to make Carter pay for his disrespect. An idea sprang to his mind, a nasty little grin spreading across his face. He glanced up at the rear-view mirror again and as he witnessed the hot tears slip down his daughter's cheeks, he felt nothing, not even a flicker of remorse. Maybe one day his Aimee would even thank him. After all, he would be saving her from living the life of a gangster's moll. A life that one day would make her as corrupt as the Carters and Johnsons. Of course there would be casualties along the way, but it was a price Kevin was willing to take – even his daughter's happiness wouldn't be enough to make him change his mind, and as for his unborn grandchild, well, in his mind he would be doing the kid a favour. By taking his or her father out of the equation then his grandchild might just have a chance in life.

Happier now, Kevin forced himself to relax, and ignoring the atmosphere in the car that his bad mood had created, he reached out to switch on the radio. Recognising the tune being played, he hummed along as though he didn't have a single care in the world, which was a lot more than could be said for Tommy and his family once he'd unleashed his wrath upon them. A laugh escaped from his lips and as Melanie turned her head to look at him, her expression one of bewilderment, he resisted the urge to laugh even harder. No one, and he meant no one, took him for a fool and got away with it, and the Carters and Johnsons were about to find out just how dangerous he really was.

* * *

As Karen Johnson waved goodbye to her visitors, she couldn't help but smile, and as her husband wrapped his arm around her, she rested her head upon his shoulder. She'd been worrying over nothing. Aimee was lovely, and not only that, but it was plain to see that the girl was smitten with her son.

'What do you reckon?' she asked, turning to look up at her husband.

Cameron shrugged. 'She seems nice,' he said as he led the way into the lounge.

Karen narrowed her eyes. 'I can sense a but coming.'

Cameron shook his head. 'Like I said, she seems nice enough, but…' He glanced towards his son. 'I wasn't so keen on her old man.'

Karen's shoulders drooped. She'd had the exact same thoughts, and as her gaze went to the drinks cabinet, she surveyed the bottles there. It hadn't escaped her notice that Kevin had been well on his way to drinking them dry. She chewed on her bottom lip. 'Maybe we should have insisted they call a taxi.'

'You did offer,' her mother, Stacey, pointed out as she cradled Jonny and Terri's son in her arms. 'That Kevin is one slimy fucker,' she added giving a shudder. 'You need to be wary of him,' she said, nodding towards her grandson. 'I don't trust the man.'

Looking up from his mobile phone, Tommy nodded back.

'I told you,' Reece said addressing Jonny. 'That Kevin is a ponce.'

Cameron lifted his eyebrows, and as he too glanced towards the drinks cabinet, he sighed. Five hundred nicker he'd paid for the bottle of whiskey that Kevin had pretty much drained, not that money was the issue, he was good for it and the alcohol could easily be replaced, it was more the principle of the matter that bothered him. And if that wasn't enough, Aimee's father had all but confirmed that he had a cocaine habit. The persistent sniffing had been the first giveaway, let alone the constant clenching and grinding of his jaw. He cast his gaze upon his son, his forehead furrowed. Tommy had never shown any indication of drug use, at least not the hard drugs anyway. He'd caught a whiff of cannabis on him every so often, but certainly not enough to cause Cameron any alarm. Tommy was, however, young, perhaps easily swayed, and seeing as he wanted to impress his girlfriend's father, would he be willing to experiment with something a lot stronger than weed? He'd have a word with his boy, Cameron decided, take him aside out of Karen's earshot and warn him to stay away from dabbling with narcotics. After all, it was no secret that drug addiction led to a slippery slope, one that was more often than not hard to crawl back from.

'I can tell you one thing,' Jonny said. 'Your nan's right, I don't trust the fucker either.' He nodded towards Tommy. 'There's no way I'm taking that Kevin out on a job with me, fuck that.'

Tommy looked up again, and before he could even open his mouth to answer, his grandmother butted in.

'I don't want to know,' Stacey said holding up her hand. 'This isn't the time or place for that kind of conversation.'

'Mum's right,' Karen agreed as she wrapped her arms around herself and gave an involuntary shiver. 'I don't want to hear it.'

Shaking his head Jonny gave a light laugh. 'What are you talking about?' he said to his former sister-in-law. 'Danny's hardly the pillar of the community, is he? He supplies firearms for a start and that's without everything else he's involved in. How exactly do you think he came by the money to buy his nightclub? Because I can tell you right now it wasn't through legal activities.'

Stacey tilted her head to the side, her expression hardening. 'Maybe so, but we certainly don't discuss business. He keeps me well away from that side of his life.'

'And as for you,' Jonny said, addressing his niece. 'Without the robberies you wouldn't have all of this.' He gestured around the lounge that wouldn't have looked out of place on the front cover of a magazine. 'And your dad,' he added referring to his eldest brother and Karen's father, Tommy Snr, 'was the one who put us on this path.'

'I already know that,' Karen hissed back at him. 'I'm well aware of what my dad was and wasn't, thank you very much. I just don't want that kind of talk here, not in front of...' She nodded towards her son. 'It's not right.'

'Give over, Karen,' Cameron laughed. 'He's an adult now, he's about to become a father for fuck's sake. And whether you like it or not he was destined for this life. He's the next generation. Were you honestly expecting him to go off in a different direction, to suddenly become respectable, get suited and booted, and work up the city or something?'

'No, of course not.' Karen pursed her lips. In truth she had expected her son to steer away from the family business, or at least she'd hoped he would. Tommy had done well at school and passed all of his exams; he'd even talked about becoming an electrician once. 'It doesn't mean that I have to like it though does it. It's bad enough that I have to be ready and waiting to give you an alibi, let alone my son too.'

Cameron waved his hand dismissively. In all the years they had been together not once had the police come knocking at their door; they were too shrewd for that to ever happen, too careful when it came to planning out the robberies.

'So, what are you saying?' Tommy asked his uncle. 'That you're not interested in the job?'

'I didn't say that,' Jonny laughed. 'What I actually said was that I'm not willing to give Kevin Fox a look in. And the less he knows about our business the better it will be for all of us.'

'He's got a point,' Reece nodded. He turned his head to look at his cousin, concern etched across his face. 'And you should steer clear of him,' he said pointing his forefinger in Tommy's direction. 'He's bad news.'

'But he's Aimee's dad,' Tommy protested. 'I can't just blank him, pretend that he doesn't exist.'

'Just be on your guard,' Cameron reiterated. 'I know his type. And just ten minutes in the man's company was enough to tell me that he's a wrong'un.'

Tommy sighed. Not that he could actually argue the point. His dad, uncle, and cousin were right: Kevin was all of those things, and a lot more besides. But despite his faults, Aimee still adored Kevin and why shouldn't she when at the end of the day he was her dad. 'Yeah,' he said somewhat reluctantly. 'You don't have to worry about me, I'll be careful.'

* * *

Slamming the front door shut behind her, tears spilled down Aimee's cheeks. 'How could you?' she cried. 'How could you say such hurtful things about me?'

Kevin groaned, and as his ex-wife fussed over their daughter, he ran his hand over his jaw, all the while biting back a retort.

'You're making me out to be some kind of slag,' she continued to sob. 'And I'm not, I've only ever been with Tommy. Tell him, will you, Mum?'

Melanie turned to look at Kevin, her eyes flashing with anger. 'Do you see what you've caused now?' she hissed. 'I knew it was too good to be true. You just can't help yourself, can you? Can't help causing upset everywhere you go.'

Kevin fought the urge to roll his eyes. Maybe his daughter was telling the truth, who knew? The only thing he did know was that Aimee took after her mother a little too much for his liking. For a start, both had the same knack of looking at him as though he was nothing more than the dirt beneath their shoes. Was it any wonder that he'd sought sanctuary down the boozer just to get away from their accusing stares. 'I'm not listening to this,' he shouted setting off for the front door. 'The pair of you are off your head,' he said tapping his temple. 'You're like a couple of witches; the only things missing are a cauldron and your fucking broomsticks.'

'Oh, that's rich coming from you.' Melanie gave a sarcastic laugh. She tapped her own temple. 'Maybe if you weren't a cokehead or pissed out of your nut on a daily basis then you'd be able to see that the only problem around here is you.'

Kevin's face turned bright red, and as the vein at the side of his neck bulged, spittle gathered at the corners of his snarled lips. 'Those fucking carters mugged me off,' he roared stabbing a finger into his chest. 'Do you really expect me to just stand by and take that?'

Confusion swept over Melanie's face. She'd thought they'd had a lovely evening, so much so that she'd hastily accepted Karen's invitation to join them for Sunday lunch. 'What are you talking about?'

'Carter,' Kevin hissed, a familiar stab of anger coursing through his veins. 'Made me look like an idiot.'

'Carter?' Melanie screwed up her face. 'You mean Tommy's uncle. But...'

'Both him and Tommy's old man.' Kevin continued to seethe. 'Trying to tell me that they run a respectable business...'

'They do,' Aimee sobbed. 'Tommy works for them at the scrapyard.'

'And you're as gullible as she is,' Kevin shouted as he nodded towards his ex-wife. 'You can't tell me a scrapyard paid for that house. And that's just one house.' He held up a finger to demonstrate his point. 'What about the rest of them, what about all the other gaffs?'

'How they make their money is none of our business,' Karen retorted as she pulled Aimee into her arms.

'It is where my daughter is concerned,' Kevin roared, his face so close to Melanie's that she could smell the foul stench of alcohol on his breath. 'And I won't have it, do you hear me?' he continued to scream. 'I won't have her around them.'

'Well, you can't stop her from seeing Tommy,' Melanie protested with a shake of her head. 'She's having his baby.'

A wicked grin filtered across Kevin's face. 'For now,' he sneered.

'I'm not getting rid of it.' Aimee continued to wail as her hand darted protectively down to her tummy. 'Tell him, Mum,' she said burying her face in Melanie's hair. 'Tell him that I'm not going to abort my baby.'

'Just get out.' With one arm still wrapped around her daughter's shoulders, Melanie fumbled with the door latch. 'Get out and stay away from us.'

'I'm going,' Kevin snarled. 'But believe me when I say this, those bastards have got a nasty shock coming their way—' He didn't manage to finish the sentence, and as the front door was slammed shut in his face, Kevin stared at the house with a measure of disbelief. Melanie had just thrown him out. Not that he could say it was the first time, or even the second or third time come to think of it. He made his way down the path all the while cursing under his breath. He'd made no idle threat; the Carters and Johnsons were about to get their comeuppance and he for one wanted a front row seat when it happened. He'd give anything to see their downfall, to see the smug grins wiped off their faces, and it would happen, Kevin was determined of that.

* * *

Aimee was inconsolable. 'Why does he always have to do this?' she wept to her mother. 'We had such a good time with Tommy and his family and now Dad has ruined everything.'

Melanie sighed. What exactly was she supposed to say? It wasn't as though she could defend her ex-husband's actions. Aimee was right, Kevin had ruined everything, he always did; it was a particular knack of his. If she didn't know any better, she'd presume that he got pleasure out of causing aggro. 'Take no notice of him,' she soothed. 'You know what he's like. He's not happy unless he's made everyone else feel as miserable as he does.'

'But it's not fair,' Aimee cried wiping the tears from her cheeks. 'Tommy's never done anything to offend him. And then the baby...' As fresh tears sprang to her eyes, her hand fluttered down to her tummy. 'What did he mean when he said, "for now"?'

Reaching out for her cigarettes, Melanie waved her free hand through the air. 'He didn't mean anything by it. He's full of hot air,' she said lighting up and inhaling the smoke deep into her lungs. 'You know what he's like, all bark and no action.'

'I suppose so.' Aimee's lips were downturned, and as she sniffed back her tears, she wiped underneath her nose. 'I don't like him sometimes, Mum,' she admitted. 'And I know it's wrong of me to say that, but I can't help how I feel. Look how many times he let me down when I was a kid, he was more interested in going down the pub than spending any time with me.'

Melanie gave a sad smile. In her eyes Aimee was still a kid, and as much as she may look like a woman, she hadn't even turned eighteen yet. But she knew exactly what her daughter meant; when it came to her ex-husband she'd had the exact same thoughts over the years. If only she could turn back time, she would have certainly spurned Kevin's advances; she knew that much. Her parents and even her friends had warned her until they were blue in the face that he was trouble, that he'd end up letting her down. Not that she'd wanted to listen back then, she'd been in love, had thought that Kevin was the be all and end all. He'd certainly pulled the wool over her eyes, and it wasn't until she'd fallen pregnant with Aimee that she'd realised what a big mistake she'd made. But by then she was stuck, trapped in a relationship with a man whose sole purpose in life was to lie and cheat.

'Listen,' Melanie said as she gently rubbed her daughter's arm. 'Give it a day or two and everything will calm down again. Your dad's got a bee in his bonnet that's all. Once he's had the time and a bit of space to think everything over, he'll be as right as rain, you just wait and see.'

'And what if he doesn't calm down?' Aimee urged. 'What if he really does hate Tommy and his family as much as he said he does?'

Melanie gave a reassuring smile. 'If there's one thing I know about your dad, it's the fact that he loves money, and seeing as your Tommy comes from money, then I can't see him staying angry for too long.'

Chewing on her bottom lip Aimee nodded again. 'He won't stop me from seeing Tommy,' she said with defiance. 'I love him.'

'I know,' Melanie sighed as she gripped onto her daughter's hand. 'Trust me darling, that's never going to happen.'

* * *

By the time Kevin reached The Cross Keys public house, the bell for last orders had just been rung. He slipped onto a bar stool and dug a hand into his pocket, pulling out some loose change. After ordering a pint, he looked around him, his shoulders remaining rigid as he surveyed the revellers enjoying what was left of the evening.

'You alright, Kev?'

Kevin turned his head, and on seeing that one of his pals had sidled up beside him, he nodded. He'd bragged to just about anyone who would listen that his luck had changed, that he was about to come into his fortune. What a joke that was. All thanks to the Carters and Johnsons he was back to square one. Forced to work a job that bored him senseless, forced to live in an overcrowded house with what could only be described as the dregs of society, and to top it off, the lifestyle and reputation he deserved were up in smoke.

'Weren't expecting to see you here tonight.' Andy McCann looked Kevin over, his glassy eyes boring into Kevin's skull. 'Thought you'd be too busy rubbing shoulders with the Carters.'

Kevin resisted the urge to scowl. The last thing he wanted was for Andy to get wind of his troubles, he'd never live it down. 'Yeah, well.' He brought the glass up to his lips and swallowed down a mouthful of the lager. 'They're not like us.' He nodded around him. 'They might have come from nothing the same as the rest of us, but having a bit of cash in their back pocket has turned their heads.'

Andy gave a laugh. 'I could have told you that.' He took a seat beside Kevin. 'Even when they lived over in Barking they thought they were a cut above everyone else. They've always swanned around as if they run the town.'

'Yeah,' Kevin agreed. He gave Andy a sidelong glance. 'It's my Aimee I feel sorry for. I mean.' He spread open his arms. 'She's stuck with the bastards for life now, isn't she?'

'Not necessarily,' Andy answered. 'There's an easy solution to the problem. She could always get rid of the kid; give it a few months and she'll forget it even existed.'

Kevin waved his hand dismissively. 'She won't even consider it.' He gave a dramatic sigh. 'I just wish there was a way to get rid of that boyfriend of hers, to get her away from him.' He paused for effect, lowering his voice slightly. 'You know what I'm like, I don't take any shit from anyone, and I told him straight,' he lied. 'Warned him off, told him to steer clear of her, not that it got me very far, mind, the bastard's got to her up here,' he said tapping his forehead. 'She thinks the sun shines out of his arse, that he can do no wrong.'

Andy raised his eyebrows. 'So, what are you gonna do?'

'I don't know.' Kevin stared down at his pint glass. 'But I can tell you one thing, I'm not prepared to sit back and watch my little girl ruin her life.'

'Sounds like you need a plan of action,' Andy commented. 'Something proactive and if you need any help.' He ran his hand over his pockmarked face, then leaned in slightly closer. 'Well you know where to come. I wouldn't be averse to seeing the flash bastards brought down a peg or two.'

'Yeah.' A slow grin spread across Kevin's face. 'I was hoping you might say that, because as it just so happens, I've got an idea.'

Andy's face lit up. 'I'm all ears,' he said leaning in even further.

4

Carla Carter entered the scrapyard office and seeing her cousin's son sitting on the sofa, his expression downturned, she did a double take.

'What's up with you?' she asked, slipping off her coat.

'Nothing.' With his chin in his hand, Tommy Jr shrugged.

'Doesn't look like it.' Her forehead furrowed, she placed her handbag on the desk then moved closer. 'Budge over,' she said, motioning to the sofa.

Tommy did as he was asked, and making way for Carla to join him, he shoved his mobile phone back into his pocket.

A moment of silence followed, and shifting her weight slightly to avoid the springs that poked through the thin leather, Carla sighed. 'Come on, out with it. What's wrong? You've got a face on you like a slapped arse.'

'I've already told you, it's nothing...' Tommy began before snapping his lips firmly closed.

Carla sighed again, and tucking a stray strand of dark hair behind her ear she gave him a gentle smile. 'This is me you're talking to. I know you, just you remember that. I used to look after you when you were little,' she said nudging him with her shoulder. 'I even used to change your nappies when you were a baby.'

Tommy screwed up his face. 'Thanks for that Carla, it's not really something I wanted to know.'

Carla laughed. 'So?' she asked again. 'Are you going to tell me what's going on?'

'It's...' Shaking his head, Tommy rubbed a hand over his face.

'Don't tell me.' Holding up her hand, Carla rolled her eyes. 'Jonny laid into you again.' She shook her head. 'When are you going to learn, eh? How many times have I told you that you need to stop winding him up? Just do as he asks without arguing or getting lairy; it's hardly rocket science, is it? Start toeing the line and he'll get off your back.'

'It's nothing like that,' Tommy protested. 'I haven't even seen Jonny today.'

'Then what is it?' Concern was etched across Carla's face. 'Is it the baby? Are you scared, is that it? I mean don't get me wrong, I totally get where you're coming from. I'm a lot older than you and I'd be petrified if I were in your shoes. Having a baby is a big responsibility, especially at your age.'

'It's not the baby,' Tommy sighed. 'I mean I am scared, of course I am,' he added, his eyes downcast and his cheeks flushing red. 'I'm only nineteen. I don't feel ready to be a dad, at least not yet anyway.'

'It's a shame you didn't think of that beforehand,' Carla retorted. 'Then you wouldn't be in this mess.' On seeing the look on Tommy's face, she wanted to kick herself for being so harsh. Mistakes happened, and she herself had made more than her fair share of blunders over the years. 'Look, it's only natural to be scared,' she said, her voice becoming gentle. 'Do you remember what uncle Jonny was like when he first found out Terri was pregnant? He was on the verge of having a meltdown,' she chuckled.

'Yeah,' Tommy laughed. 'It wasn't pretty, I know that much.'

'See?' Carla smiled. 'If Jonny had a hard time getting his head around the idea of fatherhood, then it's perfectly natural for you to feel the same.'

Tommy nodded. 'It's Aimee,' he finally blurted out. He pulled out his mobile phone again and glanced down at the screen. 'Her and her old man have had this big bust up. She reckons that she doesn't want anything to do with him any more.' He paused for a moment, his forehead furrowing. 'Only every time I go and see her, I can tell that she's been crying. I think she's a lot more upset about the situation then she's letting on.'

A daddy's girl herself, Carla nodded. 'Maybe they both need a bit of time to calm down, a cooling-off period,' she suggested. 'She's pregnant after all, her hormones are more than likely all over the place.'

'Yeah, that's exactly what I thought,' Tommy agreed. 'But when I suggested that to her, she nearly bit my head off, kept saying I didn't understand. And then today Aimee's dad messaged me out of the blue.' He gestured down to his phone. 'He wants to meet up. Reckons he wants to talk about Aimee, wants to patch things up with her.'

'So, what's the problem?' Carla asked.

'Well, what if I go meet him and then Aimee thinks I'm in the wrong, that I've gone against her or something. I'm already walking on eggshells around her. I can't seem to do anything right; she even said that I smell different, that my aftershave makes her want to throw up.'

Carla couldn't help but laugh. 'That's what happens when you're pregnant. It's called morning sickness.'

'Yeah,' Tommy conceded. 'That's what Aimee's mum said.

She told me not to take it personal.' He looked down at his phone again. 'I just don't know what to do. I mean I could tell Kevin to fuck off, but if I do that and then him and Aimee patch things up, I could end up making everything ten times worse.'

Thinking it over Carla gave a small smile. 'But what do you want to do?'

'I don't know.'

'Tommy Jr,' Carla tried again. 'You're not an idiot. So, I'm going to ask you again, what do you want to do?'

Tommy shrugged. 'What I'd like to do is smash my fist into Kevin's face. The bastard has really upset her.'

Carla shook her head. 'No matter how much you might want to, you can't do that, he's Aimee's dad.'

'Yeah, I know,' Tommy begrudgingly answered.

'Look.' Carla offered a warm smile. 'Why don't you meet up with him and see if you can help smooth things over between the two of them? You never know, this could be the push they need, and Aimee might even thank you for it.'

'I suppose so,' Tommy conceded. He pulled up Kevin's text message and chewed on the inside of his cheek for a few moments. 'I think I might go and see Mad Dog,' he said of an old family friend. 'See what he reckons I should do.'

Like Tommy, Carla was also fond of Mad Dog and his long-term partner, Lillian; they all were, and not only did they view the couple as surrogate grandparents, but they also had a lot of time and respect for them. 'Yeah, you do that,' Carla smiled. 'And while you're there tell him and Lil' that I said hello and that I'll pop in and see them soon.'

Tommy nodded, and getting to his feet he stuffed his phone back into his pocket before making his way towards the door.

'Everything will turn out okay,' Carla said, her voice gentle as she pulled on Tommy's wrist bringing him to a halt beside her.

'Not just with Aimee and her dad, but with the baby too. You're a good kid, and yeah you might be a bit uncontrollable at times – well, a lot of the time,' she corrected. 'But deep down you've got a good heart.'

'I'm hardly a kid,' Tommy chuckled. 'I'm nineteen.'

'Even so,' Carla answered, becoming serious. 'Just remember I'm here if you need me or ever want to talk.'

'Yeah, I know.' As the rest of his family traipsed into the office making the already small space even more cramped, Tommy's cheeks turned red. 'Thanks Carla,' he said tugging his arm free. 'I'll remember that.'

* * *

Kevin was grinning from ear to ear. Talk about clueless. Tommy Jr may have been a Johnson but when it came to brain cells the boy had certainly been at the back of the queue when they were being dished out. Perhaps the rumours were true after all: Tommy's parentage had left him severely lacking when it came to common sense.

He took a sip of his beer, excitement flowing through his veins. He'd always had a nasty streak inside of him, not that he didn't believe his actions were warranted, because they were. He was looking out for his daughter, his flesh and blood, what man wouldn't do the same in his shoes. Although if truth be told, Kevin was doing nothing of the sort, his actions were built on nothing more than revenge, pay back. The Carters and Johnsons had fucked him over and he was about to return the favour. Pity really, as he'd liked Tommy to begin with, he'd even been proud to be associated with him. Of course, that had all changed when Jonny Carter had taken him for a fool. Now it was game on, a survival of the fittest, or the most shrewd, whichever way you wanted to look at it, and one way or another, Kevin was determined that he would emerge as the victor.

The pub door opened, and looking up Kevin's eyes twinkled, the excitement that engulfed him rising a notch.

'Well?' he said as Andy McCann took the seat beside him.

Andy patted the bulge in his jacket pocket. 'Sorted,' he grinned.

Kevin nodded, his sly eyes wandering around the pub. 'Pass them over then,' he said, his hand snaking out for the exchange.

Digging his hand into his pocket, Andy glanced around him before pulling out an oblong shaped package that had been secured with brown parcel tape.

Weighing the parcel in his hand, Kevin gave a low whistle. He'd never seen so much coke, and as he licked his lips, he was in half a mind to rip the parcel open and cut a line there and then on the bar top.

'There's about half a kilo there.' Andy nodded down at the package, then slipping his hand back into his pocket he ever so carefully passed across a six-inch carving knife wrapped in a piece of cloth. 'That should be enough to see the kid sent down.' He swallowed heavily, his Adam's apple bobbing up and down. 'You do realise that you'll be in his debt now,' he said with a measure of caution. 'That my sister's bloke will expect a return for the goods.'

'Yeah, yeah.' Kevin waved his hand dismissively. He already knew what was expected of him. In exchange for the coke, he was to intercept a number of bank cards and credit cards from the sorting office and hand them over. The exact number of cards he was to swipe hadn't been finalised as of yet, and every time he'd asked for a rough estimation, Andy had been vague when it came to giving him an answer, but he had a sneaky suspicion that Andy's brother-in-law, Connor Bannerman would let him know in due course. Not that he could say hand on heart that he was overly thrilled at the prospect of being in Bannerman's pocket, because he wasn't. From what he'd heard about the man he was a nutcase – both him and his two brothers. Still, he reasoned, at the end of the day he knew the score, and in the long run it would be a small price to pay if it meant his plan to bring down the Carters and Johnsons was a success.

* * *

As Reece Carter studied his cousin he tilted his head to the side, his expression one of concern. 'Are you sure that this is a good idea?' he asked.

'I don't know.' Tommy Jr blew out his cheeks, and as he unlocked his car he thought the question over. As much as he wasn't really in the mood to meet with Kevin Fox, he may not have any other choice. 'Aimee's in bits,' he answered. 'And no matter how much we all think that Kevin is a waster, he's still her old man.'

Reece sighed. 'Do you want me to come with you?'

'Nah, you're alright.' Tommy gave a light laugh. 'I think we're way past the point of him wanting to batter me.' He gave a sigh. 'The worst that'll happen is that he'll bang on about this Royal Mail job and Jonny has already made his mind up. Kevin is out, no matter how much he might try to persuade me otherwise.'

'Yeah.' Reece glanced in the direction of the office to where his dad and their uncle Jonny were standing chatting. 'Well,' he said, turning his attention back to his cousin. 'Give me a buzz later and we'll go for a drink or something, we haven't been out for ages.'

'Will do.' Tommy sneaked a look at his watch. 'I don't plan on being long. I'm going to pop in and see Mad Dog first and then maybe I'll go and see Kevin. I should only be an hour or two at the most.'

'No worries.' Tapping the car roof, Reece stepped back then shoved his hands into his pockets as Tommy reversed out of the scrapyard. He continued watching him for a few moments before slowly making his way back to the office. A part of him wished that he'd insisted on accompanying his cousin. Tommy was a sucker when it came to his girlfriend, and he had a sneaky suspicion that Kevin Fox knew that. Knowing just how sly the man was he wouldn't be surprised if Kevin used Tommy's relationship with Aimee for his own gain. In other words, he'd use his daughter to get what he wanted. The burning question though, was whether or not Tommy would fall for it?

* * *

Despite being in his eighties, Mad Dog Harris was surprisingly sprightly for a man of his age, although his hair was now white, and his eyesight wasn't as good as it had once been. That wasn't to say though that he'd lost any of his faculties because he hadn't. His mind was still as sharp as ever. With a huge grin spread across his face, Mad Dog motioned for Tommy Jr to step across the threshold. 'Lil,' he called out, his thick Scottish accent still as strong as ever. 'We've got a visitor.'

Patting down her trademark platinum blonde hair Lillian entered the hallway. Nearing eighty herself, she too could easily pass for a woman a lot younger. 'Well, this is a nice surprise,' she beamed. 'Come on in.'

Tommy couldn't help but smile, and, as he followed the couple into the lounge, he looked around him, the familiar décor and furniture bringing him comfort. As a child he'd often spent time with Mad Dog and Lillian and as a result they were close.

Being Tommy Snr's eldest grandson, he knew for a fact that both Mad Dog and Lillian had always had a soft spot for him. They had loved Tommy Snr like a son, and still to this day they grieved for him, which was a lot more than his grandad's own parents had ever done. He glanced towards the mantlepiece, his gaze falling upon the photograph of his grandfather and Mad Dog, the pair of them smiling up into the camera as though they didn't have a single care in the world. He looked a lot like his grandad too, Tommy decided. Same build, same colour hair, same blue eyes. Many had said that their personalities and mannerisms were also similar, not that Tommy knew this for sure seeing as his grandad had been murdered before he'd been born and the two had never met.

'Well sit down,' Lillian smiled as she gestured to the sofa. 'You're making the place look untidy,' she winked.

Doing as he'd been told, Tommy took a seat.

'So, to what do we owe this pleasure?' Despite it being a genuine question there was a hint of humour in Mad Dog's voice.

'Do I need a reason to come and see you?' Tommy huffed. 'You're as good as my grandparents.'

'Of course you don't,' Lillian answered shooting her partner a glare. 'Ignore him, you know what a grumpy old so and so he can be.'

Tommy couldn't help but laugh, although in all honesty there was a hint of truth in Lillian's words. Mad Dog had never been what he would call a bundle of laughs. What he was though, was honest, loyal, and above all else, someone Tommy knew he could trust with his life. 'I wanted some advice,' he sighed before going on to tell them all about Kevin and his request to meet up behind Aimee's back. 'So, what do you think, should I go and meet him?'

After listening intently Lillian leaned forward in the

armchair. 'You need to follow your gut darling,' she said patting Tommy's hand. 'Besides, what harm can it do?'

'What do you mean?' Mad Dog retorted giving Lillian a scowl. Shaking his head he narrowed his eyes. 'This Kevin fella sounds like bad news if you ask me, someone you,' he said pointing a gnarled finger forward, 'should avoid like the fucking plague. I know his type, have come across a fair few fellas like him in the past.' Looking into the distance he shook his head, his rheumy blue eyes then focusing back on Tommy. 'Tell the bugger to clear off.'

'Yeah, but what about Aimee?' Chewing on the inside of his cheek Tommy sighed again. 'She's really upset, and no matter what I think of him Kevin is still her dad.'

Mad Dog narrowed his eyes again. 'Sounds like you've already made your mind up, lad,' he said huffing out a breath. 'And nothing me or Lil' say is going to sway your mind. You're just like your grandad Tommy, he could be a stubborn bugger too, would never listen to reason, even when he was in the wrong.' His gaze wandered to the photograph, his expression ever so slightly softening. 'Got him into a fair bit of trouble at times, too.'

As she too looked across to the photograph Lillian rested her hand upon her chest. 'Maybe Mad Dog is right,' she said turning her face to Tommy, concern evident in her eyes. 'This Kevin sounds like he might be trouble.'

'Yeah,' Tommy conceded. 'He is, or at least he seems to think he is. I mean he's a postman for fuck's sake, so he can't be that bad, can he? It's not like he's a career criminal or anything.'

'Doesn't hurt to be on your guard though,' Mad Dog nodded. Leaning forward in the chair he rested his elbow on his knee and beckoned for Tommy to move closer. 'Your uncle Jonny is no fool. Oh, I know he might act a bit flash at times, that he can be reckless, and that he caused your other uncles nothing but grief when he was younger, but deep down,' he said tapping the side of his nose, 'he knows the score. He was taught by the bloody best after all and if he won't have this Kevin out on a job with him, then that tells me everything I need to know: that you need to steer clear of him.'

'You're right,' Tommy answered.

'Of course, I bloody am,' Mad Dog winked. Straightening back up he laced his fingers together. 'Not that you're going to change your mind,' he added with a rise of his eyebrows. 'You're still going to walk out of here and meet up with Aimee's dad.'

Tommy gave a sheepish grin. 'Am I that obvious?' he groaned.

Mad Dog chuckled. 'You're like an open book, lad, just like your grandad was before you, and believe me when I say this, once he'd set his mind to something there was no changing it.'

Thinking it over Tommy nodded. Maybe him and his grandad were more alike than he'd originally thought.

* * *

Thirty minutes later, Tommy Jr pulled up outside The Cross Keys public house, and before he could climb out of the car Kevin exited the pub and waved his arms in the air, indicating for Tommy to stay in the car.

'Change of plan,' Kevin said as he gave the pub a cursory glance over his shoulder. 'Melanie's just turned up,' he lied. 'And the last thing I need is her giving me grief.'

Tommy frowned, and as he turned to look across at the pub his hand hovered over the door handle. 'Really? I didn't see her go in.'

'You must have just missed her,' Kevin answered nonchalantly as he climbed onto the passenger seat. 'I'll tell you what, we'll nip over to The Eastbrook, it's only five minutes down the road.'

Tommy shrugged, and starting the ignition, he stepped his foot on the accelerator. 'Was Aimee with her?' he asked, giving the pub a final glance as he drove past.

'Nah.' Kevin shifted his weight to make himself more comfortable. 'Just Mel and her fucking pals. Trust me,' he winked. 'We've had a lucky escape. Once they get on the wine, the lairy bitches will start giving it all this,' he said, using his fingers to mimic a mouth opening and closing. 'And I'm already in the doghouse where her and Aimee are concerned.'

'Yeah, I suppose so,' Tommy said as he flicked the indicator to pull into the car park situated at the front of The Eastbrook public house.

Moments later he switched off the ignition and unclipped his seat belt. 'I can't stay for too long though,' he warned nodding across to the pub. 'I've made plans with my cousin.'

Kevin nodded, and as Tommy pushed open the car door and began climbing out of the car, Kevin slipped his hand into his pocket, retrieved the package of cocaine and slid it underneath the seat. With his gaze still firmly fixed on Tommy's back he hastily reached into his pocket a second time and carefully took out the blade. It wasn't a particularly large knife, but despite its small stature he was more than certain that the weapon could cause a lot of damage. Placing the blade beside the package of cocaine, he couldn't help but grin to himself. Being in possession of a weapon alone would be enough to warrant an arrest but add coke to the mix and it would be safe to say that the Old Bill would have a field day. 'We won't be long,' he said as he pushed open the car door and heaved himself out of the car. 'We'll have a pint and then shoot off.'

A short while later they were seated at a table with pints of lager in front of them.

'So, what's going on?' Tommy asked as he eyed Kevin over the rim of the glass. 'Aimee has been in a right state, I've never seen her this upset before.'

Kevin sighed. 'It was nothing,' he answered the lie tripping off his tongue with ease. 'I said something innocent, and she took offence and blew up in my face. Before I knew what was happening Mel was throwing me out of the house.'

Tommy nodded. Just the day before Aimee had had a pop at him too. All he'd done was ask her if she wanted to go out for a drink. He understood that she was tired and feeling nauseous, but it was hardly something to throw her dummy out of the pram over.

'Her mother was exactly the same when she was pregnant with Aimee,' Kevin continued. He swallowed a mouthful of the lager and wiped the back of his hand across his lips. 'I couldn't do right for doing wrong. In the end I was too scared to even breathe around her, let alone open my mouth and speak.'

'I know the feeling,' Tommy chuckled. He picked up his glass and drained the remainder of his drink. 'Please tell me it gets better, that it doesn't last the entire pregnancy.'

'A couple of months,' Kevin confirmed with a grin. 'Three at the most.'

Tommy heaved a sigh of relief. 'Thank God for that. I was starting to think that this was it, that she'd be like this forever.'

Kevin laughed, and as he gave his watch a surreptitious glance, he looked across to the bar. 'How about another drink? One more for the road?'

'Yeah, go on then.' When Kevin made no attempt to move, Tommy scraped back his chair. 'Same again?' he asked, motioning across to Kevin's glass.

Kevin nodded. 'You go get the drinks while I nip to the gents,' he said getting to his feet.

Resisting the urge to roll his eyes Tommy made his way over to the bar. It was typical of Kevin; in all the time Tommy had known him not once had he dipped his hand into his pocket and paid for a round of drinks.

Once outside the toilets, Kevin placed his hand on the door then looked over his shoulder, the smile that had been plastered across his face moments earlier instantly slipping and being replaced with a snarl. By his estimation the Old Bill shouldn't be far off. With a bit of luck, the anonymous tip-off courtesy of Andy, was all that was needed to ensure that the filth turned up mob-handed. A slow smile crept back across his face, and as he slipped out of the side entrance, he was only sorry that he wouldn't be there to see Tommy's face once he realised that his time was well and truly up.

* * *

After pocketing his change, Tommy Jr made his way back over to where he and Kevin had been sitting, and placing the freshly filled pint glasses down on the table he took a seat. Ten minutes later he looked in the direction of the men's toilets, his forehead furrowed. What was taking Kevin so long?

He took a sip of his drink then alternated between drumming the sticky tabletop and biting the thumbnail on his free hand. Something was wrong; Kevin had been gone for ages. He looked around him, wondering if he'd maybe missed Kevin exit the toilet. With still no sign of him in the near vicinity he stood up and made his way across the pub scanning the bar area as he did so. Moments later he exited the toilets and frowned, what the fuck was going on? He patted his pockets trying to locate his mobile phone and on realising he'd left it in the car he made his way towards the entrance.

Once outside Tommy looked around him, confusion etched across his face. Kevin had made no indication that he was going to leave; in fact, it had been his idea to have another drink. Reaching his car, he pulled out his car keys and unlocked the door. As soon as he pulled down on the door handle pandemonium broke out as plain clothed police officers swarmed around him. He barely had the time to comprehend what was going on before he was shoved face first across the car bonnet, his arms were wrenched behind his back and handcuffs were being snapped on his wrists.

'What the fuck are you doing?' he roared at the officers who pinned him in place.

'Tommy Johnson?' one of the officers barked out.

As Tommy nodded his head it suddenly occurred to him that they hadn't addressed him by his actual name, Thomas – not that he could say many people did actually call him Thomas, other than his mum when she was mad at him. On a day-to-day basis he went by the name of Tommy or Tommy Jr. 'I haven't done anything wrong,' he protested. 'Get the fuck off me.'

He didn't receive a reply, and as the officers began searching his car, Tommy's eyebrows knotted together, his mind going into overdrive. Had he been followed? Was the scrapyard in the process of being torn apart, and were his family, just like him, in handcuffs too? Still, it didn't explain the misuse of his name. If the family had been under surveillance, then surely the police would know that his actual name was Thomas. Or maybe he was just overthinking the situation, clutching at straws, hoping the entire thing was one big misunderstanding, and that the Old Bill had made a cock-up of epic proportions.

As a shiver of fear ran down the length of his spine, the fine hairs on the back of his neck stood upright. Right from the start he'd known the risks that came with working for the family business, his dad and uncles had warned both him and his cousins until they were blue in the face that their chosen occupation could result in prison time. And there weren't only the armed robberies the family had committed over the years to contend with, but also the murders. Just weeks earlier his uncle Jonny had murdered a man in cold blood in the scrapyard office. Had the Old Bill somehow got wind of what had taken place? Was that why he was being arrested?

Struggling against the officers restraining him, he turned his head in time to witness a knife and a package wrapped in brown parcel tape being placed inside two evidence bags. Instinctively he knew that the package contained drugs, and his eyes almost bulged out of his head; he thrashed his body from side to side in an attempt to free himself. 'I've never seen those before in my life,' he hollered. 'You dirty bastards are setting me fucking up.'

Just as he'd known they would, the officers ignored his protests of innocence. Not that he should have expected anything different from them, it was his car after all, and both the blade and package had been found inside the vehicle that was registered to him. Helpless, he watched as they pulled down the glove box and pulled out an envelope, his heart sinking down to his stomach. He already knew what they would find inside and even more than that, he knew that the contents would make him look all the more guilty. Inside the envelope was 900 quid that he'd drawn out of his bank account and had intended to give to Aimee so that she could go out and buy a pram and some bits for the baby. He'd thought it might cheer her up, give her something else to focus on other than the argument with her dad. He scanned the car park. Had Kevin been arrested too? Was that why he'd disappeared from the pub?

After being read his rights Tommy was frogmarched towards an awaiting police van. He didn't need a genius to tell him that he was in a lot of trouble. And as innocent as he was, the evidence was stacked against him. All along, his instincts had been right, they were arresting him for intent to supply a class A drug. The mere notion was so ludicrous that if the situation hadn't been so dire he would have laughed his head off, a real belly laugh that would have had him doubled over with tears of laughter streaming down his face. If it had been fighting, or even car theft then they would have had him bang to rights, but dealing drugs, nah, that wasn't what he was about. He might have liked the occasional spliff, well, more than occasionally seeing as it was an everyday occurrence for him. But he'd never touched anything harder than weed, and certainly had never dealt any drugs; the idea had never even crossed his mind. Besides, he didn't need to, he was already earning enough money collecting debts, and at some point in the near future he would be joining his dad and uncles on the armed robberies. So, why the fuck would he need to peddle drugs like some lowlife scumbag?

As the doors of the van were slammed shut behind him, Tommy made himself as comfortable as he possibly could and bowed his head. Desperately he tried to think. The Old Bill had nothing on him, other than that the evidence had been found in his car he supposed. But what about fingerprints? Surely they would have to take that into account. He'd never even seen the knife or package before let alone touched them. And then there was the question of how the drugs had even got into the car, other than himself no one else had access to it. No, he decided, this had to be a set-up. The Old Bill must have planted the drugs. Nothing would surprise him when it came to the filth, they were well known for using underhand tactics. The only problem with that explanation though, was why would they have singled *him* out?

Leaning his head against the side panel of the van, Tommy took a series of deep breaths, his gaze drifting to the blacked-out window and his thoughts once again wandering back to Kevin. What if... No, he shook his head and dug his teeth into his bottom lip dismissing the notion. No matter how much he tried to push the thought away from his mind he was unable to rid himself of the idea that maybe Kevin was somehow involved. Could it be possible that the package belonged to Aimee's dad? It was no secret that he was a cokehead after all and other than Aimee and Reece, no one else had stepped foot inside his car. What if Kevin had seen the Old Bill outside the pub and decided to save his own skin and scarper? Not that that explained why he would have had a knife on him, unless, of course, he'd stolen the drugs. Nah, Kevin might have been a lot of things but somehow Tommy couldn't quite see him robbing a dealer of their merchandise; he didn't have the bottle for a start.

Tommy closed his eyes. Surely it was only a matter of time until the filth realised their mistake, that they'd arrested the wrong man, or at least this was what he hoped, anyway. His family were going to go ballistic. From the moment they had met him, his dad, uncle Jonny, and even Reece had stated that they didn't trust Kevin. They'd warned him to be on his guard around him and to not disclose any personal information regarding the family business. And they had been right to be cautious. Kevin had proven himself to be a snake, someone who couldn't be trusted, and even more than that, he'd shown just how much of a coward he really was.

Rage rippled through Tommy's veins and by the time the van came to a halt outside the police station he was ready to rip into someone, to tear them limb from limb, and there was no one better he'd like to get his hands on than Kevin Fox.

5

Reece Carter frowned, and pressing redial, he brought his mobile phone back up to his ear. 'He's still not answering,' he stated to no one in particular when the call rang off for the third time in as many minutes.

'Fucking hell.' Jonny rolled his eyes. 'Can't you leave him alone for five minutes?'

'Yeah,' Peter, Tommy Jr's uncle and Reece's eldest male cousin, sniggered. 'Stop calling him, for fuck's sake – he's probably out with his bird.'

Reece huffed out a breath. 'He's in the pub with Aimee's dad, actually,' he said giving both his uncle and cousin a cold stare.

Jonny snapped his head around to look at his nephew. 'What's he doing with that tosser?'

Not bothering to answer his uncle, Reece pressed redial. 'Two hours he said he'd be gone for.' He glanced at his watch. 'And that was four hours ago. We were meant to be going out tonight for a drink.'

As he chewed on the inside of his cheek Jonny swivelled his chair around so that he had a better view of the forecourt. 'I don't trust that sly fucker, Kevin Fox,' he stated glancing over his shoulder to look at his elder brother, Mitchell. 'He's bad news.' He turned back to face Reece. 'And you know what Tommy Jr is like,' he added, placing his forearms on the desk. 'He loves nothing better than causing a bit of aggro.' He stabbed his finger in Reece's direction and lifted his eyebrows. 'Trouble has a nasty habit of following the pair of you around and it's me,' he said, pointing to himself, 'who ends up getting it in the neck. Three phone calls I've had in recent weeks about you and Tommy Jr pulling shit. Three.' He held up three fingers.

Reece rolled his eyes, and avoiding making eye contact with his dad, he tuned his uncle out and went back to scrolling through his phone. Although he had to admit that there was some truth to Jonny's words. Both himself and Tommy Jr were as bad as one another – perhaps that was why they got on so well, not only were they close in age, but they also liked nothing better than to cause mayhem. They egged each other on and then when the shit hit the fan, which it often did, they looked out for one another, had each other's backs, hence the reason why they ended up getting into so many scrapes.

'Try him again.' Jonny nodded towards the mobile phone in Reece's hand. 'And tell him to get his arse back here pronto...' As his own mobile rang Jonny's voice trailed off, and leaning back in his seat he pressed answer.

Almost immediately he sat bolt upright. 'What's happened?' he asked, his gaze snapping between his brother and nephews. Listening intently for a few moments, Jonny frowned. 'Karen,' he said, his voice holding a hint of panic. 'Slow down, I can't understand a word you're saying.' He turned his chair again and craned his neck to get a better view of the forecourt before snapping his fingers towards Reece. 'Go and see if Cameron is out there.'

Jumping up from his seat, Reece's eyes were wide. 'What's happened?' he implored.

'Just go and look,' Jonny growled, frustration getting the better of him as he jerked his head towards the door.

Doing as he'd been told, Reece raced from the office.

Jonny sank back in the chair and rubbing at his temples he shook his head. 'Karen,' he soothed. 'Calm down, darling. Stop crying and just tell me what's happened.'

Concerned for his elder sister's welfare, Peter sat forward in the chair and rested his forearms on his knees. 'What's going on?' he mouthed.

Jonny ignored him, and as his niece spoke, the colour drained from his face. 'Are you sure?' he said into the phone.

The shriek that came from his niece was enough for Jonny to snatch the device away from his ear, and as he rubbed at his temples his mind whirled. All along he'd known that this day would come, that it was only a matter of time before one of them was arrested. 'What's he been nicked for?' he asked, raising his voice slightly to be heard over his niece's sobs.

Both Peter and Mitchell sprang to their feet. 'Give me the phone,' Peter demanded, holding out his hand, his voice brooking no arguments.

Reluctantly, Jonny passed his mobile phone across.

'Karen,' Peter said, his voice just as panicked as Jonny's had been moments earlier. 'What's happened?'

As Karen spoke, he clutched his hand to his forehead. 'Nah,' he said vehemently shaking his head. 'Tommy Jr wouldn't be that stupid, surely.'

Wide-eyed, Reece raced back into the office. 'Cameron's not out there,' he said, his chest heaving. Looking between his dad, uncle, and cousin, panic began to get the better of him. 'Is it something to do with Tommy Jr?' he asked.

Jonny nodded. 'He's been nicked.'

'What?' Reece's eyes were as wide as saucers. 'Why?'

'I don't know,' Jonny answered, and as Peter ended the call and handed back the mobile phone, he looked up at his nephew expectantly. 'Well?' he asked. 'What's he been nicked for?'

Peter shook his head, his face turning as deathly pale as Jonny's. 'Dealing.'

'Do fucking what?' Jonny's jaw dropped, and as he slowly turned his head, he focused his steely gaze upon Reece.

'What?' Reece repeated as he looked between his father and uncle.

As if anticipating his brother's response Jonny jumped out of his chair and bounded around the desk, knocking a stack of paperwork to the floor in his haste to stop his brother from knocking ten bells of shit out of his son. Before Jonny could reach his nephew, Mitchell had charged forward, and using his considerable strength, he slammed his son into the wall. 'Don't give me what,' Mitchell roared into Reece's face spraying him in spittle as he did so. 'What the fuck have you done?'

'N-nothing,' Reece stammered, his cheeks flushing red and his gaze automatically looking anywhere but at his father. 'I haven't done anything; I swear I haven't.'

'Don't you dare try and treat me like I'm some kind of fucking idiot,' Mitchell shouted, his expression set like thunder as he clenched the front of Reece's shirt in his fist. 'You and Tommy Jr are joined at the fucking hip. Is that what the pair of you have been getting up to?' he demanded, stabbing his finger none too gently into the side of his son's cheek. 'Are you trying to bring us all down, to get us all fucking nicked?'

'Hey.' Cautiously, Jonny put out his hand. 'That's enough,' he said inching forward, more than ready to drag his brother away from his nephew if need be. 'Just hear him out.'

Ignoring his brother's warning Mitchell tightened his grip on his son's shirt. 'Answer me!' he shouted, his eyes flashing with anger. 'Is that what you're trying to do?'

'No.' Vehemently shaking his head, Reece braced himself for his father's onslaught. 'I've done fuck all wrong and neither has Tommy Jr. If he was dealing then I'd know about it, he would have said something. Me and him are like this,' he said crossing two fingers to emphasise his point. 'He would have told me.'

'Mitch.' Jonny lifted his eyebrows and shook his head. 'He's telling the truth.'

Giving his son one final cold stare Mitchell released his grip. 'You'd better be telling the truth,' he warned, straightening up. 'Because if I find out you've just lied to me, son or not, I will end you over this – are we clear on that?'

'Crystal.' Reece nodded and as he smoothed out his crumpled shirt he took a cautious step away from his dad. 'I'm telling the truth,' he cried. 'Honest. Tommy Jr wouldn't do something like this, he doesn't touch drugs.'

About to return to his chair, Jonny paused, and spinning back around to face his nephew, the nerve at the side of his eye twitched. 'What do you mean he doesn't touch drugs?' he hissed. 'What about the fucking spliff that he had the front to spark up in my car not even two weeks ago?'

Reece swallowed and taking another step backwards he shrugged. 'Yeah, maybe a bit of weed every now and again, but nothing harder than that. Everyone does it, it's hardly a crime is it, even you and my dad do it.'

Running his tongue across his teeth Jonny glanced towards his brother and shook his head. They could hardly argue with that, and although they wouldn't call themselves heavy users, it wasn't unknown for them to have the occasional joint. 'I can't get my head around this,' he said, taking a seat and resting his elbows on the table. 'None of this is making any sense to me.'

'Yeah.' Peter looked into the distance then sighed. 'That's exactly what I was thinking.' He turned to look at his uncle. 'This has got to be a mistake. I mean admittedly Tommy Jr is a handful, and we all know that he can be a cocky little bastard, that he's got a big mouth on him, and that he doesn't think,' he said tapping the side of his head. 'But when it comes to something like this, I just can't see it, can you?'

Thinking the question over Jonny chewed on the inside of his cheek. 'No,' he admitted. He turned to look at Reece again as though trying to gauge his reaction. 'I know he needed money though,' he said lifting his eyebrows. 'That's why he came to me suggesting this post office raid.'

Peter narrowed his eyes. 'You can't seriously think that he'd stoop this low though. He could have asked any one of us for cash and we would have happily given it to him. It's not like any of us are skint, he could have come to me, you, Jake, or even his parents. He wouldn't have needed the cash from dealing.'

'True,' Jonny sighed. 'Like you said, he's a lot of things: reckless, arrogant, and for the most part, fucking stupid. But this, nah.' He turned to look at Mitchell and sucked in his bottom lip. 'Something's not adding up.'

'So what do we do now?' Peter urged.

Drumming his fingers on the desk, Jonny sighed again. 'First of all, we find Cameron and fill him in on what's happened. He should be able to find out what's going on. And then we call a family meeting.' His gaze turned towards the rickety filing cabinets piled high with paperwork. 'And thirdly we pull out every single tax return and receipt that we have for this place because I can guarantee you now just one slip up from Tommy Jr and it's game over for the rest of us, and I don't know about you,' he added with a grimace, 'but I'm not a fan of eating porridge.'

* * *

After being interviewed Tommy Jr was led back to a custody cell. The duty solicitor that had been assigned to him had advised him to say no comment to every question thrown at him, not that he'd actually considered opening his mouth. What was he supposed to even say? As much as he may have suspected Kevin of being responsible for leaving the drugs and knife in his car, he had no actual evidence to back up his claim, and even if he could prove with certainty that the coke belonged to Aimee's dad, he was no grass.

He rubbed his hand over his face, feeling sick to his stomach. He'd almost fallen off the chair when they'd told him the quantity of cocaine found underneath the passenger seat. When it came to coke, he was no expert but even he'd been shocked to learn that the package had weighed half a kilo. If Kevin had been responsible, then how the fuck had he stumped up the cash to buy it? The man didn't even like to pay for a round of drinks, let alone fork out the money for drugs that had a street value of almost fifty grand.

As the cell door was closed behind him Tommy took a seat on what he presumed was meant to be some kind of bed. Leaning against the wall, the plastic mattress hard and uncomfortable beneath him, he brought his knees up to his chest and absentmindedly rubbed at the indentations the handcuffs had left upon his wrists. His mum had been in bits when he'd called her. He could still hear the shock in her voice, could still recall hearing her sobs. Shame engulfed him, and leaning his head on his forearms he closed his eyes. All he ever seemed to do lately was make his mum cry, first when he'd told her about the baby and now this. And knowing that he was the sole reason for her tears was the equivalent of a punch to the gut.

Half a kilo. Those three words reverberated around his head. This was a lot more serious than he'd initially thought and he'd already guessed that he was in a lot of trouble. Getting to his feet he began to pace the cell. How long could they keep him locked up for? They'd already questioned him once, were they intending to haul him back into an interview room a second time?

His thoughts turned to Aimee. Just like his mum, she was bound to react badly to the news that he'd been arrested. And to make matters even worse he hadn't been detained for fighting or even car theft, which in itself would have been bad enough, but drug dealing and being in possession of a knife could possibly land him in prison for years. He shook his head. No, he told himself, it wouldn't come to that, he was innocent, and his family would never let him go down, at least not without a fight.

A familiar wave of sickness washed over him. He would never have admitted it out loud, but he was scared. What if his family weren't able to pull the strings to get him out? He glanced across to the metal door, feeling not only claustrophobic but also wishing that he'd never gone to meet Kevin. He clenched his fists, and as he continued to pace the cell, he resisted the urge to lash out, to pummel his fists into the wall. Not that the action would get him very far, and fracturing the bones in his hand or wrist on top of everything else was the last thing he wanted – or needed for that matter.

Defeated, he slumped down on the bed and chewed on his thumbnail. Think positive, he told himself. His dad would get him out. He was sure of it.

* * *

Karen Johnson's skin was ashen and, using her fingers to wipe away the streaks of mascara from underneath her eyes, in her free hand she clutched a sodden tissue. 'He wouldn't,' she cried between sobs. 'He would never touch drugs.'

Shooting his uncle Jonny a surreptitious glance, Cameron cleared his throat. Their son could do no wrong in his wife's eyes. And as much as Tommy Jr may have steered away from hard drugs, he'd been using cannabis since he was in secondary school. 'Look,' he said, in an attempt to calm his wife down. 'Stay here with your mum and I'll shoot down to the nick and try and see what's going on.'

'I'll come with you.' Grabbing her handbag, Karen slipped the leather strap over her shoulder.

'No,' Cameron reiterated, his voice brooking no arguments. 'Stay here.'

'But...' Karen's mouth dropped open. 'He's my son,' she hissed. 'I deserve to know what's going on.'

'I said no,' Cameron spat out. 'You getting hysterical isn't going to help matters. We need to keep levelheaded.'

'Do you want me to come with you?' Jonny offered.

Cameron paused. At the best of times, he and his uncle didn't have what he would call a healthy relationship. For the majority, they were at one another's throats and on more than one occasion it had almost come to blows between them. 'Yeah,' he finally answered, keen to put the past behind them and build bridges. 'You might as well.'

As her husband made to walk past her, Karen grasped hold of his hand bringing him to a halt beside her. 'Bring him home,' she choked out, her eyes wide and fearful. 'I know that he's an adult, a grown man, but he's still my baby.'

Cameron nodded, and as he glanced around the office, he rubbed his hand across his face. Somehow, he had a feeling that he wouldn't be returning with their son and he had an even greater feeling that everyone other than his wife knew that to be the case. Tommy Jr hadn't been arrested for something minor, the Old Bill had nicked him for drug dealing, and as if that wasn't bad enough, he'd also been in possession of a blade. 'I'll do my best.' He gave a gentle smile. 'But I can't promise anything, okay.'

Karen inhaled a shaky breath, and as she released her husband's hand, she wrapped her arms around herself and blinked back her tears.

'It's going to be alright,' her mother Stacey offered as she nodded after Cameron and Jonny.

'Is it?' Karen spun around, her eyes wide with fear. 'My boy has been arrested for drug dealing, how on earth is it going to be alright?'

Stacey swallowed, her own concern getting the better of her, and as her daughter broke down in tears again, she pulled her close. Karen was right – it wasn't going to be okay, and she knew that as well as she knew her own name. 'Of course it will,' she said forcing her voice to sound a lot more cheerful than she actually felt. 'Danny,' she said of her husband, 'has given Jonny the details of his brief and by all accounts he's good, one of the best in the business.'

'He'd better be.' Karen sniffed back her tears. 'Because I want my boy home.' Her eyes widened and her hand fluttered up to her chest. 'Aimee,' she blurted out. 'Has anyone told her what's happened?'

'I'll do it,' Reece volunteered. 'It might be better if it comes from me.' He gave a shrug, his lips downturned. 'She knows me.'

Karen nodded, and reaching out her hand, she patted Reece's

arm, her forehead ever so slightly creasing. 'Why weren't you with him?' she asked, cocking her head to one side. 'The two of you are always together.'

'Not always.' Reece gave her a knowing look then jerking his thumb behind him he motioned to the door. 'I'd better get off.'

Nodding again, Karen watched him go. 'Oh, Mum,' she cried as fresh tears stung her eyes. 'I can't believe this is happening.'

'I know, darling,' Stacey sighed as she slung her arm around her daughter's shoulders. 'But he will be alright. Tommy Jr is a fighter just like your dad was and if anyone can handle this then it will be him.'

Through her tears Karen turned her head to look at her mother. 'Do you really believe that?'

Stacey sighed. 'He's going to be alright, darling,' she repeated, her voice ever so slightly wavering. 'Just you wait and see.'

* * *

On the drive towards Romford police station both Cameron and Jonny were quiet. After what seemed an age Jonny cleared his throat and turned to look at his nephew.

'Be honest,' he said. 'Between me and you, do you think Tommy Jr is capable of this?'

Cameron took a few moments to think the question through. The truth was, his son had always been headstrong, a law unto himself. And seeing as both his late maternal and paternal grandfathers had been brothers, he had far too much Carter blood running through his veins to be anything different, and then when you added Johnson blood to the mix the combination was bound to be lethal. He swallowed, then glanced out of the window. 'He's a good kid,' he stated.

Jonny sighed. 'That wasn't what I asked.'

Grinding his teeth together Cameron snapped his head around to look at his uncle. 'How exactly do you expect me to answer that?' he spat. 'He's my son.'

'Yeah.' Jonny lifted his eyebrows. 'Maybe that's the problem.'

Cameron narrowed his eyes, the familiar animosity between the two men once again rearing its ugly head. 'Meaning?'

'Well,' Jonny sighed. 'You and me both know that in the wrong hands he could be dangerous. I mean, granted he has a lot of Tommy in him.' He gave a small smile as he recalled his eldest brother. 'But…'

'But what?' Cameron hissed.

Jonny gave Cameron a sidelong glance and shook his head. 'Then there's Gary…'

'Tommy Jr is nothing like my dad,' Cameron butted in.

'I suppose not,' Jonny answered as he flicked the indicator. 'But you can't tell me that Tommy Jr hasn't inherited at least some of Gary's genes, that he doesn't have the capability to be dangerous.'

Falling silent Cameron stared straight ahead of him. 'I know my son,' he finally answered through clenched teeth. 'And I know that he wouldn't peddle drugs, he has no need to.'

'Yeah.' As he brought the car to a halt outside of the police station and unclipped his seat belt Jonny nodded across to the building. 'Let's hope for all of our sakes that's the case.'

6

Placing one hand on the wall as if to stop herself from collapsing to the floor Aimee gasped out loud, her eyes filling with tears. 'No!' she shrieked as her free hand rested on the slight curve of her tummy. 'No, I don't believe you.'

Reece looked between his cousin's girlfriend and her mother. 'It's true,' he said as gently as he possibly could. 'He's been arrested.'

'I said that I don't believe you!' Aimee screamed. Rushing into the living room she scooped up her mobile phone and began frantically scrolling through her contact list before pressing dial and lifting the device up to her ear.

'He's not going to answer.' Reece rubbed his hand over his face. 'He can't.' Then licking at his bottom lip, he took a tentative step forward as though he were debating whether or not to wrench the phone out of Aimee's hand.

Shaking her head, confusion was etched across Melanie's face. 'What has he done?'

Reece opened his mouth to answer, then snapping his lips closed again he gave a shrug. 'He didn't do anything.' Which as far as he was concerned was the truth. The very notion that Tommy Jr was dealing drugs was abhorrent to him. He knew his cousin too well and knew for a fact that Tommy Jr would have told him of his intentions. That he would have asked Reece to join him and would have wanted him by his side, if for no other reason than to back him up should he run into trouble.

'Well, he must have done something,' Melanie retorted as she pulled her daughter into her arms. 'The police don't arrest you for doing nothing.'

Tears slipped down Aimee's cheeks. 'It's exactly as my dad said,' she wailed. 'He said that I'd end up on my own and that before long my Tommy would be behind bars.'

As Melanie waved her hand dismissively at her daughter's words, Reece's eyebrows knotted together. 'What did you just say?' he asked stepping forward and pulling Aimee around to face him. 'What did your old man say?'

Taken aback Aimee stared down at Reece's hand. 'I...' she began as she attempted to tug her arm free.

'Your old man,' Reece urged, his grip ever so slightly tightening. 'What did he fucking say?'

Aimee gulped. She hadn't told Tommy the real reason for her and her dad's falling out, she'd been too ashamed. Her dad had said such hurtful things that she wasn't so sure she would ever forgive him. 'He said that Tommy would end up in prison,' she answered, her voice small. Fresh tears sprang to her eyes, and as she let them slip down her cheeks, she turned to look back at her mother, her face crumbling. 'And he was right.'

Reece tilted his head to one side and as he studied Aimee his mind began working overtime. It couldn't just be a coincidence that Tommy Jr had gone out to meet Kevin and then hours later he'd been arrested for dealing, especially when the only cokehead they knew was Aimee's dad. 'Oh shit,' he muttered before racing back out of the house, leaving both Aimee and Melanie to stare after him, their mouths hanging wide open.

* * *

Slamming the car door closed behind him Cameron resisted the urge to smash his fist into the dashboard.

Jonny sighed. 'He's nineteen,' he stated. 'Right from the start you knew there was always a risk that they wouldn't tell you anything.'

'They were quick enough to tell me that he's in court tomorrow,' Cameron growled.

'True.' Giving the police station a final glance Jonny pushed the key into the ignition and started the car. Digging his hand into his pocket he pulled out a scrap of paper containing the details of the solicitor Danny McKay had recommended. 'Looks like you're going to be needing this after all.'

Cameron sighed, and taking the piece of paper, he studied the solicitor's name. 'Do you reckon he's any good?'

Jonny gave a light laugh. 'It's Danny's brief, so what do you think? And let's face it, if anyone should have received a capture over the years then it's Danny; the man is unhinged and that's putting it mildly.'

'I suppose so,' Cameron answered as he pocketed the details. 'Karen is going to go spare,' he added. 'She's expecting us to turn up with Tommy Jr in tow.'

'Yeah, well.' Pulling out into the road Jonny looked up at the rear-view mirror. 'You know what Karen is like.' He gave a shake of his head. 'She's blind when it comes to Tommy Jr; he could kill someone in front of her and she would still somehow convince herself that he's innocent. And I don't think she'll be the only one with something to say on that matter.' He gave another shake of his head and threw his nephew a sidelong glance. 'I've got a feeling that Stacey,' he said, of Tommy Jr's maternal grandmother, 'isn't gonna be too happy either.'

* * *

Bringing his car to a screeching halt on the scrapyard forecourt, Reece switched off the ignition and jumped out of the vehicle. By the time he pushed open the door to the office he was out of breath.

Alarmed, both Stacey and Karen looked up. 'What is it?' Karen asked, the words catching in her throat. 'Is it Tommy Jr?'

Reece nodded. 'Sort of,' he quickly explained. 'I went to see Aimee.'

'And?' Karen urged.

About to answer, Reece glanced over his shoulder to look at the door, and, as Jonny and Cameron walked inside the office, he turned to face them.

Karen narrowed her eyes, and pushing herself forward, she looked from her husband to the forecourt. 'Where's Tommy Jr?'

Cameron shook his head.

'No,' Karen gasped bringing her hands up to her face.

'He's in court tomorrow,' Cameron was quick to add. 'And with a bit of luck...' His voice trailed off and he rubbed at the nape of his neck, all the while shaking his head. 'Well, with a good brief on his side he should be home tomorrow.'

'Oh, darling.' Stepping forward Stacey pulled her daughter into her arms as she cried.

'That's what I've been trying to tell you,' Reece butted in. 'I went to see Aimee and she said that Kevin had been saying that Tommy Jr was going to end up behind bars.' He cocked his head to the side. 'And seeing as Tommy Jr was with Kevin this afternoon that's more than a little bit suspicious, isn't it?'

Tossing his car keys onto the desk, Jonny crossed his arms over his chest, his forehead furrowed.

'Kevin is a cokehead,' Reece continued as he looked between his uncle and cousin. 'And now Tommy has been banged up for dealing. Do you see what I'm getting at?'

Cameron narrowed his eyes. 'What are you trying to say?' he implored. 'That Kevin was involved.'

'He has to be,' Reece answered. 'Think about it. He told Aimee that Tommy was going to end up banged up. How could he have known that unless...'

'Unless what?' Jonny probed.

Reece paused. What if he was mistaken? What if he was so set on proving his cousin's innocence that he was willing to imply that Kevin had been responsible, that it had been him who'd set Tommy up? No, he decided, he was right, he knew he was, he had to be. 'It was him who planted the gear in Tommy's car. It has to be him, it's the only thing that makes any sense.'

As he thought the situation over, Jonny looked around him, his hands involuntarily curling into fists. 'The no good, sly fucker,' he seethed. 'I'm gonna fucking kill him.'

Aghast, Stacey's eyes widened. 'You don't know if that's true,' she said, rounding on Reece. 'You can't just accuse Kevin of having a hand in any of this without having any proof. The man could very well be innocent for all you know.'

'Mum,' Karen shrieked. 'If anyone is innocent then it's Tommy Jr.'

'And if I remember correctly,' Jonny interrupted, turning to face Stacey, 'you were one of the first to call Kevin a slimy fucker.'

'Yeah, well,' Stacey conceded, her cheeks flushing red. 'That doesn't necessarily make him guilty,' she argued. 'Anyone could have left the drugs in Tommy Jr's car.'

Placing her hands on her hips, Karen's nostrils flared. 'Whose side are you on?' she cried. 'This is your grandson we're talking about, not some stranger.'

Narrowing her eyes, Stacey pulled herself up to her full height and gave her daughter a cold stare. 'That's right, he's my grandson and I love him,' she stated. 'But I'm not stupid.' She tapped the side of her head. 'And neither am I blind. He's been raised amongst this lot,' she said gesturing around the office. 'He's not some innocent little boy. And you,' she said, pointing a stiff finger in her daughter's direction, 'had best remember that fact.'

Karen's jaw dropped. 'What's that supposed to mean?' she shrieked. 'Tommy—'

'For crying out loud,' Stacey implored her daughter. 'Will you just take the rose-tinted glasses off for five minutes and see the situation for what it is, instead of living in some sort of cuckoo-land? Tommy Jr may not be guilty in this instance but what about everything else he's responsible for?' She turned back to look at Jonny and stabbed her finger towards him. 'What about the cars, eh? How many exactly has he stolen over the years? Oh, and let's not forget who it actually was that taught him the tricks of the trade.'

As all eyes turned to look at him Jonny glanced away.

'And you,' Stacey continued as she turned her attention back to Reece. 'Don't think that I haven't heard the rumours, that I don't know what you and Tommy Jr get up to on a nightly basis. The pair of you love nothing more than to cause ructions and neither one of you are content unless you've battered the life out of some poor fucker.'

His cheeks flaming red, Reece followed Jonny's cue and looked down at the floor.

'Now, I've kept my mouth shut for far too long,' Stacey seethed. 'And this,' she said, throwing her arms up into the air, 'was always going to come to a head. None of you are invincible, and neither are you above the law. It's only by some miracle that one or more of you haven't been locked up before now because believe me, it's been a long time coming.'

As Karen silently wept Jonny threw Stacey a glance, his eyes hard. 'Are you finished Stace?'

Her eyes as equally hard, Stacey nodded. 'I've said my piece,' she retorted. 'And the quicker we stop treating my grandson as though he is some innocent angel who has never put a foot wrong in his life, the quicker we will be able to help him out of this mess.'

Jonny sighed, and as he looked around at his family, he shrugged. 'She's got a point.'

'Of course I do,' Stacey hissed back. 'I'm not green around the edges. My own father and brothers were no strangers when it came to doing prison time. And then there was your brother,' she said of her first husband, Tommy Carter. 'Don't for one single second think that I didn't know what he was getting up to, that I didn't know he robbed banks for a living. As I've already stated: I'm not stupid, I chose to turn a blind eye – big difference. And as for you,' she told her daughter, 'crying isn't going to help matters.' She crossed her arms over her chest, her expression stern. 'If you want to help your son then go and fetch him a shirt and tie, something that will look smart for when he's in court. And secondly, until one of us actually speaks to him and the facts have been laid out in front of us then we need to stop speculating.'

As they nodded, Stacey turned to look at her daughter, and

giving a sigh, she stepped forward and grasped Karen's hand. 'I didn't mean to come across so harsh,' she stated, her voice lowered so that only her daughter could hear. 'You know that I love the bones of that boy,' she said of her grandson. 'In a lot of ways, he reminds me of your dad.' She bit down on her bottom lip and looked into the distance. 'But sometimes...'

'Don't say it.' There was an edge to Karen's voice as she glanced towards her husband. 'Please Mum, not now, I don't want to hear it.'

Stacey gave a sad smile. 'As much as we might pretend otherwise,' she said ignoring her daughter's request, 'I can see Gary and Bethany in him too.' She gave another sigh, her shoulders slumping. 'It's only natural I suppose. They were his paternal grandparents after all.'

Karen nodded; her voice when she answered was small. 'You hated Bethany.'

'I did,' Stacey agreed. She gave a light laugh and shook her head. 'I can't say I was fond of Gary that much either, at least not once Bethany had got her claws into him. Before then though...' She sighed as she thought back to when her first husband's brother had been young. 'Let's just say that Bethany ruined him, that she fucked his head up.'

About to open her mouth to answer, Karen clamped her lips firmly together and looked away.

'It's okay,' Stacey reassured her daughter. 'I know.'

Confusion swept across Karen's face. 'But...'

'Your uncle Jimmy told me,' Stacey was quick to explain. 'I know that it was your uncle Gary who murdered your dad.'

Swallowing down the lump in her throat Karen nodded, her gaze automatically darting to her uncles, her dad's remaining brothers. 'Does anyone else know?'

Stacey shook her head. 'Your uncle Jimmy told me in confidence and I would never betray his trust.' She gave her daughter a thoughtful look. 'I only wish that you hadn't been there to witness it.'

Karen sucked in a breath. 'I didn't...' She cleared her throat again in a bid to compose herself. Other than when she'd initially told her uncle Jimmy about what she'd heard that fateful day, she had never spoken about her dad's death. All these years later it was still too painful to even think about the betrayal her dad had suffered, let alone talk about. 'I didn't actually see it happen.'

'No.' Stacey gave a gentle smile. 'But you heard the gunshot, or at least that's what Jimmy told me,' she said, studying her daughter's reaction.

'Yeah.' Looking away Karen watched her husband. There was already a lot of animosity between Cameron and her uncle Jonny, and if the truth were to ever come out, and Jonny was to find out that it had actually been his elder brother and Cameron's father Gary who had killed her dad then she had a sinking feeling that World War Three would erupt. If nothing else, Jonny would take his anger out on his nephew and in a way she couldn't blame him. Although they may not have looked identical, and it would be fair to say that her husband took after his mother rather than his father, Cameron did share many of Gary's mannerisms, so much so that at times it took Karen's breath away.

'It'll be our secret,' Stacey whispered in her ear. 'No one else ever needs to find out.'

Feeling somewhat relieved Karen nodded.

'You're a lot stronger than you think,' Stacey continued as she nodded across to her son-in-law. 'If you can build a life with the son of your dad's murderer then you can be strong for your own son too, and now more than ever Tommy Jr is going to need you.'

Karen's forehead furrowed. 'But...'

'No buts.' Stacey stood up a little straighter. 'And no more tears. You're a Carter,' she said with a smile. 'Or at least you were before becoming a Johnson. And that, my darling, means,' she said, tapping her daughter's temple, 'that you hold your head up high and that you don't take any shit from anyone.'

As she thought over her mother's words, Karen involuntarily pulled herself up to her full height. Her mum was right and, as afraid as she was for her son, crying wasn't going to help anyone, least of all Tommy Jr. 'I'll pop home and fetch him something to wear in court,' she stated.

Stacey smiled. 'You do that.' As her daughter made to walk away Stacey pulled on her elbow. 'And remember what I told you,' she said, studying Karen's face. 'No matter the outcome, you're a Carter first and foremost.'

Once Karen had left the office Stacey turned to look at her first husband's family, her voice when she spoke strong and unwavering. 'So, what's the plan?' she asked.

'That's exactly what I'd like to know.' A voice spoke from behind her.

Spinning around Stacey's mouth dropped open before creasing up into a wide smile. 'Mad Dog,' she said taking his hand in hers and giving it a gentle squeeze.

'Well?' Mad Dog asked his accent appearing even thicker than usual. 'What is the plan and more importantly what are you going to do to bring Tommy Jr home?'

* * *

Tommy Jr took one look at the solicitor his family had acquired for him and felt his heart sink down to his stomach. This had to be a joke he decided; a cruel, sick joke on his family's part.

Tugging on the cotton shirt that strained against his protruding tummy the solicitor took a seat across from Tommy and stuck out his hand. 'Richard Lewis,' he said in the way of an introduction.

Tommy shook the proffered hand.

For a few moments a silence followed, and as Richard unclipped his briefcase and pulled out several sheets of paper, Tommy studied him. Admittedly he hadn't met many solicitors in his lifetime, but he would have thought that they would look a darn sight better than the geezer sitting across from him. From the mop of unruly, dark, curly hair that fell across his forehead, to the glasses that constantly slipped down his nose, and then the shirt that sat snug upon his robust frame, it would be fair to say that Richard Lewis was a mess.

'Now then, Tommy.' Glancing up, Richard flashed a wide grin, his teeth white and straight. 'As you already know, you've been charged with two counts. Firstly' – he glanced back down to the sheet of paper, his forehead furrowed – 'possession and intent to supply a class A drug. And secondly' – he looked back down at the paper, his lips silently moving as he read out the charges – 'possession of a weapon.'

'I'm innocent,' Tommy stated, leaning slightly forward. 'I'd never even seen the knife or coke before, let alone touched them.'

'Of course you didn't.' Richard's smile widened, and folding the paper with a flourish he slipped the paperwork back into his briefcase. 'I can't see there being any issue.' He waved his hand through the air. 'By this time tomorrow you will be at home.' He gave a slight pause. 'Until the court case of course.'

Tommy slumped back in the chair, his forehead furrowing. 'Court case?'

Richard nodded. 'I'm afraid so.' He tapped the briefcase. 'A magistrate won't touch this. They'll hold a preliminary hearing of course, but ultimately, the case will be referred to a crown court.'

'But I didn't do anything,' Tommy repeated, his voice becoming louder. 'This is bollocks, I've been set up.'

'It's the standard procedure,' Richard reiterated as he got to his feet. Holding out one hand he scooped up the briefcase with the other. 'I will see you in court in the morning.' At the door he turned back around, the same infuriating smile spread across his face. 'Don't worry too much,' he beamed. 'I very much doubt that you'll be remanded into custody.'

The solicitor's reassurance did nothing to appease Tommy's concern. And as for remand, the idea that he might actually be sent straight to prison before even having a trial hadn't entered his head. If truth be told he hadn't thought that far ahead; he'd wrongly assumed that with a good solicitor on his side then the charges against him would be dropped.

Feeling even more depressed than he had previously, Tommy sank onto the chair and held his head in his hands. This couldn't be happening he told himself over and over again. Only it was and there was nothing he could do to stop the inevitable from happening.

7

The next morning Reece Carter was a bundle of nerves. He'd hardly had a wink of sleep and felt sick to his stomach. Tommy Jr wasn't only his cousin but he was also his best mate. They had more or less grown up together and their bond was tight. Reece may have been a year older than Tommy, but out of the two of them, Tommy was the main instigator when it came to them causing mayhem. Not only was Tommy a born leader, but he also wasn't afraid of getting stuck in, even when they'd been heavily outnumbered. It would be fair to say that he had a nasty temper on him too, one that made even Reece nervous at times and that, coupled with a blinding right hook, was enough to ensure that people stayed out of his way. That wasn't to say, however, that Reece considered himself to be a sheep, someone who merely followed his cousin around doing his bidding because he didn't. At the end of the day, he could hold his own; he was a Carter after all, it would be more surprising if he couldn't look after himself. But Tommy had an edge about him, a certain something that made people sit up and take notice of him. And as much as his family had never said otherwise, it hadn't escaped Reece's attention that to a certain degree they kept Tommy on a tight leash, as though they thoroughly believed that he was a ticking time bomb just waiting to go off. Underneath the friendly persona he would put on when the mood took him, he could very well be a dangerous individual. And when you considered Tommy's genes, Reece couldn't help but wonder if his dad and uncles were maybe onto something. As it was, Tommy's grandfathers had both been men not to be underestimated, and when you added Tommy's great-grandfather Dean Johnson to the equation, the risk increased tenfold. By all accounts, Johnson had been ruthless and feared by those who knew him, pretty much the same as Tommy in many respects.

Switching off the ignition he rested his hand on the steering wheel and surveyed the office. Already he could see that the scrapyard was a hive of activity, his dad, uncles, cousins, and Tommy's parents and grandmother littering the forecourt.

'He's going to come home, isn't he?'

Reece turned his head to look at Aimee. The hope in her voice tugging at his heart strings.

'Yeah, of course he will.' As he answered Reece found himself glancing away, unable to look Aimee in the eyes. The truth was, he didn't know if Tommy would be returning home with them. And as much as he hoped that this would be the case, he was unable to shift the unease that settled in the pit of his stomach.

'Tommy's parents have got him a good solicitor,' Melanie stated from the back seat.

Shifting her weight, Aimee turned her head, the quiver in her voice more than audible. 'But what if he goes to prison?'

'He won't,' Reece barked out, coming across a lot harsher than he'd intended. Momentarily closing his eyes, he shook his head. 'I'm sorry.' He held up his hands. 'I didn't mean to snap, it's just...' He shook his head then motioned to where his family were standing. 'Come on.' He threw open the car door and climbed out.

As much as his family looked outwardly calm Reece could sense the tension in the air. It was unknown territory; none of them had ever been arrested before let alone been charged with a crime, and considering their occupations that was saying something.

Lighting a cigarette he stood quietly smoking. What if Aimee was right and Tommy was sent to prison? Pushing the thought from his mind, he wandered back to his car, and leaning against the door, he shoved one hand into his pocket and absentmindedly kicked out at a stone on the ground.

'Are you alright?'

Reece looked up at his father, and giving a nod, he took a final drag on the cigarette then dropped the smouldering butt to the tarmac and ground it out underneath his heavy boot.

Mitchell Carter sighed, and coming to stand next to his son, he nodded towards the forecourt. 'Anyone would think it's a funeral the way they're carrying on.'

Reece screwed up his face. Although he had to admit his dad had a point if the glum faces were anything to go by. 'What do you expect them to do?' he growled. 'Throw a party?'

Mitchell sighed. 'Look,' he said after a couple of moments. 'None of us are choirboys. Our good luck was bound to run out at some point. I'm more surprised it's taken this long for one of us to have a capture.'

'Tommy has done fuck all wrong,' Reece hissed. Pushing himself away from the car he clenched his fists. 'It was that fucking Kevin,' he snarled. 'He's behind this.' He pointed to his stomach. 'I know he is; I can feel it in my gut.'

'Maybe.' Taking out his own cigarettes Mitchell nodded. 'Without proof though,' he said, lighting up and exhaling a cloud of smoke above his head, 'there's fuck all we can do about it – at least for now anyway.'

Reece's jaw dropped. 'So, we let him get away with it? We let him fuck Tommy over, is that what you're suggesting?'

'I didn't say that.' Mitchell gave a light laugh, and nodding towards where his brothers and nephews were standing, he clasped his son by the shoulder. 'Can you honestly see any of that lot letting this drop?'

Thinking the question over, Reece shook his head. His dad had a point he supposed. His family may have had their fallouts over the years, and plenty of them, but at the end of the day they looked out for one another. It was what families did, wasn't it? They had each other's backs, just as he and Tommy Jr did.

* * *

Beads of sweat dotted Richard Lewis' top lip, and shaking his head, he gave Tommy Jr a sympathetic smile. 'He's a hard nut to crack, Tommy lad,' he stated.

Tommy narrowed his eyes, feeling even more fed up with the brief his family had acquired for him than he had the day before. 'Who is?' he asked.

Giving a dramatic sigh, Richard lifted his briefcase onto the table that separated them and shook his head. 'Hodson,' he answered looking up.

Confusion swept across Tommy's face, and as his eyebrows scrunched together, he cocked his head to one side. 'Who the fuck is Hodson?'

'Arthur Hodson,' Richard sighed. 'The magistrate who will be sitting in on your case.'

The hairs on the back of Tommy's neck stood upright. 'What does that mean for me?' he implored, the words coming out in a rush. 'I mean, I can still go home, can't I? You said yourself that this was just a preliminary hearing, that I won't be detained.'

Richard paused, pushed his glasses up the bridge of his nose, a habit that was beginning to get on Tommy's nerves, and he pressed his lips together. 'I think' – he took a sheet of paper out of the case and placed it on the table before snapping the briefcase closed – 'that maybe you should prepare yourself for the worst. Like I said.' He lifted his hand in the air as if to ward Tommy off. 'Hodson is a hard nut to crack. I've come up against him a few times and wouldn't be surprised if he made an example out of you. He has a reputation, doesn't take any nonsense and when it comes to narcotics,' he said glancing away. 'Well, let's just say that he doesn't tolerate drug dealing in any way, shape, or form.'

The air left Tommy's lungs, and turning away from Richard, he squeezed his eyes shut tight and groaned. 'That's just great,' he said with a hint of sarcasm. 'Some fucking brief you are.' Spinning back around, his eyes flashed dangerously. 'I thought you were supposed to be some kind of big shot. And I can guarantee,' he said stabbing his finger in Richard's direction, 'that my family paid some fucking wedge to get you here. You're a fucking joke mate, a first-class fucking joke.'

Clearing his throat, Richard's shoulders drooped. 'I'll see you in court,' he said quietly. 'Oh, and Tommy,' he added as an afterthought. 'Try not to lose your temper and whatever you do, watch your attitude. I don't want to give Hodson an even greater reason to take a dislike to you.'

Tommy didn't bother to answer, and as Richard hastily retreated out of the door, he clenched his fists, the scowl across his face deepening. He had a nasty feeling, no, it was more than a feeling, it was more like an impending sense of doom that surged through his entire body. No matter how much he might rein his temper in he wouldn't be going home and there was nothing he, or anyone else could say on the matter to change that fact.

* * *

An hour later Richard Lewis' face was so deathly white that he resembled a corpse, and rubbing at his neck that still bore the indentations of Cameron Johnson's fingers, he gasped for breath.

'You need to be reasonable,' he spluttered out. 'I wasn't even made aware of the case until late yesterday afternoon.'

'Reasonable,' Cameron spat as he began to pace the pavement directly outside the court. 'Fucking reasonable!'

Richard swallowed, and still rubbing at his neck, he glanced around him. 'I've had less than twenty-four hours to prepare a defence.'

Cameron charged forward again, his expression one of anger. 'And my son,' he roared, 'is about to be locked up like a caged animal.'

'On remand,' Richard corrected, nerves getting the better of him as he blinked up at Cameron in rapid succession. 'He pleaded not guilty and until a jury says otherwise that's how he'll be treated.'

'He'll still be detained,' Cameron hollered, his hand involuntarily curling into a fist. 'Which part of that don't you understand? Or maybe...' he said, inching even closer, his expression one of anger. 'I need to punch it into your skull; maybe then you'll understand the severity of the situation. It's alright for you, you get to walk away from this, but what about my son, what about my wife?' he roared, jerking his thumb in Karen's direction. 'She's in fucking bits.'

Stepping forward Jonny shoved Cameron away from the solicitor, and coming to stand between the two men he breathed heavily through his nostrils, the muscles across his shoulder blades remaining taut as though he were half expecting Cameron to lunge forward a second time and follow through with his threat to knock the brief on his arse. 'How long until he gets a trial? What are we talking here, weeks, months?'

Thinking the question over, Richard ever so slightly raised his eyebrows, his wary gaze watching Cameron Johnson's every move. 'Could be anything up to a year.'

'A year,' Karen gasped, the despair in her voice more than apparent. Turning to her husband she gripped hold of his arm; her fingers grasping his shirt and balling the material in her fist. 'No,' she cried, her eyes wild with fear. 'Do something,' she implored him. 'You promised me that everything would be okay, that our son would be coming home with us.'

Shrugging his wife's hand away from him, Cameron rounded on the solicitor, his nostrils flaring. 'You can't be serious,' he demanded. 'He's done fuck all wrong.'

'I'm afraid so.' His cheeks flushing red, Richard nodded. 'I did warn you that it wouldn't be an open-and-shut case, that Hodson would—'

Cameron's arm shot out, and slamming Richard into the wall again, his lips curled into a snarl. 'I couldn't give a flying fuck about Hodson or whatever the fuck his name is,' he seethed. 'I paid you an extortionate amount of dough to make all of this disappear, for the charges against my boy to be dropped.'

Richard's eyes bulged, and as he cowered away from Cameron, Jonny swore under his breath. 'For fuck's sake,' he hissed as he wrenched Cameron away a second time. 'You're not making this any easier. Carry on like this and you'll end up in the cell next to your son.'

'This is bollocks,' Reece shouted.

Giving his nephew a look of warning, Jonny stabbed his

finger in Reece's direction. 'Enough,' he growled. 'I know that tempers are beginning to flare but will all of you just calm the fuck down...' As the electronic gates adjoining the court opened and a prison van containing Tommy Jr sped past them, the words died in his throat. And as his niece's gut-wrenching sobs filled the air, he snapped his head back towards Richard. 'Tell us what we need to do,' he begged of him. 'And we'll do it.'

Richard straightened out his shirt, and pushing his glasses up the bridge of his nose, he sighed. 'Finding out how exactly the narcotics and knife could have made their way into Tommy's car would be a good starting point. I'm going to need something, anything, that I can work with,' he said, giving both Cameron and Karen a cautious glance. 'Something that will make a jury doubt the prosecution's claims that Tommy's intention was to supply a class A drug.'

Jonny nodded, and as he looked around at his family, he had a sinking feeling that the solicitor's request would be a lot easier said than done. That wasn't to say, however, that it would be entirely impossible. After all, he came from a big family, and seeing as there were so many of them, nothing escaped their notice. 'Consider it done,' he answered with a lot more confidence than he actually felt.

8

Pentonville Prison. Those two words alone were enough to send a shiver of fear down the length of Tommy Jr's spine. He didn't know what was awaiting him, neither did he know what was expected of him. He wasn't so sure that he'd ever met anyone who'd served time inside. Wracking his brain, he tried to think back. Other than his nan's dad and brothers, men he'd never even met, he could think of no one else. Well, there was Max Hardcastle of course, he'd spent years banged up for a murder he'd committed as a teenager, but Tommy had only met the man a couple of times, never mind had the opportunity to question him about his time spent incarcerated.

The van came to a shuddering halt, and as the sound of metal doors opening echoed around him, Tommy braced himself. He couldn't show his fear – that much he did know, and as a new inmate he was bound to be viewed as fair game, someone the other prisoners would try to push around.

He swallowed deeply and, digging his fingernails into the palm of his hands in an attempt to stop his hands from shaking, he got to his feet. Moments later he was led out of the van, and before he could even get a glimpse of his surroundings he was ushered through a door and into a reception area. Bleak was the only way he could describe the room. Whitewashed iron bars covered the grimy windows, the walls were painted off-white and the concrete floor beneath his feet a dark grey.

After being booked in, interviewed, and assigned a prison number he was led through another set of locked doors, the keys dangling from the prison officer's belt a constant reminder that he was trapped and that there was no way of escaping.

'You're on D wing,' the screw barked out at him with an accent Tommy couldn't quite place as he led them through a series of corridors.

As much as the information meant nothing to him, Tommy nodded. Reaching yet another barred gate he stepped into what he presumed was another reception area, his gaze automatically drifting upwards to look at the metal bars that separated each floor and wing. Giving an involuntary shudder he followed the screw, the noise coming from the other inmates suddenly loud to his ears.

Coming to a halt outside a cell, he waited for the door to be unlocked then walked inside.

The cell was so small that if he spread out his arms, he would be able to touch the walls on either side of him. Taking in his surroundings, his gaze lingered on an iron bunkbed, both beds unoccupied, much to his relief.

'Do I...' He cleared his throat, then turning around to face the screw, he forced his voice to sound a lot more confident than he actually felt. 'Do I get a phone call?'

The prison officer nodded. 'Everything will be explained when you have your induction.'

Tommy nodded again, and, as the door was closed and the clank of metal against metal indicated that he'd been locked inside, he took a step closer to the bunkbed and wearily slumped down on the edge of the bottom bunk. Beside him was a plastic bag and peering inside he took note of the bedding, plate, cutlery, and essential toiletries that had been supplied to him. For some reason he felt even more depressed, the welcome pack a stark reminder that he wouldn't be going anywhere, anytime soon, no matter how much he might want to.

* * *

A few hours later Cameron Johnson looked down at his mobile phone, and seeing the unfamiliar number flash across the screen, he leapt to his feet and exited the scrapyard office.

On hearing his son's voice, he glanced over his shoulder ensuring that his wife wasn't within earshot of his conversation. 'Are you alright, boy?' he asked as he wandered across to the far side of the forecourt.

As Tommy Jr answered, Cameron's shoulders slumped, relief flooding through him. 'Listen,' he said, giving the office another cautious glance. 'I know the brief came across as a shower of shite, but Danny reckons he's top notch, that he really knows his stuff.' He waited for his son to answer then got down to business. Now that he'd had the chance to calm down, he could see that Richard Lewis had been right. They needed something, anything, that could be used during the trial to discredit the prosecution's claims, and so it was imperative that Tommy Jr be honest with him, no matter how much Cameron might not like his answers. Aware that the phone call could very well be monitored and as a result implicate his son even further, Cameron resisted the urge to ask him outright if he'd been responsible for the drugs and blade found in the car. Not that he actually believed this to be the case, but still, he supposed, there was always that tiny chance that perhaps Tommy Jr may not be quite as innocent as they all believed him to be. After all, his son was legally an adult and it had been years since he or Karen had actually felt the need to know Tommy Jr's every movement; who knew what he got up to once he was out of their sight?

'As soon as I can, I'm going to come and see you,' he stated. 'I'll book a visit.' He paused and glanced back at the office knowing that his wife would be angry with him, but in the circumstances what else was he supposed to do? He needed answers from their son and having Karen with him on a visit wasn't the best way to go about it. No doubt she would be an emotional wreck, the shock of seeing her only child incarcerated was bound to break her heart. Not that he could entirely blame his wife, he too would find it difficult, especially when it came to the end of the visit and there was nothing else he could do but to leave Tommy Jr behind. 'I'm going to bring one of your uncles with me,' he said hoping that Tommy Jr would understand what he was trying to tell him: that the visit wouldn't purely be a social visit but a chance for them to find out what the hell had gone down.

All too quickly the call came to an end and hastily saying his goodbyes Cameron switched off the phone and made his way back towards the office, deep in thought. The drugs and knife had come from somewhere, that much he did know. It stood to reason that someone had been responsible for supplying the goods, the only question though, was who?

* * *

As Kevin Fox tucked a box of chocolates underneath his arm it took all of his willpower to keep the smug grin off his face. Banging his fist on Melanie's door he smoothed down his hair and forced a mock sad expression to spread across his face.

The moment Melanie opened the front door, he placed his hand upon his chest. 'I've just heard the news,' he said with a shake of his head. 'I can't fucking believe it. I mean...' He looked down at his ex-wife, his sly eyes closely gauging her reaction to him turning up on the doorstep both unannounced and unwelcome. 'I know I said that he'd end up behind bars but I didn't actually think it would happen. I thought he was too shrewd for that, that he had his head screwed on,' he said pointing to his temple.

Melanie sighed. 'I suppose you'd better come in,' she said moving aside to give Kevin enough room to squeeze past her.

Stepping across the threshold, Kevin glanced towards the staircase. 'How is she?'

'How do you think?' Melanie puffed out her cheeks. 'She's in bits.' She ran her hand through her short hair not caring one iota that it stood up on end, resembling a brush. 'She's having Tommy's baby for Christ's sake, and she's terrified that he won't be there when she gives birth. Keeps saying that she can't live without him.'

'That's the shock talking.' Kevin shook his head dismissing his daughter's distress, all the while suppressing the grin that threatened to portray the part he'd played in Tommy Johnson's downfall. 'I could batter him for this,' he blurted out. 'What the hell does he think he's playing at?' He shot another glance towards Melanie and puffed out his chest. 'I won't have anyone upset my little girl, least of all him. And what if she'd been there when the Old Bill nicked him? She could have been arrested too; they could have charged her as being an accessory.'

Crossing her arms over her chest Melanie cocked an eyebrow. 'Don't you go upsetting her any further,' she warned stabbing a finger towards her ex-husband. 'As far as she's concerned, he's innocent.'

Kevin screwed up his face. 'How the fuck is he innocent?' he barked back. 'He was found with a blade and half a kilo of coke in his car.'

As she studied Kevin, Melanie rocked back on her heels. 'How do you know that?' she demanded. 'I didn't even know what he'd been charged with until Aimee came out of court.'

Realising his mistake Kevin hastily backtracked. 'It's the talk of the boozer.' He waved his hand dismissively. 'You know what that lot are like. They love nothing better than to stick their big hooters into everyone else's business, and seeing as our Aimee is associated with Tommy they've done nothing but question me all afternoon.'

'I suppose so,' Melanie sighed. On hearing footsteps descend the stairs, she shot Kevin another look of warning. 'Don't wind her up. She's been through enough as it is.'

'What do you take me for?' Kevin hissed back. 'I'm her dad, I wouldn't dream of upsetting her.'

Moments later Aimee entered the lounge and on seeing her father she faltered, her back becoming ramrod straight, and her eyebrows pinched together. 'What are you doing here?'

Kevin stepped forward, and spreading open his arms, he gave a sad smile. 'I came to see how you are doing, of course.' He shook his head giving his daughter a sad smile. 'Your mum told me what happened, that you've been in bits. I'm so sorry, darling. I just wish there was something I could do, something to make all of this go away.'

There and then Aimee's face crumpled and as tears sprang to her eyes she stepped into her dad's arms and broke down.

'Come on now,' Kevin murmured in her ear. 'Everything's going to be okay.'

'No it won't,' Aimee wailed, her heart breaking that little bit more. 'I want him to come home.'

'And I'm sure that he will... eventually.'

Aimee cried even harder. 'I need him dad,' she sobbed. 'I love him.'

Biting back a retort Kevin stood back slightly, and holding his daughter by her forearms, he looked into her eyes. 'He's no good, sweetheart. He'll end up bringing you down. It's all his type ever do. And you've got the baby to think about now. Is this the kind of life you want for yourself or your child? Trust me when I say this, darling, you don't need the likes of him, me and your mum will see you alright, we'll look after you. Maybe him being locked up was a blessing in disguise. A way for you to get that little prick out of your life for once and for all.'

'Kevin,' Melanie warned.

'No,' Kevin barked back. 'She needs to know the truth, to see the situation for how it really is. All of this pussy footing around is doing her no good. I could have told you from the start that something like this would happen. The Carters, the Johnsons, they're all the fucking same; they're nothing but scum. This poor little mare is carrying Johnson's kid, so where the fuck are Tommy's parents, eh? Why ain't they looking after her, making sure that she's alright? If you want my opinion,' he said, stabbing his finger towards his ex-wife, 'I very much doubt she'll even hear from any of them, it'll be a case of out of sight, out of fucking mind.'

'Or maybe,' Melanie hissed. 'They've got a lot on their plate seeing as their only son has been locked up for something he didn't do.'

Kevin began to laugh. 'Don't give me all of that old fanny. He's as guilty as they fucking come. The coke and knife were found in his car, so how else do you explain that eh?'

Melanie snapped her lips closed, and turning to look at her daughter, she shook her head, her shoulders slumping in defeat. 'I don't know,' she sighed.

'Exactly,' Kevin stated. 'You don't know.' He looked down at his daughter, and pulling her close again he nuzzled his face in her hair in an attempt to hide his grin. 'It'll be alright, darling,' he soothed. 'You've got your old dad, and, unlike that cunt Tommy Johnson, I won't be going anywhere.'

* * *

Perched on the edge of the desk in the scrapyard office anger settled across Reece's face. 'I can't believe this is happening,' he declared. 'That brief you hired was shit,' he said flashing Cameron an accusing stare. 'Tommy Jr should have never been sent down.'

'The brief,' Jonny said through clenched teeth, 'is one of the best in the business. He came highly recommended.'

'Yeah, well if he's that good,' Reece spat back, 'then why is Tommy in prison right now? His prints weren't even on the package or knife, they've got nothing on him.'

Clutching his forehead Jonny let out an incredulous laugh. 'What do you mean they've got nothing on him? The coke and blade were found in his car for fuck's sake. Besides,' he sighed, 'you heard what the brief said. We need to find something he can work with.'

Reece screwed up his face. 'Yeah, well that's not good enough. We need to do something now; we need to get him out.'

Gritting his teeth, Jonny shook his head. 'What exactly do you suggest we do?' he barked back. 'Send him a cake with a file in it? Or how about we order a helicopter and have it fly over the prison and airlift him out.'

'I was only saying,' Reece grumbled. 'No need to bite my head off.'

Fast on his way to losing his patience with his nephew Jonny gave Reece a cold stare. 'Stop coming out with stupid shit then and I won't need to bite your head off.' He rubbed at his temple. 'Other than finding out where the coke came from and how it happened to get into Tommy Jr's car, there's nothing else we can do.'

Thinking the situation over Mitchell sat forward and rested his forearms on his knees. 'We're not talking about a wrap here,' he said looking around him. 'We're talking about half a kilo…'

'Yeah, and?' Cameron interrupted, his back instantly up.

'Let the man finish.' Crossing his arms over his chest, Mad Dog Harris raised his eyebrows, his voice hard. 'I know that Tommy Jr is your son but you're not the only one who cares about him. Same goes for you,' he said, turning his attention to Reece. 'Throwing out insults isn't going to help anyone, least of all Tommy Jr.'

Thoroughly chastised both Cameron and Reece nodded.

'Carry on,' Cameron mumbled jerking his head in Mitchell's direction.

'As I was saying.' Momentarily, Mitchell paused. 'Half a kilo,' he said continuing. 'That's got to be worth, what, fifty, sixty grand on the streets.'

'Yeah, about that, I suppose,' Jonny agreed. 'Although I can't say I know much about this sort of thing. Dealing that shit has never been our game.' He looked across at his nephews, wondering if perhaps they knew a bit more than he did. 'It could be worth even more.'

'Well.' Mitchell spread open his arms. 'We're talking big time then. Surely to fuck that's got to narrow the list of suspects down a bit, hasn't it? This is no small-time dealer, some hood rat on the street. And that's another thing,' he added, jerking his head around to look at Cameron. 'Say for argument's sake Tommy Jr had had a hand in this then I'm going to take a wild guess and say that he wouldn't have been able to stump up the cash to buy the gear outright.'

'No.' Cameron narrowed his eyes. 'I mean he isn't skint, not by any means, but he doesn't have that kind of money lying around.'

'What are you trying to say?' Jonny asked his brother.

For a few moments Mitchell was quiet. 'Fifty grand is a lot of dough,' he answered. 'And someone, somewhere is going to want their cash.'

Still unsure where his brother was going with the conversation, Jonny mirrored Mitchell's stance and sat forward. 'So...?'

'So.' Mitchell looked around him. 'How many dealers do we know? And I'm not talking about the kids racing around the estates on their bikes peddling pills or selling the odd bit of weed. I'm talking about the bastards who are at the top of their game, the ones who are supplying these little hood rats on a large scale.'

Sinking back into the chair Jonny wearily closed his eyes and as Mad Dog let out a low whistle from across the office, he rubbed his hand over his face. There was only one name that sprang to his mind, only one family who, like his brother had just stated, were at the top of their game. 'The Bannermans,' he groaned. 'Or in other words, aggravation that we can all do without.'

Mitchell nodded. 'Got it in one.'

As he looked around him, Reece screwed up his face, his forehead furrowing. 'Who are the Bannermans?'

Jonny groaned a second time and glancing from his brother to his nephew he sighed. 'Your worst fucking nightmare, sunshine,' he answered with a grimace. 'That's exactly who the Bannermans are.'

9

With one hand behind his head Tommy Jr lay on his back and stared up at the metal bars of the top bunk. After a restless night, the majority of which he'd tossed and turned trying to make himself as comfortable as he possibly could, he'd pretty much given up on drifting off to sleep.

With no idea of the actual time, he sat up, swung his legs over the side of the bunk, planted his feet firmly on the floor, then moved his neck from side to side, in an attempt to ease out the tension across his shoulder blades – not that the action helped him in any way. His entire body felt as though it was so tightly coiled that just one wrong move would be enough to do himself some damage.

The sound of keys jangling and cell doors being opened echoed around him, and turning his head in time to witness the thin metal slot situated across the top half of the door slide down before being slammed closed again, the door was unlocked. From his position Tommy peered towards the landing and as men of varying ages trudged along the walkway he got to his feet and inched closer to the open door. Leaning against the iron frame he watched the comings and goings, unsure exactly of what he was supposed to do now. He thought back to his induction, not that he could say he'd been able to take much of it in, the entire time the screw had been talking had passed him by in a blur. He did recall something being mentioned about the exercise yard though, and stepping outside the cell, he glanced over his shoulder, taking note of the numbers screwed to the cell door.

After a cautious glance around him, he began to follow the other prisoners, a part of him wanting to keep his head down low, keep himself to himself, and not make eye contact with anyone. And then there was another part of him, the part which wanted to remind himself of exactly who he was. He was a Johnson, not that he expected this information to mean much to anyone else. His family may have been widely known, perhaps even feared in some circles, but here in prison he was sure it meant fuck all. Here, he was nothing but a small fish in a big pond, and for the first time in his life his surname wasn't about to get him off the hook or even go in his favour.

A short time later, Tommy stepped outside into what he guessed was the exercise yard. The entire area was as bleak as the inside of the prison, if that was even possible. Everywhere he looked was either brickwork, or concrete, the walls surrounding the yard at least twenty feet high and topped with barbed wire bringing further testament to the fact that he was trapped. Shoving his hands into his pockets he began to move forward relishing the feel of a light breeze that spread across his skin. He'd not even completed a day inside yet and already he wanted out, wanted to go home. And as much as working at the scrapyard bored him half to death most of the time, he'd give anything to be getting up to go to work right about now. Even the thought of a bollocking from his uncle Jonny for not pulling his weight, or his mum nagging at him because he'd dumped the wet towels in the corner of the bathroom again rather than hanging them up to dry would have been welcome rather than enduring another minute in this hell hole.

Once he'd walked the entire perimeter of the yard Tommy leaned against the wall and took note of a man of similar age, height, and stature standing a few feet away from him. With light brown hair, brown eyes, and a smattering of freckles across his nose and cheeks he nodded a greeting.

As Tommy returned the nod the man moved closer, copying Tommy's stance as he leaned back against the wall and rested one foot up on the brickwork as though to steady himself.

'Shit ain't it?' he commented as he nodded around them.

'Yeah, you could say that,' Tommy answered with a sigh.

'How long are you in for?'

Tommy turned his head and gave a small shrug. 'I'm on remand. How about you?'

'Five years.' His lips turned up into a smile as he gave a cheeky grin. 'Could have been a lot worse, I was expecting to get at least ten.'

Tommy nodded, and as he swallowed, he looked away. If found guilty, he was expecting a similar sentence, maybe even more. The mere thought was enough to make him feel sick.

'Dylan,' the man said as he motioned to himself.

'Tommy.'

They fell into a comfortable silence and clearing his throat Tommy gestured around them. 'How long have you got left?'

Dylan gave a light laugh although it sounded hollow to Tommy's ears, and as he ran his hand through his light brown hair he straightened up, his demeanour suddenly becoming more guarded, as he glanced across the yard and studied two men standing across from them. 'Five.' He shrugged, his eyes narrowed into slits. 'I've only been here for a couple of days, transferred from Isis.' He gave another shrug. 'I was hoping to stick it out there for a bit longer seeing as I've only just turned nineteen and it's a youth offenders nick, but no, the bastards shipped me out to this shithole instead.'

Whistling through his teeth Tommy shook his head. He couldn't even imagine spending another day of his life locked up, let alone the next five years.

'I dunno why they didn't just ship me out to a proper nick and be done with it,' Dylan continued to grumble.

Screwing up his face Tommy glanced around him, his gaze taking in the high walls and barbed wire. 'This is a proper nick, ain't it?'

Dylan laughed and turning his head he gave Tommy a quizzical stare. 'It's a holding prison...' His voice trailed off and pushing himself off the wall his shoulders tensed. 'And like I said,' he added, staring ahead of him, 'seeing as I've been lumped with five years it would have made more sense in the long run.'

Following Dylan's gaze, Tommy took note of the two men standing across from them and ever so slightly frowned. All thanks to the family he came from he knew trouble when he saw it. He'd been on the receiving end of men like these two before and knew their type. If nothing else, the menacing stares they gave were a dead giveaway to the fact they had some sort of problem with Dylan, and he knew from experience that it was only a matter of time before tempers began to flare and that they began throwing their weight around. From as far back as he could remember there had always been someone who had a beef, whether that be with himself, his dad, uncles, or cousins, hence why he and Reece had got into so many fights over the years. 'Mates of yours?' he enquired.

'Nah.' Dylan shook his head, his body stiffening as though he half expected the men to charge over and start laying into him. 'I've never seen them before.'

Tommy nodded, and as he and Dylan continued chatting, he inadvertently kept one eye on the men, watching their every move. A short time later they made their way back inside, and as they went, Tommy turned to look back over his shoulder. Whoever the men were, they had certainly unnerved Dylan, and as he gave his new pal a sidelong glance he couldn't help but wonder what he'd done, not only to get himself locked up, but to also put a target on his back in such a short space of time.

* * *

Entering the scrapyard office, Jonny immediately rocked back on his heels. 'What are you doing here so early?'

Peter sighed, and taking a sip of his lukewarm coffee, he grimaced before slumping back on the sofa. 'I couldn't sleep, you know, what with...' Turning his face away he sucked in his bottom lip, his cheeks turning red.

'What?' Shrugging off his jacket Jonny tossed his car keys onto the desk, all the while studying his eldest nephew.

'All this that's going on with Tommy Jr,' Peter answered. He straightened up, placed his elbows on his knees, and shook his head. 'You know as well as I do that nothing we do or say is going to make a difference. That however much we might want to, we're not going to get him out of the nick. The filth have him bang to rights.' He clenched then unclenched his fist, as though debating whether or not to voice his true thoughts. 'And no jury in the country,' he added after a few moments, 'is going to believe he didn't know the gear was in his car, it's just not possible, is it? I mean c'mon think about it, how could he have not known? It's like Mitch' said last night, this is not a wrap we're talking about, something that could have slipped out of someone's pocket, it's half a kilo for fuck's sake, it's hardly something you'd be able to miss.'

As he continued to study Peter, the nerve at the side of Jonny's eye pulsated. 'What exactly are you trying to say?'

Thinking the question over, Peter slumped back against the cushions again and pinched the bridge of his nose. 'He's my nephew,' he said. 'And I love him, of course I do, but...'

'You don't believe him,' Jonny volunteered.

'No.' Peter shook his head. 'I want to, I really want to, but...' He blew out his cheeks and rubbed his hand across his jaw. 'The coke was in his car, and we both know there is only one way it could have got there.' He glanced towards the door and threw up his hands. 'My mum and sister might think the sun shines out of Tommy Jr's arse but you know as well as I do that he's a lot like my dad, and if that wasn't bad enough, add Gary to the equation and we've got a real problem on our hands. At the best of times Tommy Jr is a handful, always has been, but he's not a kid any more, and we're long past the days where a slap on the wrist is going to scare him into toeing the line. He's too old for any of that, he's a man now.' He paused for breath and looked down at his clenched fist before looking back up. 'And as much as I don't want to admit it, I just can't help but think maybe there's a lot more of Gary inside of him than any of us realise.'

Jonny sighed. As much as he didn't like to admit it the exact same thoughts had crossed his mind too. His eldest brother, Tommy Snr – Tommy Jr's maternal grandfather – had been a risk taker, and although drugs hadn't been something he'd ever shown much of an interest in, who knew what the future could have held if he hadn't been murdered? And when it came to the third eldest of his brothers, Gary, nothing would surprise him where he was concerned. At the best of times Gary had been volatile and not content until he'd riled someone up. He could barely recall any of his brothers having a good word to say about him, and as much as Tommy Snr may have tolerated Gary and had even gone as far as to fight his corner at times, he had a feeling that his eldest brother hadn't liked him, not really, not deep down. 'I take it you don't think Aimee's old man was involved then?'

Shaking his head again, Peter got to his feet. 'Reece is clutching at straws. Him and Tommy Jr are tight, more like brothers than cousins. It's only natural that he would want to blame someone and yeah, Kevin might be a cokehead but for all we know, Tommy Jr could have been his dealer. It would certainly be one way of explaining why Kevin had been with him before getting nicked, and of course, why the coke was in his car.'

Thinking it over Jonny reluctantly agreed. Still, though, it didn't explain where the drugs had originally come from. If Tommy Jr had been dealing then someone must have supplied them to him, that much was a given. 'I think it's about time we paid the Bannermans a visit.'

'Yeah,' Peter groaned. 'I had a nasty feeling you might say that.'

* * *

Four hours later, Jonny was deep in thought, and as he sat outside The Jolly Fisherman public house in Barking, he absent-mindedly drummed his fingers on the steering wheel. When it came to the Bannerman brothers, he couldn't say he knew a great deal about them, other than the fact they were lunatics of course, but other than that their paths had never crossed. Having had no personal dealings with them he wasn't so sure of how to even contact them, and the only thing he did know for a certainty was that the brothers had been born and raised in South London, which made him question how exactly Tommy Jr could have even come into contact with them. Perhaps they'd had a chance meeting, or maybe someone had introduced them, or, and it was a big 'or' considering the circumstances, perhaps Tommy Jr was innocent after all. One thing he did know, however, was a man who would know exactly where the brothers could be found. He looked back to the pub, and resting his elbow on the window frame, he went from tapping the wheel to chewing thoughtfully on his thumbnail.

'Are we getting out or not?' Beside him in the passenger seat, Cameron shifted his weight, the impatience in his voice more than evident. 'You said this is where we could find him, didn't you?' he asked when Jonny didn't answer. 'So what are we waiting for?'

Jonny remained quiet, and as he glanced across to his nephew then looked behind him at his other two nephews, Peter, and Reece, he inwardly groaned. Perhaps he should have taken Mitchell and Sonny up on their offer to accompany him. Even bringing Mad Dog Harris along for the ride would have been the better option, if for no other reason than the fact they wouldn't have flown off the handle should the man refuse to help them, which given his relationship with the Bannermans was a very possible outcome.

He gave a sigh, then pushing open the car door, he climbed out. As they approached the pub, Jonny paused and turned back to look at his nephews. 'Just let me do the talking,' he warned them. 'And whatever you do, don't start getting lairy because believe me, it's not going to end well.'

As his nephews narrowed their eyes Jonny sighed a second time. 'He has a reputation,' he quickly explained. 'Or at least he used to.' His thoughts wandered to the flower shop the man they'd come to see co-owned with his wife. It was hardly the type of occupation you'd expect for a man who had once served time inside for murder. And in Jonny's eyes the shop was nothing more than a front, it had to be, pretty much the same as their scrapyard in that respect. And despite the fact the man portrayed himself to be on the straight and narrow, in Jonny's opinion he was still a dangerous individual, one who wouldn't think twice when it came to shoving a blade into their guts, should they upset him in any way, shape, or form.

'Come on.' After giving his nephews one last look of warning, Jonny pushed open the door to the pub and walked inside.

As was typical of the boozers in Barking, The Jolly Fisherman was packed solid, the clientele the kind you would expect to find of a weekday lunchtime. Weaving his way through the pub, Jonny stopped by the bar, and digging his hand into his pocket, he pulled out his wallet, his gaze searching for the man they had come to see.

He ordered a round of drinks then taking a deep breath he motioned for his nephews to follow him. Exactly where he'd known he would find him, Harry Bannerman, or Fletch as he was more commonly known, stood beside the pool table, deep in conversation with the heavy-set man standing next to him. As Jonny approached, Fletch turned his head, probably more so out of habit than for any other reason. After all, his reputation preceded him and even now it was clear to see that he was on his guard and aware of his surroundings, however much he might have outwardly appeared to be at ease.

A smile broke out across Fletch's face, and shoving out his arm he grasped Jonny's hand in his, the handshake firm.

'Fletch.' Jonny returned the smile and turning to the man beside Fletch he gave a nod. 'Stevie.'

As he studied Jonny, the hint of a smile still remained across Fletch's face. 'Long time no see. And,' he said leaning slightly forward, 'a little birdie told me that there's been some developments in the Carter family.' His smile broadened. 'I never thought that I'd see the day Jimmy would retire or that you'd be the one to take over the reins. Bet that went down like a lead balloon with Sonny and Mitchell. I've got to admit,' he said flashing a knowing wink. 'I would have loved to have been a fly on the wall that day.'

'Yeah.' Jonny gave a light laugh although it would be fair to say that Sonny and Mitchell had been given no other alternative but to agree with their elder brother Jimmy's decisions. At the end of the day, none of them would have dared go up against him. Jimmy had been the head of the family; not only had his word been final, but it had also been one that they didn't argue with, and it had been that way ever since he'd taken over from Tommy Snr.

Narrowing his eyes the playfulness was gone from Fletch's expression, and as he glanced towards Cameron, Peter, and Reece his eyebrows knotted together. 'For you to come in here mob-handed I'm gonna take a wild guess and say this isn't a social visit.'

'No, it's a personal matter.' Jonny cleared his throat. 'I need an address mate,' he said. 'And pronto.'

'For?' Cocking his head to one side Fletch ran his tongue over his teeth, his shoulders becoming tense.

Jonny swallowed, and lifting his eyebrows he looked Fletch dead in the eyes. 'Your cousins.'

The laugh that came from Fletch was loud. 'Leave it out,' he said looking between Jonny and all three of his nephews. 'Is this some kind of joke?'

Jonny shook his head. 'Do I look like I'm laughing?'

On seeing the seriousness in their expressions, the laughter died from Fletch's throat, and shaking his head he leaned casually against the pool table and crossed his arms over his chest. 'You've come to the wrong man,' he said turning slightly away from them. 'Ask someone else.'

Anticipating this exact answer, Jonny sighed. After all it was no secret that despite sharing the same blood, both Fletch and his cousins were not on good terms. He'd even heard rumours that Fletch had once battered one of his cousins half to death. How true the whispers were though, he had no idea; he'd certainly never asked Fletch outright if there was any weight to the accusations. But as the old saying went, there was no smoke without fire and knowing Fletch from old, he'd put nothing past him.

'Look,' Jonny tried again. 'As I've already said, this is personal.' He jerked his thumb towards Cameron. 'My nephew, his son, is in a lot of shit and...'

Fletch screwed up his face cutting Jonny off. 'And as *I've* already said,' he growled. 'You've come to the wrong man.'

'You know them,' Jonny persisted standing his ground. 'Or at least you know where I can find them.'

'That's right,' Fletch answered through gritted teeth, his eyes flashing dangerously. 'I do know them, and I know exactly what they're capable of. So do yourself a favour, turn around, walk out of here, and forget we ever had this conversation.'

As Jonny opened his mouth to throw back a retort Stevie moved closer and held up his hands. 'Do as he says.' Forever acting the peacemaker, he threw his best mate a wary glance, knowing full well that Fletch, just like his cousins, had a short fuse and that it wouldn't take much for him to see red and start throwing punches. And considering the fact Fletch was still on licence and could be recalled back to prison should he end up in an altercation and the police were called, it was in his best interests that he stay away from trouble. 'The Bannermans are unhinged, and whatever problem you think you might have with them, it is better off being forgotten about.'

'And what about my son?' Cameron protested, moving forward so that he and Stevie were standing toe to toe. 'Do you honestly expect me to let this go? Because believe me when I say this: we won't be leaving here until we have an address for those bastards.'

Giving an agitated sigh and wishing not for the first time that he'd brought Sonny and Mitchell along with him instead, Jonny yanked on his nephew's arm, forcing Cameron to move several paces back. 'I warned you,' he hissed in his ear. 'To let me deal with this.'

His lips still curled into a snarl; Cameron's chest heaved. 'I'm not leaving here,' he reiterated. 'Not until we know where to find the Bannermans, those bastards set my boy up.'

'Yeah, well.' Taking a step back Jonny straightened out his shirt. 'If you want answers than you'd best keep that big trap of yours shut.' He threw Fletch a cautious glance over his shoulder before turning back to face Cameron. 'He knows them better than anyone,' he said lowering his voice. 'And if he's warning us to walk away that's got to tell you something.'

Cameron swallowed, and looking towards his two cousins he reluctantly nodded.

With the situation somewhat calmer, Jonny turned back to face Fletch. 'I'm asking you as a mate,' he beseeched him. 'You've known me – known my family,' he corrected, 'for a long time. We go back years. I even used to go fishing with Spence' when we were kids,' he said, referring to Fletch's younger brother. 'And I wouldn't be here now if there was anyone else I could ask.'

At the mention of his late brother, Fletch swallowed deeply, his heart sinking down to his stomach. Spencer's death had hit him hard, and all these years later he still couldn't help but blame himself for not being there when Spencer had needed him.

'You're a father,' Jonny continued. 'If this was one of your kids you can't tell me that you wouldn't do the same, that you wouldn't fight tooth and nail for them.'

Fletch's thoughts wandered to his son and two daughters. 'I'd kill for them,' he stated. 'No questions asked.'

Jonny nodded. 'Then help us out,' he pleaded. 'This is Tommy's grandson we're talking about here; he's only a kid and he's facing years banged up for something he may not have even been involved in.'

Thinking the situation over Fletch was quiet for a few moments then digging his hands into his pockets he sighed. 'I could give you an address,' he finally answered. 'But I very much doubt that you'll find them there. They don't stay in the same place for too long; how else do you think they've managed to stay one step ahead of the Old Bill?'

Jonny's shoulders slumped. Not that he could say he was overly surprised. Given the Bannermans' chosen occupation, they were hardly going to let all and sundry know where they could be found.

'That doesn't mean to say that I don't have a way of tracking them down,' Fletch added breaking Jonny's thoughts. 'After all.' He gave a low chuckle. 'It's like they say, keep your friends close and your enemies closer. And trust me, when it comes to those cunts, they're no friends of mine.' He gave a shrug. 'Let's just say that I like to keep tabs on them; it's one way of making sure that our paths aren't likely to cross now or at any point in the future.' He picked up his bottle of lager and pointed it in Jonny's direction. 'Give me a couple of days and I'll see what I can find out.'

Breaking into a smile Jonny clasped hold of Fletch's hand. 'Cheers, mate,' he winked. 'I owe you one.'

'Don't thank me,' Fletch answered, his voice becoming serious. 'Because take it from me, by the time they're finished with you, you're gonna wish you'd never gone looking for them.'

10

Eager to get inside the visiting room to see his dad and uncle, Tommy Jr could barely keep still. Shifting his weight from one foot to the other, he glanced over his shoulder to see Dylan standing several places behind him in the queue.

'My brother's coming in to see me,' Dylan grinned as he stretched himself up to his full height and peered over the heads of the other prisoners in an attempt to see into the waiting room. 'I've not seen him since being sent down.'

Tommy couldn't help but smile, Dylan's excitement was infectious and as he too looked towards the waiting room, he ran his hand over his short, cropped hair. It had only been a matter of days since he'd last seen his family, but it felt more like months.

A short while later he made his way over to where his dad and uncle Jonny were sitting and as both men got to their feet and pulled him in for a bear hug his smile widened.

'Are you okay?' Cameron asked, his eyes not leaving his son's face.

Tommy nodded. 'I'm doing alright.' He took a seat opposite

them, and leaning his elbows on his knees he sat slightly forward and laced his hands together, hoping more than anything that it would hide the slight tremor there. The last thing he wanted was for his dad and uncle to see just how nervous he was. Not that there was any reason for him to actually feel nervous; he was innocent, and he'd scream that fact from the rooftops if needs be. 'I didn't do anything,' he blurted out. 'I was set up.'

'I know, boy,' Cameron answered. 'You don't need to tell me that.'

Nodding again Tommy turned to look at his uncle, searching his face for confirmation that he too believed him.

After what seemed an age Jonny gave a brisk nod. 'Tell us what happened. From start to finish.'

Tommy took a deep breath and waiting for one of the prison officers to pass them by he lifted his eyebrows not knowing where to even begin. 'Kevin messaged me,' he eventually answered. 'Him and Aimee had had this big bust up and so he wanted to talk. We went to The Eastbrook, had a drink, and then I'd gone up to the bar to get us another round of drinks, but when I came back Kevin had disappeared.'

Jonny narrowed his eyes. 'What do you mean he'd disappeared?'

'Exactly what I said,' Tommy continued as he looked between the two men. 'He was nowhere to be seen, I searched everywhere for him.'

Sinking back into the seat Jonny ran his tongue over his teeth and glanced towards Cameron. 'Then what happened?'

'Well, I made my way outside, I thought maybe he might be in the car park having a smoke and then when I still couldn't find him, I went to get my phone from my car so that I could give him a call and find out where he was, and before I knew what was happening I was surrounded by the Old Bill and they had me in cuffs. I didn't know what to think,' he added, running his hand over his face. 'I thought that maybe we'd all been nicked, that the scrapyard had been under surveillance.'

'And the gear?' Jonny asked.

Vehemently shaking his head, Tommy's eyes were wide. 'I'd never seen it before. I swear on my life,' he went on, his voice ever so slightly rising. 'I didn't put it there.'

'Then how did it get there, eh?' Jonny asked not taking his eyes away from his great-nephew.

'He's already told you,' Cameron barked out. 'He doesn't know.'

Holding up his hand Jonny flashed Cameron a glare. 'I'm asking him not you,' he stated motioning towards Tommy.

Frustration getting the better of him, Tommy swallowed. 'I don't know,' he cried. 'I thought that maybe...' He glanced away.

'What?' Cameron coaxed.

'I don't know.' Tommy momentarily paused. 'I thought that maybe Kevin had left it there. I mean it's the only thing that makes any sense. No one else has been in my car other than Aimee and Reece and they wouldn't have left the gear there.'

The nerve at the side of Jonny's eye twitched. 'What about the Bannerman brothers?'

Confusion swept across Tommy's face and before he could answer Cameron interrupted a second time.

'He's already told you he thinks that Kevin was responsible for putting it there,' he growled.

Shooting his nephew another glare Jonny turned back to face Tommy. 'Answer the question. Have you been in contact with the Bannerman brothers?'

His forehead furrowing Tommy shook his head. 'No,' he said screwing up his face. 'I've never heard of them.'

As he studied his great-nephew Jonny gave a small nod.

Visibly relaxing Tommy slumped back in the chair. 'I've gone over and over it in my mind,' he said throwing up his arms. 'And there's no other way the coke could have got into my car unless Kevin put it there.'

As he waited for one of the prison officers to pass them by again, Jonny lifted his eyebrows. 'And how the fuck would Kevin have been able to afford half a kilo of coke?'

Tommy shook his head, his shoulders immediately slumping. 'I don't know,' he admitted uncertainty creeping back in. 'But I can't think of any other explanation. I mean maybe he could have got it on tick.'

'That's a lot of coke to get on tick,' Jonny sighed. 'And who in their right mind would willingly hand over that much gear?'

Falling silent Tommy chewed on his thumbnail. His uncle was right, no one would be stupid enough to hand over fifty grand's worth of coke, at least not without some kind of guarantee that the money would be repaid. And seeing as this was Kevin they were talking about, the chances of repayment were slim to say the least.

'Are you sure that you've never heard of the Bannerman brothers?' Jonny probed.

'No.' Shaking his head again Tommy looked from his dad to his uncle. 'Who are they?'

'It doesn't matter,' Jonny said chewing on the inside of his cheek.

'Obviously it does,' Tommy demanded. 'That's the third time you've asked me the same question.'

'They're dealers,' Cameron volunteered. 'Come from over South London way.'

Screwing up his face again Tommy shook his head. 'Like I said, I've never heard of them.'

'And what about Kevin?' Jonny asked. 'Could he know them?'

As he thought the question over Tommy chewed on his thumbnail again. 'I don't know… maybe,' he finally answered. 'I mean he reckons that he has a lot of mates, that he's well connected, and that back in the day he was a face.' He lifted his shoulders up into a shrug. 'But come to think of it I've only ever seen him speak to Andy.'

'Who's Andy?' Cameron enquired.

'His pal from the boozer,' Tommy answered, turning to face his father.

'And what do you know about this Andy?' Jonny asked.

'Not a lot,' Tommy shrugged. 'I've only met him a couple of times and even then, I didn't really speak to him. He's got this look about him, you know the look I mean, like he's sly, someone who can't be trusted, a weasel.'

'Yeah, I know the type.' For a few moments Jonny was thoughtful. 'Looks like we'll need to add this Andy to our list of people to see then, doesn't it?'

Cameron nodded and as a bell rang to indicate that visiting was coming to an end, panic clouded Tommy's expression.

'You do believe me, don't you?' he asked, the words tumbling out of his mouth so fast that he barely paused for breath. 'That I had nothing to do with any of this?'

'I believe you,' Cameron answered as he clasped his son's shoulder and gave it a gentle squeeze.

'And what about Mum?' His voice cracking, Tommy swallowed down the hard lump in his throat. 'Is she okay?'

'She will be.'

As the two men got to their feet Tommy followed suit. 'And what about Aimee? Have you seen her?'

'She's fine.'

'And Reece?'

'Everyone is okay,' Cameron reassured his son.

'You'd tell me if they weren't though, wouldn't you?'

Cameron gave a small smile. 'Just worry about yourself.' He cast a glance around the visiting room, his gaze taking in the other prisoners. 'No one has tried to push you around, have they?' he asked, concern sweeping across his face.

'Nah, nothing like that.' Tommy shook his head and as he nodded in Dylan's direction he gave a small smile. 'I've made a mate, been hanging out with him.'

Heaving a sigh of relief, Cameron gave a small smile, and as he pulled his son in for a final hug, he spoke low in his ear. 'Look after yourself and remember to keep your wits about you.'

'I will do,' Tommy answered. 'I don't have any other choice, do I?'

As his dad and uncle walked away from him, Tommy sunk back onto the chair. Despair flooded through his veins, and as he rubbed his hand over his hair again, he went over their conversation. Just who were the Bannerman brothers, and why had his uncle kept asking if he knew them? Glancing back across the visiting room, he locked eyes with Dylan. He may not have heard of the brothers, but he'd bet on his own life that someone in here knew who they were.

* * *

'Well?' Jonny asked as soon as he and Cameron had exited the prison. 'What do you reckon?'

'He was telling the truth,' Cameron was quick to answer as they walked towards where Jonny had parked his car. 'He'd have no reason to lie. It's like Stacey said, he's hardly an angel, he's been nicking cars since he was at school, and sooner rather than later he was bound to end up coming out on a job with us.'

'Yeah,' Jonny answered as he pressed the key fob to unlock

the car. 'I was thinking the same thing.' He rested his arms on the open door and surveyed Cameron across the car roof. 'And what about Kevin, do you think he could be involved?'

Anger flashed across Cameron's face. 'If he set my boy up, I'll kill him,' he stated.

Jonny gave a low laugh. 'Yeah, well that's a given.' He looked into the distance. 'Problem is though,' he said with a rise of his eyebrows. 'Why would Kevin set him up? I mean, what exactly would he have to gain from any of this? His daughter is having Tommy Jr's kid, so why would he want him taken out of the equation?'

As he opened his mouth to answer, Cameron quickly snapped his lips closed again. Jonny had just hit the nail on the head. For what reason would Kevin have wanted to set his son up? 'I don't know,' he finally admitted as he climbed into the car. 'But I'm going to find out, even if it kills me.'

'Yeah, well,' Jonny remarked as he started the ignition. 'Let's just hope it doesn't come to that, for both of our sakes.'

* * *

Tommy Jr's earlier euphoria at seeing his dad and uncle had all but evaporated, and as he trudged back to his cell with Dylan falling into step beside him, he'd never felt more depressed.

'Shit ain't it?'

Tommy nodded, not trusting himself to speak for fear that his voice would come out as a squeak.

'It does get easier though,' Dylan shrugged.

'Does it?' Tommy asked after clearing his throat, not for one single moment actually believing that saying goodbye to his family could get any easier.

'Yeah,' Dylan nodded. 'The first time my mum and sister

came in to see me I nearly burst into tears afterwards.' He gave a laugh and shook his head as though recalling the moment. 'Got to toughen up though eh, and seeing as I've got five years to get through, I can't end up a blubbering mess every time someone comes to see me, I'd end up going doo-fucking-lally.'

Tommy couldn't help but laugh and Dylan was right he supposed, he needed to get used to his family leaving him behind, however hard it might be. 'Hey,' he said keen to change the subject. 'Have you ever heard of the Bannerman brothers?'

Dylan snapped his head around. 'Yeah,' he answered screwing up his face. 'Of course I have, they're from my neck of the woods.' Leaning back slightly he studied Tommy's face. 'Why, you're not related to them are you?'

'Nah.' Tommy shook his head.

'Thank fuck for that.' His forehead furrowing Dylan continued to study Tommy, curiosity clearly evident across his face as he chewed on the inside of his cheek. 'Because the last thing I want, or need for that matter, is to be associated with those nutters.' He paused then looked Tommy up and down. 'So, do you work for them then?' he asked, lowering his voice. 'I've heard they have a lot of kids in their employment, kids who would happily do a stretch for them if they get caught selling their shit.'

Shaking his head again Tommy sighed. 'No, I'm not related to them, and I definitely don't work for them.'

Dylan whistled through his teeth, and taking a step to the side as if pretending to create a distance between them, he flashed a grin. 'Don't tell me,' he groaned, clutching a hand to his forehead, 'that you've done something to piss the no-good bastards off?'

'As if,' Tommy laughed. 'I'd never even heard of them until today.'

'Pity,' Dylan shrugged, the smile slipping from his face. 'I'd give anything to see those fuckers brought down.'

'I take it they're not mates of yours then,' Tommy chuckled.

'Not fucking likely,' Dylan answered, his lips curling into a snarl. 'I wouldn't piss on the bastards if they were on fire.'

'My uncle mentioned them,' Tommy continued. 'And I wondered who they are, that's all.'

'They're lunatics,' Dylan blurted out. 'Amongst other things,' he added, glancing over his shoulder to make sure no one else was within earshot of their conversation. 'My old man has had a couple of run-ins with them over the years; things got pretty nasty between them a while back and a turf war was on the cards.'

Tommy narrowed his eyes. It was the first time that Dylan had made any mention of his father, or even given a glimpse of his life before being banged up. He'd briefly mentioned his mum, sister, and his elder brother, but never his dad. 'Who's your old man?' he asked as they stopped in front of his cell. 'I might have heard of him.'

'No one.' Shaking his head dismissively Dylan tapped the side of his nose. 'At least no one you'd know anyway.'

His eyes still narrowed, Tommy watched as Dylan sauntered off in the direction of his own cell. 'I thought we were pals,' he called after him good naturedly. 'So what's with all the secrecy?'

Spinning around Dylan gave a cheeky wink. 'Trust me mate, when it comes to something like this my lips are firmly sealed,' he declared pretending to pull a zip across his lips. 'Besides,' he added as an afterthought as he glanced around him, his voice becoming a lot more serious. 'You never know who's listening and I'd rather not put myself on anyone's radar.'

Entering his cell Tommy made his way over to the bunk and collapsing onto the bed he lay back and placed one hand behind his head. Maybe Dylan was right not to divulge who his father was; after all, he wasn't about to tell anyone who his own family were. The last thing he wanted to do was create even more problems for himself, and considering his family's line of work, there was always a very real possibility that at least one of them had had a run-in with one of the inmates. And seeing as Tommy could very well be locked up for the next few weeks, months, or even longer, it was hardly the time or place to settle old debts.

11

Beads of cold sweat broke out across Andy McCann's top lip. Draining the remainder of his lager he placed the empty glass on the bar and swiped his fingers over his lips, all the while keeping his beady eyes glued to the entrance door. He'd seen hide nor hair of Kevin Fox, not since he'd handed over the coke, and the kid, Tommy Johnson, had been nicked and subsequently sent to prison. Ever since then, his sister's bloke, Connor Bannerman, had been on his case. Both he and his brothers wanted payment for the goods they'd provided or rather they wanted the credit cards and bank cards that Kevin had promised to intercept for them from the post office. And as much as Andy liked to pretend he was some kind of tough man, he had to admit, the mere thought of putting himself on the Bannermans' radar was enough to make him want to quake in his boots. He knew for a certainty that the fact Connor was shacked up with his sister wouldn't be enough to soften any blows they chose to dish out, and if he knew the brothers half as well as he thought he did then he had a nasty feeling they wouldn't hold back. They could very well use him as an example to others; after all, it had been his idea to plant the cocaine and weapon in the kid's car, it had been him who'd approached Connor Bannerman, him who'd all but told his sister's boyfriend that he and his brothers would be fools to turn down such a good opportunity. Credit card fraud was big business, everyone knew that, and the credit cards coupled with the bank cards Kevin could get his hands on, were guaranteed to earn them a fair few bob – admittedly not as much as the distribution of narcotics, but they would easily double their money on the cocaine they'd handed over.

One thing Andy hadn't envisioned, however, was for Kevin to ghost him. He'd thought that they were mates, drinking buddies, and like a fool, he'd trusted him. More than that, he'd thought they'd shared a common goal, one that was to see the Carters and Johnsons brought down a peg or two. But if that was the case then why the fuck had Kevin done a disappearing act?

After ordering a second drink, Andy slipped the change into his pocket and greedily gulped down the alcohol. Nerves were beginning to get the better of him, and as he chewed on the inside of his cheek, the sensation of cold dread inched its way up his spine. Unless he was very much mistaken, and Kevin didn't put in an appearance and pronto, then he was a dead man walking. A cold shiver engulfed him, and as his mind wandered to the methods of torture the Bannerman brothers wouldn't be averse to using on him, he fought the urge to vomit. It was no secret that the brothers were widely known as men you didn't cross, and that only an idiot would dare go against them.

Pulling out his mobile phone, Andy pressed redial and brought the device up to his ear. Just as it had all the other times he'd attempted to phone Kevin, the call rang off. Anger thundered through his veins, and resisting the urge to smash the phone against the bar, he slipped the device back into his pocket. He was going to muller Kevin when he eventually got his hands on him and relish every second of seeing his so-called pal brought down. As he contemplated the predicament, and more importantly, how he was going to talk his way out of the imminent danger he found himself to be in, the door swung open and Kevin breezed across the threshold as though he didn't have a single care in the world.

As usual there was a cockiness to Kevin's swagger, an arrogance that at that precise moment in time grated on Andy's nerves. If he hadn't been so relieved to see his friend he would have bounded across the pub and planted his fist on the side of Kevin's jaw.

'Where the fuck have you been?' he hissed when Kevin finally made his way over to him. 'I've been going off my fucking head.'

Kevin brought his shoulders up into a nonchalant shrug, his lips curling into a snarl. 'Where do you think I've been?' he hissed back. 'I've been consoling my daughter.'

Andy narrowed his eyes. Despite the charade he may have put on, he knew for a fact that Kevin didn't give two shits about his daughter, at least not in the way most fathers would. He gave a nod of his head, his anger slowly dissipating. 'Is she okay?'

'What do you think?' Kevin barked out. 'She's in fucking pieces.' He clicked his fingers towards the barmaid then dug his hand into his pocket and pulled out his wallet. Once his drink had been ordered he leaned casually against the bar, and as a smug grin made its way across his face, he gave a wink. 'Good thing she's got her old dad to help her out, eh?'

Andy couldn't help the laugh that escaped his lips and giving a shake of his head he mirrored Kevin's stance. 'I take it she fell for it then?'

'Hook, line, and fucking sinker. Naturally, she now thinks I'm the best thing since sliced bread, and all the while that little prick Tommy Johnson is out of her life the better it will be for all concerned.'

'Talking of Johnson.' Taking a step closer Andy lowered his voice. 'My sister's bloke has been on my case; he wants the bank cards.'

Kevin's expression hardened and squaring his shoulders he picked up his glass and drained his drink in one large gulp. Slamming the empty glass back down on the bar he dragged the back of his hand across his lips. 'He'll get his bank cards,' he growled, 'when I'm good and fucking ready.'

Panic swept across Andy's face and his eyes were filled with despair. 'That wasn't the deal,' he shrieked.

'It is now,' Kevin retorted with a nonchalant shrug. Digging his hand into his pocket again he pulled out a ten-pound note and waved it in the air in a bid to attract the barmaid's attention again. 'Don't you think I've got enough on my plate?' he added. 'What with my Aimee and everything that's gone on. Like I've already stated, she's been in bits and it's me,' he said jerking his thumb towards his chest, 'who's been left to pick up the pieces.'

Andy's mouth fell open and as he stared at his friend the panic that curled around his insides was quickly replaced with anger. 'You do realise this is the Bannermans you're dealing with?' he hissed through clenched teeth. 'That they're not known for their patience.'

Kevin shrugged a second time and as he tapped the side of his nose he smirked. 'And I think you're forgetting,' he hissed back, 'that without me there won't be any bank cards.'

Shaking his head, Andy held up his hands and was in half a mind to flee from the pub in an attempt to create a safe distance between them, not that fleeing would do him much good in the grand scheme of things. When it came down to it, his front door would be the first that the Bannermans would come knocking on. 'They're gonna come for you mate,' he said matter-of-factly, as he began backing away. 'And when they finally catch up with you take it from me, you're gonna wish you'd never been born.'

A hearty laugh escaped from Kevin's lips. 'Yeah?' he chuckled his voice full of bravado. 'Well fuck 'em, because from where I'm standing,' he called after Andy's retreating back, 'I think you'll find that they need me a lot more than I'll ever need them.'

* * *

By his own admission, Nathan Bannerman was a nasty piece of work and as he leaned against a table littered with drug paraphernalia he slipped a cigarette between his lips, his movements both slow and unhurried as he lit up and inhaled a lungful of smoke. Standing at well over six feet tall, with wide shoulders and a muscular build he directed his hard stare upon the youngest of his brothers, Connor.

Right from the start he'd been opposed to the deal that Connor had put forward. Half a kilo of coke may have been the equivalent of peanuts to them, but at the end of the day fifty grand was fifty grand and being the greedy bastard he was, that money was better off being in his pocket rather than in the pocket of some random geezer they barely even knew. Even the lure of an endless supply of both credit and bank cards hadn't been enough to initially sway his mind. Narcotics was their game and supplying everything from pills to crack cocaine to heroin was how they made their money. What the fuck did they know about credit card fraud, and more to the point, where would they find the time to branch out? As it was, they spent a large chunk of their lives doing everything in their power to stay one step ahead of the Old Bill and as a result were forced to uproot and move premises on a regular basis.

Taking a final drag on his cigarette he exhaled a cloud of smoke above his head, then flicking the cigarette butt onto the concrete floor he ground it out underneath his heavy boot. 'What's the lowdown on the credit cards?' he asked, cocking an eyebrow as he looked across to his youngest brother.

Connor Bannerman's cheeks reddened, and, resembling a deer caught in the headlights of a car, he looked between his two brothers. 'I'm working on it,' he answered, giving a nonchalant shrug.

Kissing his teeth, Nathan scowled, irritation rushing to the fore. 'What do you mean you're working on it?' he barked out, all the while ignoring the knowing look his middle brother Lee shot towards him.

'Exactly what I said,' Connor shrugged again. 'I'm working on it.'

'In other words,' Lee piped up as he lounged back on a chair, his legs casually crossed over at the ankles as a smirk played out across his lips. 'We've been done over like fucking kippers. I told you this would happen, that that tosser, Andy,' he sneered, 'couldn't be trusted.'

Connor shot Lee a scathing look, and before he could open his mouth to fling back a retort Nathan was upon him, his hands curled into tight fists as he grasped his brother by the front of his shirt and yanked him roughly around to face him.

'We had a deal,' Nathan hissed. 'A deal that I wanted no part of. Now I'm going to ask you one last time and you'd best think long and hard before you answer me because I'm this close,' he said placing his thumb and forefinger an inch apart to emphasise his point, 'to losing my rag. Where the fuck are the credit cards?'

A nervous grin swept over Connor's face. 'I already told you,' he answered, averting his gaze. 'I'm working on it.'

Nathan narrowed his eyes, and releasing Connor, he

continued to study him for a few moments, his hard stare boring into his youngest brother's skull. 'Then work on it faster.'

Connor nodded, and as he swallowed, his smile slowly ebbed away. 'I will do. Relax bruv and chill out. As I keep on telling you, everything is under control.'

'It had better be. Oh, and one more thing,' Nathan added as he walked across the lock-up and resumed his position against the table. 'This place is a fucking shithole,' he said, gesturing to the work surfaces complete with several weighing scales that were coated in white residue. 'If the filth were to turn up, they'd have a fucking field day. Get it cleaned up, now.'

The snort of laughter that came from Lee's direction was enough to make Connor swing his head towards him, and screwing up his face his fingers automatically inched up to his face, his thumb slowly rubbing across the length of the pale pink scar on his forehead, an enduring reminder of his last interaction with their cousin, Fletch. 'I'm not your fucking lackey,' he snarled. 'Get someone else to do it.'

Amusement was clearly visible across Nathan's face, a rare occurrence considering he barely smiled. 'I'm telling you,' he ordered, his voice brooking no arguments. 'Now get it done. Oh, and Connor,' he said becoming serious. 'Just a little heads-up, if I don't have those credit cards in my hand within the next twenty-four hours then me and you are going to have a problem, a big problem, is that understood?'

Connor didn't bother to answer and as his gaze darted around around him, his expression was a mixture of both contempt and humiliation. The fact Nathan had spoken to him as though he were nothing, a no one, in front of their entire workforce, rankled. He was as much a Bannerman as Nathan and Lee were, and as such, deserved respect. 'Get this place cleaned up,' he ordered kicking out at the nearest chair, his fists more than ready to lash out at the occupant if he so much as dared to argue or answer him back.

As the man, and several of their minions, jumped up from their seats and began the process of clearing the tables, Nathan and Lee shared a glance. Despite Connor's reassurance that everything was under control Nathan had a nasty feeling that it was anything but and an even nastier feeling that maybe Lee was right, and they had been done over like kippers. Anger consumed him; no one, and he meant no one, took them for fools and got away with it. They came from a long line of men who had reputations, men who had ruled over South London with an iron fist, and like fuck were they about to roll over and do nothing while those around them took the piss and robbed them blind. And there was no greater piss-take than someone robbing them of fifty grand.

A rare smile tugged at the corners of his lips. As it was, it took a great deal of effort on his part to keep Lee under control. Unknown for his patience, his middle brother was the human equivalent of a ticking time bomb, and it was no secret that Lee had a screw loose, that he was unhinged and took great delight in causing others significant harm. 'He's got twenty-four hours,' he said jerking his head in the direction of the door that moments earlier Connor had slipped out of. 'And if those credit cards don't materialise then I think it's about time you paid that brother-in-law of his, a friendly visit, or not so friendly as the case might be.'

Still lounging back on the chair, Lee's eyes lit up, the prospect of dishing out violence making him almost giddy with excitement. 'Now you're talking,' he grinned cracking his knuckles. 'I'm looking forward to getting stuck in.'

'Yeah, I thought you might be,' Nathan answered with a roll of his eyes. 'I wouldn't expect anything less from you.'

* * *

Aimee was on a mission and after stepping off the bus in Dagenham she looked up at the public house before her. Taking a deep breath, she pulled back her shoulders and forced herself to move forward. Her dad had spouted so much shit in her ears over the past few days that she didn't know whether she was coming or going. Anyone would think that Tommy Jr was the devil incarnate the way he was carrying on. Her mum hadn't been much of a help either, despite her recent turn around; in the past she'd always had it in for Tommy and had been more than vocal about him when it came to slagging him off, stating that she didn't trust him or think he was good enough for her only daughter. She'd even gone as far as to say that he would end up letting her down, and inevitably shatter her heart into a million pieces. Well maybe her mum had been right about that, her heart had been broken, so much so that she'd cried herself to sleep ever since Tommy had been arrested and sent to prison.

Pushing open the door to the pub she stepped inside. As irrational as she knew she was being, nerves were beginning to get the better of her, and as she took a faltering step forward, she was in half a mind to turn on her heels and run back out the door as though her life depended on it. Maybe she shouldn't have come, or maybe she should have gone to the scrapyard instead. She gave an involuntary shudder. No, the pub was definitely the better option. She wanted to catch Reece on his own, or rather she wanted to see him without the rest of his family being present. Being around Tommy's family still made her feel nervous. She'd only met them a couple of times and their last meeting at the court hearing hadn't exactly been a happy one. If anything, it had been harrowing; her stomach had been tied up in knots the entire day, and the lump in her throat so large that she'd barely been able to swallow let alone speak.

Her gaze scanned the pub, and spotting Reece across the far side she made her way over to him, her strides purposeful and appearing a lot more confident than she actually felt.

'Reece.'

Spinning around, for the briefest of moments confusion was etched across Reece's face although he did his best to hide it from her, Aimee noted. 'Aimee,' he exclaimed, his gaze shifting nervously around him. 'What are you doing here?'

Aimee swallowed deeply. He looked so much like her Tommy that she felt the urge to cry all over again. Lifting her hand to her forehead she rubbed at her temples, a part of her wishing she hadn't come, that she hadn't wanted to know the truth. 'I wanted to talk,' she finally answered her voice faltering. 'To ask you something.'

After giving the request a moment's thought Reece nodded and guiding Aimee towards a table he pulled out a chair and sat down. 'Would you like a drink?'

Shaking her head Aimee gave a small smile, her hand resting on the slight curve of her abdomen. 'I can't. I'm pregnant, remember.'

'Yeah.' Reece gave a light chuckle. 'What with everything that's gone on...' He momentarily paused before carrying on. 'I kind of forgot.' He looked over his shoulder in the direction of the bar. 'How about a soft drink then?'

Shaking her head again, Aimee sat forward and rested her elbows on the table, keen to get down to business. 'Have you heard from him at all, Tommy I mean?'

'Nah, not yet.' Sucking in his bottom lip, Reece shook his head and sighed. 'His dad and our uncle Jonny went to see him this morning though.'

Her expression one of hurt, Aimee nodded. She'd thought that Tommy would want to see her too and the fact he didn't stung. 'Is... is he okay?'

Reece shrugged. 'I think so.' He looked down at his watch. 'Or at least I haven't heard otherwise. The visit should be over by now though,' he said, taking another peek at his watch.

An awkward silence followed and after a few moments Reece cleared his throat. 'Was there something else...?' His voice trailed off and shifting his weight as though to make himself more comfortable he lifted his eyebrows. 'You said you wanted to talk.'

Aimee nodded and lacing her hands together she rested her chin on her clasped fingers, her eyes filled with anguish. 'Tell me the truth,' she croaked out. 'You know Tommy, maybe even better than I do.' She gave a small smile, her eyes searching Reece's face. 'Did he do it? Was it him who put the drugs and knife in the car?'

Narrowing his eyes Reece slumped back in the chair. 'What the fuck!' he exclaimed. 'Do you honestly think that Tommy would be that stupid?'

A lone tear slipped down Aimee's cheek. 'I don't know what to think,' she admitted. 'My head is all over the place.'

His lips curling into a snarl, Reece made to get up. 'If anyone should believe him then it should be you,' he spat out. 'Cheers for that, Aimee,' he added with a shake of his head. 'I'll let him know what you really think of him shall I? That his bird thinks he's nothing more than some scumbag dealer.'

'No! Please don't tell him that.' Fresh tears blinded Aimee's vision, and as she tugged on Reece's hand in an attempt to stop him from walking away from her, she silently pleaded with him to sit back down. 'I love him, Reece.' Her shoulders began to heave and holding her head in her hands she sobbed. 'I just want him to come home.'

'He will do.' His cheeks turning red, Reece's startled gaze darted around him hoping more than anything that no one else was able to see their interaction. 'Come on, Aimee,' he pleaded clutching hold of her hand. 'Don't cry. My family are doing everything they can to get him out.'

'But what if...' Her voicing cracking Aimee swiped the tears from her cheeks. 'My dad...'

Reece's expression hardened, his back straightening as he snatched his hand back. 'What about your dad?' he spat.

Oblivious to the change in Reece, Aimee gave a shudder. 'My dad seems to think that Tommy is guilty.' She exhaled a breath. 'And that he could be sent away for years.' She placed her hand on her tummy again, her gaze drifting downwards. 'I'm having Tommy's baby,' she said looking back up. 'I can't do it all by myself. I need him.'

Slumping back in his seat again Reece dragged his hand through his hair. 'He's gonna come home,' he reiterated. 'He has to, he's innocent...'

'But my dad...'

'Fuck your dad,' Reece snarled. 'He knows fuck all. In fact,' he growled, 'it wouldn't surprise me if it was him who left the gear in Tommy's car.'

Confusion swept across Aimee's face, and sitting up a little straighter, her forehead was furrowed. 'What do you mean by that?' she demanded.

Snapping his lips closed, Reece looked away.

Aimee's heart began to beat faster, her mind whirling. 'What do you mean, Reece?' she repeated. 'What does my dad have to do with any of this?'

'He was with Tommy Jr,' Reece blurted out. 'Just before he was nicked, they'd been in the boozer together.'

'No.' Shaking her head, Aimee clambered to her feet. 'You're lying.'

'Why would I lie?' Spreading open his arms, Reece looked up at Aimee, his expression one of defeat. 'Why would I need to lie to you? Your old man was with Tommy Jr.' He sat forward, his words low and deliberate as he spoke. 'He was in his car.'

As her mind continued to whirl, Aimee's mouth fell open. Her dad had neglected to tell her that he and Tommy had been together before his arrest. Her hands shaking, she slumped back onto the chair and began to recall her dad's words, how he'd told her time and time again that both Tommy and his family were scum, that she was better off without him, that her baby would be better off without Tommy in the picture. Had it all been a lie? Had her dad played on her vulnerability and actively set out to poison her mind against Tommy? 'I feel sick,' she groaned pressing her hand to her lips before jumping back out of her seat and bolting in the direction of the ladies' toilets. The fact her dad, the one man she was supposed to be able to trust above anyone else had lied to her face, and not just once but over and over again, was enough to break her heart in two. All along she'd known that he was no good, that he had no morals, and as much as she hadn't wanted to believe that he could be so vindictive, so spiteful, she knew in her heart that it was true.

Dropping to her knees, she gripped hold of the toilet bowl with clammy fingers and emptied the contents of her stomach. Retching so hard that she could barely breathe, tears slipped down Aimee's cheeks. Her dad had betrayed her, he'd betrayed Tommy too, and as much as he may not have been an angel, he didn't deserve to be imprisoned, especially when he'd done nothing wrong.

From behind her the door leading to the toilet opened and moments later, she heard a gentle voice call out her name.

'Aimee, are you okay, sweetheart? Reece said that you weren't feeling very well.'

Recognising the voice, fresh tears sprang to Aimee's eyes, and as the landlady, Rina came into view she leaned her head against the wall of the cubicle, wrapped her arms around herself and began to sob. 'My dad lied to me,' she cried.

'Oh, darling.' Crouching down Rina gently swiped the damp hair away from Aimee's forehead then pulled her into her arms.

'My dad lied,' Aimee whispered.

'I know, sweetheart,' Rina soothed as Aimee held on for dear life. 'I know.'

* * *

Aimee wasn't the only one who felt sick to their stomach. Walking from the pub to his home a short distance away, Andy's eyes were like golf balls. Jerking his head from side to side, his nerves were in tatters as he surveyed the area before him, his steely gaze on the lookout for any signs of Connor Bannerman being in the near vicinity. Nausea washed over him, and clutching a hand across his abdomen, he resisted the urge to vomit, half expecting Connor to appear out of nowhere and batter him to death. Fear radiated off him and by the time Andy had made it to the entrance door of his block of flats he was beginning to think that his heart would give out and that he would keel over and die, which in the circumstances may have actually been a blessing in disguise when he considered the alternative.

Sooner or later Connor Bannerman was going to come looking for him, that much was a given and seeing as Kevin had all but refused to keep up his end of the bargain, the consequences were bound to be severe and would fall upon Andy's shoulders. Not that he wouldn't happily give up Kevin's name, because he would. At the first chance he had, he'd open his mouth and sing louder than a canary if needs be, he'd even give up his own mother if it meant taking the heat off himself.

Taking the stairs two at a time, he raced towards his flat, eager to get inside and firmly lock the front door behind him. Maybe he should just come clean, get on the blower to Connor and let him know the score, profess his innocence, and plead for forgiveness, maybe even send him Kevin's way. With a bit of luck perhaps Connor would feel pity for him; he very much doubted this would be the case, but he could at least hope.

His hands trembling, on the third attempt he managed to slip his key into the lock and unlock the door. Hastily closing it behind him, he leaned back and rested his head against the cool wood, his heart beating ten to the dozen. Wishing not for the first time that he'd never become involved in Kevin's scheme to bring down the Carters and Johnsons, he pushed himself away from the door and rubbed his hand over his face, the stubble littering his jawline rough to his touch.

Paranoia had well and truly set in and making his way through to the lounge he made a beeline for the window. Once there, he yanked the yellowing, tobacco-stained net curtain aside, not caring one iota as the thin material ripped in his haste to scan the area below. With no sign of Connor Bannerman, neither in the car park or the street on either side of the flats, he let out a collective breath. He needed to get a grip and fast and digging his hand into his pocket, he pulled out a battered pack of cigarettes. Lighting up, he took a deep drag, the smoke barely having the time to drift down from his nostrils before taking a second and third drag in quick succession.

'They're gonna kill you one day. They're not called cancer sticks for nothing.'

The hairs on the back of Andy's neck rose and as the blood drained from his face a cold shiver ran down the length of his spine. Frozen to the spot he ever so slightly turned his head towards the living room door, his lips still open in preparation to take another puff on the cigarette.

'That's if I don't kill you first, of course,' Connor Bannerman grinned maniacally.

12

A silent scream lodged in the back of Andy's throat, his bowels threatening to give way at any given moment. 'How...' He swallowed deeply, the prickle of fear that edged down his spine increasing in intensity. 'How did you get in here?'

Connor chuckled, the harsh sound reverberating around the sparse room. 'How do you fucking think?' He held up a key, the very same key that Andy had given to his sister for safekeeping.

'What do you want?' Andy stammered dropping the smouldering cigarette to the floor and stamping on it before it had the chance to burn down to his fingertips.

Not bothering to answer, Connor screwed up his face and took a moment to survey the lounge, his obvious disgust becoming all the more visible as he took in the squalor. 'You're no better than an animal,' he barked out, stepping further into the room, one hand clenched into a tight fist. 'You live in a fucking shithole.'

Andy glanced around him, his terrified gaze taking in the filth as though seeing it for the first time through a stranger's eyes. Littered on the floor were several empty pizza boxes, greasy takeaway containers, empty beer cans, and several overflowing ashtrays, the cigarette butts flowing onto the floor. He'd been meaning to tidy up, really he had, only there was always somewhere he had to be or something more important to do. 'I...' He swallowed again unable to get the words out.

'You what?' Connor sneered.

'I...' Desperate for an escape route, Andy slid his back along the wall. If he could make it to the front door then just maybe he'd stand a chance of escaping Connor's clutches.

As if anticipating Andy's movements, Connor took a step backwards blocking the only exit.

Andy's gaze snapped towards the window. Being four floors up, he could hardly leap out of the window to his safety.

A smirk tugged at the corner of Connor's lips. 'Do it,' he goaded, his eyes flicking towards the window. 'Jump, I fucking dare you.'

'I...' Looking from the window and then back to Connor again, Andy shook his head. 'C'mon,' he all but screamed. 'It'd be suicide.'

Connor grinned, the same maniacal grin that was enough to send a shard of terror ricocheting through Andy's body. 'Yeah, it would be,' he answered, cocking his head to one side, his eyes hard. 'Not that that would be a bad thing, mind. I mean, who would actually miss you?' He moved forward bridging the gap between them. 'Especially when you're nothing but a snidey cunt. You owe me fifty grand,' he growled. 'Did you honestly think that I'd let that go, that I wouldn't come looking for you?'

Andy shook his head, gulping down the bile that threatened to spew from his mouth.

'That I was going to stand by and let you mug me off?' Connor continued to roar moving even closer.

'No!' Andy shrieked back. Placing his hands protectively over his head, he cowered away from Connor, the fear he felt so tangible that he could almost taste it. 'I didn't try to mug you off,' he pleaded. 'I wouldn't do that. It's all Kevin's fault,' he cried, the words spilling out of his mouth in a rush in his attempt to save his own skin. 'If you want to blame someone then blame him – it was all his idea, I wanted no part of it, I swear to you.' It was a lie of course, one that he had a nasty feeling Connor was able to see straight through.

Connor's arm shot out and grasping a handful of Andy's hair in his fist he proceeded to drag him through the flat, out the front door, and down several flights of stairs all the while ignoring Andy's screams for help and his desperate attempts to free himself. Moments later he bundled Andy none too gently into the boot of the car then made his way around to the driver's side. After a quick scan of the area to make sure there hadn't been any witnesses or busybodies wanting to poke their noses into his business, he unlocked the door and slipped behind the wheel. Starting the ignition, he turned on the car stereo in a bid to drown out Andy's cries, safe in the knowledge that if anyone had actually seen their interaction that they wouldn't be calling the police. Luckily for him, violence was a common occurrence on the Dagenham council estate where Andy lived, and it wasn't unheard of for a punch-up or a slanging match to take place. It was part and parcel of everyday life, so much so that residents would more often than not have the sense to turn a blind eye for fear of any repercussions, knowing that the last thing they would want was to be embroiled into the drama, there were exceptions of course, but thankfully they were few and far between.

Moments later he pulled out of the car park. Twenty-four hours Nathan had given him to sort out the fiasco concerning the credit cards and bank cards, well he could do one better than that – he'd personally bring the bastard responsible for his humiliation and promptly drop him at his eldest brother's feet and let him deal with the problem as he saw fit. Seeing as this was Nathan, he had a feeling his brother was about to go to town on Andy, not that Connor felt any form of pity for him because he didn't, why should he when the low-life bastard had tried to treat him like an idiot? In fact, he wouldn't be surprised if Andy disappeared just like all the others who had dared to cross both his and his brothers' path.

* * *

The sound of the front door slamming shut was enough to make Melanie frown, and tossing a damp cloth onto the kitchen worktop, she made her way into the lounge her forehead furrowing as she took note of her daughter's pale, drawn face. 'Are you feeling queasy again?' she asked, giving Aimee a sympathetic smile. 'I know it's tough going but it won't last the whole pregnancy. Just a few more weeks and then it should start easing off. I was the same when I was expecting you, I felt dog-rough for the first few months, couldn't keep a single thing down no matter how much I tried...'

'Where is my dad?' Aimee gritted out as she brushed past her mother and peered into the kitchen.

Taken aback by her daughter's harsh tone Melanie raised her eyebrows. 'He's not here,' she sighed. 'But I do want to have a little chat, just you and me before he gets back, I've got something to tell you.' She gave a small, timid smile and motioned to the sofa, beckoning for Aimee to take a seat. 'It's about your dad and...' As her voice trailed off, she smoothed down her short hair and sat down. 'We've been talking and, well, seeing as he is here every day anyway, and that we've been getting on so much better lately I thought that, well – we thought,' she corrected, reaching out for her daughter's hand and tugging her down beside her. 'He really is trying to make amends, darling, to be a better dad to you, and to be a good husband to me.'

Her back becoming ramrod straight, Aimee screwed up her face. 'He's not your husband,' she barked out. 'You're divorced.'

'I know,' Melanie sighed again. 'But that's the thing I'm trying to get at, I know that we've had our problems, our ups and downs, but he's changed, darling, he's a different man now, he's more...' She looked into the distance, a soft expression spreading across her face. 'More responsible, I suppose. He's seen the error of his ways and all he wants is his family back, for all of us to live under the same roof again.'

The disgust written across Aimee's face was more than visible. 'And you actually fell for that?' she asked, incredulous. 'He hasn't changed at all, he's still the same selfish bastard that he's always been.'

Melanie's face fell and as she picked at an imaginary thread on her shirt she looked up and gave Aimee a scathing look. 'No matter what he's done in the past he's still your dad.'

The hairs on the back of Aimee's neck prickled. 'What have you done, Mum?' she croaked out.

Melanie swallowed, then took a deep breath before flashing another nervous grin. 'I said that he could move back in,' she said holding up her hand as if to ward off her daughter's protests. 'Only temporarily at first, just to see how things go between us and if everything works out well then we can make it more permanent.'

'You've done what?' Aimee shouted ripping her hand free and jumping to her feet. Tears stung her eyes, blinding her vison, and swiping them away, she placed one hand on her chest in an attempt to steady her racing heart. 'How could you?' she cried. 'How could you let that bastard move back in here?'

'Look,' Melanie sighed as she rubbed her hand over her forehead. 'I know in the past that he barely, if ever, put us first, but he's changed,' she protested. 'I can feel it in my gut,' pointing to her stomach she searched her daughter's face. 'He's trying, really trying, to prove that he's a better person and look how much he cares for you. Over the past few days, he's been there for you, Aimee, for the first time in his life he's trying to be a proper dad to you. He's wiped away your tears, hugged you, made sure that you were okay, made you his priority.'

'He lied to us,' Aimee interrupted stabbing her finger towards the front door. 'He's been lying to us from day one. Tommy's cousin has told me everything, how my dad,' she snarled screwing up her face, 'was with Tommy right before he was arrested, that they'd been to the pub together, that my dad had been in Tommy's car. For all we know the coke could have belonged to him, you know what he's like, he's always buzzing off his nut, either that or pissed.'

Melanie's mouth dropped open. 'But...'

'Can't you see what he's done, Mum?' Through her tears, Aimee gave a half laugh and threw her arms up into the air. 'He played us, pretended to care about us when he doesn't and you fell for it, *I* was even starting to fall for it,' she added, poking a finger into her chest. 'He knew exactly what he was doing, he wanted Tommy away from me and he succeeded, he then tried to poison my mind against him!' she cried. 'He did exactly what he threatened to do and took my Tommy away from me and our baby. He's sick in the head,' she continued, her shoulders heaving as she struggled to contain her emotion. 'He's twisted... What kind of father would do something like that?'

Snatching up her cigarettes, Melanie's hand shook, her mind reeling. 'That doesn't mean anything,' she said dismissively. 'So what if your dad was with Tommy – it doesn't mean he was responsible for him being arrested. You're overreacting as per usual, putting two and two together and coming up with five. Your dad might be a lot of things, but he isn't a monster.' Lighting the cigarette, she took a deep pull, welcoming the burn as the smoke hit her lungs. 'Neither is he that fucking clever, he can just about function on a day-to-day basis let alone mastermind Tommy's arrest.'

Slumping onto the sofa Aimee held her head in her hands. 'Then why didn't he say anything, Mum, why didn't he mention that him and Tommy had been together? He had ample opportunity to say something, but he didn't, did he? He said, zilch, fuck all, nothing.'

'And why do you think that is?' Even as she answered, Melanie knew that she was making excuses for her ex-husband, that deep down in her heart she wanted to believe he had changed. 'Because of this,' she snapped. 'He didn't want you to think badly of him; you're his little girl and he loves you more than anything in this world.'

Aimee narrowed her eyes. 'Do you really believe that?' she asked with a shake of her head. 'Truly, Mum, hand on heart, do you honestly think that my dad cares one iota about me, or even us?' she said, wagging her finger between them. 'You know as well as I do that he's never been there for me or you; he refused to even put his hand in his pocket and buy me shoes when I was a kid, and what about all the other women eh, how many times did you catch him shagging some tart from down the pub?'

Melanie opened her mouth to answer before quickly snapping it closed again. No matter how many excuses slipped out of her mouth Aimee made a valid point. Kevin had never been there for them and had all but ignored the fact he had a wife and child at home while he'd chased after anything with a pulse. Countless times she'd caught him cheating on her, to the point that he'd become brazen about it, not even bothering to hide the evidence that he'd taken another woman to bed. And when it came to Tommy, why had Kevin not mentioned that the two of them had been together before Tommy's arrest? And how was it that he'd known about the coke found in Tommy's car, or to be precise, the quantity of cocaine that had been found? Stubbing out the cigarette Melanie wearily got to her feet. She had the beginning of a blinding headache and running her hand over her face, her shoulders were slumped. She was a fool to have trusted Kevin again, to have believed his lies, especially when she'd told herself time and time again that he was no good and that she was better off without him. 'I think I'm going to have a lie down for a bit,' she said averting her gaze. 'Clear my head.'

'And what about my dad?' Aimee glanced towards the living room window; her eyebrows pinched together as she chewed on her bottom lip. 'What should I do if he turns up?'

Thinking the question over Melanie resisted the urge to shrug, what was she supposed to even say? She was already feeling foolish enough for believing that she and Kevin could have a second chance, or third or fourth as the case happened to be. 'Tell him that I want a word,' she said, jerking her head towards the staircase.

As she studied her mother's face, Aimee nodded. 'I'm sorry, Mum,' she said.

Nodding her head in return, Melanie sighed. 'Not as much as me, darling,' she answered. 'I'm a fool when it comes to that man, always have been. He knows exactly how to pull the wool over my eyes and has done since the very first day that I met him. Like they say, a leopard will never change its spots, only I stupidly thought that your dad could change, that he could be the man I wanted him to be.' She rubbed at her eyes, smearing her mascara. 'I'm a bloody idiot,' she cried. 'A stupid bloody idiot who should have known better.'

'No, you're not.' Grabbing hold of her mother's hand, Aimee offered a small smile as fresh tears filled her eyes. 'If anyone is an idiot then it's Dad.'

* * *

At the scrapyard office, Jonny Carter was quiet, and, as he drummed his fingers on the desk, he was deep in thought, relishing a few moments of peace before the rest of the family descended upon him wanting to know what had been said on the visit with Tommy Jr.

Sitting opposite him, Cameron was equally quiet, his expression glum, as though he had the weight of the world resting upon his shoulders, which was understandable, Jonny conceded, seeing as Tommy Jr was his only child and looking at serving a hefty lump if found guilty.

Moments later the door crashed open, and Reece bounded across the threshold. Looking between his uncle and cousin he lifted his eyebrows. 'Well,' he asked, 'how is he?'

'He's okay,' Cameron sighed. 'A lot better than I was expecting.'

'So...?' Perching on the arm of the sofa Reece's gaze flicked between the two men. 'What did he say? Did he tell you what happened?'

Holding up his hand, Jonny shook his head. 'I'm not going to keep repeating myself,' he said motioning to the cars pulling onto the forecourt. 'When the rest of the family get here, we'll explain everything.'

Reece's forehead furrowed. 'But he is innocent, right?' he asked with a measure of trepidation. 'He told you that he'd been with Kevin, that it was him who stashed the gear in the car.'

'What did I just say?' Jonny growled. 'I'm not going to keep repeating myself.'

'Alright,' Reece grumbled huffing out a breath. 'No need to bite my head off, I was only asking.'

Jonny sighed, and as his expression softened, he shook his head. 'I'm sorry,' he said. 'I know that you and Tommy Jr are close...'

'He's my best mate,' Reece interrupted.

'Yeah, I know.' Jonny gave a small smile, regretting his harsh tone. 'Like I said, I'm sorry.'

The door opened, and as the rest of the family traipsed inside, Jonny got to his feet, shook Danny McKay's hand then resumed his position, resting his forearms on the desk.

'Well?' Stacey asked looking from her husband to her grandson's father, Cameron, and great uncle, Jonny. 'How is he?'

'He's good. Keeping his head down or at least trying to anyway,' Jonny groaned. 'But seeing as this is Tommy Jr we're talking about, it's only a matter of time until someone rubs him up the wrong way and he kicks off.'

After a few moments of silence, Jonny cleared his throat and continued. 'As for the coke, he's adamant that he had nothing to do with it.'

'I knew it.' Reece jumped off the arm of the sofa and gave a triumphant grin. 'I told you that he was innocent.'

'Yeah, alright smart arse, sit back down.' Jonny rolled his eyes all the while ignoring the red hue that spread across his cheeks. Like Peter, he too had had his doubts over Tommy Jr's innocence, not that he'd been stupid enough to vocalise those thoughts out loud of course. 'He mentioned something about a mate of Kevin's, Andy something or other.' He glanced towards Cameron for confirmation then raised his eyebrows. 'Obviously, we'll need to have a word with him, see what he knows.'

'Why?' Reece blurted out. 'Why don't we just go straight for Kevin?' He looked around him and scowled. 'He's the bastard we should be going after, he's the reason Tommy Jr is banged up.'

'Because,' Danny answered, tapping his temple. 'Kevin didn't miraculously come up with fifty grand to buy the gear all by himself, did he? Think about this logically, someone must have helped him.'

'You mean like the Bannerman brothers?' Reece sighed.

'Yeah, maybe,' Jonny agreed. 'But even then, I still can't see them just handing over half a kilo of coke, not without a guarantee that it would be repaid and considering it's now in the hands of the Old Bill, that's not likely, is it?'

'Nah, I suppose not,' Reece agreed.

'None of this makes any sense to me,' Stacey said shaking her head. 'From what you've said about these Bannerman brothers they're not stupid.'

'That's up for debate,' Danny mumbled.

Stacey glowered at her husband.

'They're dealers,' Jonny volunteered. 'Hardly the pillar of the community, are they?'

Stacey couldn't help but laugh. 'And you lot are armed robbers, you're not exactly what I'd call law-abiding citizens either, so what makes you any different from them?'

'We don't peddle shit to kids for a start,' Jonny growled. 'And yeah, fair enough we might take one or two things that don't belong to us, but no one gets hurt in the process.'

Stacey raised her eyebrows. 'Try telling that to the poor fuckers who have shotguns shoved into the side of their heads, because I'm pretty sure they wouldn't agree.'

'You've got some front, Stace,' Jonny shot back. 'Your husband is the one who supplies us the shotguns.'

Holding up his hand Danny shook his head, his hard eyes enough to tell Jonny that he was going too far.

'We're going a bit off subject here,' Cameron barked out. 'I think we're all more than aware that our chosen occupation isn't exactly what you'd call legal.'

'He's right, Mum,' Karen said as she came to sit beside her husband. 'We're meant to be talking about Tommy Jr, not the robberies.'

Stacey huffed out a breath. 'So you think this Andy might know something then?' she asked.

'Only one way to find out isn't there,' Jonny grinned. As the sound of a car entering the forecourt reached his ears he turned in his chair, craning his neck as he did so to get a better view of the occupant. 'Right, you lot, out.' He started getting to his feet.

Danny narrowed his eyes. 'Is that who I think it is?' he asked, nodding towards the figure stepping out of the vehicle.

'Yep,' Jonny answered. 'And you know as well as I do that he won't appreciate an audience.'

Stacey's jaw dropped. 'Why the bloody hell would Fletch come here?' Confusion creased her face and as she turned to look at her husband her eyes widened. 'Please tell me that this isn't what I think it is,' she said turning back to face her former brother-in-law. 'That you're not going after the Bannerman brothers.'

Jonny lifted his eyebrows. 'What did you expect us to do, Stace? Tommy Jr is family; we're not going to sit idly by and do fuck all, are we?'

Her face pale, Stacey nodded, taking a moment to study Jonny. 'You've got too much of your brother inside you,' she said in a low voice as Danny began to usher both her and the rest of the family outside.

It wasn't the first time that someone had likened Jonny to his eldest brother and knowing that Tommy Snr had been considered a legend amongst his family and peers, he couldn't help but beam.

At the door, Stacey paused, her expression becoming serious. 'And we all know how that ended,' she warned before following her husband outside.

Within a matter of moments, the smile slipped from Jonny's face. The stark warning coming across exactly how it had been intended: the equivalent of a punch to the gut.

13

Andy was so scared that he'd wet himself, and as the hot urine trickled down his legs and seeped into the denim of his jeans, he'd never felt more humiliated. He was a grown man for fuck's sake, someone who could hold his own, yet at the sight of Nathan and Lee Bannerman looking down at him as the car boot was sprung open, he'd cried like a baby and was still crying as they dragged him out of the motor, into a lock-up and then unceremoniously dumped him onto a dusty, concrete floor.

'Please,' he sobbed holding up his hands. 'Don't hurt me. We... we can talk about this.'

'Talk,' Lee scoffed. 'Why the fuck would we want to talk?' Crouching down, he grasped a handful of Andy's hair in his fist and yanked his head backwards so that he could look him in the eyes. 'Believe me, there ain't fuck all for us to talk about, unless,' he grinned, 'you want to talk about how you mugged us off, because if that's the case then I'm all ears.'

As Andy cried even harder an impending sense of doom consumed him. They were going to kill him, he knew that as well as he knew his own name, and as he glanced around him, his terrified gaze taking in a series of weapons, he prayed that his death would be quick and not prolonged and that his mother, despite their strained relationship, would have something left of him to bury.

'It was Kevin,' he choked out. 'Kevin Fox. It was all his idea.' Snot and tears mingled together, coating his cheeks and upper lip. 'He... he was meant to get the bank cards for you. I swear,' he continued to wail. 'I swear on my life that it was Kevin who mugged you off, not me.'

Throwing Andy away from him, Lee straightened up, reached for a claw hammer, then without hesitation brought it down across Andy's kneecap.

The scream that escaped from Andy's lips was deafening, and as he rolled around the floor cradling what was left of his splintered kneecap, he sobbed so hard that he could scarcely catch his breath, let alone breathe and continue pleading for his life.

'That's just for starters,' Lee stated as he slowly circled Andy's broken form. He looked up and cocked his head to the side. 'How many bones are there in a human body?'

'Two hundred and six,' Connor volunteered.

Lee whistled through his teeth. 'Two hundred and six,' he repeated with a wicked gleam in his eyes. 'That's a lot of bones I'm going to smash to smithereens. And if you're still alive once I'm finished, which let's face it is highly unlikely, then I'm going to start cutting you, just small slices at first,' he grinned. 'To prolong the agony and then I'll move onto hacking off body parts, your fingers, toes, nose, ears.' His gaze wandered down towards Andy's nether regions. 'Well, I think you get the picture. Once I'm done with you there'll be nothing left. At least nothing recognisable anyway.'

Vomit spewed out of Andy's mouth, and as he continued to heave, the sound of Lee's laughter rang loudly in his ears. Many a time he'd heard the rumours surrounding Lee Bannerman, that he was a nutcase, that he was unhinged, and never had he believed the gossip to be as true as he did right now. Lee Bannerman was more than just a nutcase, he was an absolute lunatic, a maniac who should be locked up for the protection of others.

'Please,' he cried again in a last-ditch attempt to save his life. 'Speak to Kevin, he'll get you anything you want.'

Lee narrowed his eyes. 'I thought you just said that he'd mugged us off.'

On the verge of passing out, it took all of Andy's effort to shake his head. 'He'll get you the cards,' he said, his body trembling so violently that he could barely speak.

'Yeah you're right about that,' Lee grinned. 'One way or another we will get what we're owed.'

Hope spread through Andy's veins and as he peered up at Lee he blinked rapidly. Perhaps he'd been wrong, and he wasn't about to die after all. Relief surged through him, he could live with a broken kneecap, six weeks in a plaster cast was fuck all when he considered the alternative. Even the thought of living the remainder of his life with a permanent limp had to be a lot better than ending up in some shallow, unmarked grave, or a ditch on the side of some remote road.

'Not that you'll be alive to see it.' Lee smiled down at him breaking his thoughts. Bringing the hammer down a second and third time in quick succession, Andy's screams filled the air, not that they deterred Lee; if anything they seemed to spur him on as though the sound of bones breaking brought him a great sense of enjoyment.

Five minutes later as Lee pulled back his arm in preparation to deliver another sickening blow, he suddenly paused, his eyebrows scrunching together as he dropped the weapon to his side and bent slightly forward to peer down at Andy. 'For fuck's sake,' he shouted. 'Has he croaked it?'

Both Nathan and Connor moved forward, their eager gazes searching for the rise and fall of Andy's chest.

'Looks like it,' Nathan remarked giving a nonchalant shrug. 'He definitely isn't breathing; I know that much.'

Breathing heavily, Lee wiped the sweat from his forehead before throwing the hammer across the lock-up. 'The tosser,' he hissed. 'I knew I should have started slicing the fucker sooner.'

Nathan and Connor shared a wary glance.

'Never mind, bruv,' Nathan commented as he slung his arm around his brother's shoulder and gave it a tight squeeze. 'We're not done yet,' he reminded him. 'Once this Kevin has repaid his debt you can have a free rein, fuck the bastard up, really go to town on him.'

Lee's eyes lit up and rubbing his hands together he kicked out at Andy's still form one last time. 'I will do,' he answered pointing a blood-stained finger in his younger brother's direction. 'So you'd best find that bastard and quick.'

Silently groaning, Connor averted his gaze. Not only would he have to deal with his girlfriend once she'd learned that her only brother was on the missing list, but he had a nasty feeling that locating Kevin wouldn't be as easy as Lee or even Nathan seemed to think it would be. How could it, when all they had to go on was a name? There must be hundreds of Kevins out there, maybe even thousands, and to top it off they didn't even know what he looked like or where he lived. They knew he worked for the Royal Mail, but Andy had failed to tell them where exactly.

He could try questioning his bird, he supposed, see what she knew about Kevin. And seeing as he was a good pal of Andy's, she must know who he is, and more importantly where he could be found. But asking Julie for information was hassle he could do without. Not only would he look suspicious, but she was bound to question his motives, especially when she realised her brother had disappeared off the face of the earth. She might even put two and two together and start pointing fingers.

Cursing Lee for snuffing out Andy's life before they'd the chance to extort valuable information out of him he stormed out of the lock-up, kicking the door closed behind him. Considering his brother's psychopathic tendencies, he could be so dense at times, that Connor questioned the fact of whether or not they were actually related.

* * *

Strolling into the scrapyard office, Fletch took a moment to look around him. It had been years since he'd last visited the Carters' place of work, and even then, it had been a case of business rather than pleasure all thanks to his former boss Billy King's illegal activities. Not that he could say much had changed over the years, at least not that he could see anyway. The sofa appeared to be the same, albeit it was now threadbare with visible springs poking through the thin leather fabric, and as for the rest of the furniture, the desk, chair, and filing cabinets, he took a wild guess that they too hadn't been changed over the years either. The only new addition he could see was a potted plant slung into the corner of the office, the pot cracked and the plants' leaves brown and dropping.

'Thanks for coming,' Jonny said, gesturing to the sofa for Fletch to take a seat. 'I take it you found an address for your cousins.'

A look of anger flashed across Fletch's face. 'Don't call them that,' he spat. 'Those bastards are fuck all to do with me.'

Realising his mistake, Jonny's cheeks turned red. He better

than anyone knew what it was like to be related to someone you despised, and he'd despised his elder brother Gary with an absolute passion, they all had. 'Sorry,' he said, keen to make amends. He motioned to the sofa again and waited for Fletch to sit down before continuing. 'I take it you found an address for the Bannermans?' he asked, rewording the question.

Fletch sighed and shifting his weight to avoid the raised springs he leaned forward, resting his forearms on his knees. 'Not yet. I'm still working on it. They're not so easy to track down and the last known address I had for them turned out to be deserted.'

Jonny groaned, disappointment evident across his face.

Still unsure he was actually doing the right thing when it came to locating the brothers, Fletch chewed on his bottom lip. 'Are you sure about this?' he asked, looking between Jonny and Cameron. 'That you actually want to find them? Like I've already said, they're not the kind of men that any sane man would want to mess with, let alone actively seek out.'

'We don't have any other choice,' Jonny sighed slumping back in the chair. 'You know as well as I do, that they're the main contenders when it comes to drugs, that they're at the top of their game and responsible for the majority of narcotics being peddled in London and half of Essex.'

Fletch raised his eyebrows and ignoring the spring that poked into his backside he shook his head. 'For fuck's sake,' he groaned. 'Is that what this is all about? You want an in or want to start peddling shit and are worried that they'll step on your toes?'

'Like fuck we do,' Jonny snarled. 'I wouldn't touch that shit, let alone dream of selling it.'

'Then I don't understand,' Fletch exclaimed screwing up his face. 'I mean I remember you mentioning something about your nephew that he'd been caught dealing...'

'Great-nephew,' Jonny butted in. 'My brother, Tommy's grandson. And he wasn't caught dealing.' He swallowed, then looked away, his cheeks flushing red, knowing full well that for all intents and purposes Tommy Jr looked as guilty as they came. 'He was caught with half a kilo of coke in his car.'

'Same thing, isn't it?' Fetch asked, raising his eyebrows. 'I mean,' he continued eyeing the two men. 'You can't claim half a kilo for personal use, only an idiot would buy into that, and despite what we,' he said wagging his finger between them, 'might think of the Old Bill, they're not as stupid as they look.'

Jonny gritted his teeth. 'Tommy Jr is adamant he knew nothing about the coke and seeing as those bastards are suppliers then I'm guessing they might have had a hand in it or at the very least know something.'

Fetch let out a low laugh and shook his head. 'That's some fucking assumption you're making.'

'Maybe.'

'No maybe about it,' Fetch retorted. 'As I've already told you, you're playing with fire, all of you,' he said, turning his hard stare to Cameron. Getting to his feet, he walked across the office, pulled down on the door handle then turned back around. 'I hope you know what you're doing, what you're getting yourselves involved in because this isn't going to end well,' he added looking between Jonny and Cameron. 'For any of you.'

'We don't have any other choice...' Jonny began.

'Yeah, so you keep on saying,' Fletch interrupted. Pinching the bridge of his nose he shook his head again. 'Don't get me wrong. I get it, I really do. We're no different when it comes to family, especially our kids, we'd do anything for them and trust me I've had to fight tooth and nail for mine, and I mean that literally.'

Jonny lifted his eyebrows, his immediate thoughts going to

the rumours he'd heard of Fletch almost battering one of his cousins to death. Maybe there was some truth to the gossip after all.

'Let's just say that the Bannermans almost destroyed my family,' Fletch continued. 'Given half the chance they would have killed my kids and not given a single flying fuck. They abducted my daughter, held her hostage, and were more than prepared to slit her throat if they didn't get what they wanted, which was me by the way, or should I say they wanted my blood on their hands. Those are the kind of men you're dealing with, men who have no care for anyone or anything. They're more than just unhinged, they're dangerous fuckers.'

'And yet the fact you're still here to tell the tale is enough to tell me they can be beaten.' Jonny ran his tongue over his teeth, one eyebrow cocked. 'That they're not invincible.'

'No maybe not,' Fletch conceded. 'But neither are any of you.'

Swallowing heavily, Jonny averted his gaze, the truth of Fletch's words settling in the pit of his stomach like a lead balloon.

'Look I get that your nephew, or rather your boy,' he said jerking his head in Cameron's direction, 'is banged up, but he'll survive. I've been there, done it, and got the fucking T-shirt. Spent the best part of my life locked up and I deserved it too considering the crime I'd committed,' he said, holding up his hands. 'Not that I'm sorry for it and given half the chance I'd do it all over again but that's neither here nor there. At the end of the day, I came out of it alive which is a lot more than can be said for you and your family if you see this through and go after the Bannermans.' Pausing for breath he looked around him taking note of the tired décor and then the yellowing, dog-eared paperwork piled high on top of the filing cabinets. 'Stick to robbing banks.' He gave a light chuckle. 'Despite owning this place, and the debt collecting, I take it that is still your game.'

Somewhat reluctantly, Jonny nodded.

'Yeah, I thought as much,' Fletch answered giving him a knowing look. 'Believe me, you don't want this. Maybe if...' He sucked in his bottom lip and sighed. 'Well, maybe if it had been your brothers, I mean Tommy, and Jimmy, or maybe even Gary, seeing as he wasn't the full ticket, then just maybe it would be a different story, perhaps they would have been able to take them on.'

The nerve at the side of Jonny's jaw ticked, his expression suddenly becoming hard. 'I'm not some pussy,' he spat out. 'I do know how to look after myself.'

'I didn't say you couldn't.' Fletch gave a half laugh. 'It's just, well, you know what Tommy was like, he could be cunning when he needed to be.'

'Yeah.' Getting to his feet, Jonny's shoulders were tense as he rounded the desk. 'I think you've made your point.' He waved his hand in the direction of the door. 'Thanks for the pep talk, but I think we can handle it.'

Taking note of the fact that he was being dismissed, Fletch huffed out a breath. 'Just think on it before you go looking for them, that's all I'm asking,' he reiterated. 'Doesn't hurt to be prepared.'

'Trust me, we will be.' Pulling open the door signalling that their meeting was over, Jonny gave a wide smile, one that didn't quite reach his eyes.

With a weary shake of his head, Fletch stepped out of the office knowing that there was nothing left to say. He'd given a warning, several warnings to be precise, and if the Carters didn't take his words seriously, then what else was he supposed to do other than let them get on with it and learn from their mistakes, ones that were bound to end in a massacre.

Once Fletch had left the office Jonny resisted the urge to slam the door closed after him.

'What do you reckon?' Cameron asked as he nodded in the direction of the forecourt.

His back up, Jonny scowled, more determined than ever to not only go after Kevin, and his sidekick Andy, but also the Bannerman brothers. 'He was talking bollocks, that's what I think,' Jonny hissed. 'He might bow down to the cunts, might quake in his boots whenever their names are mentioned but believe me when I say this: I fucking don't.'

Cameron nodded, and as he stared at the now closed door, he had a sinking feeling that maybe Fletch was right, that they had every reason to be cautious and that given the brothers' reputations for violence, they should be more than careful and keep their wits about them when it came to dealing with them.

* * *

Kevin was whistling a merry little tune as he made his way down the pathway leading to his ex-wife's home, or should that be *his* home, seeing as he would soon be moving back in, and in his opinion, not before time either. He'd put a lot of effort into sweet-talking Melanie, he'd helped around the house, bought her bottles of wine, and the odd takeaway, he'd even brought her breakfast in bed on occasion. When it came to his daughter, Aimee had been a harder nut to crack, but crack her he had, although it would be fair to admit that he'd needed to lay on the charm a little thicker. Not only had he held her while she'd cried but he'd also whispered in her ear over and over again that he would never let her down, unlike her so-called boyfriend,

Tommy Johnson. Of course it was all an act, one that he would soon drop once his feet were firmly planted underneath the kitchen table.

Letting himself into the house he frowned at the quietness. Usually, the TV or stereo would be on, or Mel would call out from the kitchen asking if he'd like something to eat or drink. He walked through to the lounge rubbing his hand over his stomach, he could murder a bacon sandwich right about now, his mouth watering as he imagined himself sinking his teeth into thick slices of buttered bread and crispy rashers of bacon.

On seeing the look on his daughter's face Kevin immediately rocked back on his heels. The glare Aimee shot towards him was enough to chill him to the very bone. He supposed Mel had told her that he was moving back in, and being the stroppy, spoilt little mare that she was, she wasn't happy about it.

'I suppose your mum has told you the good news then,' he said slipping off his jacket and draping it over one of the dining chairs. 'That your old dad is moving back in.'

Aimee nodded, her hard stare continuing to bore into his skull.

Kevin rolled his eyes. 'Fuck me, who pissed in your cornflakes this morning, eh?' he grumbled. 'It wouldn't hurt to smile once in a while. Every time I look at you, you've got a face on you that'd be enough to curdle milk.'

'And unless it's escaped your notice, *Dad*,' Aimee spat back, accentuating the word. 'I've not had much to smile about of late, what with the father of my child being imprisoned an' all.'

Agitation rippled through Kevin's veins. 'Are you still on about that?' he asked, shaking his head as though disappointed in his offspring. 'You're like a broken bleedin' record darlin', give it a rest. How many times do I need to tell you that you're better off without the prick? He's nothing but scum, same goes for the rest of his family.' He stabbed a nicotine-stained finger forward, his lips curling into a snarl. 'You've had a lucky escape, girl, and it's about time you realised that.' He began kicking off his boots, then ambled over to the sofa and flopped down, making himself at home as he picked up the remote control, switched on the television then pulled out his cigarettes and lit up. 'From the very moment I met him I could see straight through his bullshit,' he said giving his daughter a sidelong glance. 'I'm astute, me,' he said tapping the side of his nose. 'Always have been. And every other word that came out of that mouth of his was a load of old pony. He was a flash cunt too, thinks he's better than the rest of us. Well, he's not so flash now is he,' he smirked. 'Shitting and pissing in a bucket on a daily basis and eating slop that I wouldn't even give to a dog morning, noon, and night.'

Aimee screwed up her face. 'Is that why you were in the pub with him then, Dad? You know, right before he was arrested?'

A cold chill spread throughout Kevin's body. Recovering quickly, he shook his head, his expression becoming one of anger. 'What are you talking about? I wasn't in any boozer with him.'

'Yes, you were. Reece told me that you'd messaged Tommy asking to meet up, that you'd wanted to talk, about me, apparently.'

'Then Reece is talking bollocks.' Kevin waved his hand dismissively then puffed frantically on his cigarette, the only outward sign he gave to suggest that his daughter's words had rattled him. Inside however, he was seething, he'd not banked on Tommy telling anyone that they'd planned to meet up. 'I didn't see hide nor hair of the lad, why would I? I can't stand the trappy little bastard.'

Getting to her feet Aimee gave a sweet, albeit menacing smile. 'I wouldn't get too comfy if I were you.' She jerked her head towards the lounge door. 'Mum wants a word, and before you ask,' she added. 'I told her everything.' She leaned in a little closer, her eyes flashing dangerously. 'How you've been lying to us. You see, Dad, you're not as clever as you think you are. My Tommy would never touch hard drugs. Yeah, I'll hold my hands up and admit that he smokes the odd spliff every now and again, but coke?' She shook her head. 'That's not his scene and never has been. But it is yours, isn't it? You love nothing more than to shove a bit of Charlie up your nose.'

Subconsciously Kevin ran his hand underneath his nose, checking that he hadn't left any white residue behind after his last hit.

On seeing the action Aimee's lips twisted into a scowl; her obvious disgust written all over her face. 'I should have joined the dots sooner. That coke was yours, wasn't it? You were the one who put it in Tommy's car, you were the one who set him up.'

Kevin jumped up from the sofa. 'You know fuck all!' he roared. Grasping Aimee by the shoulders he shook her roughly, spraying her in foul smelling spittle as he did so. 'Have some fucking respect. I'm your dad, not some mug off the street.'

Terrified, Aimee gasped, a scream lodging in the back of her throat as she tried in vain to prise her father's hands away from her. 'Stop,' she cried. 'You're hurting me.'

Not releasing his grip Kevin sneered. His face just inches away from Aimee's as he continued to roar. 'I hope they throw away the key,' he taunted her. 'I hope that bastard spends the rest of his life banged up, rotting away to nothing. It's what he deserves for what he did to me, what his family did to me. That Royal Mail job was my idea. Mine,' he shouted. 'That money was supposed to set me up for life, I could have had everything I'd ever wanted if it wasn't for those wankers. Well...' He gave a nasty little chuckle. 'I'm the one who'll have the last laugh. You mark my words, girl, I'm not done with them yet; in fact, this is just the beginning. I'll see all of them brought down if it's the last thing I ever do, every single last one of them.'

Aimee's eyes widened and realising that he'd said too much, Kevin shoved his daughter away from him not giving a single care as she fell awkwardly onto the sofa. Running his hands through his hair, his face red and blotchy, and his nostrils flaring, Kevin looked not only deranged but also downright dangerous.

'So, it's true,' Aimee cried. 'You were the one responsible, you set Tommy up!'

'Who else did you think it was?' Kevin hissed. 'They deserve to suffer just like I have to suffer. I've got fuck all, not a fucking bean to my name, while they swan around giving it large, splashing their cash around and driving their flash, top-of-the-range motors, and don't even get me started on their gaffs. The bastards live a life of luxury, while the rest of us,' he shouted poking himself in the chest, 'have to scramble around in the dirt without a pot to piss in.'

Tears slipped down Aimee's cheeks, her terror more than palpable as she looked up at her father. 'You won't get away with it,' she sobbed. 'I'll go to the police; I'll tell them what you did. I'll tell them everything.'

Kevin clenched his hand into a tight fist and yanking Aimee towards him he continued to bellow in her face, 'Is that so?' He pulled back his arm, ready to strike. 'Do you honestly think they would believe you?'

'What the bloody hell is going on in here?' Melanie screeched at the top of her lungs.

Immediately, Kevin's arm dropped to his side. 'Nothing,' he answered, his hard glare still directed at his daughter. 'We were just having a little chat, that's all. Setting down one or two ground rules for when I move back in.'

Looking from her ex-husband to her daughter Melanie's eyes were wide. 'Aimee?' she said pulling her dressing gown tighter around her body as she stepped closer. 'What's going on?'

Breathing heavily, Aimee cowered away from her father, her terrified gaze still looking up at him as though half expecting him to follow through with his threat and lash out at her. 'He...' she began, barely able to get the words out. 'He...'

'He what?' Rounding on Kevin, Melanie placed her hands on her hips. 'What have you done to her?' she shouted, her tone accusing.

'I've done fuck all to her.' Kevin waved his hand through the air as he tried desperately to come up for an excuse for his outburst. Falling short he stumbled away from his daughter, creating a distance between them. 'You know what she's like at the moment, she's hormonal. You only have to look at her and she either bites your head off or bursts into tears.'

'Aimee,' Melanie tried again, 'is this true?'

'I...' Pulling herself into a sitting position Aimee wrapped her arms around her legs, her face deathly white and her body trembling. 'Just tell him to go, Mum,' she begged lowering her head onto her knees. 'Please.'

Melanie's mouth opened and closed, resembling a fish out of water. 'I think maybe,' she finally said, turning to look at Kevin, 'that it'd be best if you leave.'

Kevin's eyes bulged. 'You're throwing me out!' he gasped, looking around him. Melanie may not have had much but at least her home was clean which was a darn sight more than could be said about the mould-infested room he rented. Then there were the other home comforts he'd come to enjoy over the past week, a home-cooked meal, his washing and ironing done. And then there was the money aspect that came with shacking up with Mel. Other than pay out for the odd bottle of wine or takeaway, he'd had more cash in his back pocket, or rather, more money to splash out on in the pub buying all and sundry drinks, acting the Billy big bollocks, not forgetting the cocaine that he loved to shove up his hooter on a daily basis, as his daughter had so rightly pointed out. 'You're actually kicking me out on my ear!' he shouted. 'You're putting her,' he said, nodding towards Aimee with a sneer, 'above me?'

Pulling herself up to her full height Melanie's expression became hard. 'Always,' she said slowly as though the very idea of putting Kevin above her daughter was ludicrous. 'She's my daughter, my own flesh and blood.'

'Oh, I see.' Kevin gave a sarcastic laugh. 'We're back to that again, are we? The two witches ganging up on me, your favourite pastime.'

'No, Kevin,' Melanie said as she yanked open the lounge door and pointed towards the front door. 'I'm just tired of your bullshit, the constant lies.'

Kevin's jaw dropped, his gaze bouncing between his ex-wife and daughter. 'What has she been telling you?'

'Everything,' Melanie answered. 'But you already knew that, didn't you? I heard exactly what you said. How you set Tommy up, how you threatened your own daughter with violence.'

The blood drained from Kevin's face and backing several feet away he shook his head. 'No one will believe you. The Old Bill will laugh in your face. I've got a cast-iron alibi; someone who will swear on the bible that I was in The Cross Keys the entire afternoon, that I never left, not even for as long as to take a piss.'

'Maybe,' Melanie shrugged as she moved closer towards him, a steely glint in her eyes. 'But how about the Johnsons and Carters, do you think they would believe you?' Walking across the lounge Melanie unzipped her handbag and pulled out her mobile phone. 'Shall we ask them?' She ran her tongue over her teeth, her eyes flashing dangerously. 'Shall we see what they think about you and Tommy meeting up before his arrest, because I'm pretty sure they will be interested in everything I have to say?'

His jaw dropping again, Kevin could only gape at Melanie, his eyes going from his ex-wife's face to the phone in her hand. He'd not banked on Tommy's family ever finding out the truth, that he was solely responsible for Tommy's incarceration, with a little help from Andy and the Bannerman brothers of course. A coward through and through, he could virtually taste his fear. 'You wouldn't dare,' he croaked out. 'Me and you have got history; we were married for fuck's sake; we've got a kid together, and' – he pointed towards Aimee – 'we've got a grandchild on the way.'

Melanie let out a sarcastic laugh. 'Are we talking about the same grandchild you wanted our daughter to terminate? And as for being married, you mean nothing to me now, you might as well be dead for all I care. I was a fool to believe that someone like you could change, because as I've told you time and time again, Kevin Fox, you will never change, not as long as you have a hole in your arse, you're not capable of it. You haven't the first idea of what it is to be a father or husband. In fact, if you weren't so pathetic, I'd pity you.'

Kevin gulped, her harsh words sending a shot of terror ricocheting throughout his body. Sure, he could recall Melanie saying the exact same thing to him in the past, he'd even laughed it off, but never had the words been said with such loathing, such contempt. Composing himself, he held his head high. 'Then maybe it's best I do leave. I know when I'm not wanted, when I've overstayed my welcome.' He shoved his feet into his boots, snatched up his cigarettes and lighter, then slipped on his jacket. 'And as for you and her,' he spat nodding towards Aimee. 'You're welcome to one another. I hope you're happy now,' he added glaring at his daughter. 'This is what you wanted, isn't it? Your old dad kicked out on his ear, without a penny to his name, and for what, eh? So that you and that bastard Tommy Johnson can ride off into the sunset and play happy families together. Well let me tell you now, girl—'

'Oh, just get out,' Melanie hissed, cutting him off. 'We don't want to hear it. Go on,' she said, her voice rising several decibels. 'Piss off and don't come back.'

With the last of his remaining dignity still intact, Kevin turned on his heels, charged down the small hallway, and flung open the front door with such force that he almost ripped it off its hinges. 'This isn't over,' he warned, before slamming the door shut behind him. 'Not by a long shot.'

14

The change in atmosphere was so subtle at first that Tommy Jr wondered if it was actually a figment of his imagination. He likened the change to an excited buzz, one that he couldn't quite put his finger on, nor find a source for.

As he wandered in the direction of Dylan's cell a hushed silence fell over the landing. Excited, glee-filled eyes watching his every move. Glancing over his shoulder, Tommy narrowed his eyes. Something was clearly going down, but what that was, he had no idea.

'What the fuck is going on out there?' he asked as he flopped down onto the bed beside Dylan.

Dylan turned his head, his gaze scrutinising what he could see of the landing from his position. 'Fuck knows?' he shrugged, his attention snapping back to the television as he continued playing a video game. After shouting out a number of expletives he passed the controller across to Tommy. 'Here,' he said with a huff. 'See if you have better luck than me.' Leaning back, he sucked on a vape, the blueberry scented vapour filling the air as he exhaled. 'You need to kill that one,' he said nodding towards the screen as Tommy's character chased after a zombie.

'Yeah, I know, I know.' Tommy clenched his jaw, his expression one of concentration as he pushed the buttons on the controller. 'For fuck's sake,' he whined moments later as his character fell to the ground signalling the end of the game. 'It's always the fucking same.'

Dylan chuckled. 'It's rigged,' he exclaimed taking back the controller and tossing it onto the bed beside them. 'It's gotta be.'

'Yeah, I suppose so,' Tommy continued to grumble. Leaning back, he pulled out his own vape, puffing on it as he looked over the photographs taped to the wall. 'You got any visits booked?'

'Nah,' Dylan shrugged. 'But hopefully my mum and sister might come and see me soon. It's been a while since I last saw them. My mum... well.' He sighed then gave another small shrug. 'She's not been all that good lately, she suffers with her nerves, some days she can't even get out of bed. Not that you'd know it to look at her,' he added glancing behind him to the photographs.

Tommy nodded. Curiosity getting the better of him, it was on the tip of his tongue to ask if Dylan's dad would be putting in an appearance. Thinking better of it he carried on vaping as a comfortable silence stretched out before them.

'I'm hoping that my bird will come and see me,' Tommy said after a few moments. 'I miss her.'

'Yeah, I bet you do,' Dylan winked. He nodded down at Tommy's hand and squashed his lips together in an attempt to hide his grin. 'You'd best get used to that hand, pal, it's the only action you're gonna be getting for the foreseeable future.'

'Fuck off,' Tommy chuckled, rolling his eyes.

A commotion coming from the landing made both Tommy's and Dylan's heads snap towards the door. Footsteps could be heard, heavy footsteps by the sound of it, and they were close too, a little too close for Tommy's liking.

Sitting bolt upright, Tommy's forehead furrowed. 'What the fuck's going on...?' he began, as several men burst into the cell, their faces covered by the T-shirts they had pulled over their noses and lower faces in the way of a disguise. Not that they should have bothered – almost immediately Tommy recognised them as being the same men Dylan had had some sort of beef with in the yard on his first morning at the prison.

As if in slow motion, the seconds that followed were a blur. If it hadn't been for the harrowing screams that came from Dylan or the burning sensation across Tommy's own skin as splashes of scalding water dotted his arm and wrist before he had the chance to leap out of the way, he would have thought the entire situation to be nothing more than a dream, or nightmare as the case happened to be.

Steam billowed from Dylan's face and torso, the stench of burning, scalding skin thick in the air. Scooting up the bed Tommy's eyes were wide, his mouth hanging open as his mind tried desperately to make sense of what was going on. He hadn't seen the blade, the attack had been too quick for him to even get a glimpse of it, but what he could see was the blood. Deep pools of claret that seeped from Dylan's twitching body down onto the mattress below.

'Jesus fucking Christ,' Tommy screamed as the men ran from the cell. Spurned into action he launched himself forward, all the while ignoring the blisters that were already forming on his forearm.

Too afraid to even look at his friend's face, to see his skin melting he tentatively reached out, his fingers trembling. He had to stem the blood he knew that much, only he didn't know where to begin; all he knew for sure was that there was too much of it, too many stab wounds for him to even count. Plunging his hands on Dylan's torso he pressed down hard, not even knowing if he was actually helping matters or making the situation ten times worse. Within a matter of seconds his hands were coated red, and the scent of iron mingling with the stench of burning skin made him want to gag.

'I need some help in here!' he screamed, pressing down even further on the wounds, his wide eyes fixed upon the door, in the hope that a screw would hear his desperate calls. 'He's going to fucking die.'

It took what felt like an age for one of the prison officers to poke his head around the door, and as his shocked, pale face went from Tommy to Dylan, he momentarily froze.

'Don't just stand there, help him!' Tommy roared.

As though spurred into action, the prison officer shouted out for assistance then bounded into the cell, shoving Tommy roughly out of his path and dropping to his knees in front of Dylan's still-twitching form.

As the officers took over in their attempts to save Dylan's life, Tommy slumped back, his head hitting the wall next to the photographs of Dylan's family. Even from where he was sitting, he knew that their attempts would prove futile, that no one would be able to survive the injuries that Dylan had been subjected to.

Tears filled Tommy's eyes, and hastily swiping them away he breathed heavily, the hard lump in his throat almost preventing him from swallowing. He had to be in shock, he decided, and as one of the officers tried to question him, he was barely able to register the words, let alone have the capacity to answer. He was numb, his entire body shaking – so much so that his teeth chattered. The only thing he wanted to do was to speak to his mum and dad, or to hear Aimee's voice. Even then, he didn't think he would be able to string a sentence together, at least nothing that was comprehensible. It was as though his mind had been paralysed, his brain a jumbled mess of incoherent thoughts. Nausea washed over him, and before he could be led from the cell bile rose up his throat, the smell of death becoming so heavy that he could scarcely breathe.

'He's dead, ain't he?' he eventually managed to choke out, his voice barely louder than a whisper. He didn't receive a reply, not that he'd particularly expected one. He didn't need a genius to tell him the outcome, he already knew in his heart that despite his and then the prison officers' best efforts to keep Dylan alive, he was already gone.

A sombre mood took over the cell, the earlier panic that came from the screws suddenly evaporating. He watched as one of the officers glanced at his watch, to take note of the time of death Tommy guessed, and felt his legs buckle from underneath him. He had to get out of the cell, away from the blood, away from the sight of Dylan's corpse sprawled out on the floor, his scalded, blistered face barely even recognisable. In a daze Tommy stumbled forward, the sound of his heartbeat ringing so loudly in his ears that for the briefest of moments he wondered if he'd actually lost his hearing.

'Move!' he roared as he elbowed the officers out of his way and fought his way outside onto the landing. Once there he gulped in air and looked around him, his hard gaze scanning the faces of those who stared back at him. Morbid fascination was etched across the prisoners' faces as they craned their necks to get a better view of the crime scene.

Tommy's blood boiled. 'What do you want, a fucking picture?' he snapped as he barrelled his way through the crowd. Still covered in Dylan's blood, he made his way to his own cell, his head held high, his back ramrod straight, and the muscles across his shoulder blades taut. It wasn't until he was alone that his shoulders drooped, and he let out a long, ragged breath. Rubbing his hands vigorously over his face, he was oblivious to the fact that streaks of Dylan's blood were now smeared across his face. As for his own injuries, he could barely feel any pain, and if it wasn't for the fact that his skin had turned bright red and that large blisters were beginning to form on his arm and wrist, he would never have known that he too had been scalded in the attack. Still breathing heavily, he began to pace the length of his cell as he tried in vain to comprehend what had just taken place, to try and make sense of what he'd just bore witness to.

As though on autopilot he snatched up the telephone receiver, his hands shaking so much that it took him two attempts to type out the numbers on the keypad. Finally, he held the phone up to his ear, and, on hearing his dad's voice when he answered, a lone tear slipped unashamedly down Tommy's cheek.

'Dad,' he choked out, the emotion in his voice making it thick and barely audible. 'I need to see you.'

* * *

Four days later, as Jonny and Cameron took their allocated seats in the visiting room of Pentonville Prison, apprehension hung over them like a thick black cloud. Tommy Jr had given no indication as to what was troubling him, despite his father's best attempts to coax it out of him. If anything, Tommy Jr had appeared to clam up even more, refusing to even utter a single word, or give his father any kind of explanation for what was wrong.

Not only had Tommy Jr's desperate telephone call to Cameron been cause enough for alarm but there had also been various rumours circulating the criminal underworld that a notorious villain who hailed from South London had discovered his son had been murdered while residing at His Majesty's pleasure. By all accounts, Jason Vickers was on the warpath, which was understandable considering his youngest son's life had just been extinguished in one of the worst ways imaginable.

As the prisoners began to make their way into the visiting room, Cameron cleared his throat, nudged Jonny in his side, then anxiously got to his feet.

Following suit, Jonny stood up, the heaviness in the pit of his stomach growing in intensity as he took a moment to study his great-nephew. Gone was Tommy Jr's usual cheeky grin and cocky stance; in their place was a man Jonny barely recognised, a man whose body was rigid, his lips set into a thin line, and his face pale. But it was the change in his eyes that Jonny found even more alarming, they resembled hard flints mixed with something else that he couldn't quite put his finger on, determination maybe, or perhaps even fear.

'You have to get me out of here,' Tommy said, his voice barely louder than a whisper as his father pulled him in for a bear hug.

Cameron narrowed his eyes. 'What's going on?' he asked as Tommy went on to embrace his uncle.

With a shake of his head Tommy sat down, his gaze darting around the visiting room.

'Tommy Jr?' Cameron asked again, his tone almost pleading. 'Talk to me. Tell us what happened.'

Tommy swallowed, then after giving the visiting room a final sweeping glance, he ran his hand over his cropped hair. 'I have to get out,' he repeated, sitting forward, his voice low. 'I'm a witness.' He shook his head and swallowed again, his knee bouncing up and down. 'Do you understand what I'm telling you?'

Jonny and Cameron shared a glance, their eyebrows raised as they tried to make sense of what they were being told.

'They're not going to let that go, are they? They'll come for me next. I mean that's how it works, isn't it?' Tommy continued, the words tumbling out of his mouth in a rush as he looked between his father and uncle. 'They're not going to let me walk around, knowing that I know who they are, that I saw...' He took a series of deep breaths as though trying to calm himself, his eyes becoming even more wild as he chewed on his thumbnail. 'Maybe if I could get to them first then I'd stand a chance.' He nodded to himself, as though a plan of action was forming in his mind. 'Yeah, I'll do that, I'll take them out before they get to me, before they...'

Alarmed, Cameron shoved his hand on top of his son's bouncing knee. 'Take who out?' he urged him. 'You're not making any sense, Tommy Jr.'

'There was so much blood,' Tommy whispered oblivious to his father's question. 'And I tried...' He looked down at his hands, turning them over and studying them before inspecting his fingernails, as if half expecting to find traces of blood still coating his nails and skin. 'I tried to stop the bleeding, but I couldn't and then...' His voice faltered, and tugging down the sleeve of his sweatshirt to hide the blisters that littered his forearm and wrist he shook his head again. 'I really tried, Dad.'

Cameron's mouth opened and closed, the words barely able to form in the back of his throat before Jonny whipped out his arm, caught hold of Tommy's wrist in a vice like grip and pushed up the sleeve of his jumper, his eyes widening to their upmost as he took in the sight of his great-nephew's injuries.

'What the fuck is this?' he hissed. 'Who did this to you?'

Shoving his uncle away from him, Tommy yanked down his

sleeve. 'It's nothing,' he said sinking back in the chair, his wide eyes scanning the room again.

'Have you had those looked at?' Snapping his head towards the prison guards Jonny was on the verge of calling them over, to demand an explanation from them as to what the fuck had gone down.

'I wasn't the target,' Tommy shrugged causing Jonny to turn back and look at him.

'No.' Jonny cocked his head to the side, his mind ticking over as he slowly began to put the pieces of the puzzle together. 'But Jason Vickers' boy was, wasn't he?'

Confusion was etched across Tommy's face.

'Jason Vickers,' Jonny said again through gritted teeth. 'His boy was topped in here a few days ago and from what I've heard they did him over good and proper. The usual trick, sugar and boiling water, and as if that wasn't enough, they stabbed the poor bastard an' all.'

Tommy took a shuddering breath then nodded. 'Dylan,' he croaked out. 'His name is...' He paused, taking a moment to correct himself. 'His name was Dylan... He was my pal.' He sniffed then looked back down at his hands. 'I couldn't stop it; I didn't know how to.' He brought his hand up to his forehead, closed his eyes, and massaged his temples. 'The blood was just pissing out of him and...'

'It's alright,' Cameron soothed. 'We get the picture. You tried to help him.' He leaned forward, grasped his son by the back of his neck, tugged him closer so that he could speak privately in his ear. 'It wasn't your fault, son.'

'I know it wasn't,' Tommy nodded, pulling himself out of his father's grasp. 'You either have to get me out of here or I'll do the bastards,' he warned. 'I mean it,' he said his lips curling into a snarl. 'I'll fucking do them.'

Jonny blew out his cheeks. 'We're working on it,' he promised his mind still reeling. 'And as for...' He clicked his fingers as though trying to recall the name of Jason Vickers' son.

'Dylan,' Tommy volunteered.

'Yeah, Dylan,' Jonny continued. 'From what I've heard it was an isolated incident, more than likely some kind of feud concerning his old man.'

'Fat lot of good that will do me,' Tommy seethed, his voice rising. 'Which part of this don't you understand? I was there, I was sitting right next to him. I'm a witness.'

'Okay, okay.' Jonny glanced around him in the hope that no one else had been able to hear Tommy Jr's outburst. 'I get what you're saying, but...' He held up his hand as though trying to placate his great-nephew. 'You need to calm down, you have to think rationally, don't go doing anything stupid, something that will get you locked up for even longer.'

Crossing his arms over his chest, Tommy scowled. 'This is bollocks,' he snapped. 'I shouldn't even be in here; I did fuck all wrong.'

'I know,' Cameron sighed. 'And believe me, we're doing everything we can to get you out.'

As one of the prison officers called out that visiting was over, Tommy nodded. 'Then let's just hope,' he muttered, 'that I won't be coming home in a body bag same as Dylan.'

* * *

Danny McKay rubbed his hand over his face. Not only had he always vowed that he would kill for his wife should anyone ever have the audacity to lash out at her or cause her any harm, but he also didn't like to see her upset in any way, shape or form. And in recent weeks his Stace had been more than just upset, she'd been so distraught that it pained him to even look at her.

'I know that he's no angel,' she said again as she looked up at him from her position on the sofa. 'And that admittedly he has his moments, probably far more than I'd care to mention. I'm not an idiot, nor blind to his faults, and any mother or grandmother who is unable to see any wrong in their child is a dangerous woman.' She gave a shudder. 'I know that he has a temper on him, and that it doesn't take much to rile him up, but deep down, he's got a good heart. When he was younger, he used to come and stay with me most weekends, all because he didn't like the thought of me living alone.' She gestured around the lounge, the fine lines around her eyes becoming more prominent ever since Tommy Jr's incarceration. 'He used to say he didn't want me to be lonely, and that he was worried about me living somewhere so secluded.' She gave a small smile. 'Although it could be because I spoiled the little bugger rotten whenever he was here. He was my first grandchild you see, and I've loved him since the very moment he was placed in my arms.'

Danny nodded. He too was fond of Tommy Jr, and Stacey was right, he was a good kid albeit cocky at times, not that he'd expect him to be any different when you looked at the family he'd been born into.

'There must be something we can do,' Stacey sighed. 'Some way that we can get him out of prison.'

Taking a seat beside his wife, Danny wrapped his arm around her shoulders and pulled her close. 'Let me have a word with Jonny,' he said. 'I'm not promising anything,' he declared when Stacey looked up at him in surprise. 'So don't go getting your hopes up but there is a way of guaranteeing the case will be thrown out of court, not in the legal sense of course, but the outcome would be the same.'

'But...' Turning to face her husband, Stacey's jaw dropped. 'How?'

'Don't ask questions, Stace, especially ones that you won't like the answer to. Like I said, it isn't strictly legal, in fact, if you want me to be honest it's highly illegal and I'd rather you not know the ins and outs, it's better that way, and the last thing I would ever want is for you to become an accessory.'

Taking her husband's words on board, Stacey took a deep breath before relaxing back into his embrace. 'I don't care what you have to do,' she said sincerely. 'I just want my grandson to come home.'

* * *

As Jonny pulled on to the forecourt outside the scrapyard office, Cameron cleared his throat.

'He's not coping in there, is he?' he said, referring to Tommy Jr.

Jonny sighed. He'd had the exact same thoughts, only he hadn't wanted to say the words out loud, knowing full well that they wouldn't be appreciated, and that Cameron would more than likely bite his head off. As it was, their relationship was fraught, and more often than not they were at loggerheads, the slightest thing setting either one of them off. Things had got so bad between them in the past that they had almost come to blows. In recent weeks they had come to some sort of understanding, a truce if you like, and let bygones be bygones. 'I don't think so,' he admitted. 'But then again, it's understandable. He witnessed his pal being topped, that'd be enough to push any man over the edge.'

Cameron nodded, his gaze drifting towards the office. 'Karen can't know anything about this,' he warned. 'She's barely holding it together as it is and, well...' He cleared his throat again and shook his head. 'What with my dad and his troubles, I mean we've always been on the lookout for any signs that Tommy Jr was maybe...' He swallowed and averted his gaze. 'Well, you know, following on in my dad's footsteps, that perhaps he was struggling up here,' he said, tapping his forehead. 'That he might need some kind of psychiatric intervention.'

Jonny screwed up his face. His brother Gary, Cameron's father, had had more than just a few troubles. He'd been a stark raving lunatic and that was putting it mildly. 'He's nothing like Gary,' Jonny barked out. 'That fucker was off his head. He had no care for anyone or anything, well other than your mother of course – as far as he was concerned, she was the be all and end all.' He shook his head. 'If he hadn't croaked it in the gas explosion, then sooner or later he would have ended up being sectioned.'

Unease spread through Cameron's body, and as a red hue spread up his neck and face, he shifted his weight. Not only had his parents' relationship been predominantly one-sided, but he had also been there to witness both his mother's and father's demises. The gas explosion had been nothing more than a cover up. If truth be told, his parents had been dead long before the explosion and subsequent fire that had ripped through his maternal grandfather's house. He knew this for a fact, seeing as he'd watched his uncle Jimmy murder them in cold blood. It was only by some miracle that Jimmy hadn't murdered him too. Perhaps Jimmy had taken pity on him, or maybe he'd had an inkling that Bethany and Gary had never had any real care for him. His mother had viewed him as nothing more than an inconvenience, a burden, a child she had been forced into giving birth to but had never wanted. And when it came to his father, in Gary's eyes he was nothing more than a means to an end, a valid reason to keep in contact with the woman he was obsessed with. Whatever his uncle's reasons, Cameron was only thankful that Jimmy had chosen to spare him that fateful day.

'If anything, Tommy Jr takes after Tommy Snr,' Jonny continued, breaking Cameron's thoughts. 'They're like two peas in a pod.'

'I suppose so,' Cameron nodded, then unclipping his seat belt, he pushed open the car door. 'Let's hope it stays that way,' he said, climbing out. 'And that this stint inside doesn't fuck him up, because I can tell you now, he wasn't acting right today. I've never seen him behave like this before and if I'm being perfectly honest, I'm more than just a little bit worried about him.'

'He'll be okay,' Jonny stated with a measure of confidence as he looked up at the rear-view mirror. 'He's bound to have off days, especially after what he's just been through.' Stepping out of the car, he nodded towards Danny McKay's motor as it pulled in behind him. 'Because if he didn't,' he said, giving Cameron a sidelong glance, 'let's face it, we'd be even more concerned.'

Moments later, Danny joined them. 'I was hoping to catch you.' He nodded towards the office. 'I've got a proposition to put to you, one that I've got a sneaky suspicion you're going to snap my hand off for.'

15

In disbelief Jonny shook his head, his eyes wide as he studied Danny. 'And you're only just mentioning this to us now,' he growled.

Danny nodded and taking a seat on the worn leather sofa he kicked his legs out in front of him. 'Stacey has been on my case,' he shrugged. 'And you know what I'm like. I can't abide to see any woman upset, especially my wife and she's been in fucking pieces these past couple of weeks.'

His jaw dropping, Jonny rubbed at his temples. 'I can't get my head around this.'

Screwing up his face, Danny lounged back, making himself all the more comfortable. 'It's not that hard to get your head around, Tommy Jr is her grandson...'

'I'm not talking about Stacey or how upset she is,' Jonny spat. 'I'm talking about the fact you've been sitting on this information for almost two weeks and have said fuck all, to any of us,' he added waving his hand in Cameron's direction.

Danny narrowed his eyes. 'It's not exactly something you slip into conversation is it...'

Jonny let out an incredulous laugh. 'Let me get this straight – and feel free to correct me if I'm wrong,' he seethed. 'You've got the Old Bill in your pocket and didn't think to mention that little fact, that it might not be of some fucking use to us.'

'One Old Bill,' Danny corrected. He glanced away, his cheeks flushing red. 'Well, maybe two. But that's neither here nor there,' he said holding up his hand as if to stop Jonny from retorting. 'The point I'm trying to make is that seeing as this person is in a position of power, they could very easily make something disappear.' He lifted his eyebrows. 'Such as evidence, for example.'

'Fuck me.' Shaking his head again, Jonny's eyes were wide. 'I can't believe we are even having this conversation.' He narrowed his eyes. 'Are you going soft in your old age, or fucking senile?'

'Leave it out,' Danny scoffed. 'There's fuck all wrong with me.'

'Well you could have fooled me,' Jonny answered. 'Because the Danny I know would have been all over this like a rash, not waited weeks before casually letting slip that there might be a way for us to get Tommy Jr out of the nick.'

'Come on,' Danny sighed. 'You know what I'm about. It's not like this is the first filth I've had in my pocket over the years, is it? It's widely known that the Old Bill are even more corrupt than the so-called villains; all you have to do is tap into the bastards' weaknesses.' He paused for breath and sat forward. 'So, are you interested or not?'

'What do you fucking think?' Jonny threw his arms up into the air. 'Of course we're interested. How soon can you get things sorted?'

'All it will take is one phone call.' Pulling out a burner phone, Danny flashed a wide grin. 'Like I said, this geezer is so deep in my pocket that it'd be a miracle if he ever managed to claw his way back out. And unless he wants one or two of his less than desirable pastimes made public knowledge, then trust me, he'll do exactly as I say.'

'And you reckon this could work?' Cameron asked, cocking his head to one side as he studied Danny intently. 'That it would be that easy, that the case would be thrown out of court?'

'Of course it would,' Danny replied. 'Without the evidence there isn't a case and what's more my brief would have a fucking field day with something like this,' he winked. 'It's right up his alley.'

Jonny chuckled. 'And there was me thinking that he was a pile of shit, that he didn't know his arse from his elbow.'

'Then clearly you've underestimated him,' Danny answered. 'Because believe me when I say this – Richard Lewis is one of the best in the business and seeing as I'm sitting here now and not banged up, that should tell you everything you need to know.'

Without needing to think Danny's proposition over Jonny nodded. 'Then do it,' he said motioning to the phone in Danny's hand. 'And make it quick. The sooner we get Tommy Jr out of that shithole, the better it will be for everyone.'

* * *

Despite his uncle's warning to keep his head down low, rage rippled through Tommy Jr's veins. Like fuck was he about to go down without a fight or become another statistic and leave the nick in a body bag. Keeping one eye on the two men responsible for Dylan's death he made his way around the exercise yard, the carefree way in which they laughed and joked around making him feel sick to his stomach.

Clenching then unclenching his fists in rapid succession Tommy's lips curled up into a snarl. Taking a moment to look around him, he took note of where the screws were positioned.

He'd have one chance he decided, just one chance to steam in and cause as much physical damage as was humanly possible before being hauled off and carted away to the isolation block. The cold sensation of the makeshift blade tucked inside the sleeve of his sweatshirt beckoned to him. He'd slice the bastards wide open, and not stop until they were bleeding out on the floor like the pigs they were, gasping for air and choking on the blood that clogged up their throats.

With his jaw clenched tight, Tommy began to make his way across the yard, his strides long and purposeful. He didn't care that he was putting himself on their radar, that he was making it known that he knew who they were and what they'd done. The last thing he was ever going to do was pussy foot around the bastards, or sleep with one eye open, too afraid that he'd become their next victim and that a kettle of boiling hot water would be flung over his nuts while he was caught off guard or sound asleep. It wasn't in his nature to back down, to anyone; he was a fighter, always had been and the two pricks before him were about to learn that fact the hard way.

He'd barely made it halfway across the yard when a body stepped in front of him blocking his path – a large, muscular body. 'You don't want to do that, son,' he said, jerking his head behind him. 'Not here.' He motioned to where the prison guards were standing. 'Too many witnesses.'

'Get out of my way,' Tommy growled. 'Those bastards...'

'Yeah,' the man said, a small, lazy grin etching its way across his face. 'I know what they did. They've hardly been discreet about it, have they?' He gave a light chuckle and shook his head. 'They haven't got a scooby, not a brain cell between the pair of them and believe me it's only a matter of time until they get their comeuppance. In fact, I have it on good authority that enquiries as to who they are, are already being made.' He gave a carefree shrug. 'If they make it to the end of the week still in one piece it'll be a miracle.'

Breathing heavily through his nostrils Tommy took a step back. Although he'd never spoken to him before, he'd seen the man around, not that he would have been able to miss him. Standing at over six feet tall, with light brown skin, dark brown eyes, and medium length dreadlocks, the man's easy grin disguised the fact that he knew how to handle himself. After being recently transferred from Belmarsh Prison, his name had preceded him, and not only was his reputation thought to be warranted, but he was also liked by the majority of prisoners, and well respected too.

'Cain,' the man said, pushing out his fist.

Tommy huffed out a breath. 'Tommy,' he reluctantly answered, his own fist half-heartedly bumping against Cain's.

'Yeah, I know who you are.'

'How the fuck would you know who I am?' Tommy screwed up his face.

'It doesn't matter how,' Cain winked. 'Let's just say we have a mutual acquaintance. Someone who asked me to check in on you.' He motioned behind him again. 'As much as you might want to, this isn't the time or place for you to get your own back.' Casually strolling away, he looked over his shoulder. 'Revenge is a dish best served cold,' he called out. 'Remember that, son, and you'll go far in life.'

As he stared after Cain's retreating back, Tommy frowned, so many different questions buzzing around his head. For a start, who was their mutual acquaintance, and more importantly, why would he want Cain to check up on him? By the time he'd turned back around, the bastards responsible for Dylan's death were gone, along with the rest of the prisoners.

'Come on, Johnson,' one of the prison guards shouted out.

'Move yourself. We don't have all day waiting for you to get your arse in gear.'

There and then, Tommy wanted to kick himself for the missed opportunity, and as he began making his way back inside, he couldn't help but scowl. Cain was wrong, this wasn't only about revenge, it was as much about asserting himself, a way of proving to those around him that he wasn't some pussy scared of his own shadow.

* * *

Chief Superintendent Saunders stared down at the phone in his hand, a prickle of fear running down the length of his back. The colour had long drained from his face, and slumping back in the chair, he wiped his hand across the cold beads of perspiration that lined his forehead. Underneath his armpits, sweat had also begun to pool and damp patches were beginning to stain his crisp white shirt.

Opening his desk drawer, he tossed the phone inside and chewed absentmindedly on his thumbnail. He had always known that this day would come, only he'd pushed the terrifying reality of what that would actually mean – not only for himself, but also for his career – to the back of his mind, hoping above all else that his relationship with Danny McKay, if you could even call it a relationship, would miraculously disappear into a puff of smoke. A case of out of sight, out of mind.

He got to his feet, walked across his office, unbuttoned his damp shirt then peeled it away from his body. Pulling on a fresh shirt he took his time doing up the buttons. He needed time to think, not that McKay had actually given him much time. Twenty-four measly hours, that was it, and if he didn't jump to McKay's demands then the bastard would be contacting Saunders' superiors, not to mention the newspapers, and every social media platform available to mankind. His mind wandered to the photographs McKay had in his possession, extremely explicit photographs that showed Saunders in all different manners of compromising situations. Insurance McKay had called them, or rather, the means to commit blackmail.

He was starting to sweat again, and cursing under his breath, Saunders rested one hand on the door handle as he began to take a series of deep breaths. 'Think,' he told himself. 'Bloody think.' It was no use, not a single intelligible thought sprang to his mind, at least none that was going to get him off the hook. He'd been caught bang to rights. He was stupid, that was what he was, a stupid, stupid man with little to no self-control. But in his defence, how was he supposed to resist, when those sweet, voluptuous curves, had been begging for him to take them? He blamed his predicament on his time spent working in the vice squad; the girls, or the tarts as they'd often called them, had been more than happy to spread their legs for a copper, some had even boasted about the fact, as though bedding the filth gave them some sort of kudos. And when it came down to it, who was he to refuse them? He hadn't been alone in using the women for sex, they had all done it, all of them, even those who were married. They'd viewed the easy sex as a bonus, a way to round off a busy week. Only, unlike his colleagues, he'd never stopped or seen the error of his ways. Even as he'd climbed the ranks, he hadn't been able to stop seeking out sex workers. He often likened it to an addiction, one that he had absolutely no control over.

His career on the line, Saunders pulled open the door and strolled outside, his demeanour that of a man in control, unlike the sweating, terrified mess he was fast becoming beneath the facade. He gave his secretary a brisk nod then made his way down several short flights of concrete steps, the sound of his shoes as he made his way down to the basement area ringing loud in his ears.

It wasn't entirely unusual for him to pay the evidence room a visit, although it would be fair to say that his visits were few and far between and that he usually had a genuine reason to actually make his way down there. His expression stern, he pushed open the door and waltzed inside, his steely gaze fixed on the sergeant as he caught him taking an unauthorised tea break.

The sergeant jumped to his feet so fast that he almost knocked his chair over. 'I was just...' He wiped the crumbs from the front of his shirt then nodded down at his mug of tea and open packet of digestives. 'Didn't get a lunch break,' he muttered. 'Short staffed.'

Saunders pursed his lips, his scowl more than evident. 'Get this place cleaned up,' he barked out. 'Now.'

The sergeant, whose name Saunders for the life of him couldn't remember, raced from the room, liquid spilling over the rim of his mug as he went, his footsteps loud and hurried as he bolted up the stairs in the direction of the canteen.

Alone, Saunders looked around him. It had been a good while since he'd last been inside the evidence room, and he briefly wondered if the filing system had been upgraded during his absence. He began walking up and down the aisles, searching. Johnson, McKay had said in his phone call. Thomas Johnson to be precise. Finally, he found what he was looking for, and taking down a small box, he turned to look either side of him, his ears pricked for any telltale signs that the sergeant could be on his way back. With trepidation he opened the box, unsure exactly of what he would find inside. Staring down at the bagged contents he almost reeled backwards his heart thundering inside his chest. Every fibre of his being screamed at him that this was wrong, that he was breaking the law. That he wasn't only playing with fire, he was tampering with evidence, and even worse than that, he was about to erase all traces of it.

Gingerly, he took a deep breath and reached inside the box, his fingers stiff as he pulled out the first of the evidence bags, with what looked very much like a six-inch blade nestled inside. The second evidence bag was far worse. Narcotics, and if he had to take a wild, professional guess, he'd bet his life on it that it was cocaine.

Reminding himself that there was no other alternative, Saunders stuffed the package into his pocket; it was a tight squeeze, the oblong shape barely able to fit. Next, he slid the knife down the waistband of his trousers, ensuring that it was covered and couldn't be seen by his colleagues, then replacing the lid upon the empty box he returned it back to the shelf.

By the time the sergeant ambled back into the room Saunders was tapping his foot impatiently. 'You took your time,' he hissed, giving his wristwatch a stern tap.

Flustered, the desk sergeant bowed his head. 'Had to mop up the tea,' he quickly explained jerking his thumb behind him. 'I left a trail of it going up the stairs and what with health and safety...' On seeing Saunders' expression, the sergeant's voice trailed off, and peering around the room, he stood up a little straighter. 'Was there something I could help you with, sir?'

Saunders' eyes hardened. If he hadn't been in such a rush to discard the evidence, he would have enjoyed bringing the sergeant down a peg or two, to read him his rights, and remind him that not only were beverages not permitted in the evidence room but it was also against the policy to take an unofficial tea break. 'No,' he barked out. Forcing a stilted, almost menacing smile across his face, he turned on his heel, left the evidence room and made his way back up the stairs.

Once he was back inside the sanctuary of his office he

returned to his desk and took out his mobile phone, his hands beginning to shake as he scrolled down to his call log then pressed dial. 'It's done,' he said once Danny McKay had answered, his voice so low that for the briefest of moments he'd thought that perhaps McKay hadn't heard him. He cleared his throat, trying desperately to claw back some needed respect. 'The photographs...' he began, hating himself for how weak and submissive his voice sounded. 'You will destroy them?' When he received no reply, he took the device away from his ear and stared down at the screen, goose flesh spreading up the length of his arms as he took note of the fact that McKay had already dismissed him and ended the call, hurtling Saunders into even further despair.

16

Looking over his shoulder in an attempt to check that the coast was clear, Kevin nipped inside the side entrance of The Cross Keys pub. Satisfied that there was no sign of Cameron Johnson or any of the Carters for that matter in the near vicinity, he made his way over to the bar, dug his hand into his pocket and then pulled out a crisp twenty-pound note. He didn't actually believe that Mel would follow through with her threat and inform Tommy's family of what he'd done. She might have been a lot of things, mainly a mouthy bitch, but she wasn't spiteful, or at least she hadn't been in the past. But that was before she'd found out that he'd orchestrated Tommy's arrest. His daughter, on the other hand, was a different kettle of fish altogether. She was so far under Tommy Johnson's spell that he'd put nothing past her, especially when ratting him out would give her some clout amongst her boyfriend's family.

Once his drink had been ordered, Kevin leaned casually against the bar and took a moment to look around him, hoping more than anything that Andy would put in an appearance and pronto. More than ever, he needed an air-tight alibi, and seeing as Andy was as much embroiled in the plan to bring down the Carters and Johnsons as he was, it was also in his best interests that they get their story straight.

Gulping back his drink, Kevin slammed the empty glass on the bar then dug his hand into his pocket again. 'Here,' he called out to the barmaid. 'Has Andy been in today?'

The barmaid pursed her lips as she tried to think. 'Not that I can remember.' She nodded down at the glass. 'Same again?'

Kevin nodded and after watching the barmaid saunter across the bar and pour his drink he turned his gaze to the door. He and Andy were cut from the same cloth, the boozer was more like their second home. Melanie even used to joke that if they installed beds he'd never leave, which in a way was partly true, he wouldn't need to, everything he could possibly ever want would be laid out before him, an endless supply of booze, crumpet by the bucket-load, and then as much gear as he could lay his hands on, providing he had the cash to pay for it, of course. A scowl worked its way across his face. Talking of cash, all thanks to his daughter's tantrum, he was back to square one without a proverbial pot to piss in. A familiar bitterness began to build inside of him, a sensation of both anger and loathing that consumed every fibre of his being. Fuck 'em all, he seethed, his ex-wife and daughter included. As far as he was concerned, the Johnsons and Carters were welcome to the stony-faced, miserable bitches.

The door opened, breaking Kevin's thoughts and as a familiar figure stepped across the threshold he straightened up.

'Oi, Jules,' he called out, using his forefinger to beckon the woman over. 'Come here a minute.'

Julie McCann, Andy's sister, tottered across the pub in a pair of stilettos and an impossibly short skirt. 'Wotcha Kev,' she beamed up at him once she'd reached his side, her voice gravelly as though she'd smoked far too many cigarettes.

Returning the grin, Kevin surreptitiously looked her up and down. She was a bit of alright was Andy's sister, always up for a good time and she had a great pair of knockers on her, certainly not the kind of woman he would kick out of bed in a hurry, not that his efforts of chatting her up had ever got him very far. Time and time again, she'd rebuked him, blaming her reluctance to jump into the sack with him on the basis that he already had a wife. Even after his divorce, she'd refused him, claiming that she didn't want to ruin their so-called friendship. As an afterthought Kevin's gaze darted back to the door, hoping that she was alone and that her bloke, Connor Bannerman, wasn't following on behind. Not that Kevin actually knew what Bannerman looked like seeing as Andy had never introduced them. 'You on your own tonight?' he asked, testing the waters.

Julie nodded. 'I'm looking for my brother, actually. He owes me some dough.'

As he turned to look back at the door Kevin's forehead furrowed. 'He ain't been in today.'

'No, of course he bleeding well hasn't,' Julie retorted, the smile slipping from her face. Unzipping her handbag, she pulled out her mobile phone. 'I'm gonna end up mullering him. He knew I needed that cash; I'm meant to be going out tonight with my mates and was relying on that money,' she whined.

Kevin blew out his cheeks. 'So, you're not out with your fella tonight then?'

Shaking her head Julie chewed on her bottom lip. 'He's busy,' she sighed. 'Got some business to attend to and apparently that's more important than taking me out.' Bringing the device up to her ear her expression hardened. 'Answer the phone, you tosser,' she muttered into the device. As the call rang off, she mumbled a number of expletives, each and every one of them aimed at her brother, before slipping the phone back into her handbag. 'Looks like I got all dolled-up for nothing,' she said, fluffing out her hair. 'I could honestly murder him at times.'

'Not literally, I hope,' Kevin chuckled. 'He is your brother after all.'

Julie gave him a pointed look, her eyebrows raised. 'Listen,' she said one hand on her hip. 'If he turns up, tell him to stop fucking about and to give me a call.'

'Yeah, I will do,' Kevin nodded. And as Julie wandered back across the pub, his gaze once again drifted towards the entrance. Despite owing his sister money it wasn't like Andy not to be in the boozer. He was always in there, so much so that the guvnor often joked he was part of the furniture. Chewing on his bottom lip, a flicker of concern edged its way down Kevin's spine. What if... no, he shook his head, he was being paranoid that was all. Only now that the thought had edged its way into his brain, he was unable to shift it. What if Andy had somehow come across the Bannermans? Or what if they'd come looking for him? Yeah, that was more likely, Andy had warned as much, that it was only a matter of time until they turned up demanding the bank and credit cards that he'd promised them. He snapped his head in Julie's direction, the blood draining from his face. She'd said that her fella had business to attend to, what if that business concerned the cards, and what if the Bannermans were coming for him next?

His Adam's apple bobbed up and down as he gulped. Fear getting the better of him. Well, he wouldn't be hanging around to find out, he knew that much, and snatching up his drink, he drained the contents, ignoring the burn as the whiskey slipped down his throat. Giving Julie one final gander, he hurried across the pub and slipped outside.

So consumed with thoughts of both Andy and the Bannerman brothers, he didn't notice the motor parked several feet away from the pub, neither did he notice the occupant as he jumped out of his car.

In all reality the Bannerman brothers were the least of his problems. The real threat came from the Johnsons and Carters. In particular Reece Carter, who at that precise moment in time was hellbent on making Kevin pay for his devious actions.

* * *

Reece Carter's face was twisted into a snarl, and as he snatched up a claw hammer from the passenger seat, fury rippled through his veins. His family may have been content to sit idly by and do fuck all, but he wasn't. Tommy Jr was his best mate, and that dirty, lowlife bastard Kevin Fox had done him wrong. They even had the proof, well maybe not concrete proof as such but the fact Kevin had been in Tommy's car just minutes before his arrest was all the proof Reece needed. Kevin had been involved and nothing and no one would be able to convince him otherwise.

About to slam the car door closed, he felt a tap on his shoulder. Spinning around his jaw dropped, his gaze automatically flicking back to Kevin as he walked briskly away from the pub, turned the corner and then was gone from his sight.

'Hey, I thought it was you.'

As quickly as he could, Reece composed himself. 'Aimee,' he said, his voice coming out a lot higher than he'd intended. 'What are you doing here?'

Aimee chuckled. 'I live around here.' She leaned back slightly pursing her lips. 'The question should be, what are you doing here?' She turned her head to look at the pub, her eyebrows knotting together. 'Why are you here?' There was an accusing tone to her voice. 'This isn't your local,' she said gesturing behind her towards the pub.

'I erm.' Reece swallowed, all the while covertly dropping the claw hammer back onto the seat out of Aimee's view. 'I...'

'What the fuck, Reece!' Aimee blurted out. 'Did you come here looking for my dad?'

'No.' Visibly swallowing, Reece shoved his hands into his pockets. Of course it was a lie and if truth be told it wasn't the first time he'd come looking for Kevin either, only the sly bastard had been keeping his head down low and until now had managed to stay out of sight. 'I was just going to have a drink that's all.' He nodded towards the pub. 'Since when did that become a crime?'

'Oh my God.' Bringing her hand up to her forehead Aimee's eyes were wide. 'Did my mum phone you?' she demanded. 'She did, didn't she?' Panic was written all over her face and when she spoke, the words tumbled out of her mouth in a rush. 'I know he did something bad,' she cried. 'And I know that what he did is unforgiveable and that he should be punished for it, but he's still my dad. Please, Reece.' She looked up at him, her eyes searching his face. 'I'm begging you not to do this. Don't hurt him.'

Reece narrowed his eyes. 'I was right, wasn't I?' he hissed, triumph settling in his gut, although it was somewhat of a hollow victory, he concluded. 'It was your old man who set Tommy up.'

Aimee took a shuddering breath, tears swimming in her eyes. 'Please, Reece,' she whispered with a shake of her head. 'Please don't.'

It took every inch of Reece's willpower not to shove Aimee away from him and chase after Kevin. 'Was I right?' he growled. 'Was it your dad who left the coke and blade in Tommy's car?'

As her mouth opened and closed in rapid succession, Aimee brought her hands up to her face and sniffed back her tears. 'He's got problems,' she said in her father's defence. 'The booze and sniff have changed him. He tried to attack me, he...' She grappled to find the right words. 'He's deluded up here,' she said, pointing to her forehead. 'He thinks that your family did him wrong, something or other about the post office, that it was all his idea, that he—'

Reece let out a nasty chuckle cutting her off. 'It's not me you should be begging to. What do you think the rest of the family will do to the bastard? Or how about Tommy once he gets out of prison? – which he will do,' he said with confidence. 'Do you really think that he'll let this slip or that he'll clap your old man on the back and tell him no hard feelings?' He moved in closer, his voice hard. 'There's a very different side to your boyfriend,' he said, shaking his head, his eyes cold. 'One that you've never, ever seen. Why do you think that they,' he said, referring to his family, 'keep such a tight rein on him? I'll tell you why, shall I?' he said, tilting his head forward. 'Because he's a dangerous fucker, that's why. He won't give a flying fuck that Kevin's your old man; the minute he gets out of the nick, he's gonna be gunning for him.'

Aimee gasped, her eyes wide with fear. 'You're lying,' she choked out. 'My Tommy's not like that; he's good, he's kind.'

Reece scoffed. 'I thought we'd already established that I'm no liar.' He straightened up and turned his head to look in the direction that Kevin had disappeared, all the while inwardly cursing Aimee for turning up and interrupting his plans to bring the spineless bastard to his knees. Pulling open the car door he climbed behind the wheel and turned the key in the ignition. 'You just wait and see,' he concluded. 'Whether you like it or not your old man is finished.'

* * *

Reece wasn't the only one gunning for Kevin. As Connor Bannerman pulled into the car park of The Cross Keys pub, he was on the verge of erupting. Within hours of Andy's demise, his bird was already on his case bitching about her brother. At some point he'd expected her to wonder where he was, only he hadn't thought it would be so soon, that if anything, it would at least take a few days if not a week or so before she noticed he was on the missing list.

Climbing out of the car, he locked up, then made his way over to the pub. As soon as he stepped inside, Julie was upon him.

'Babe,' she said with that familiar whine in her voice, the same one that was beginning to grate heavily on his nerves. 'I can't find my brother.' She fluttered her eyelashes as she looked up at him, her lips forming into a glossy pout. 'He was meant to give me my dough back that I loaned him and without that money I can't go out tonight.'

Ah and there it was, the crux of the matter. She wasn't particularly worried that Andy hadn't put in an appearance. All she wanted was money from him, as though he was nothing more than her personal cash cow. Well unfortunately for her that would soon be coming to an end. Give it a day or two and he'd be giving her the push. It was time to move on to pastures new and having Julie clamped to his side like a leech wasn't the way to go about it. As it was, he was sick to the back teeth of her. 'How much?' he groaned shoving his hand into his pocket and pulling out his wallet.

Julie swallowed; her eyes fixated on his wallet. 'Hundred nicker.'

Peeling off five twenty-pound notes, Connor pressed the money into her hand, making a mental note of the fact that this was the last penny she would be getting out of him.

'Thanks, babe.' She reached up to kiss him on the lips, her eyes sparkling as she went on to tuck the money inside her handbag. 'Fuck knows what my brother is playing at.' She glanced towards the door. 'No one has seen him. Even Kevin hasn't got a scooby where he is.'

Connor's ears pricked up. 'What did you just say?'

Tearing her gaze away from the door she turned back to look at him. 'I said that even Kevin hasn't seen him today and they're usually joined at the bleedin' hip.'

Connor's heart began to race, one hand involuntarily curling into a fist. 'Where is he?' As much as he tried not to, he was unable to keep the growl from his voice nor keep the anger inside of him from bubbling to the surface.

'I...' Standing on her tiptoes, Julie scanned the pub. 'I don't know.' She frowned. 'He was here just now; I was speaking to him.'

'Where does he live?'

Julie spun around, her eyebrows raised. 'How should I know?' she barked out. 'He's Andy's pal not mine.'

Connor's lips twitched into a smile, one that was so forced he was sure that Julie would be able to see straight through him. Or maybe not; she was so self-absorbed that even on a good day she was barely able to see past her nose. 'I just thought that maybe if you gave me his address I could go and have a word with him, see what he knows.'

Julie grinned, and moving closer, she slung her arm around his neck. 'Aww, babe,' she crowed, her sickly-sweet perfume invading his nostrils. 'Don't worry about it. I'm sure that Andy will turn up sooner or later.'

'Yeah,' Connor nodded. 'Course he will.' Which was a lie seeing as the last time he'd laid his eyes upon Andy he'd been as dead as a dodo.

'Right, I'd best be off.' He gave the pub one last slow glance, as if Kevin, whoever the fuck he was, would miraculously materialise before his eyes. 'If this Kevin does come back, give me a bell and I'll have a word with him.'

Julie giggled. 'Why are you so concerned with Kevin?'

'I'm not,' Connor protested.

'You're not jealous, are you?' she teased, curling a lock of dark hair around her finger and pushing her ample breasts towards him. 'Worried that you've got competition?'

Connor almost laughed in her face. Jealous. Was she feeling alright? He couldn't give two hoots about her, and had only turned up at the pub to see if she suspected that her brother was dead and that his corpse was more than likely buried in a shallow grave right about now or maybe floating in the Thames. 'Nah.' He tapped the tip of her nose. 'Why would I be?'

Still giving him a knowing look, Julie shrugged. 'No reason.' She gave a sigh. 'Nothing has ever happened between me and Kev you know, so there's no need for you to worry. I'm all yours,' she crooned, running her fingers up his arm. 'Although it's not for the want of him trying, mind you. He's always had a bit of a thing for me.'

'Right.' Detangling himself from her arms, Connor nodded and began moving away. 'I'll see you later.' Not that he actually had any intention of seeing her. With a bit of luck she'd end up drinking herself into a stupor and then the only thing he'd have to contend with were her drunken texts that he would promptly delete without even reading. Now more than ever he was itching to get shot of her, and as soon as she'd pointed him in Kevin's direction, he would kick her unceremoniously to the kerb, and not before time either. Right from the start she'd been nothing more than a stopgap, something to ease his boredom and pass the time away. She was easy too and had jumped into bed with him within hours of them meeting. Hardly the type of woman he was planning to take up the aisle or take home to meet his old mum.

'He could be at his ex-wife's house I suppose,' Julie called after him.

Connor came to a halt and as he turned around his left eyebrow was cocked. 'And where does she live?'

Julie bit down on her bottom lip, her forehead furrowing. 'Not far, just around the corner.'

Spreading open his arms Connor stepped closer. 'Door number?'

'Number ten, I think. Corner house. You can't miss it, the gate is hanging off its hinges, and there's a bush to the side of the front door.'

Connor nodded. 'Frequent visitor, is he?'

'I dunno,' Julie shrugged. 'I suppose so. I mean it's where his daughter lives so he's bound to drop by every now and again.'

Connor forced a smile. 'I'll pop around there, see if this ex-wife of his is any the wiser to his whereabouts.'

Without giving Julie the chance to answer, he walked from the pub and jumped back into his car. He was close to finding the bastard, so close that he could feel it in his gut. Fifty grand may have meant fuck all to him and his brothers when you considered their wealth, but at the end of the day it was the principle of the matter that irked. Kevin owed them; they weren't a charity, nor did they give out large quantities of cocaine to all and sundry for free. He likened them to being businessmen, their business being that of supplying narcotics to those in need, a business that required payment up front for the goods they provided.

He let out a groan and rubbed the palm of his hand over his face, his fingers seeking out the pale pink scar on his forehead, something he did whenever he was feeling stressed, the smooth skin bringing him some sort of comfort. Was it any wonder that Nathan and Lee were so pissed with him? All thanks to the proposition Andy had presented to him, he'd thrown caution to the wind, bypassing the need for payment up front fully believing the credit cards and bank cards Kevin would acquire for them would more than double their money. He should have known from the off that it wouldn't be that easy, that there would be a catch. What he hadn't envisaged, however, was for Kevin and Andy to mug them off. No, he'd stupidly believed that their surname alone would be enough to guarantee payment, that only a fool would try to have them over.

Starting the ignition, he pushed his foot down on the accelerator and sped out of the car park, the tyres kicking up dust and rubble in his wake. Within a matter of minutes, he'd found the house where Kevin's ex-wife and daughter lived, and switching off the ignition, he sat for a few moments surveying the property, his hands gripping onto the steering wheel so hard that his knuckles had turned white. A few moments later he jumped out of the car, strolled casually down the pathway and banged his fist on the front door, all the while keeping his gaze firmly fixed on the window for any telltale signs of the net curtains twitching, indicating that someone was home.

When he received no reply he made his way back to the car, the anger inside of him increasing. Once they had finally located Kevin, his brother Lee wouldn't get a look in. He was personally going to tear the thieving bastard to shreds, rip him limb from limb, if for no other reason than to pull back some much-needed respect from his brothers. He'd been made to feel humiliated, and now that Andy's life had been extinguished, that only left Kevin Fox to deal with.

After giving the house one final hard stare, he turned the key in the ignition, pulled away from the kerb, and headed in the direction of the A13, itching to get back on home turf and away from the stench that was East London. He'd never liked the area, it was a shithole, always had been. Was it any wonder his cousin Harry, or Fletch as he was more commonly known, lived there? Out of habit his hand inched upwards, his fingertips caressing the scar again. He should have steered clear of Julie the very moment she told him where she lived. Should have known she would bring him nothing but trouble. He thought too much with his dick, or at least this was what his brother Nathan told him, and maybe he was right in this instance. Look at the trouble chasing after a bit of skirt had caused him – skirt that he didn't even want in the long term, might he add.

By the time he was nearing South London, Connor was so enraged that he could practically taste his anger. As he pulled up outside the lock-up, he jumped out of his car ready to tear into someone, preferably Lee should he open that big trap of his and start giving him crap or spouting any snide comments.

'Where the fuck have you been?' his brother Nathan barked out.

'Out,' Connor snapped.

'No shit,' Nathan retorted. 'Cheers for leaving us to do the donkey work.'

'Yeah,' Lee grinned waggling his eyebrows. 'You missed out on all the fun.'

Connor narrowed his eyes, his gaze drifting down to the floor beneath his feet. There was a lot more blood than he originally remembered, much more.

'Turns out he wasn't dead after all,' Lee chuckled.

Connor's head snapped upwards. 'What do you mean he wasn't dead? I saw him with my own two eyes.' He nodded down at the floor where he'd last seen Andy's body laid out. 'He'd kicked the bucket.'

Lee shrugged. And it was only then that Connor noticed the blood that speckled his brother's face and arms. 'What the fuck did you do?' he yelled.

His grin intensifying, Lee slung his arm around his younger brother's shoulders. 'Do you mean before or after I extracted valuable information out of him?'

Opening his mouth to answer, Connor quickly closed it again and shook his head, barely able to take in what he was being told. How was it possible that Andy had still been alive? He hadn't been breathing, or at least that's what he'd thought.

'By all accounts, our pal Kevin frequents a boozer called The Cross Keys. And according to that pile of shit Andy, he's a regular.'

Connor could only gape at Lee in horror, almost afraid of what he was going to say next. 'And? What else?'

'That's it,' Nathan interjected. 'It's a starting point.'

Rubbing at his temples, Connor shook his head again. He already knew the name of the pub Kevin frequented. Not only that, but he also knew where his ex-wife and kid lived too, and he hadn't had to torture anyone for the privilege. 'And you didn't think to ask for a description?' he hissed. 'Or where exactly he worked?'

Lee's forehead furrowed. 'Nah.' He gave a grin revealing a row of even, white teeth. 'I was having too much fun by that point.' He mimicked slicing into something. 'If you get my drift.'

'Yeah, I get it alright,' Connor grumbled. Shrugging Lee's arm away from him he looked down at the blood staining the floor. From the look of things Lee had had more than a bit of fun if the amount of claret was anything to go by. Inwardly he groaned. How the fuck in God's name had this become his life?

17

It wasn't often that Jonny could say he was impressed but this was one of those times. Richard Lewis was nothing short of a genius. Not only had he managed to wipe the floor with the prosecution, but even Jonny himself had started to believe Richard's spiel, he was that good.

According to Richard's defence, the cocaine and weapon believed to be found in Tommy Jr's car had never existed. The entire debacle was nothing more than an elaborate plot schemed up by corrupt officers to persecute a young man, and an innocent young man at that, let's not forget. And for no other reason than because his face didn't fit, that he was young and wealthy and that he drove a car the officers could only dream of owning on their salaries, not forgetting the large amount of cash Tommy Jr had had on him at the time, fuelling the fire of their obvious jealousy.

Within a matter of minutes, the case against Tommy Jr had crumbled and the prosecution team and police officers were left with egg on their faces, and steam practically billowing from their ears and nostrils.

Outside the court Jonny was all smiles as he waited alongside the rest of the family for Tommy Jr to be released. Although he was under no illusion that if it hadn't been for Danny McKay then Tommy Jr would never have gained an early release from prison. Without his intervention the case would have ended up going to trial and seeing as the evidence, innocent or not, had been stacked against him he didn't think much of Tommy Jr's chances. It was almost inevitable that he would have been facing a guilty verdict and then a subsequent lengthy sentence.

'Here he comes,' Reece shouted, barely able to contain his excitement.

All heads turned in time to witness Tommy Jr walk out of court, a wide smile plastered across his face.

He looked more grown up, Jonny decided. As though his short time spent incarcerated had somehow turned him from a boy into a man.

A cheer went up, and as the family crowded around, Jonny couldn't help but grin. 'Are you alright, boy?' Jonny asked as he pulled his great-nephew into his embrace.

Tommy nodded.

'I told you that we'd find a way to get you out,' he beamed. 'And I meant every fucking word.'

Tommy nodded again. 'I want to have a chat with you in private,' he said quietly in Jonny's ear. 'I'll pop into the office later on after I've spent a bit of time with my mum and dad, and Aimee.'

'Are you okay?' Jonny asked, concerned. Leaning back slightly, he studied Tommy Jr's face. 'You've got nothing to worry about, you know that don't you?' he said, jerking his thumb behind him at the court. 'The charges were quashed.'

'Nah, it's nothing like that.' Tommy let out a long breath and wiped the palm of his hand over his cropped hair. 'I'm happy to be out, over the fucking moon in fact.' He gave a wink. 'We'll talk later. Okay?'

'Yeah.' Jonny flashed a small smile, a combination of both intrigue and worry washing over him. 'I'll be in the office whenever you're ready.'

* * *

Despite his reputation, Aimee had never been afraid of Tommy Jr; he'd not given her any reason to be. In the time she had known him he'd only ever been gentle with her, the perfect boyfriend in every way imaginable, so much so that her friends often swooned over their relationship, telling her that she was so lucky and that they would give their right arms to trade places with her. And they were right to feel envious. Her and Tommy got along so well that it was sickening. They never argued, and what's more, they even shared the same sense of humour and were always laughing together.

Sitting beside him in his parents' car, their hands entwined, Aimee bit down on her bottom lip, her gaze fixed on the passing traffic as they made their way towards the area where Tommy lived. His parents were taking them out for a meal to celebrate his release from prison, something quiet they'd said, knowing that Tommy hadn't wanted his family to make a big fuss.

'Are you alright, babe?' Tommy asked quietly in her ear.

Aimee turned her head, forcing a smile. He looked so sincere that she wanted to cry, and as he went on to stroke the curve of her expanding tummy, she blinked her tears away. 'Of course I am,' she answered giving his hand a reassuring squeeze.

Tommy grinned, and as he went back to speaking to his parents, she resumed her position, her gaze fixed on the side window, the cars that whizzed by becoming nothing more than a distant blur. Only deep down inside, she wasn't okay. As much as she didn't want them to, Reece's words reverberated inside her head. 'He's a dangerous fucker. He won't give a flying fuck that Kevin's your old man; the minute he gets out of the nick, he's gonna be gunning for him.' She gave a shudder. No matter how badly her dad had treated her, or the cruel words he'd said, she didn't want to see him harmed, even after the despicable things he'd done to Tommy. It had been no lie when she'd told Reece that her dad was messed up, that he had problems, because he did. He was an addict, maybe an alcoholic too, or at least a functioning one, seeing as for the first time in his life he'd managed to hold down a job. And then there was the fact that she knew her dad had been responsible for planting the coke and knife in Tommy's car. And as much as Reece might have suspected her dad's involvement, he had no actual proof, unlike her. Her dad had confessed everything, and as much as the words had been said in anger, she knew he'd been telling the truth. He despised Tommy and his family, so much that he'd deliberately set out to destroy them. She inwardly shuddered. It was a big secret to keep, a burden that weighed heavily on her conscience.

At the restaurant Aimee remained tense, and as much as the meal was delicious, Aimee found that she had no real appetite. She prodded the food around her plate, blaming her reluctance to eat on morning sickness although in truth she hadn't felt nauseous for weeks. That gained her a sympathetic smile from Tommy's mum.

'I remember it well,' she said patting her son's arm. 'But it will all be worth it when you hold that baby in your arms.'

Aimee nodded, her cheeks flushing red at the blatant lie. As happy as she was to see Tommy home, she was scared and not just a little bit scared, but really scared. Throughout the meal she couldn't help but watch him from out of the corner of her eye.

Was he really as dangerous as Reece had indicated? Did he really have another side to him?

From what she could tell, her Tommy hadn't changed, he was still as attentive as ever, still laughed and joked with his parents, still clutched hold of her hand, his thumb rubbing gentle circles across her palm. Only everything had changed, he'd changed, and she was starting to wonder if she even knew him or at least knew the real him.

It was a relief when Cameron asked for the bill. All she wanted to do was go home, to get away from them, even Tommy. She needed time to think the situation through. Oh, she still loved him, of course she did, and she had a feeling that she always would. He was her first love so how could she not love him? Not only that, but she was having his baby, and she loved their baby with all of her heart.

She was so confused. So many conflicting emotions running through her mind. Maybe the pregnancy hormones were to blame, or maybe it was because her eyes were now fully open. Perhaps her dad had been right all along. No, she pushed that thought away – her dad wasn't right, he was wrong, he had to be.

By the time Tommy's parents had pulled onto their driveway so that Tommy could collect his own car and drive her home, Aimee was beside herself. The thought of spending time alone with him, just the two of them together, brought her nothing but sheer terror. What if she slipped up? What if she implicated her dad's involvement? What if Tommy then took it upon himself to hunt him down and seek retribution?

As much as she knew she was being irrational, the fear was very real. Perhaps she should say nothing at all; at least then she wouldn't be able to say anything incriminating.

Five minutes later Tommy briefly took his eyes off the road to look at her. 'Are you okay?' he asked. 'You've been really quiet.'

'I'm fine.'

Tommy sighed then rubbing his hand over the back of his neck he squirmed in his seat. 'I didn't do it; you know that don't you? I mean the gear and the blade. I didn't put it in my car. I'm not a dealer.' He scrunched up his face. 'I wouldn't touch that shit.'

Aimee turned her head to look at him and gave a soft smile. 'I know. I never doubted you, not for one single moment.'

Tommy blew out his cheeks. With one hand on the steering wheel, his free hand reached out for hers again.

It was on the tip of Aimee's tongue to ask him if what Reece had told her was true. Perhaps Reece had only said those things in anger, and he had been angry at the time, very much so. Instead, she said nothing, too afraid of his answer, not that she thought he would actually tell her the truth. It was only natural that he would lie and deny that he was a violent thug. As it was, during their time together, she'd seen him with more than his fair share of injuries, a bruised cheekbone, split lip, grazed knuckles to the point that she would roll her eyes whenever he turned up with a new mark on him, she'd even laughed it off. But she wasn't laughing now. There was a ring of truth to what Reece had told her, no smoke without fire as they say. And then there were the rumours that Tommy's family were involved in armed robberies. She'd never believed them, hadn't wanted to, and yet the more she thought about it the more everything made sense. At least that was something her dad had been right about. It wasn't possible that a scrapyard could pay for their wealth, the houses, the cars, or their bank balances.

The rest of the journey was spent in silence, an uncomfortable, heavy silence that filled the car making both her head and her heart ache. She had a big decision to make. Could she really turn a blind eye? Did she even want to? And, more importantly, could she spend her life with a man who was not only supposedly violent but also involved in illegal activities?

* * *

After waiting for Aimee to open her front door, turn and give him a wave, then close the door behind her, Tommy Jr sat in his car for a few moments watching the house. She'd been quiet today, a little too quiet for his liking. He got that maybe she was feeling overwhelmed; it had been a hard day after all, for all of them. The court hearing could so very easily have gone tits up, and instead of sitting in a swanky restaurant with his parents and Aimee, eating food fit for a king, he could have been banged up in his cell, tucking into what could only be described as inedible slop with no hope of release.

Shaking his head, he changed gears, flicked the indicator, pulled away from the kerb and then drove in the direction of Barking. After a quick glance at the time, he put his foot down on the accelerator, hoping that his uncle Jonny would still be at the scrapyard and even more than that, he hoped he would be alone.

Ten minutes later he brought the car to a halt, switched off the ignition, and stepped outside the car. It was hard to believe that he could have missed spending time at the yard, especially when he'd always grumbled about it in the past when it came to getting up for work, and yet he had missed it. He'd spent the majority of his life there and had a lot of fond memories of the place.

Strolling across the yard, his strides were confident, assured, and pushing open the door he stepped across the threshold.

From behind the desk Jonny looked up, flashing a wide smile. 'I was about to give up on you,' he chuckled giving his watch a quick glance. 'Thought you were probably too busy enjoying your first night of freedom.'

Tommy returned the smile, and walking inside, he took a seat on the arm of the sofa and took a moment to look around him. Nothing had changed, the place even smelled the same; a slight muskiness that mingled with the familiar scent of his great-uncle's expensive aftershave.

'You said you wanted a word.' Jonny cocked his eyebrow, his head ever so slightly tilted in Tommy's direction.

'Yeah,' Tommy nodded, his voice coming across as strong. 'I wanted to talk about Kevin.'

Jonny's eyebrow rose even further, and sitting up straighter he steepled his fingers. 'Go on. What about him?'

The smile fell from Tommy's face. 'No one touches him,' he declared. 'I want your word on that.' He stabbed his finger towards the door. 'I need you to tell them, all of them,' he said, referring to the rest of their family, 'not to go after him.'

Jonny opened his mouth to protest, and before he could speak, Tommy lifted his hand in the air.

'I mean it,' he hissed, the steely glint in his eyes becoming even more prominent. 'No one lays a finger on him. No one except for me.'

18

As much as Jonny wanted to say that he was surprised, he wasn't, not really. It made sense that Tommy Jr would want revenge and that he would personally want to take matters into his own hands. At the end of the day, Kevin Fox had done him wrong, and as much as the family may have been in uproar, they hadn't been the ones imprisoned, nor had they been forced to witness the horrific murder of a friend.

'Okay,' Jonny nodded. 'If that's how you want to play it.'

'It is,' Tommy Jr reiterated locking eyes with his uncle. 'And as for the Royal Mail job, it's still gonna go ahead.'

Jonny narrowed his eyes and sinking back in the chair he studied his great-nephew. There was something different about him, he decided. Something he couldn't quite put his finger on. He opened his mouth to answer then paused for a moment and absentmindedly rubbed his hand over his chin. 'Fuck me, Tommy Jr, you've only just been released,' he said shaking his head. 'If something goes wrong and we're caught you'll end up back inside, with no hope of getting out.'

'And this time I'll deserve it,' Tommy protested. 'If I end up back inside, I'll have no one to blame but myself. I'll happily put my head down and do the time.'

Unsure, Jonny ran his tongue over his teeth. 'Maybe wait for the dust to settle first...'

'No.' Getting to his feet Tommy walked across the office and placed his hands on the desk, frustration beginning to get the better of him as he leaned forward. 'You're not listening to me. We are doing this. No waiting or pussy footing around. We strike while the iron is hot.'

Thinking it over, Jonny shrugged. 'I doubt anyone else will agree to it, not this soon. The filth were crawling all over you, they even tore apart your mum and dad's gaff looking for evidence.'

'Then make them agree to it,' Tommy implored his uncle. 'You're the head of the family now. You run this place, you're in charge. They do what you say, not the other way around.'

Jonny lifted his eyebrows. There was some truth to Tommy Jr's words. He was in charge and had been ever since his eldest brother Jimmy had retired and moved to Spain. 'Look, I get that you're pissed off but that's to be expected. What's with the rush, eh? Give it a couple of months or so and then maybe we'll consider it.'

'What do you think?' Tommy flung back at him. 'That bastard Kevin fitted me up.'

'Yeah, I get that,' Jonny nodded. 'Believe me, I do.'

Tommy's lips curled into a snarl. 'So, you'll agree to it then?'

Giving a hesitant nod, Jonny slumped back in the chair. 'I'll think about it, okay? I can't be any fairer than that.'

'No!' Tommy roared, thumping his fist on the desk, upsetting the paperwork and several Biro pens. 'Which part of this don't you understand? I'm not fucking about here. I've had near on two weeks with fuck all to do but think about this shit.' He tapped his temple. 'With or without you on board, that job is going ahead even if that means I have to carry it out alone.'

For a few moments Jonny was quiet, his forehead furrowed. 'Is there any point in me trying to talk you out of this?' he finally asked.

Tommy shook his head. 'No, so if I were you, I'd save your breath.'

'Yeah, I thought as much,' Jonny sighed, with a slight smile. 'You've got too much of me inside you, that's your trouble. I was a stubborn bugger at your age an' all, thought I was invincible.'

'Is that right?' Tommy snarled. 'And there was me thinking I took after my grandad, Tommy Snr.'

The smile slid from Jonny's face. 'True,' he sighed. 'You're like the spit out of your grandad's mouth.'

Straightening up, Tommy crossed his arms over his chest. 'Are you with me then or not?'

'Do I have any other choice?' Jonny groaned.

'No. Not really,' Tommy answered allowing himself a small smile.

'Right, well in that case it looks like we've got a job to plan out, doesn't it?'

Elation spread through Tommy's veins. He hadn't expected it to be easy when it came to convincing Jonny and his instincts had been right. Jonny had put up a fight, one that Tommy had been willing to go to battle with him over. And his threat hadn't been idle, he'd been more than prepared to do the job alone if that's what it took, and he would have done too, he'd have moved heaven and earth if he'd had to, if it meant seeing his revenge through to the bitter end.

'Oh.' As Tommy made for the door he abruptly spun around. 'One more thing.'

Jonny leaned back in his chair again; his expression that of a man who was stunned, as though he couldn't quite believe what he'd just been coerced into. 'What?'

'The Bannerman brothers. You were right; Kevin wouldn't have been able to stump up the cash to buy the gear, the ponce doesn't even like to buy his own drinks, let alone fork out fifty odd grand just to fuck me over.' His eyes hardened. 'Set up a meeting with them. As far as I'm aware, those bastards owe me an' all.'

* * *

Melanie took one look at her daughter's face and frowned. 'What's wrong?' she asked closing the magazine she'd been reading and placing it on the arm of the chair.

Aimee shrugged. 'Nothing,' she answered shrugging off her jacket, her lips downturned.

Melanie's frown deepened. 'You and Tommy haven't had a falling out, have you?'

'No of course not.' Aimee averted her eyes and slumping onto the sofa she tucked her legs underneath her. 'It's just...' She swallowed then huffed out a breath. 'What if he isn't the person I thought he is?'

'Where is this coming from?' Sitting forward in the chair Melanie clasped hold of her daughter's hand. 'Are you talking about the court case, because he was cleared of any wrongdoing, darling. And if anyone was in the wrong then it was your dad; he was the one who singlehandedly caused this entire mess.'

'I know all of that.'

'Then I don't understand.'

'What if?' Aimee paused trying to find the right words. 'What if there's another side to him, one that I've never seen before?'

Melanie was thoughtful. 'Do you love him?'

'Of course I do.'

'Then I really can't see the problem. He treats you well, I'd even go as far as to say that he worships the ground you walk on.'

'He does,' Aimee chuckled. She leaned back against the sofa and gave her mother a soft smile. 'You've changed your tune; you couldn't stand him not so long ago. You used to say that he wasn't good enough for me.'

Waving her hand dismissively, Melanie pursed her lips. 'I've never disliked him. I was just worried, that was all. I didn't want you to make the same mistakes that I had.'

'And do you think I have?' Aimee asked. 'Made the same mistakes as you, I mean.'

Thinking the question over Melanie gently brushed a lock of loose blonde hair away from her daughter's face. 'No, darling, I don't. He's nothing like your dad.'

It was the exact answer Aimee had been expecting. She already knew that Tommy and her dad were poles apart. That Tommy would never hurt her like her dad had, at least not intentionally anyway. She took a deep breath, and as her mum pulled her towards her, she nestled in closer. What had she been thinking? She loved Tommy and he loved her. What else could they possibly ever need?

As Melanie got up to make them both a cup of tea, Aimee sucked in her bottom lip. If she and Tommy truly had a future together then she had to come clean, had to tell him the truth, starting with what her dad had done. It was too big a secret to keep to herself and one way or another her reluctance to spill the beans would end up tearing them apart or at the very least cause resentment if he was to find out that she'd known about her dad's involvement and hadn't told him. It was bound to.

Her mind made up, Aimee took the mug her mother handed to her and blew on the steaming, hot tea. Yes, she decided. She would tell Tommy everything. All she could hope and pray was that he wouldn't be so angry that he'd hunt her father down and cause him harm. Yet another thing she didn't want on her conscience.

* * *

Later that evening Tommy Jr drove into The Cross Keys car park, switched off the ignition, and leaned back in his seat.

Beside him in the passenger seat Reece frowned. 'Are we getting out or not?' he asked, nodding towards the pub.

'Yeah, in a bit,' Tommy answered. 'I just need a few minutes to think.'

'About what?'

Tommy ignored the question, and as he chewed on his thumbnail his gaze was firmly fixed on the pub ahead of them.

Reece blew out his cheeks. 'What are we waiting for? Because let me tell you now I was ready to smash that bastard's nut in with a claw hammer. I would have done too if Aimee hadn't turned up and ruined everything. The no-good ponce deserves a hammering after the stunt he pulled.'

The nerve at the side of Tommy's eye twitched. 'What did you just fucking say about Aimee?' he growled snapping his head around.

The anger in Tommy's voice was enough to tell Reece that he wasn't happy. Holding up his hands he moved as far away from him as he possibly could, which considering they were in a car wasn't far enough, especially when he knew for a fact his cousin had a wicked temper on him and that he'd think nothing of smashing him in the face regardless of the fact that they shared the same blood. 'She didn't see anything, honest. Although she did guess why I was there,' he said lowering his voice a fraction. 'She pulled me up on it.'

Tommy clenched his jaw. No wonder Aimee had been so quiet when he'd seen her earlier. 'Cheers for that, Reece,' he snarled punching his cousin on the arm. 'Thanks a fucking lot.'

'Oi.' Rubbing at his arm Reece screwed up his face. 'Leave it out, Tommy. If anything, I was looking out for you which is a lot more than anyone else did.'

'Well don't,' Tommy snapped. Shoving open the car door he climbed out, his face set like thunder. 'In future don't do anything unless I ask you to. And do not go after Kevin. I'm being deadly serious,' he warned. 'Because if I find out you've so much as laid a finger on him then I swear before God I'll swing for you myself and believe me, I'm gonna go to town on you. Is that understood?'

'Yeah alright,' Reece grumbled. 'Fuck me, you've been proper aggy since coming out of the nick. What's with you? I thought you'd be happy now that you're out of that shithole, that you're a free man.'

Tommy sighed. He was happy or at least as happy as could be. No matter how much he tried not to think about it, he was still plagued by the memory of Dylan's death, and on a nightly basis he would have nightmares. The sound of Dylan's harrowing screams haunted him, and the image of his face melting down to nothing but muscle and bone would make him sit bolt upright in bed, sweat pouring down his face and his heart hammering inside his chest. If that wasn't bad enough the putrid scent of burning skin and flesh combined with the unmistakable stench of blood that had gushed from Dylan's body hung over him as though it were ingrained inside his nostrils, the smell so rancid that it took everything inside of him not to press his fist to his lips in an attempt to stop himself from physically gagging.

'Why are you even defending the cunt?' Reece continued, oblivious to the turmoil that ran through Tommy's mind. 'It's because of him you were banged up in the first place.'

'Because I said so, alright.' Tommy blew out his cheeks, his earlier anger quickly dissipating as they began to make their way towards the pub. 'Look.' He motioned towards Reece's arm. 'I'm sorry. I didn't mean to lash out. I've got a lot on my mind; I saw some things inside and...' He swallowed then looked away, unable to utter the words out loud, least of all to Reece. As close as they were he didn't want his cousin's pity, nor did he want him to start asking too many questions. It had been hard enough telling his dad and great-uncle Jonny that he'd watched a friend die, let alone the rest of the family. 'I know you were looking out for me, and I shouldn't have swung for you, we're best mates, ain't we?' he said nudging his elbow into Reece's side.

Reece shrugged. 'I was only doing what you would have done if it had been me.'

'Yeah, I know.'

Pulling open the door to the pub just minutes before the bell for last orders rang out, Tommy stepped inside, his hard gaze settling on a familiar figure sitting at the bar.

'Tommy,' Reece hissed as he yanked on his cousin's arm. 'Just don't go doing anything stupid, not here in the boozer. If you whack him the Old Bill will be called. You could end up back behind bars.' He glanced around him taking note of how many people were still in the pub. 'You'd be better off getting him outside, take him somewhere secluded and then steam into him.'

Tommy gave a light laugh although there was no humour behind it. 'I'm not going to lamp him one,' he said making his way forward. 'All I'm planning to do is have a nice friendly chat with my bird's dad.'

Reaching the bar Tommy leaned casually against the bar top. 'You alright, Kev?'

Kevin's shoulders tensed, and turning his head, the colour drained from his face. 'Tommy,' he said with a measure of caution, his startled gaze flicking between Tommy and Reece. 'How...?' He swallowed deeply as though trying to compose himself. 'When did you get out?'

'Today. This afternoon to be precise,' Tommy answered. 'All charges against me dropped. I thought that Aimee would have told you the good news.' He gave a calculated smile then straightening up turned to face the bar. Making a show of excluding Kevin as he ordered a drink for both himself and Reece, he pocketed his change then resumed his position once again.

Kevin nodded and swallowing deeply he reached out for his pint glass. Finding it empty he placed it back on the bar and eyed up the drinks the barmaid was pouring for Tommy and Reece. 'I'm glad. I mean you should never have been sent down in the first place.'

Tommy's face hardened. 'Too fucking right I shouldn't have,' he snarled. 'I did fuck all wrong.'

'Nah, of course you didn't.' Kevin nodded around the pub. 'That's exactly what I told this lot in here. It was bang out of order if you ask me. Fucking ludicrous. And nothing more than an excuse for the Old Bill to throw their weight around. As if someone like you would need to peddle drugs, you earn a decent enough wage working for your family.'

Grinding his teeth together, Tommy's fists inadvertently clenched. 'Talking of being nicked,' he said forcing the words to come out a lot more jovial than he intended. 'What the fuck happened to you?'

The smile slid from Kevin's face and wiping away a layer of

perspiration from his top lip he swallowed again before answering. 'What do you mean?'

Tommy laughed. 'You know exactly what I mean. When I was being nicked where the fuck were you, because from what I remember you were nowhere to be seen?'

'I...' Kevin averted his gaze. 'I...' he began again.

'You what?' Tommy goaded. 'Decided to just let me take the fall for something I was innocent of?'

'No,' Kevin vehemently shook his head. 'It wasn't like that.'

'Wasn't it?' Tommy lifted his eyebrows. 'You could have fooled me.' He gave Kevin a cold stare. 'So, come on, I'm all ears. What *was* it like?'

'Well.' Kevin cleared his throat. 'I went for a piss didn't I and when I came back out you'd already been nicked.'

'Really?' Tommy narrowed his eyes. 'Must have been some fucking piss then because you were gone for more than twenty minutes.'

'What *is* this, eh?' Feeling a moment of bravado, Kevin puffed out his chest. 'Fuck me, I would have been quicker if I'd known you were timing me.' He shook his head. 'Anyway, that's all in the past. You're out now, it's time to move on, to look forward to the future. Give it a few more months and you'll be a dad up to your eyeballs in shitty nappies.'

At the mention of his unborn child, Tommy's lips curled into a snarl. If found guilty then Kevin would have also robbed him of the opportunity of witnessing his baby's birth. 'The Royal Mail robbery,' he said changing the subject in an attempt to keep his temper from erupting. 'It's on.'

Kevin's face lit up, and, as he glanced between Tommy and Reece again, he rubbed his hands together. 'Now you're talking. When is it going down?'

Uncurling his hands to stop himself from smashing his fist

into Kevin's face, Tommy shrugged. 'You'll find out soon enough.' He drained the remainder of his lager and placed the empty glass on the bar then jerked his head towards the door indicating to Reece that it was time to leave.

'And how much will I get?' Kevin called out to Tommy's retreating back.

Tommy ignored the question and pushing open the door he stepped out of the pub.

'We ain't really gonna give that ponce a cut of the robbery, are we?' Reece asked.

Poking his finger against Reece's temple, Tommy Jr gave a nasty grin. 'What do you fucking think?'

19

The next morning Aimee made her way into the scrapyard. She could just as easily have called Tommy Jr and told him to pop by her house but instead she wanted to surprise him. She'd even brought him some breakfast from the café on her way. Two bacon rolls and a large cup of tea. If anything, she was feeling a little bit guilty. The previous evening she'd pretty much given him and his parents the cold shoulder, more concerned with getting away from them than celebrating Tommy's release from prison.

Spotting Tommy's car on the forecourt she smiled as she neared the portable cabin that the family used as an office.

'Hey.' Stepping out of the office Tommy bounded down the steps and walked towards her. 'What are you doing here?'

Aimee could barely contain her giggle. He looked so handsome that she was practically weak at the knees. 'I came to surprise you.' She handed over the paper bag containing the bacon rolls and watched as his eyes lit up.

'Cheers, babe.' As Tommy peered inside the bag, the scent of bacon assaulted his nostrils, and his mouth watered. 'I was just telling Reece that I'm so hungry I could eat a scabby horse,' he laughed. Taking out one of the rolls he surveyed it for a moment then took a large bite. While chewing he swiped the crumbs away from the corner of his lips and gave a contended groan. 'You definitely know the way to a man's heart,' he beamed.

'I got you this as well.' Passing across the polystyrene cup she smiled. 'I put three sugars in it too before you ask, just the way you like it.'

Tommy took a sip. 'You're a diamond,' he winked.

Aimee's heart swelled. This was the Tommy she knew and loved. Cheeky, with just a hint of cockiness about him, but not so much that he came across as arrogant. 'I just wanted to have a little chat,' she said as he continued eating. 'To apologise for yesterday. I'm sorry if I seemed a bit off or came across as rude.'

As he watched her shift her weight from one foot to the other a frown creased Tommy's forehead. 'There's nothing to apologise for. It was a big day, for all of us,' he said jerking his thumb towards the office. 'The case could have gone either way, and if it wasn't for Danny's brief I'd still more than likely be banged up.' He gave a sheepish grin. 'I actually thought the geezer was a pile of shit at first, and that the family had only hired him as some kind of wind up or sick joke, or at least I had until we got into court. He absolutely wiped the floor with them. Did you see the Old Bills' faces?' he laughed. 'They were raging. At one point I thought they were going to haul me over the dock and start laying into me.'

'It wasn't that,' Aimee interrupted, her gaze drifting towards Reece as he stood leaning against the door of the office watching them. 'I mean don't get me wrong it was nerve-wracking, I felt sick to my stomach the entire time we were in court. But that wasn't the reason why I was so quiet.'

'Okay,' Tommy nodded, and placing the polystyrene cup on

the floor, he returned the bacon roll to the paper bag in order to give her his full attention. 'So what's going on then, babe?'

Aimee swallowed, nerves getting the better of her. 'It's my dad,' she blurted out before she had the chance to change her mind and keep schtum.

'What about him?' Tommy's voice was strained, the muscles across his shoulder blades becoming noticeably rigid.

'He...' She took a deep breath and shook her head not wanting to say the words out loud.

'Aimee,' Tommy growled. 'If you've got something to say then spit it out. What about your dad?'

Giving a helpless shrug, fear struck at Aimee's heart. What if she'd read the situation wrong? What if Tommy's carefree attitude was nothing more than an act? Or what if the next words to come out of her mouth were enough to drive him over the edge and make him see red? Her heart in her mouth, she dug her fingernails into the palm of her hand wishing that she'd said nothing at all, only it was far too late for her to start backtracking, she'd already piqued his interest and if she knew him half as well as she thought she did then there was no way in hell that he would let it drop now, or at least not until she'd told him what was on her mind.

'Come on, babe,' Tommy coaxed. 'Since when did me and you keep secrets from one another, eh?'

'It was him,' Aimee blurted out. 'My dad was the one who set you up. He left the coke and knife in your car.' Reaching out, she clutched hold of Tommy's hand and gave it a tight squeeze, her eyes beseeching. 'Please don't hurt him,' she begged. 'Promise me, Tommy. I know that he's done wrong, and as much as I might not like him at times, or approve of the way he behaves, he's still my dad.'

Tommy was so taken aback that he pulled his hand free and

took a step backwards. 'How...?' Lost for words he rubbed at the nape of his neck. 'How do you know this?' He snapped his head around to look at his cousin, glaring at him. 'Who told you that your dad was involved? Was it Reece?'

'No.' Aimee shook her head. 'My dad did, he admitted everything to me. We were arguing and it just slipped out. I don't think he even meant to tell me; he was just so angry at the time that he couldn't help himself. Tommy,' she pleaded a second time. 'Promise me that you won't go after him, that you're not going to hurt him. He's not well. Up here I mean,' she said tapping her temple. 'He does things without thinking. If you want to blame anyone or anything then blame the drink and drugs. He probably didn't even realise how serious the situation would turn out to be, or that you'd be arrested and sent to prison. He needs help.'

Tommy narrowed his eyes. 'What the fuck are you talking about?' he hissed. 'He planted half a kilo of coke in my motor, I was hardly going to be let off with just a slap on the wrist, was I? Your old man knew exactly what he was doing, he knew that I'd be sent down, he was banking on it, why else do you think he asked to meet with me? From start to finish the entire thing was a set-up.'

Aimee's face fell, and as a shiver of fear ran down the length of her spine, she clutched hold of his hand again. 'Please, Tommy, I'm pleading with you, don't hurt him. I'll even get down on my hands and knees and beg if I have to, if that's what it takes. He's my dad.'

Tommy sighed. 'Leave it out, Aimz'. What do you take me for, eh? I'm not some thug who goes around beating people up just for the sheer fun of it. I'm not sick in the fucking head.'

'I know you're not.' Her fears temporarily subsiding, a moment of relief surged through Aimee's veins. Maybe she had been right to tell him the truth after all, to clear the air between them. She glanced towards the office. 'It's just that Reece said there was another side to you, one that I've never seen before and that you could be dangerous if you wanted to be. That this is the reason why your family keep you on such a short rein because they know what you're capable of.'

Following her gaze Tommy shot his cousin another glare. 'Then Reece has got a big mouth,' he snarled. Turning back to look at Aimee his expression softened. 'Do you honestly think that I'd do something to hurt you or that I'd deliberately set out to upset you?'

Aimee shook her head. 'No, at least not intentionally anyway.'

'Well, there you go then.' He pulled her close and kissed the top of her head. 'I'll hold my hands up and admit that I'm pissed off, who wouldn't be, in my position? It's because of your dad that I was banged up. But I promise you, babe, hand on heart,' he said placing his hand on his chest. 'I'm not going to lay a finger on him.'

'Really?' Stepping back slightly so that she could look up at him, there was hope in Aimee's voice. 'You won't go looking for him or try to threaten him?'

'I swear,' Tommy winked. 'On my life. In fact, I'll go one step further and give you my word. I'm not going to touch him, and neither will anyone else,' he added jerking his thumb towards the office.

A weight had been lifted from Aimee's shoulders, and throwing her arms around Tommy's neck, she kissed his cheek. She'd been silly to doubt him and should have known all along that Reece had only said the things he had in anger. Of course, her Tommy wasn't dangerous, she knew him, he had a good heart. And yes, it would be fair to say that he and Reece did get into fights on occasion, but that didn't mean he was a menace to society. He was just in the wrong place at the wrong time and if anything, trouble came looking for him not the other way around. 'I'm sorry,' she sighed.

'Don't be.' Tucking into his bacon roll again, Tommy flashed a carefree grin. 'Like you said, Kevin is your old man, it's only natural you would want to protect him even if the sly bastard deserves a pounding after what he caused.'

* * *

For the first time in what seemed like forever, Kevin had a smile upon his face. Not only did he have a spring in his step, but he was also feeling giddy with excitement. All of his dreams were about to finally come true. He was gonna be raking it in. In fact, he was going to have so much dough that he would be able to afford anything and everything he'd ever wanted. No more scrimping and scraping to buy a pint of lager down the boozer, or a wrap of cocaine. If he wanted to, he'd be able to buy sniff by the bucketload, and as it just so happened, that was his exact plan.

Entering his place of work, he turned his head to look at his colleague for the night. A right miserable bastard if ever he'd seen one. 'You alright, pal?' he called out as he slipped off his jacket, took a seat, kicked his legs up onto a coffee table, and then lit up a cigarette.

Stanley Wilson wrinkled his nose, his lips pursed. 'Can't you read?' he declared nodding towards the no smoking signs dotted around the room.

Kevin shrugged and taking a deep drag on the cigarette he blew the smoke in Stanley's direction. 'Mind your own business and keep that out of it,' he said tapping his nose.

Waving the smoke out of his face Stanley sighed and as he

went back to reading his newspaper Kevin couldn't help but chuckle. Looking around the room his gaze fell upon a series of iron cages, his expression becoming deadly serious. The old codgers he worked with wouldn't know what had hit them once Tommy Jr and his family descended upon them. The mere thought of what was to come was enough to make him want to laugh out loud again, and as he continued smoking his cigarette, he began mentally spending his share of the robbery. Yeah, he decided. It was about time his life took a turn for the better. He was done with scrambling around in the dirt, living from day to day without a penny to his name. He was about to become someone, someone to be looked up to. And who knew, perhaps this was only the beginning, maybe after the robbery the Carters would take him under their wing, show him the ropes, and take him out on other robberies?

With a smile etched across his face, Kevin stubbed out his cigarette, placed his hands behind his head, and closed his eyes all the while ignoring the disapproving tut that came from Stanley. It was on the tip of his tongue to tell the old bastard to fuck off. Instead, he kept his lips firmly closed; the fucker would soon get what was coming to him and in Kevin's opinion that time couldn't come soon enough.

* * *

Cameron narrowed his eyes and as he threw his son a wary glance he shook his head. 'Have you lost your mind? He's only just come out of prison,' he argued waving his hand in Tommy Jr's direction.

'Dad,' Tommy sighed. 'How many more times do I have to tell you? It was my idea.'

Cameron snorted and as he turned his head to look back at

Jonny his eyes were as hard as flints. 'And you're actually allowing this, are you?' he asked, his tone accusing. 'You're actually condoning this madness?'

Jonny sighed. 'At the end of the day he's going to do it with or without us.' Leaning back in the chair he spread open his arms. 'And considering he's never carried out a robbery before, and no, before you say it – stealing cars doesn't count,' he said, giving Tommy a hard stare. 'Then even you have to admit it's better this way, that at least we'll be there to guide him, to show him how it's done, to limit the risk.'

Still grumbling, Cameron shook his head. 'I can't get my head around this,' he said, clutching his forehead. 'I can't believe what I'm hearing.' He rounded on his son. 'Are you seriously trying to fuck up your life, have you learned nothing? You could end up back inside as quick as this,' he said snapping his fingers together to demonstrate his point. 'Is that what you actually want, to lose your freedom all over again, to break your mother's heart and for your child to grow up without his or her father around, because believe me, son, you're going the right fucking way about it?'

'For fuck's sake, Dad.' Tommy gritted his teeth. 'Will you just chill out for five minutes and back off? Nothing is going to go wrong. Kevin set me up last time, it had fuck all to do with the robberies.'

'I still don't like it,' Cameron grumbled. 'And I still think it's a big risk.'

'You don't have to like it,' Jonny shot back at him. 'Besides it's a poxy sorting office, something we'd be able to turn over with our eyes closed. And from what Kevin told Tommy Jr, there's hardly any security on the premises. It'll be a piece of piss.'

'It had better be,' Cameron warned.

'It will be.' Leaning back in his chair, Jonny took a moment to look at his two brothers and then the remainder of his nephews. 'So are we all in agreement then, the job goes ahead?'

'Yeah, I suppose so,' Mitchell Carter nodded. 'Like you said, we could do this with our eyes shut, and it's hardly something that's gonna take a lot of planning out.'

Jonny nodded, and turning his attention to Tommy, he flashed him a wide grin. 'I'll leave it in your capable hands to get us a post office van. Besides,' he winked, 'it's about time you got off your arse and started pulling your weight around here.'

* * *

Like his great-uncle Jonny, Tommy Jr had nimble fingers. Car theft, in his opinion, was not only what he considered to be a doddle but also something that he excelled in. For the past thirty minutes or so he'd been trailing a Royal Mail transit van and each and every time the van would stop, then so would he, although it would be fair to say that he made sure to pull in a safe distance away so as not to arouse any suspicions.

Beside him in the passenger seat, Reece glanced at his watch. It was nearing lunch time and seeing as the van had come to a halt alongside a row of shops he tapped his fingers impatiently on his knee.

'He's gotta stop for lunch soon, surely,' he said giving Tommy a sidelong glance.

'Yeah,' Tommy answered, his hand on the door handle in preparation to jump out. 'You'd think so.'

Intently they continued watching and waiting, and as soon as the postman strolled inside a café Tommy flung open the door and jumped out of the car. 'Meet me back at the yard,' he said over his shoulder as he set off for the van.

Reece nodded and scrambling over the central console he

took his position behind the wheel, his gaze glued upon the café for any indication that the postie was making his way back outside.

'Come on,' he muttered as Tommy set to work. 'Hurry the fuck up.'

Within a matter of seconds Tommy was inside the van.

Holding his breath, beads of perspiration dotted Reece's forehead, and as his gaze flicked between the café and then the van, he gripped onto the steering wheel for dear life, his foot hovering above the accelerator, ready to make his getaway.

'Come on,' he shouted a second time. 'Move.'

The door to the café opened, and as the postman stepped back outside, Reece's eyes were as wide as golf balls. 'No, no, no,' he hissed under his breath. 'This ain't good.' Putting the gear into first, he pulled out onto the road, adrenaline pumping through his veins. What the fuck was Tommy playing at? And why was it taking him so long?

By the time Reece had pulled up alongside the van, Tommy waved him on, and as he continued to drive, he looked up at the rear-view mirror, sighing with relief to see the van just feet behind him and the postman standing on the pavement holding his head in his hands.

* * *

Twenty minutes later Tommy Jr drove into the scrapyard, pressed his foot on the brake, and then switched off the ignition. Leaping down from the van he slammed the door closed behind him, then began to pull out a large sheet of tarpaulin.

'What the fuck took you so long?' Reece stormed across the yard. 'You were seconds away from being caught red-handed.'

Tommy screwed up his face. 'What are you talking about?'

'The postie was on his way back,' Reece seethed. 'If you'd left it any longer, he would have seen you.'

'Yeah, and?' Gesturing towards the tarpaulin Tommy gave a nonchalant shrug. 'Are you gonna help me or are you planning on just standing there watching me?'

Reece huffed out a breath and yanking on the thick plastic he shook his head. 'You were taking too long,' he continued to grumble.

Tommy's eyes hardened and as Jonny began to make his way over to them he shot his cousin a look of warning. 'I had it under control, alright? So can you just drop it?' he hissed quietly so that their uncle was unable to hear them. 'I knew what I was doing.'

Oblivious to the tension between both his nephew and great-nephew, Jonny nodded, clearly impressed as he looked the van over. 'Any problems?' he enquired as they pulled the sheet over the van concealing it from view.

'Nah.' Giving Reece a surreptitious glance Tommy shook his head, his cheeks flushing red at the blatant lie. 'It was exactly as I thought it would be. A piece of piss, like taking candy from a baby.'

'Right then.' Jonny rubbed his hands together. 'I'm gonna shoot off and meet up with Danny McKay to collect the guns. Make sure you're back here by six tonight,' he warned wagging his finger between them. 'And don't be late.'

As Jonny walked off in the direction of his car, Reece turned back to look at Tommy, his eyebrows raised.

Tommy rolled his eyes, agitation evident in his voice. 'What?'

'You know what,' Reece answered. 'You had trouble getting the van started didn't you, you just don't want to admit it? I mean, you must have done, you're a natural when it comes to driving, and we all know that one day you'll take over from Jonny and that you'll become the family's next getaway driver. So what was taking you so long?'

Anger flashed across Tommy's face. 'I told you to fucking drop it,' he hissed, his cheeks turning red. 'There's fuck all wrong with the van, I got it started straight away.'

'But...'

Tommy bounded forward so that he and Reece were standing nose to nose. 'Do yourself a favour, Reece, and shut the fuck up before I end up putting you on your arse.'

Reece held up his hands and taking a step back he looked from Tommy to the van. 'Okay,' he said in surrender. 'I'll keep my mouth shut. If you reckon there's nothing wrong with it, then I'll have to take your word for it.'

'Yeah, you do that.' Giving a satisfied nod Tommy averted his gaze before making his way inside the office. Once there, he stared out of the window, his eyes firmly fixed on the post office van. As much as he hated to admit it, there was a hint of truth to Reece's accusation. He had had trouble starting the vehicle, so much so that he'd been on the verge of giving up and abandoning the van. It wasn't until his fifth or maybe even sixth attempt that he'd finally got the engine to splutter to life and even then, it had seemed a little too sluggish for his liking. No wonder the postman had left the key in the ignition. He thought it strange at the time, until he realised the van had an issue, and that should someone try to drive off in it, they'd soon come to realise that the bastard thing didn't actually have much power behind it, and that was only if they could even get it started in the first place.

He swallowed down his concern and making his way back outside he ignored his cousin as he walked towards his car.

Reece cleared his throat. 'You'll be needing these.' He tossed across the car keys. 'And don't forget,' he said in an attempt to clear the air between them. 'We need to meet back here at six.'

'Yeah, I heard what he said,' Tommy snapped, referring to their uncle. 'I'm not deaf or despite what you might think of me, stupid.'

'I didn't say you were.' His eyes narrowed; Reece crossed his arms over his chest. 'What the fuck is with you, Tommy? We used to be best mates but all you've done since getting out of the nick is have a pop at me. I'm sick to the back teeth of walking on eggshells around you, too scared to even open my mouth and say anything because you'll end up biting my head off.'

Tommy paused. Guilt eating away at him. It was true, he did seem to be losing his temper a lot more than he had previously, especially where Reece was concerned; maybe it was because they were so close, or at least they used to be. 'I'm sorry, I...' He shook his head unable to come up with a reason or excuse for his outburst. 'I didn't mean...'

'Sorry doesn't cut it,' Reece growled back at him. 'I couldn't wait for you to get out of prison,' he said screwing up his face. 'I was the one who fought your corner even when they,' he said, nodding towards the office, 'thought that you might not have been as innocent as you said you were. I was fucking there for you, and this is all the thanks I get for it.' He shook his head, his lips curling into a snarl. 'Do you know what? I'm starting to wish that you'd stayed inside, at least then I wouldn't be your punching bag or have to take this shit from you on a daily basis, at least then maybe you and me would still be pals.'

As Reece stormed inside the office Tommy closed his eyes, his shoulders drooping. He needed to sort himself out and fast before he and Reece ended up hating one another, which considering his behaviour of late, was a very real possibility. Pulling open the car door, he slipped behind the wheel, sat there for a few moments then started the ignition. As much as he'd promised Aimee he wouldn't lay a finger on her father, the anger inside of him was too great to ignore. Kevin was the sole cause of his misery. It was because of him that he and Reece were at loggerheads, and because of him he was barely able to sleep through the night without reliving Dylan's death, over and over again.

He rubbed the palm of his hand over his face then glanced up at the rear-view mirror. He barely even recognised himself of late. There was a hardness to his eyes that he'd never seen before, and he had to admit he didn't like it. Reece was right, he'd changed, and not for the better either, yet another thing he blamed Kevin for.

By the time Tommy had reversed out of the scrapyard he was more determined than ever to bring Kevin Fox to his knees. He had no other choice on the matter, because if he didn't, the rage that coursed through his body would eat away at him until there was nothing left, or at least nothing recognisable anyway.

Knowing exactly what he needed to do Tommy forced his body to relax. One way or another Kevin was going down, and no one or nothing would be able to stop that fact, not even Aimee.

20

After leaving the hairdressing salon where she worked, Aimee walked towards the bus stop, contemplating whether or not to call a taxi rather than get the bus home. Delving into her handbag she pulled out her mobile phone then chewed on her bottom lip. What with the baby coming, her and Tommy Jr needed to save as much money as they possibly could and wasting her hard-earned cash on a taxi when she could just as easily take the bus, however tired she might be, seemed like a waste.

Looking up she surveyed the road ahead and with no sign of a bus coming along any time soon she groaned out loud. She was dead on her feet, her body so tired that all she wanted to do was snuggle down on the sofa and take a nap.

Sod it, she decided. She'd call a cab and worry about the money later. Just as she was about to press dial a car pulled up beside her. In that moment Aimee didn't know whether to laugh or cry, and as Tommy leaned across the passenger seat and pushed open the door for her, she beamed down at him.

'Oh my God, you're a life saver,' she said as she climbed inside the car. 'I'm so bleedin' tired I think that I could sleep for a week.'

Tommy chuckled. 'I was passing by and thought I'd see if I could catch you and give you a lift home.'

As she clipped her seat belt into place Aimee turned her head to look at him. 'And where were you going, eh?' she teased.

Laughing even harder, Tommy caught hold of her hand and gave it a squeeze. 'Yeah, alright,' he admitted. 'You caught me out. I already knew what time you finished work. I wanted to surprise you.'

'Well, thank you,' Aimee smiled as she slipped off her shoes and made herself comfortable. 'Are you planning to stay over at mine tonight? My mum said that she was thinking of getting a takeaway, Chinese I think, unless you fancy something different.'

Tommy shook his head, the playfulness leaving his face. 'I can't,' he answered taking his eyes off the road to look at her. 'I'm working.'

Aimee narrowed her eyes, her gaze snapping towards the time on her phone. 'What do you mean, you're working? Since when have you ever worked late at night?'

For a few moments Tommy was quiet, then clearing his throat, he gave Aimee another glance. 'Do you remember the other day when you came to see me at the scrapyard?'

Aimee nodded.

'And I said that we didn't have secrets between us.'

'Yeah,' Aimee answered as unease began to coil around her insides. 'What about it?'

Tommy shifted his weight. 'Well…'

'Tommy, what is it?' Aimee implored, her heartbeat picking up pace. 'You're beginning to scare me now.'

Momentarily pausing, Tommy shook his head. 'You're not daft, babe.' He turned to look at her again as if to gauge her reaction. 'A part of you must have been wondering about my family, where all of their money comes from.'

'The scrapyard.'

Tommy shook his head. 'The scrapyard is nothing but a front. I mean, don't get me wrong, it does bring in some money, but nowhere near enough to keep any of us afloat.'

Aimee's face paled. 'What are you trying to say?' she asked as nausea washed over her.

'There's a job going down, tonight.' He gripped onto the steering wheel and took a deep breath. 'An armed robbery. And I'm gonna be there, along with the rest of the family.'

As Aimee gasped, she brought her hand up to her face. 'No,' she said, her fingers trembling and her eyes wide and fearful. 'No, Tommy. No.'

Tommy clutched hold of her free hand again and gave it another gentle squeeze. 'I'm only telling you because I don't want it to ever come between us. And I didn't want you to find out from anyone else.' He lifted his eyebrows. 'You must have known that the scrapyard didn't pay for my parents' house, or any of my uncles' houses, come to that.'

'But I don't understand.' Her mind reeling, Aimee shook her head. 'You told me that your dad owned businesses, that they'd been left to him by his grandfather.'

'He does,' Tommy sighed. 'And none of those are strictly legal either. In fact, they're as dodgy as fuck and mainly used for money laundering purposes.'

'But...' Still shaking her head, Aimee could barely comprehend what she was being told. 'Your mum is so nice; how could she be involved in something like this?'

Tommy laughed. 'My mum was a Carter before she got

married,' he said. 'It was her old man, my grandad, who put the family on the road as bank robbers. Not that she approves, mind you. In fact she positively loathes my dad's occupation and goes mental at him if he even so much as dares to ever bring it up in front of her.' He squeezed her hand again. 'I don't want that for us. For me and you, I mean. I want you to know what I'm about, even if you don't like it. I'm not an angel, babe, and I'll never pretend to be one,' he said, turning to look at her again. 'And you were right what you said the other day. The family does keep me on a short rein.' He gave a hollow laugh. 'They reckon I've got too much Carter blood inside of me, what with my grandfathers being brothers an' all.'

Placing her hand upon her abdomen, Aimee shuddered. 'You could go to prison again,' she cried.

'Yeah,' Tommy agreed. 'But only if we're caught, and so far the family have been lucky. They know the risks involved, and they've always been careful,' he reassured her. 'The Old Bill have never so much as brought any of them in for questioning.'

Aimee screwed up her face. 'Yet, you mean.'

'Yeah, I suppose,' Tommy agreed. He gave a sigh. 'Look. I know it's a lot for you to get your head around, but this is me being honest with you. I mean we'll get married one day won't we, and well... you'll have to know what I do for work then. I'll hardly be able to keep it a secret once we're living together.'

Aimee's jaw dropped. 'You've always said you didn't want to get married.'

Tommy shrugged. 'Not right now I don't, but one day in the future I do.'

'Oh, Tommy.' Shaking her head, there was fear in Aimee's eyes. Deep down she had always known that his family were involved in illegal activities, it was the only thing that made any real sense and it was ludicrous to even suggest that they would be able to afford to own their houses solely on the money they earned from a scrapyard, especially when they were more like mansions rather than your usual run-of-the-mill ex-council houses. And that was without the lifestyles they lived, the cars, and then the money they were able to flash around in abundance. 'I'm scared,' she admitted.

'Don't be,' Tommy said, in an attempt to placate her. 'I'll be careful. I promise. And I would never do anything to implicate you. I will never tell you anything that could get you into any trouble.'

Aimee took a shuddering breath. 'And you're not going to hurt anyone, are you? Promise me,' she pleaded with him. 'Because I don't think that I could bear that. I don't think I could be with a man who was violent.'

'Of course I won't,' he lied as his mind wandered to her father, or to be more precise, the hatred he felt towards him. 'You should know me better than that.'

'I do.' As the car came to a halt outside her mother's house she unclipped her seat belt. 'Will you let me know that you're okay?' Her voice came out as a squeak as she swallowed down the hard lump in her throat. 'Afterwards I mean, once it's done so that I know you haven't been arrested.'

'Always,' he said as he leaned across the seat to kiss her cheek. 'You'll be the first person I call. I promise.'

Aimee nodded, and as she looked at him, she searched his face. For what reason she didn't know; perhaps she needed some sort of clarification that he was still her Tommy, that he was still the man she loved, despite his admission that he was about to follow on in his family's footsteps and become an armed robber. A cold chill swept over her. It didn't even occur to her to ask where exactly he and his family were planning to target, and if she was being totally honest with herself, she didn't want to know. All that mattered was that he came back to her in one piece, and nothing more than that.

* * *

As Nathan Bannerman took a sip of his brandy he kissed his teeth. For the past hour both he and his two brothers had been drinking heavily. That wasn't to say, however, that he was anywhere near on his way to feeling under the influence. If anything, he was still as sober as a judge and he had a sneaky suspicion that whether he liked it or not he was going to stay that way.

Swirling the amber-coloured liquid around the glass, he brought it up to his lips and took a generous swig, his hard gaze fixed on his youngest brother.

Out of the two, it had always been Lee who'd given him the most grief. His middle brother, the one who was volatile, dangerous, the human equivalent of a ticking time bomb. In recent weeks, however, it was Connor who had given him the most cause for concern. Connor didn't think, or rather he did think, but mainly with a part of his anatomy that had no place to make business deals, especially when that said deal came to the hefty sum of fifty grand.

'Have you been on the blower to that bird yet?' he asked, his voice coming across far too calm considering the anger that rippled through him.

Connor looked up, his cheeks once again flushing red, a trait that was fast on its way to getting on Nathan's wick. 'Nah.' Connor gave a shrug and wrinkled his nose. 'I'm giving her the elbow.'

The nerve at the side of Nathan's eye twitched, the only outward sign he gave to suggest that he was in grave danger of losing his rag. 'Are you for fucking real?' he hissed. 'Her brother ripped us off and now you decide you want shot of her.'

Connor rolled his eyes and as he looked between his two brothers he leaned forward. 'That's what you wanted, isn't it?' He tipped the glass towards them. 'You were the ones who kept telling me she's a skank and that I should fuck her off.'

'She is a skank.' Lee gave a smug grin. One of his favourite pastimes was to wind up his younger brother, and Connor being Connor always bit. 'I've told you time and time again that she would spread her legs for just about anyone.' As he waved his hand towards Connor amusement danced across Lee's face. 'And the fact she ended up in your bed only serves to prove my point.'

'Fuck off.' Sinking back in his seat Connor scowled. 'Why don't you go find someone to slice up instead of trying to wind me up something chronic?'

Lee laughed out loud. 'Oh, the night's still young,' he winked glancing around them.

Rolling his eyes again, Connor followed his brother's gaze. The club they were in was packed to the rafters and he felt a moment of pity for whoever it was that should cross paths with his brother. Not that Lee would need much of an excuse to kick off. All it would take was for someone to accidentally bump into him or so much as dare to look in his direction and before they knew what was happening Lee would not only be screaming blue murder but actually ready to commit it too.

'Besides,' Connor said giving his brothers a smirk. 'I don't need Julie. Not when I already know where Kevin's ex-wife and kid live.'

Both Nathan and Lee shared a glance.

'I don't fucking believe this.' Lee threw his arms up into the air. 'And you didn't think to share that information? You know, to help us out here so that we can recover the fifty grand that all thanks to you has gone walkabout.'

Connor swallowed, knowing in that instant that he'd fucked up. He'd wanted to be the one to rip into Kevin, and even more than that, he'd wanted to be able to claw back some much-needed respect.

'Fuck this.' Lee jumped to his feet; his fists clenched at his sides. 'You're lucky that you're my brother,' he yelled, 'because right now the only thing I want to do is smash your fucking face in.'

Pulling on his brother's shirt, Nathan shook his head. 'Not here,' he said, motioning around them. 'We don't air our dirty laundry in public. And as for you,' he said, addressing Connor, his expression becoming suddenly unreadable. 'You're lucky that I've got him on such a tight leash. Because I make him right. Not only did you make a fuck up of epic proportions, but you've also made us look like fools.' Standing up he released Lee and stabbed his finger towards the entrance. 'Move,' he hissed. 'Before I batter you myself.'

* * *

Making a beeline for his usual spot inside the sorting office, Kevin kicked his feet up on the coffee table, and with a cigarette in his hand, he made himself as comfortable as he possibly could.

By the time Stanley Wilson had made his way into the control room, the cigarette had burned down to Kevin's fingers, his head rolling back against the backrest of the sofa and his mouth gaping wide open as he snored loudly.

Shaking his head, Stanley poked Kevin with the toe of his

steel-capped boot. 'Wake up!' he shouted. 'You're not being paid to sleep on the job.'

Kevin awoke with a start, and wiping the dribble from his chin he looked around him. 'I wasn't asleep. I was resting my eyes,' he protested, sitting up and brushing the cigarette ash from the front of his shirt before dropping the butt into a waste basket.

Stanley shook his head. 'You're a liability,' he scowled, stabbing his forefinger in Kevin's direction. 'First thing tomorrow morning, I'm going to report you. This place could have been robbed and you, you great slummock would have snored your way through the entire thing.'

'And you're a fucking jobsworth,' Kevin scowled. From the corner of his eye, he watched as Stanley flicked on the kettle. 'While you're up,' he smirked, 'Do the honours and make me a cuppa. And don't be stingy with the milk either.'

Kevin's audacity was enough to make Stanley's jaw drop. 'Make your bleeding own,' he retorted, taking a moment of satisfaction to see the look on Kevin's face as he took out just the one mug and teabag from the cupboard then set about making his own tea.

* * *

Despite his earlier confidence, Tommy Jr couldn't help but feel nervous. It wasn't so much the actual robbery that was making him feel jittery, it was the post office van. Shooting Reece a glance, a hot flush crept up his neck. What if they couldn't get the van started? He'd end up looking like a right prat.

Taking the balaclava Jonny handed to him, Tommy stuffed it inside his pocket. Next, he took the gloves that were being handed out. Trying them on for size he gave a satisfied nod before pulling them back off and shoving them into his other pocket.

Placed upon the sofa were three shotguns. Not that he actually expected to be given one. He'd never even held a real gun before, let alone actually fired one. Eyeing up two rucksacks beside the door, he motioned to the bolt cutters laying on top of them.

'What are they for?'

'What do you think?' Jonny answered. He gave a wicked grin. 'To cut off the bastard's fingers. You'll be surprised how hard it is to cut through gristle and bone but with these beauties it will be like a hot knife gliding through butter.'

Tommy blanched, and as he screwed up his face, his uncle Peter clasped him on the shoulder.

'He's joking,' he laughed. 'They're for the cages. How else do you think we're going to get them open?'

Forcing his expression to relax, Tommy felt not only like a fool but also an amateur, which he was he supposed, seeing as this was to be his first heist. He looked towards his cousin again, this time the two of them locking eyes.

'I think that's about it,' Jonny declared, and as he began to pull on his gloves he motioned to the desk. 'Don't forget to leave your phones behind. The last thing we need is to be traced back to the sorting office.'

As they each pulled out their mobile phones, switched them off and then placed them on the desk, Jonny nodded.

'Right then you lot,' he said. 'Let's do this.'

As they traipsed out of the office Tommy's stomach was churning. The van was going to let him down, he knew it was, he could feel it in his bones. As the rear doors were opened, he climbed inside, hesitating slightly before inching forward. A large part of him wanted to jump back out, make a run for it, and hide. Or at least stay hidden out of sight until his uncle had managed to get the transit started.

'Go on,' one of his uncle's urged pushing him forward, his voice holding a hint of amusement, as though he wrongly presumed Tommy's reluctance was because he was nervous about taking part in his first heist. 'What are you waiting for?'

Taking his position alongside the rest of the family, Tommy sat down on the hard floor, and as the doors were slammed shut engulfing them in darkness, he momentarily screwed his eyes shut tight. 'Please, please, please,' he whispered to himself. 'Please start.'

He could feel a slight movement as Jonny and Mitchell climbed into the front of the van, then the sound of the driver's door, and passenger door being slammed closed. And then... other than his heart beating so hard and fast that he thought the organ would burst out of his chest, there was nothing but an eerie silence.

As the seconds ticked by Tommy held his breath, his ears straining to listen out for the telltale rumble of the van's engine starting up. Unfortunately for him the only noise echoing throughout the vehicle was that of the ignition being turned over and over, and over again.

In that instant Tommy's heart sank. This couldn't be happening, he told himself. Only he knew it was. Even Reece had guessed that there was a problem with the van and he hadn't been the one driving it.

'Tommy Jr,' he heard Jonny roar from the front seat. 'I'm gonna fucking kill you!'

Sensing each of his family members snap their heads towards him Tommy pushed himself further away from them, all the while bracing himself for his uncle's onslaught, and he knew it was coming, it was bound to. He'd well and truly fucked up.

He didn't have to wait long. Within a matter of seconds Jonny was yanking open the rear door, his face set like thunder. 'What the fuck is this?' he seethed as he jumped up into the van and clambered over the rest of the family just to get to him.

Tommy looked up and seeing the look upon his great-uncle's face he swallowed deeply.

'It's a bit temperamental.'

'A bit?' Jonny yelled. 'It won't even fucking start.'

Getting to his feet before he was dragged up, Tommy shrugged. 'It started first time for me,' he lied, avoiding eye contact with Reece.

'Then you'd best get up front and get this pile of shit moving,' Jonny hissed pushing Tommy back out of the van. 'Otherwise, me and you are going to have a big problem.'

Doing as he'd been told, Tommy climbed up into the front of the van. He was beginning to sweat, and wiping his hand over his cropped hair, he took another deep breath then reached for the key and gave it a tentative turn. Immediately the engine purred to life.

Sinking back in the seat Tommy exhaled a breath, not even daring to turn his head and look at his uncle for fear that there was still a very real possibility that he would swing for him.

Beside him on the front seat, Mitchell blew out his cheeks. 'This pile of shit is going to let us down,' he stated with a shake of his head. 'How the fuck are we supposed to make our getaway when the getaway van is on its last legs?'

Jonny huffed out a breath, his fists involuntarily clenching. 'I could seriously fucking kill you, Tommy Jr,' he hissed.

Tommy swallowed again. 'You just have to have the right knack,' he said flicking his wrist to demonstrate his point. 'Give the key a nice gentle little twist.'

Shaking his head, Jonny gave his great-nephew a final glare

before slamming the door closed and walking around to the passenger side. 'Then you'd best hope and pray,' he said, climbing in, 'that that gentle little twist of yours fucking works because if it doesn't, I'm telling you now you'd best run as fast and as far away from me as you can possibly get. Have you got that?'

'Yeah,' Tommy answered sounding a lot more confident than he actually felt as he pushed his foot down on the accelerator and drove out of the yard. 'I've got it.'

21

No matter how tired she may have been previously, Aimee was now wide awake. She didn't think she would be able to sleep even if she wanted to, not after Tommy Jr had dropped his bombshell on her.

He was an armed robber, or at least he would be once the night was over. The mere thought was enough to make her shudder. Sitting up in bed, she brought her knees up to her chest and chewed on her thumbnail, her eyes glued to her mobile phone awaiting his call to tell her that he was alright and hadn't been arrested.

'Are you okay, darling?' Poking her head around the bedroom door, Melanie gave a gentle smile. 'I saw that your light was still on and thought I'd best check up on you.'

'Oh, Mum.' Scrambling off the bed, Aimee threw herself into her mother's arms.

'Hey,' Melanie gasped. 'What's all this?'

Aimee sobbed, and as the tears began to flow, she had a feeling that she would be unable to stop them even if she wanted to.

'What on earth is wrong?' Wrapping her arms around her daughter, Melanie's face was etched with concern.

'It's Tommy,' Aimee cried through her tears. 'He...' She shook her head, not wanting to say the words out loud. How was she supposed to tell her mum that he was an armed robber, knowing full well that she would view him in a different light, that maybe she would even refuse point blank to let him enter the house again? 'Oh, Mum,' she wailed. 'I don't know what I'm supposed to do.'

'Hey, stop this.' Holding Aimee at arm's length, Melanie shook her head. 'I can't help you, darling, not unless you tell me what's wrong.'

'I can't.' Tears slipped down her face. 'He...'

As the sound of knocking on the front door drifted up the stairs, Aimee stiffened, her face becoming all the more pale and her eyes widening. 'It's my Tommy,' she croaked out, pulling away from her mother and bolting down the stairs.

Stunned, Melanie brought her hand up to her forehead. 'Aimee,' she called out. 'Will you please explain to me what the hell is going on...'

The front door crashing against the wall, followed by Aimee's startled scream made Melanie's blood run cold. Darting down the stairs after her daughter, she came face to face with the Bannerman brothers, the menacing look on their faces enough to send a shard of terror ricocheting through her body.

* * *

Kevin was sulking, and as Stanley blew on his tea, it took everything within his power not to smash the mug into the old bastard's face.

'You could have made me a cup,' he scowled. 'It wouldn't have bloody hurt you.'

Stanley ignored him, and as he continued blowing on the hot liquid, he took a seat then pulled out his newspaper. After a few moments he looked up. 'It's your turn to do the rounds, isn't it?' He glanced at his watch. 'The quicker you get going the quicker you'll be back here doing sod all as per usual.'

Kevin heaved himself off the sofa. 'I'm not your lackey,' he complained. 'Do this, Kevin, do fucking that, Kevin. Why don't you stick a broom up my arse while you're at it and I'll sweep the bleedin' floor for you an' all?'

Lifting his eyebrows Stanley pursed his lips. 'Chance would be a fine thing. You barely move all night.'

A buzzer sounded, and after giving the grainy monitor screen a customary glance, Stanley lifted his eyebrows even further. 'Are you going to answer that?' he asked, tossing across a heavy set of keys.

Kevin huffed out a breath and stomping across the room he came to a halt in front of the control panel, not even bothering to look at the monitor screen, let alone ask for the van driver's identification, before pressing down on the buttons that opened the electronic gates and allowed the post office vehicles to drive into the depot. 'I should be getting paid extra for this,' he grumbled. 'It's me,' he said poking himself in the chest, 'who does all of the work around here, while you just sit there, reading your newspaper, and drinking your poxy tea, doing fuck all.'

As annoyed as he was, Stanley chuckled under his breath. With only a few months left to go before he retired, it was about time he put his feet up, especially when the likes of Kevin Fox thought they could sleep on the job and get paid for doing the bare minimum night after night.

A silence fell over the depot, and looking up again, Stanley cocked his head to the side, his ears straining for any sound of movement coming from the yard adjacent to the room where the packages and parcels were secured overnight. Usually, the drivers and their mates would have come into the room by now, their chatter loud as they placed the goods inside the metal cages, then set about making endless cups of tea and helping themselves to his biscuits.

Putting down his newspaper, Stanley cautiously got to his feet. 'What's going on out there?' he said, giving Kevin a sidelong glance.

Kevin spun around, his gaze automatically drifting towards the corridor that led out to the yard. 'What?' he said. 'I can't hear anything.'

'Exactly my point,' Stanley whispered. He pulled out his phone, his finger hovering over the call button. 'They should have been in here by now.'

'Woah,' Kevin said warily, eyeing the phone in Stanley's hand. 'Don't do anything rash. There's no need to be calling the Old Bill. You know what they're like,' he said nodding towards the yard. 'They're playing silly buggers, having a laugh, a bit of banter. I bet you any money that they're out there now pissing themselves with laughter. They more than likely think we're in here scared shitless and that they've got one over on us.'

A frown creased Stanley's face. 'Maybe,' he said, lowering the phone to his side.

'Course they are. They're a bunch of wind-up merchants. Do you remember that time when they—'

Before Kevin could finish the sentence a number of masked men, brandishing shotguns, burst into the room.

The following sequence of events happened so fast that

Kevin barely had the time to think let alone comprehend what was going on. And as much as he may have been expecting their arrival, the reality of having Tommy and his family bursting into the control room barking out threats was enough to make his bowels loosen.

Sinking down to his knees, he winced as a gun was slammed into the side of his head, his expression becoming one of confusion. He understood that they would want to make the situation look believable, and that they had to ensure Stanley's suspicions weren't aroused. But even so, there was no need for them to be so heavy handed.

As his arms were wrenched behind his back, and thick plastic cable ties were being secured around his wrists, Kevin's frown deepened. 'Oi,' he hissed under his breath. 'That's a bit fucking tight, ain't it?'

He didn't receive a reply, and as he was shoved none too gently forward, his body connected with the floor, the left side of his face and shoulder taking the impact. 'Oi,' he hissed again, his voice low so that Stanley was unable to hear. 'Watch it. You could have done me some damage.'

* * *

Behind the balaclava pulled down over his face, Tommy Jr's eyes were hard, and his lips curled into a snarl. Was Kevin taking the actual piss? He'd like to cause the tosser a lot more than just some damage. If he had his way, he'd beat the smug bastard to a pulp and not even break out in a sweat, or give a flying fuck, for that matter. It was only his promise to Aimee that was stopping him from laying into her old man.

With his foot pressed down on Kevin's back, Tommy

observed what was going on around him. He had to give it to his family, they were definitely professional and knew what they were doing when it came to carrying out armed robberies. Within a matter of seconds, his dad, uncles, and great-uncles, had taken control of the room.

Watching as they cut through the wires of the recording equipment dotted around the room, they then began the process of cutting through the thick iron cages, before proceeding to load the rucksacks with the goods being stored inside. As an assortment of what Tommy guessed to be jewellery, watches, and gold bullion was flung into the bags, he forced his shoulders to relax. His uncle Mitchell had been right; so far the heist had been a piece of piss and with only Kevin and some old codger who looked to be at least in his late sixties to early seventies the only ones there to stop them, what could possibly go wrong?

Minutes later his uncles were hauling the rucksacks up onto their shoulders and heading for the door, keen to make their getaway. Following suit, Tommy released his foot from Kevin's back and made to step over him.

'Hey, Tommy,' Kevin urged. 'When do I get my cut?'

The hairs on the back of Tommy's neck stood to attention, and snapping his head in the direction of Kevin's colleague, he curled his hands into fists. Was this prick actually for real? Not only had he just implicated himself, but he'd also referred to him by his name.

White, hot fury rippled through Tommy's veins, and crouching down, he grasped Kevin by his hair, yanked him upright, then pulled back his fist. Before he even had the chance to throw a punch he was being pulled back, the hand clutching at his elbow strong and unwavering. Turning his head, Tommy locked eyes with his cousin.

As Reece shook his head in a warning, he jerked his head behind him and gestured that it was time for them to leave. That no matter how angry he might be, and rightly so in the circumstances, they needed to get out of there and fast.

Reluctantly Tommy threw Kevin away from him, not caring one iota as he fell back on the floor in a crumpled heap. 'I'm gonna have you,' he seethed, his voice barely louder than a whisper. Straightening up, he began backing away, his murderous gaze remaining locked on his girlfriend's father. As he should have known right from the very start, Kevin was more than just a liability. Not only did he have a big mouth, but he was also seriously lacking when it came to brain cells.

By the time Tommy was jumping up into the van, he was more than just a little angry, he was absolutely raging. Kevin had just single-handedly fucked up the entire heist. 'I'm gonna kill him,' he seethed. 'That big-mouthed cunt is gonna get what's coming to him.'

Beside him, Jonny snapped his head around, his forehead furrowing. 'What the fuck happened?'

Tommy swallowed, then taking a deep breath, he cracked his knuckles in an attempt to relax his fingers. 'He called me by my name,' he said, inching out his hand and tentatively turning the key in the ignition. To his relief the van started straight away, and pressing his foot down on the accelerator he sped out of the depot. 'The stupid prick even had the audacity to ask when he was going to get his cut.'

Jonny cursed under his breath. 'Are you sure?' he said turning to look over his shoulder at the depot.

'Of course I'm fucking sure,' Tommy retorted. 'I heard him say it.' Giving his uncle a sidelong glance he shook his head, the muscles across his shoulder blades taut. 'One way or another, that sly bastard is going down,' he spat. 'Even if I have to kill him myself.'

* * *

In a state of shock, Stanley pushed himself up into a sitting position. In all of his years of working for the Royal Mail this was the first time he'd ever witnessed an actual robbery. And despite the many training courses he'd attended, nothing could have prepared him for the reality of having a shotgun slammed into the side of his face.

His body trembling, he leaned his head against the wall and concentrated on regulating his breathing. The only consolation he was able to take from the situation was that he hadn't been physically harmed. His nerves, on the other hand, had taken a battering, one he wasn't so sure he would ever be able to recover from.

Turning his head, he narrowed his gaze on Kevin. The great slummock had put their lives at risk, and although Stanley hadn't been able to hear exactly what had been said between the two men, he knew for a fact the fool had said something to antagonise one of them; why else would he have reacted the way he had?

'Didn't you learn anything while training for the job?' he spat out. 'You could have got us both killed.'

Kevin groaned, and as he too pulled himself up into a sitting position, he tugged at the restraints secured around his wrists. 'I can't feel my fucking hands,' he cried. 'The bastards have cut off my blood supply.'

Stanley rolled his eyes. He should have known Kevin's only thought would be of himself. With great difficulty, he staggered to his feet, then ambled across the room, the sight of the empty cages infuriating him. He should have called the police the moment he suspected something was amiss, and he would have done too, if Kevin hadn't persuaded him not to. 'This is all your fault,' he snapped.

Kevin's jaw dropped. 'Me,' he exclaimed. 'What the fuck did I do?'

'Did you ask for ID before opening the gate?'

Just as he'd known he would, Kevin gave a sheepish shrug of his shoulders, his cheeks flushing red.

'I thought as much,' Stanley spat. Thankful that his wrists had been bound in front of him rather than behind his back like Kevin's had, he ever so carefully scooped up his mobile phone from the floor and set the device on the desk. Heads were going to roll, and like hell was he going to take the fall for Kevin's blatant, idiotic mistake, especially when he was so close to retirement, and, until now, had a clean record. He took a deep breath, his gaze drifting towards the monitor screen. Many a time he'd complained about the picture quality, he'd even written an official report to head office stating that it was a security issue, not that they had done anything about it. He lifted his face to the ceiling, momentarily closed his eyes, then puffed out his cheeks. 'If anyone asks,' he said turning back to look at Kevin, 'you were shown what you believed to be identification.' He nodded towards the grainy screen. 'With a bit of luck, we'll come out of this with not only our pride, but our jobs still intact.'

Kevin beamed. 'Sounds like a plan,' he winked.

'Yeah,' Stanley grumbled. 'I had a feeling you might say that.'

As he dialled the emergency services, Stanley slumped onto a chair. Never before had the prospect of retirement seemed so appealing to him.

* * *

As she looked from her daughter to the three men, Melanie gripped onto the banister rail for dear life. 'Who are you and what are you doing in my house?' she asked, the words coming out so strained that she barely even recognised her own voice.

A silence followed, and as her heart continued to beat wildly inside her chest, Melanie took a tentative step down the stairs. 'I asked you a question,' she cried. 'What are you doing in my house?'

This caused a reaction, or rather a snort of laughter, and as Melanie snapped her head around to look at the culprit, her forehead furrowed.

'We're looking for your old man.'

Melanie frowned. 'Kevin?' she exclaimed, her startled gaze going between the three men. 'But he doesn't live here.'

'No, maybe not,' Nathan Bannerman answered as he took a seat on the sofa and made himself at home. 'But from my understanding he's a regular visitor.' He spread open his arms and offered a menacing grin. 'So, do yourself a favour and get on the blower to him. Tell him that the Bannerman brothers want a word.'

Melanie hesitated, her mind whirling.

'He told you to get your old man on the phone,' Lee roared as he yanked Aimee towards him and held a knife to her throat.

The terrified scream that came from her daughter was Melanie's undoing, and as her entire body shook, she raced across the lounge, fumbled to open her handbag, then took out her mobile phone. Her fingers shaking so much that it took her several attempts to unlock the device.

'Chop, chop.' Nathan grinned at her. 'Otherwise...' He gave a mock sad smile and motioned a slicing action across his throat. 'All it will take is a nod from me and you can say goodbye to this kid of yours. Pity, really,' he said giving Aimee a fleeting glance.

'She's a pretty girl and I'd hate to see her become disfigured in any way.'

Swallowing down a sob, Melanie paused. 'It's nearly out of battery,' she cried gesturing down at her phone.

'Then you'd best hope and pray that bastard you were married to answers.'

Melanie gave a hopeless nod, and pressing dial, she brought the device up to her ear. The call rang off, and as she turned back to look at the men, the fear in her eyes increased. 'He isn't answering.'

Nathan tilted his head to the side, his hard gaze penetrating through Melanie's skull as though he were debating whether or not she was telling them the truth. 'Shame,' he eventually answered as he slowly turned to look at his brother.

'Mum!' Aimee screamed as the point of the knife clutched at her throat dug in a little deeper.

On seeing a trickle of blood make its way down her daughter's neck, terror gripped at Melanie's heart. 'No!' she screamed. 'Wait, wait. Please don't hurt my daughter,' she pleaded. 'I'll keep trying him.'

Lifting his hand in the air to stop his brother from committing murder, Nathan grinned. 'You do that,' he answered, kicking his long legs out in front of him.

Yet again Kevin didn't answer the call, not that Melanie should have expected any different from him. In the past he'd gone days at a time without returning her calls, sometimes even weeks. 'Please,' she pleaded. 'Don't hurt her. Please. I'm begging you. She's pregnant.'

Nathan let out a nasty chuckle. 'Even more of a reason to get your old man here then, eh? Otherwise, it looks like you'll have the death of both your daughter and grandchild to worry about.'

The threat to her unborn child sent a shard of panic surging through Aimee's veins, and thrashing her body from side to side she slapped and punched whichever part of Lee's arms, face, and body that she could reach. As a final, last-ditch attempt to save herself and her baby, she flung her head back, the hard bone connecting with the bridge of Lee's nose.

A loud crack resonated through the air, and as Lee brought his hand up to stem the blood gushing from his nostrils, his lips twisted into a snarl. 'You bitch,' he bellowed. 'You stupid little bitch. Fucking grab her, will you?' he yelled at his younger brother.

Before Connor could reach for her, Aimee had raced from the room with Melanie hot on her heels, their squeals of terror becoming even louder and all the more desperate as they ran into the kitchen and slammed the door closed behind them. Spying the kitchen table, she rushed forward, swiped the contents to the floor, and then began pushing it in the direction of the door.

'For God's sake, help me, Mum,' she pleaded.

Spurned into action Melanie helped push the heavy pine table forward, the two women panting for breath by the time they had wedged the table underneath the door handle. Even still, Aimee doubted it would be enough to keep the men out. Moving across the kitchen, she pulled open a drawer and pulled out two kitchen knives. Passing one across to her mother, she jumped in fright as the wooden door began to splinter with each and every kick against the door that the brothers gave.

'They're going to kill us,' she cried. 'We're going to die.'

'No we're not,' Melanie soothed, although her eyes told a very different story. Like her daughter, she was scared half to death, and as she wrapped her arms around Aimee she sent up a silent prayer before glancing towards the back door. If they could make it outside then perhaps they could raise the alarm. Perhaps they would be saved.

'Give me the phone, Mum,' Aimee pleaded. 'Please.'

Melanie passed across her phone, and as the two of them ran out into the back garden, Aimee tapped frantically at the keypad. After a few moments she brought the device up to her ear.

'Tommy,' she choked out. 'Help me. They're going to kill us.'

22

Entering the scrapyard office, Tommy Jr's earlier anger had somewhat dissipated. He was still livid with Kevin, mind you, but the anger that had been at the forefront of his mind had now been replaced with excitement. He'd just taken part in his first heist, and as he eyed the rucksacks, he couldn't help but grin. Even his initial worry about the van letting him down had been erased from his mind, and as he watched his uncles lay the shotguns back on the sofa, he fought the urge to laugh out loud. Euphoria rippled through his veins; a feeling that he had a sneaky suspicion he could more than get used to.

'You did good.' His uncle Jake smiled at him. 'Now you're a proper Carter,' he winked.

'Johnson, you mean,' Cameron scowled.

Jake waved his hand dismissively. If Cameron's grandfather Dean Johnson hadn't despised Tommy Snr so much then Cameron would have been given the Carter surname, as was his right, rather than his mother's maiden name. Flashing Tommy another wink, he wrapped his arm around his nephew's shoulders. 'Your grandad Tommy would be proud.'

Tommy beamed even wider. His uncle was right, despite his surname being Johnson, he actually felt more like a Carter, he always had, and he definitely took after the Carter side of the family rather than the Johnson's, he knew that much.

As they began to collect their mobile phones from the desk, Tommy hung back slightly and as he locked eyes with his cousin he gave a small smile. 'Cheers,' he said. 'You know... for stopping me from whacking that pile of shit, Kevin.'

Reece shrugged and for the briefest of moments Tommy thought that his cousin would rebuke him until he flashed a grin.

'That's what mates do isn't it, look out for one another?'

'Yeah.' Tommy grinned back, thankful that the air had been cleared between them. Collecting his mobile phone, he powered the device on. A moment later he frowned. He'd had a missed call from Melanie. Bringing the phone up to his ear he listened intently to a voice message, his face becoming all the more pale with every second that passed.

'Fuck.' He brought his free hand up to his head, his eyes growing wider. 'Fuck!' he shouted again.

All heads turned to look at him.

'What's the matter with you?' Jonny asked, his eyes narrowed.

Tommy shook his head, and replaying the message he clenched his jaw.

'Tommy,' Reece repeated. 'What's wrong?'

Shaking his head again, Tommy stuffed the phone into his back pocket. 'It's Aimee.' He swallowed then looked around him, his eyes falling upon the shotguns. 'She's in trouble.'

'But...' Before Reece could finish the sentence, Tommy had charged forward, grabbed one of the guns and then bolted out of the office.

'Ah, fuck,' Reece groaned. Chasing after his cousin, he too

snatched up a gun then dashed outside. 'Tommy,' he shouted. 'Wait up. I'm coming with you.'

* * *

Aimee was near-on hysterical, and as she and her mother were standing huddled together in the back garden, she was unable to stop her body from shaking. No matter how much or how hard they had screamed for help, none of their neighbours had poked their heads outside to see what was going on; she wasn't so sure that any of them were even home, seeing as their houses were in darkness. They had even tried to climb over the six-foot fence into their neighbour's garden but with nothing to stand on to propel them over, that exercise had proven to be fruitless too. And when Melanie had suggested she lift her daughter up and push her over the fence Aimee had point-blank refused to leave her mother's side.

Looking down at the mobile phone in her hand Aimee fought the urge to cry all over again. Her mum hadn't been lying when she'd said that the battery was low. As soon as she'd finished leaving Tommy a voicemail the battery had died, and no matter how many times she'd tried to power the phone back on there had been no sign of it springing back to life.

'Mum,' Aimee cried. 'What are we going to do?'

Melanie took a deep breath, and as she looked towards the fence again, she gave her daughter's hand a tight squeeze. 'I know that you don't like it, darling, and that you don't want to leave me but there's no other alternative. You have to get help; you need to phone for the police.'

'No, Mum,' Aimee wailed. 'I can't, what if they...'

'Yes, you can,' Melanie interrupted, her voice stern. Grasping her daughter by the shoulders she looked into her eyes. 'You have to, darling,' she said. 'Because if you don't, then...' Her voice trailed off and she glanced towards her house. It was only a matter of time until the men managed to force their way into the kitchen, and once they had, who knew what they were going to do next, what they were capable of? Perhaps they would follow through with their threat and kill the both of them. 'You have to,' she reiterated. 'We've got no other choice, and you need to think about the baby.'

Aimee swallowed and wiping the tears from her eyes she placed her hand on her abdomen and nodded. 'Okay, Mum,' she sniffed, eyeing the fence with a measure of trepidation. 'I'll do it.'

* * *

By the time Tommy Jr had brought his car to a screeching halt outside Aimee's house, his great-uncle Jonny was pulling in behind him alongside several of his other uncles.

Jumping from the car, he raced down the pathway and banged his fist on the front door before standing back slightly and looking up at the windows.

'What the fuck is going on?' Jonny demanded, once he'd joined his two nephews.

'I don't know.' Bringing his hand up to his head, Tommy's eyes were wide. 'She said that she needed help, that someone was going to kill her. She sounded fucking petrified.' Pulling out his mobile phone he dialled Aimee's number. Just as it had each and every time before, the call rang off. 'She's in there,' he said glancing back up at the window he knew to be Aimee's bedroom. 'She has to be.' Passing the shotgun across to Jonny, Tommy took several paces back, then bounding forward, he put all of his weight behind his body and shoved his shoulder against the door, the impact made little to no difference, and stepping back,

Tommy repeated the action over and over again until finally the door flung open, almost ripping the frame from its hinges.

Bursting into the living room with his family behind him, Tommy's expression was murderous. 'Who the fuck are you?' he shouted as he pulled the gun out of Jonny's hands and turned it on the three men, who at that precise moment, were in the process of kicking down the kitchen door.

The men turned their heads. If they were surprised by the Carters' arrival then they didn't show it, Tommy noted.

'I asked you a fucking question,' Tommy continued to roar. 'Who the fuck are you and what the fuck are you doing in my bird's house?'

As he eyed the guns that both Tommy and Reece were brandishing, Nathan Bannerman straightened up, his eyes narrowed. 'And who the fuck are you?' He tilted his head to the side, his hard eyes raking over Reece, Jonny, Peter, and Jake. 'And more to the point, which one of you cunts is Kevin Fox?'

Tommy snarled. He should have known Kevin would have been the one they were looking for. The bastard had a habit of rubbing people up the wrong way, himself included. He glanced towards the kitchen, sensing a moment of relief in the knowledge that they hadn't managed to reach Aimee or her mother. Or at least he didn't think they had.

Using the gun, he motioned for the men to move away from the door that led into the kitchen. 'Move,' he hissed. 'Because believe me, I won't hesitate when it comes to blowing the three of you away.'

His eyes still narrowed, Nathan gestured for his brothers to step aside, and once they had been steered across the living room, he held up his hands. 'You've made your point,' he sneered. 'So, I'm going to ask you again one last time before I end up losing my rag. Which one of you bastards is Kevin Fox?'

'None of us,' Jonny spat. Continuing to study the three men, he lifted his eyebrows. 'I take it you're the Bannermans.'

Tommy gave a hollow laugh. 'This gets even better,' he said, his hand steady as he brandished the firearm towards them. 'I'm gunning for you bastards. It's because of you I was banged up.'

Confusion was etched across Nathan's face. 'Who the fuck are you?'

For the briefest of moments Tommy was thrown off. 'You know exactly who I am!' he shouted, his temper in grave danger of erupting. 'You were the ones who set me fucking up.'

* * *

Just as she was about to cock her leg over the fence, Aimee froze. 'That's my Tommy!' she cried.

Melanie's head snapped towards the house. 'Are you sure?' she asked, biting down on her bottom lip not wanting to get her hopes up.

'Of course I'm sure, I'd know his voice anywhere.'

Scrambling down from the fence, Aimee ran towards the house. 'Tommy,' she called out as she began heaving the table away from the door. 'We're in here.'

* * *

Tommy Jr turned his head to look in the direction of the kitchen, a moment of relief spreading through his veins. Aimee was okay.

'Tommy,' she called out again.

'It's alright, babe,' he shouted turning his hard glare back to the Bannerman brothers. 'I'm here.' Jerking his head towards the kitchen he motioned for Reece to help Aimee and her mother. 'Get her and Mel out of here,' he ordered.

Reece spun around, and giving a shake of his head, his eyes were wide. 'Leave it out, Tommy.'

'I told you to get her out of here,' Tommy growled, his voice brooking no arguments.

After giving his uncle Jonny a wary glance, Reece nodded before ushering both Aimee and her mother out of the house.

With Aimee now safe, Tommy allowed his shoulders to ever so slightly relax, not that the hand holding the gun wavered; if anything it became all the more steady, determined. 'You owe me,' he said. 'You, Kevin, and that piece of shit, Andy, because I know for a fact Kevin wouldn't have been able to pull this off alone. You were the ones who gave him the coke and in my book that makes you as equally responsible for my downfall.'

Nathan, Lee, and Connor shared a glance.

'So. This is how we're gonna play this out, because believe me, I've had fuck all to do but think about this shit for weeks.'

Nathan held up his hand. 'I don't know what you're talking about...'

'Of course you fucking do,' Tommy roared, moving forward. 'You gave Kevin the coke and then him and Andy...'

'Andy's brown bread,' Lee volunteered. 'Did him over myself.' He gave a grin and made a slicing action. 'Was a good night,' he chuckled. 'I mean it was a bit messy as I'm sure you can imagine, given the amount of claret that pissed out of the bastard, but it was worth it just to see the look on his face as I snuffed out his life.'

Taken aback, Tommy couldn't help but stare at them. He opened his mouth to fling back a retort before hastily snapping it closed again, his mind whirling. He'd heard rumours that they weren't the full ticket, and even Dylan had said as much, but until now he hadn't realised they were actually deranged.

'Andy owed us,' Nathan continued. 'Or rather, Kevin does.

Fifty grand, for half a kilo of coke. The very same coke I've got a feeling you're referring to.'

Jonny let out a low whistle and lifting his eyebrows towards Tommy he shook his head, silently warning him to be careful.

'Yeah, well.' Tommy cleared his throat. 'You won't be getting the coke back, the Old Bill have it.'

'I gathered as much,' Nathan replied. 'Which now leaves us in a bit of a quandary, doesn't it? Someone has to pay and seeing as that only leaves Kevin.' He spread open his arms, gesturing around the room. 'Well, you can see our point, the reason why we're here hunting the fucker down.'

Against his better judgement Tommy nodded, not that this meant they would be getting their hands on Kevin. If anyone was going to finish the lowlife bastard, then it would be him. 'Either way, Kevin is a dead man walking.'

'Yeah, you've got that much right,' Connor chipped in.

Cautiously, Tommy lowered the gun to his side. 'And seeing as it was me he fitted up, then it's only right I should be the one who decides how his life comes to an end.'

'Tommy Jr,' Jonny warned.

Holding up his hand in a bid to quiet his uncle down, Tommy shook his head. 'I promised Aimee that I wouldn't lay a finger on him.' He turned back to look at the Bannerman brothers. 'And at the end of the day, I intend to keep that promise.' A smile made its way across his face. 'And as it just so happens, I won't need to kill him.'

Unsure where the conversation was going Nathan narrowed his eyes.

'Not when you've got the means and the business to do it for me,' Tommy continued. 'And seeing as your business consists of supplying gear to cokeheads and that the said gear could easily be laced with something designed to kill a man then...' He lifted his shoulders. 'I think you get my point. And what's more it would be viewed as nothing more than an accidental overdose, happens all the time. My conscience will be clear, or rather as clear as it ever could be under the circumstances, seeing as it was my idea an' all.'

A laugh escaped from Nathan's lips and flicking his head towards Tommy he lifted his eyebrows. 'What's your name?'

'Tommy Johnson.'

Nathan nodded, somewhat impressed. 'I've got a feeling I'm gonna need to keep my eye on you.' Stepping forward he stretched out his hand and as they shook on the deal he gave a wink. 'Nice doing business with you.'

Tommy Jr returned the nod, his eyes remaining as hard as flints. 'Likewise.'

23

As they made their way to their cars, Jonny was seething.

'Have you lost the fucking plot?' he hissed.

Tommy Jr rolled his eyes. 'No, actually, I haven't. I know exactly what I'm doing.'

'Really,' Jonny exclaimed. 'Because from where I'm standing I've got to say I'm starting to wonder if you've gone fucking cuckoo. You do realise you've just made a deal with the Bannerman brothers.'

'Yeah,' Tommy nodded. 'A deal to get rid of that lowlife Kevin.'

Exasperated, Jonny threw his arms up into the air. 'And what happens when they decide they want us?' he said, poking himself in the chest, 'to do more deals with them. Do you honestly think they'll take no for an answer? All thanks to you, they've got one over us, and not only that but they've also been made privy to our business.'

Tommy shook his head. 'It won't be like that,' he answered his voice low as he watched Aimee step out of his car. 'I'm not an idiot, Jonny, I do know what I'm doing.'

As he gave his great-nephew one last scathing look, Jonny shook his head. 'You'd better know what you're doing,' he warned.

'I do,' Tommy replied, and as Aimee ran towards him, he plastered a wide smile across his face.

'Oh, Tommy,' Aimee cried as she flung herself into his arms. 'I was so scared.'

'I know, babe,' he soothed. 'But it's all sorted now.'

As Jonny scoffed, Tommy ignored his uncle.

'Will you stay here tonight?' Glancing towards the house Aimee gave an involuntary shiver. 'I don't think I'd be able to sleep if it was just me and my mum alone in the house.'

Turning to look over his shoulder at the house, or rather the front door that he'd pretty much destroyed in his haste to get inside, Tommy nodded. 'Yeah, of course I will. We'll need to patch the door up though.'

Aimee was thoughtful for a moment. 'I think my mum is going to get onto the council, tell them we've been vandalised, or that someone tried to break in.'

'Yeah, sounds like a plan,' he said as he watched his family begin to get into their cars. 'Oi, Reece,' he called out. 'Wait up a minute.' Releasing his arms from around Aimee he kissed the top of her head before jogging down the path. Once he'd caught up with his cousin, he gave a small, almost nervous smile. 'Are me and you cool?' he asked.

Reece huffed out a breath.

'Look,' Tommy quickly added. 'I didn't mean to snap earlier. I know I've been doing a lot of that of late, and yeah, I admit I've been an absolute bastard to be around, but in my defence I've had a lot on my mind, and when I was inside I saw something.' He shook his head as an image of Dylan laid out on the floor, his body contorting as hot, steam smouldered from his face and head sprang to his mind. 'When I feel ready to, I'll tell you about it; I'll tell you exactly what happened, but not yet, I can't,' he said shaking his head.

Reece narrowed his eyes.

'As for tonight,' Tommy sighed. 'I was just worried; you know, about Aimee and everything, it was nothing personal, I didn't mean to have a pop at you. I just didn't want Aimee to hear anything being said about Kevin.'

As Reece glanced in Aimee's direction he nodded. 'Yeah, I get it.'

'So, me and you...' Tommy probed.

Reece gave a small chuckle. 'We're still pals.' He gave a shrug. 'No matter how much you might piss me off at times, we're family, ain't we? I haven't got any other choice on the matter.'

It wasn't exactly what Tommy wanted to hear, but at the same time at least Reece wasn't telling him to fuck off. 'I'll speak to you tomorrow, yeah?'

'Yeah,' Reece nodded, his gaze bouncing back to Aimee. 'Look after her because that girl loves you.' He gave a cheeky wink. 'Fuck knows why, but she does.'

Tommy chuckled. 'I will do.'

As he made his way back to Aimee's house, for the first time in weeks Tommy's heart felt lighter, as though a weight had been lifted from him. He gave a small smile. He couldn't even begin to imagine how he'd feel once Kevin had been taken care of, and as far as he was concerned, Kevin's demise couldn't come quick enough.

* * *

The next morning, after leaving the Royal Mail depot, Kevin was not only elated but he also fully believed himself to be the dog's bollocks. He was on cloud nine and nothing and no one would be able to dampen his mood.

After answering each and every one of the Old Bills' questions, he and Stanley had been given the go ahead to go home. He'd been so convincing that perhaps he should have taken up acting as a career; he'd even put on tears, and at one point he'd pretended to be shell shocked – so much so that one of the officers had needed to ask him the same question three times.

Strutting down the street towards his bedsit he dug his hand into his pocket and pulled out his cash. There wasn't much, a couple of tenners and a few pound coins. He dug his hand in a little deeper this time pulling out a twenty-pound note. A grin spread across his face. He had enough to buy himself a wrap of coke and a couple of beers, maybe a whiskey chaser too.

Nearing his front door, he began to whistle a cheerful tune. All he needed was a couple of hours' kip, a shower and shave and then he would be ready to celebrate his good fortune. Resisting the urge to rub his hands together he unlocked the door, his nose wrinkling at the sour stench that hit his nostrils. Still, he reasoned, as he trudged his way up the stairs towards his room, it wouldn't be for long. Within a matter of weeks, he was bound to be given his share of the robbery and with a bit of luck he'd have the money to rent somewhere a bit more upmarket, somewhere more suited to his new position in life, and seeing as he was now someone who should be looked up to, he'd need to start looking and acting the part. As much as he still didn't like them, he had to give it to the Johnsons and Carters; they certainly knew how to conduct themselves. Not only did they look pristine, but they also exuded wealth. You certainly wouldn't have caught any of them living in a dingy, mould-infested room, wearing the same sweat-encrusted clothes day after day.

Once inside his room, Kevin stripped down to his underpants

and after kicking his uniform across the floor he laughed out loud. He'd even been given a week off work on full pay, to recover from his ordeal. He began to laugh even harder, and flopping down onto the unmade bed, he lay on his back and positioned his arms behind his head. Yeah, he decided: a couple of hours of well-earned sleep and he'd be ready to take on the world and what's more, he couldn't wait.

* * *

As he and his family stepped inside the Bannermans' lock-up, Tommy Jr took a moment to look around him. He wasn't sure exactly what he'd been expecting to find, but it certainly hadn't been this. To his shock, the Bannermans ran their business with a military precision. Not only was the lock-up clean, bordering on spotless, but the amount of men they had working for them had taken him by surprise.

Tearing his gaze away from the work benches, or rather the drug paraphernalia that littered the work surfaces, he moved forward.

'Is it done?' he asked.

Nathan Bannerman nodded, and crossing his arms over his broad chest he motioned down to a packet of white powder before them. 'It's done.' He gave a slow grin. 'Believe me, there's enough shit in there to kill an entire fucking army.'

It was exactly what Tommy had been hoping to hear, and as he turned his head to look at his uncle Jonny, he clasped his hands together. 'Well, I suppose that's that, then.'

'Yeah,' Jonny agreed and nodding towards the door he indicated that it was time for them to leave.

As they reached the door Tommy paused. 'One more thing,' he said, spinning around. 'Who'll be dropping off?'

Connor Bannerman jerked his thumb behind him and as Tommy looked the young man over, he gave an approving nod. For all intents and purposes, the kid, not much younger than himself, looked no different from any other hood rat dropping off gear. Not only that but he had the appearance of someone able to blend into a crowd, his features nondescript and his clothing the same as any other kid who hung around the Dagenham council estate.

Satisfied, Tommy smiled. And as he and the rest of the family walked back to their cars, he blew out his cheeks. There was no going back now, not that he actually wanted to, mind.

'Are you okay?'

Tommy nodded. 'Yeah, why wouldn't I be?'

Jonny lifted his eyebrows and pushing his hands into his pockets he leaned back against his car. 'It's not every day you mastermind the murder of someone and let's face it, this isn't just anyone we're talking about, it's your missus' old man. That's bound to have an impact.'

Shrugging, Tommy looked his uncle dead in the eyes. 'I couldn't give a flying fuck about Kevin, why would I?'

Taking the words on board, Jonny shook his head. 'It's just. I don't know...' He looked away for a moment. 'A lot for me to get my head around, I suppose. I mean just a couple of months ago you would never have dreamed of topping Kevin.'

Tommy laughed. 'I'm not the same person I was a couple of months ago.'

'Yeah,' Jonny nodded. 'I've gathered that much.'

As Tommy began to climb into the car, Jonny couldn't help but study him, his forehead ever so slightly furrowed. It was no lie, his great-nephew had changed beyond recognition, and if he was being entirely truthful, he wasn't so sure it was a good thing. If anything, the changes in Tommy made him feel slightly uneasy, you could even say wary. And even more than that, he couldn't help but feel as though he was working alongside his brother Tommy all over again. Tommy Snr hadn't given a fuck about anyone, other than his family of course, but when it came to outsiders, he wasn't only ruthless, but also a force to be reckoned with.

* * *

As she looked up at the house before her, Aimee chewed on her bottom lip. A part of her didn't even know why she was bothering, neither did she fully understand why she kept on giving him chance after chance. Only deep down, she did know why. Kevin, despite his issues and let's face it he had many, was still her dad, and even more than that, she still loved him.

Lifting her hand, she knocked on the door, then shifting her weight from foot to foot, she fought the urge to run away. No matter what, she needed to see him, if for no other reason than to clear the air between them.

A few moments later the door opened, and wiping the sleep from his eyes, Kevin gave a yawn.

'Hello, Dad.'

A look of surprise creased Kevin's face and as he glanced down the pathway his gaze settled back on his daughter. 'What are you doing here?'

Aimee gave a light chuckle. 'Thanks, Dad. It's nice to see you too.'

Kevin waved his hand through the air. 'I didn't mean it like that. It's just a surprise, that's all.'

'Can I come in?'

'Of course you can,' Kevin beamed as he ushered his daughter across the threshold.

Once inside her father's room, Aimee looked around her. It broke her heart to see him living the way he did. The bed sheets alone looked filthy and that was without empty cups and takeaway containers littered around the room. Making a mental note to give his room a good spring clean she turned to face him.

'I hate this,' she admitted. 'Me and you at loggerheads.'

Kevin had the grace to look down at the floor.

'You're my dad,' Aimee continued, her voice thick with emotion. 'And you've hurt me, really hurt me.'

Looking up Kevin swallowed down the lump in his throat, his expression contrite. 'I'm sorry,' he said sincerely. 'I'm so sorry, darling. I fucked up and I know that. I wasn't thinking straight. I took my anger out on the wrong person.'

Aimee nodded. 'Tommy could have still been in prison, and it would have been your fault,' she cried.

'I know,' he said quietly. 'And I don't blame you for hating me.'

'I don't hate you,' Aimee sighed. 'I don't always like you, but I could never hate you.'

Kevin gave a smile. 'Well, we can work on that.' Spreading open his arms, he lifted his eyebrows. 'How about we let bygones be bygones? A fresh start, what do you say?'

Aimee didn't need to be asked twice, and as she stepped into her father's embrace, she gave a small smile, a part of her hoping that she wouldn't regret forgiving him so easily.

* * *

Later that night Tommy Jr sat inside his car outside The Cross Keys. Beside him on the passenger seat Reece couldn't help but fidget.

'Are you sure that you don't want me to come in with you?' he asked nodding across to the boozer.

Glancing at his watch Tommy shook his head. 'I need to do this alone.' Turning his head he gave his cousin a smile. 'Thanks, though.'

'For what?' Reece asked, scrunching up his face. 'I haven't done anything.'

'For having my back,' Tommy laughed. Giving his watch a second glance, he pushed open the door and stepped out of the car. 'I won't be long.'

Reece nodded. 'Just be careful,' he called after him.

Lifting his hand in acknowledgment Tommy strolled across the car park. On entering the pub, he made a beeline for Kevin.

'You alright, Kev?' he asked as he leaned casually against the bar.

Spinning around Kevin gave a wide grin. 'Course I am.' He waggled his eyebrows. 'Couldn't be fucking better.'

Tommy laughed. 'Yeah, that makes two of us,' he winked. 'In fact, I've got an even greater feeling that me and you will soon have some celebrating to do.'

Kevin's eyes lit up and leaning in closer he lowered his voice. 'You're referring to the robbery I take it?'

'We hit the jackpot, mate.'

Kevin's mouth dropped open. 'How much are we talking?'

Pretending to take a moment to think, Tommy cocked his head to the side. 'At least sixty k each, maybe even more.'

'I knew it.' Letting out a low whistle, Kevin rubbed his hands together. 'And when do I get my cut?'

'Soon,' Tommy answered. And as the door to the pub opened, he straightened up. 'In fact, I've arranged a little present for you, something to tide you over until the money comes through.' He motioned behind him to where the Bannermans' foot soldier was stepping through the door.

Kevin's eyes widened and for the briefest of moments he was lost for words. 'Cheers, Tommy,' he eventually answered. 'I really appreciate that. I'm on my arse at the moment, haven't got a pot to piss in.'

'No need to thank me.' Tommy clapped Kevin on the back. 'Enjoy,' he grinned. 'And just remember, there's plenty more where that came from.'

As he began to walk across the pub Tommy passed the foot soldier, neither one of them making eye contact or even acknowledging the other.

Moments later he was climbing back into his car.

'Well?' Reece asked. 'Is it done?'

Tommy Jr nodded and as he started the ignition he gave his cousin a sidelong glance. 'Yeah,' he answered, his voice lacking any emotion. 'It's done.'

EPILOGUE

Swallowing deeply, Aimee turned her body from side to side as she studied her reflection in the mirror, her hand gliding over her small bump. Tears sprang to her eyes and swiping them away, she looked down at her tummy.

'I still can't believe it,' she said.

From behind her Tommy Jr wrapped his arms around Aimee's shoulders, his gaze finding hers in the mirror. 'I know, babe,' he sighed.

Turning around, Aimee looked up at him, and after straightening out his black tie, she ran her fingers down his white shirt, smearing away any imaginary creases. 'He was really looking forward to becoming a grandad,' she sniffed.

'I know,' Tommy continued to soothe.

As she turned back to look at her reflection Aimee grimaced. 'Do I look okay?'

Tommy nodded and it was no lie, she looked amazing; even dressed in black his Aimee was a stunner.

'The cars are here.'

Both Aimee and Tommy turned their heads to look at Melanie.

'Thanks, Mum.' Aimee gave a small smile. 'We'll be down in a moment.' Taking a deep breath, she scooped up her handbag. 'This is it, I suppose.'

Tommy nodded again, and as Aimee began to walk from the room, he caught hold of her wrist bringing her to a halt beside him. 'It's gonna be okay, you know that, right?'

Aimee flashed a smile. Her first genuine one in what felt like weeks. 'Yeah,' she answered, her gaze drifting to the window, or to be more precise the black hearse parked outside. 'I know it will.'

* * *

Thirty minutes later they took their seats in the chapel. Staring straight ahead of him, Tommy Jr eyed the coffin. As far as coffins went it was cheap compared to some that Aimee and her mother had viewed. But in the end, they had decided on a plain pine one, preferring to buy an elaborate wreath to say their goodbyes, even though Tommy had told them they could choose whatever they wanted, and seeing as he was personally footing the bill, he'd meant every word. Under the circumstances it was the least he could do.

Kevin's death had come as no surprise, or at least it hadn't to anyone who'd personally known him. It was no secret that he was a user, that he'd shovelled cocaine up his nose by the bucket-load, and that it was only a matter of time until he'd actually succumbed to an overdose.

As it turned out, the coke he'd sniffed that particular night had been laced with a mixture of lethal toxins, almost enough to have killed an army of men. And according to the pathologist,

Kevin would have died within seconds of taking a hit. That had brought Aimee some comfort, and as much as she'd sobbed in Tommy's arms, she'd told him that she was pleased to know her dad hadn't suffered, and that his heart would have given out long before he'd ever come to realise that something was amiss.

Once the service had ended, they made their way outside to look at the flowers, and there were a lot of them, Tommy observed; far more than he'd been expecting, although it would be fair to say that the majority of them had come from his own family.

As they continued to look at the flowers, Tommy locked eyes with his uncle Jonny. In a way, Kevin had got off lightly, he'd died doing something he'd loved, which was a darn sight more than the bastard had actually deserved. Still, he reasoned, at least he'd managed to keep his promise to Aimee. He'd told her that he would never lay a finger on her father, and he hadn't, in the end he hadn't needed to. All thanks to the Bannerman brothers, he'd been able to seek his retribution, and just as he'd known it would, Kevin's death had been ruled as an accidental overdose.

'Are you ready, babe?'

Tommy looked up.

'I think my mum wants us to make our way over to the pub for the wake.'

'Yeah,' Tommy nodded, and giving the flowers one last lingering look, he grabbed hold of Aimee's hand.

Kevin had made a fuck up of epic proportions. Not only had he messed with the wrong man, but he'd also severely underestimated Tommy. He wasn't about to back down from anyone, in fact he had his sights set on the crown, and one day, once his uncle Jonny had retired, Tommy Jr was determined to take over from him. He'd already proven that he had what it took to lead the next generation of Carters. Not only had he been behind the

Royal Mail heist, but he'd also managed to execute the perfect crime, a murder that was unlikely to ever come back to haunt him, not now or at any point in the distant future. Even more than that, he had a sneaky suspicion that this was only the beginning, and fuck anyone who got in his way, because he wasn't planning on playing fair. He'd do anything, and everything, in his power to ensure that both himself and his family remained at the top of their game, no matter how many so-called villains, gangsters, or wannabes he would need to wipe out in the process.

ACKNOWLEDGEMENTS

Thank you to the team at Boldwood Books for your continued support. And a special thank you to my editor, Emily Ruston, for everything you do. Thank you to Debra Newhouse and Susan Sugden.

Thank you to my girls, Joana, Thanu, Liz, Katie, and Chantel; your support and encouragement means everything to me.

Thank you to Deryl Easton and the NotRights Book Club. You have been there from the very beginning and your support is invaluable.

And lastly, a special thank you to my family for continuing to believe in me.

ABOUT THE AUTHOR

Kerry Kaya is the hugely popular author of Essex-based gritty gangland thrillers with strong family dynamics. She grew up on one of the largest council estates in the UK, where she sets her novels. She also works full-time in a busy maternity department for the NHS.

Sign up to Kerry Kaya's mailing list for news, competitions and updates on future books.

Follow Kerry on social media here:

facebook.com/kerry.bryant.58
x.com/KerryKayaWriter
instagram.com/kerry_kaya_writer

ALSO BY KERRY KAYA

Reprisal

The Fletcher Family Series

The Price

The Score

Carter Brothers Series

Under Dog

Top Dog

Scorned

The Reckoning

The Carters: Next Generation Series

Downfall

Retribution

The Tempests Series

Betrayal

Revenge

Justice

PEAKY READERS

GANG LOYALTIES. DARK SECRETS. BLOODY REVENGE.

A READER COMMUNITY FOR GANGLAND CRIME THRILLER FANS!

DISCOVER PAGE-TURNING NOVELS FROM YOUR FAVOURITE AUTHORS AND MEET NEW FRIENDS.

JOIN OUR BOOK CLUB FACEBOOK GROUP

BIT.LY/PEAKYREADERSFB

SIGN UP TO OUR NEWSLETTER

BIT.LY/PEAKYREADERSNEWS

Boldwood

Boldwood Books is an award-winning fiction publishing company seeking out the best stories from around the world.

Find out more at www.boldwoodbooks.com

Join our reader community for brilliant books, competitions and offers!

Follow us
@BoldwoodBooks
@TheBoldBookClub

Sign up to our weekly deals newsletter

https://bit.ly/BoldwoodBNewsletter

Printed in Great Britain
by Amazon